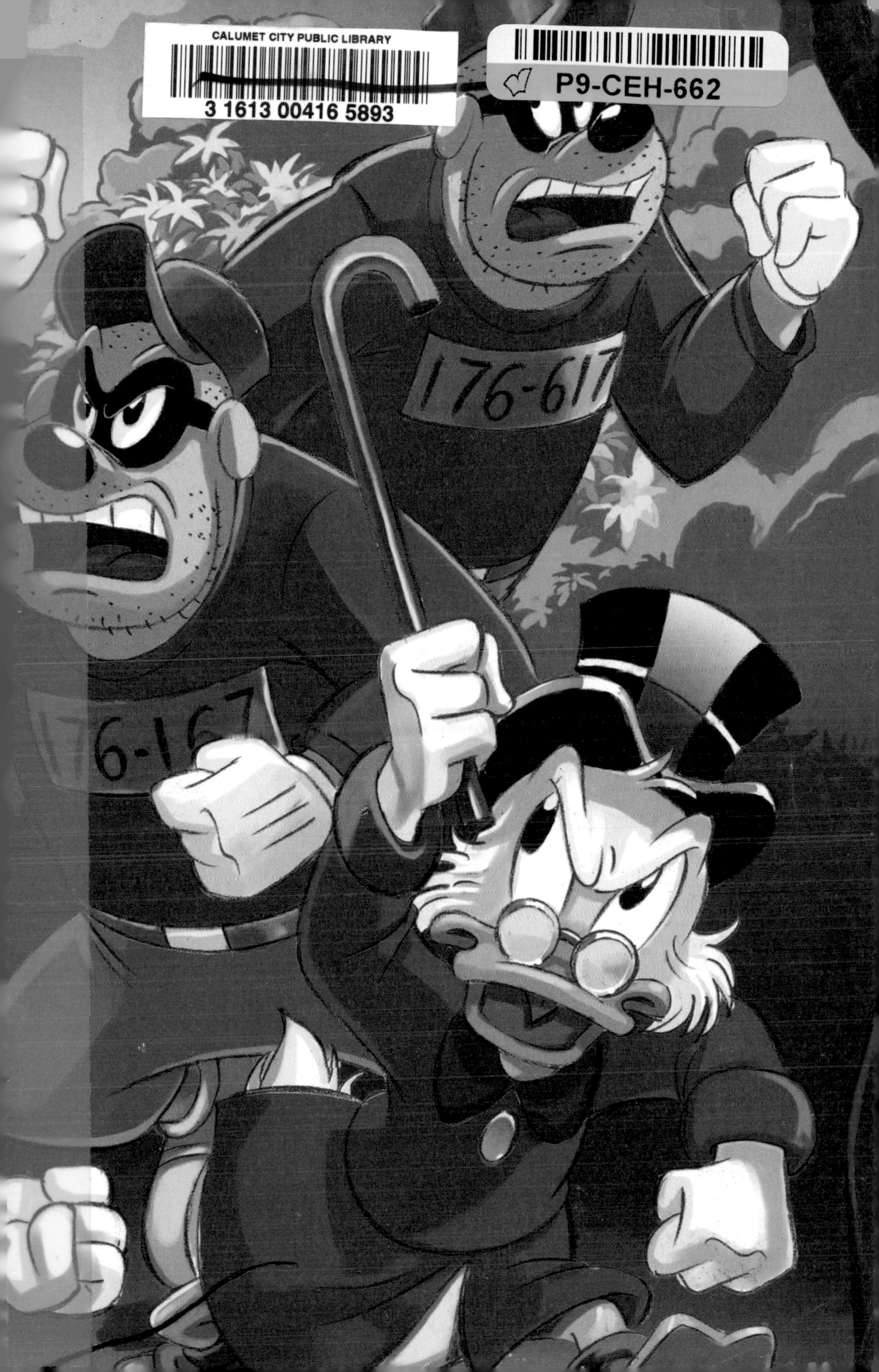

Ross Richie - Chief Executive Officer
Mark Waid - Chief Creative Officer
Matt Gagnon - Editor-in-Chief
Adam Fortier - VP-New Business
Wes Harris - VP-Publishing
Lance Kreiter - VP-Licensing & Merchandising
Chip Mosher - Marketing Director

Bryce Carlson - Managing Editor
Ian Brill - Editor
Dafna Pleban - Editor
Christopher Burns - Editor
Christopher Meyer - Editor
Shannon Watters - Assistant Editor
Eric Harburn - Assistant Editor

Neil Loughrie - Publishing Coordinator
Travis Beaty - Traffic Coordinator
Ivan Salazar - Marketing Assistant
Kate Hayden - Executive Assistant
Brian Latimer - Lead Graphic Designer
Erika Terriquez - Graphic Designer

DISNEY'S HERO SQUAD: ULTRAHEROES VOLUME THREE — THE ULTIMATE THREAT —

December 2010 published by BOOM Kids!, a division of Boom Entertainment, Inc. All contents © 2010 Disney Enterprises, Inc. BOOM Kids! and the BOOM Kids! logo are trademarks of Boom Entertainment, Inc., registered in various countries and categories. All rights reserved.

Office of publication: 6310 San Vicente Blvd Ste 107, Los Angeles, CA 90048-5457. A catalog record for this book is available from OCLC and on our website www.boom-kids.com on the Librarians page.

For information regarding the cpsia on this printed material call: 203-595-3636 and provide reference # east – 70231

FIRST EDITION: DECEMBER 2010

10 9 8 7 6 5 4 3 2 1

WRITERS:
GIORGIO SALATI, RICCARDO SECCHI,
TITO FARACI

ARTISTS:
ETTORE GULA, ROBERTA MIGHELI,
STEFANO TURCONI

TRANSLATOR:
SAIDA TEMOFONTE

EDITOR:
CHRISTOPHER BURNS

LETTERER:
DERON BENNETT

COVER:
MAGIC EYE STUDIOS
COLORS - JAKE MYLER

DESIGNER:
ERIKA TERRIQUEZ

SPECIAL THANKS:
JESSE POST, STEVE BEHLING, ROB TOKAR,
AND BRYCE VANKOOTEN

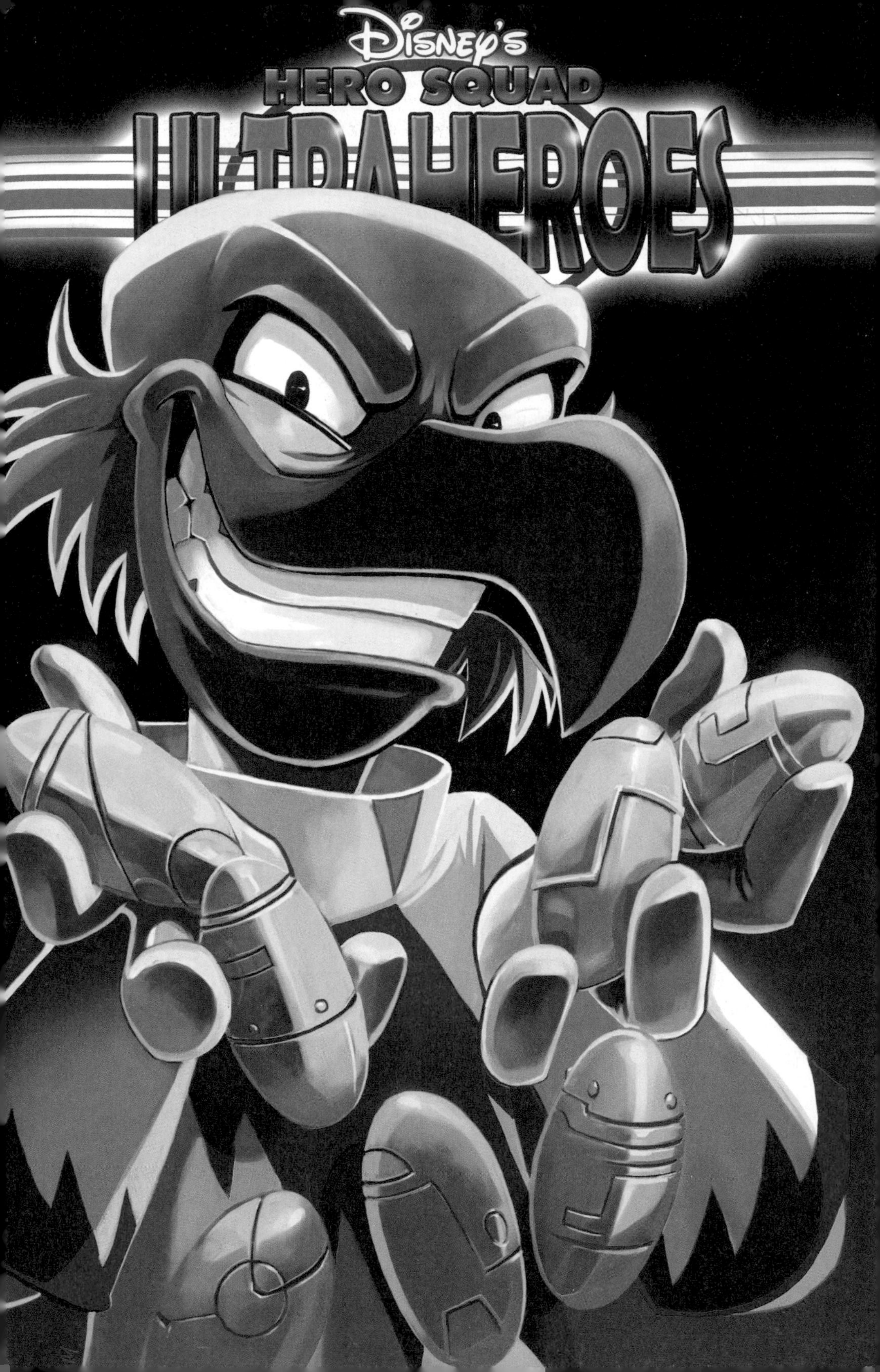
Disney's
HERO SQUAD
ULTRAHEROES

PREVIOUSLY IN DISNEY'S HERO SQUAD: ULTRAHEROES VOL. 2...

THE VILLAINOUS EMIL EAGLE HAS REVEALED HIS TRAITOROUS INTENTIONS BY DOUBLE-CROSSING THE SINISTER 7, AND STEALING THE ULTRAPODS FOR HIMSELF. HOWEVER, BEFORE HE CAN REBUILD THE ULTRAMACHINE, HE HAS TO DEFEAT EEGA BEEVA, WHO GUARDS THE FINAL COMPONENT: HIS ROBOT ASSISTANT, LYTH...

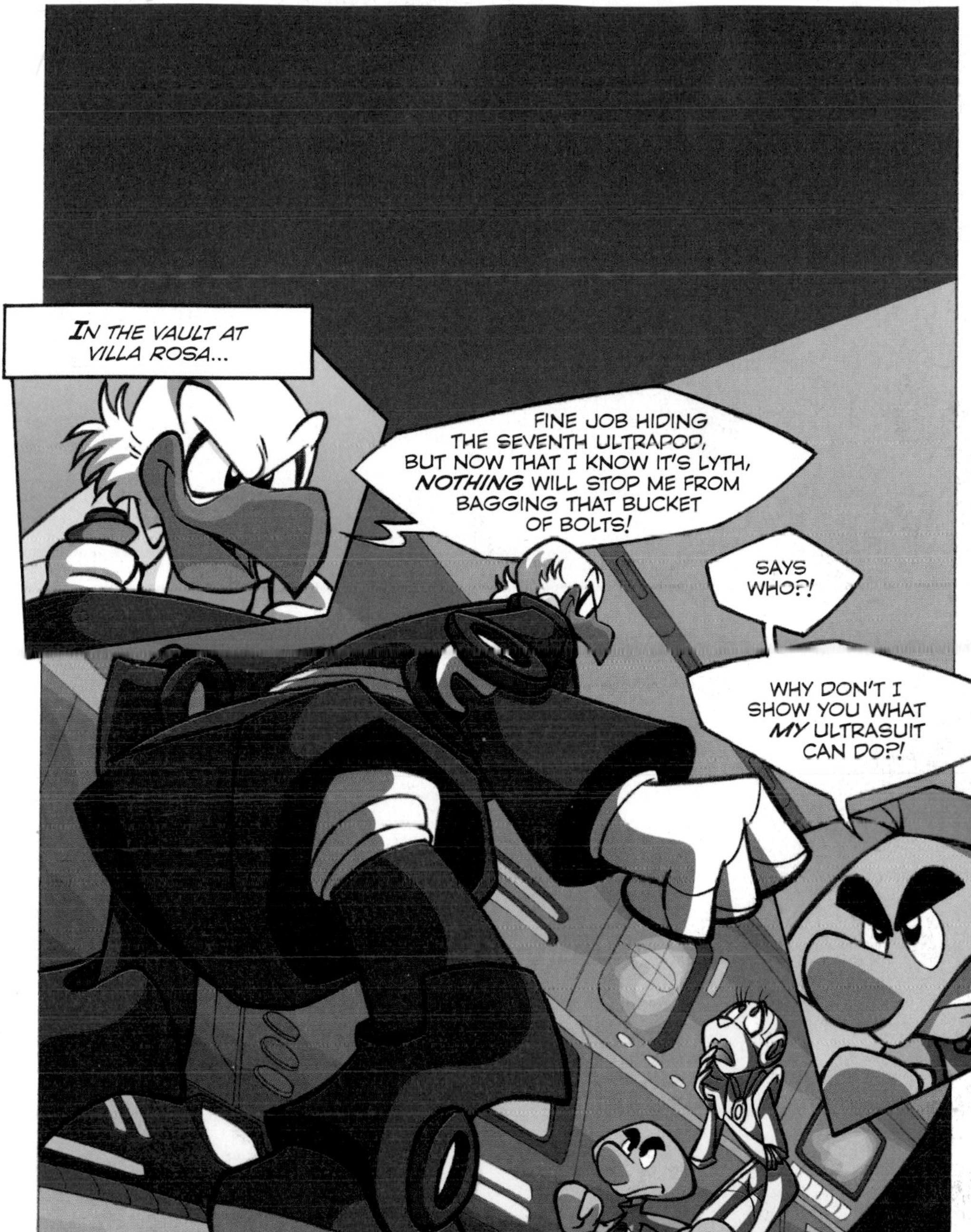
IN THE VAULT AT VILLA ROSA...
FINE JOB HIDING THE SEVENTH ULTRAPOD, BUT NOW THAT I KNOW IT'S LYTH, *NOTHING* WILL STOP ME FROM BAGGING THAT BUCKET OF BOLTS!
SAYS WHO?!
WHY DON'T I SHOW YOU WHAT *MY* ULTRASUIT CAN DO?!

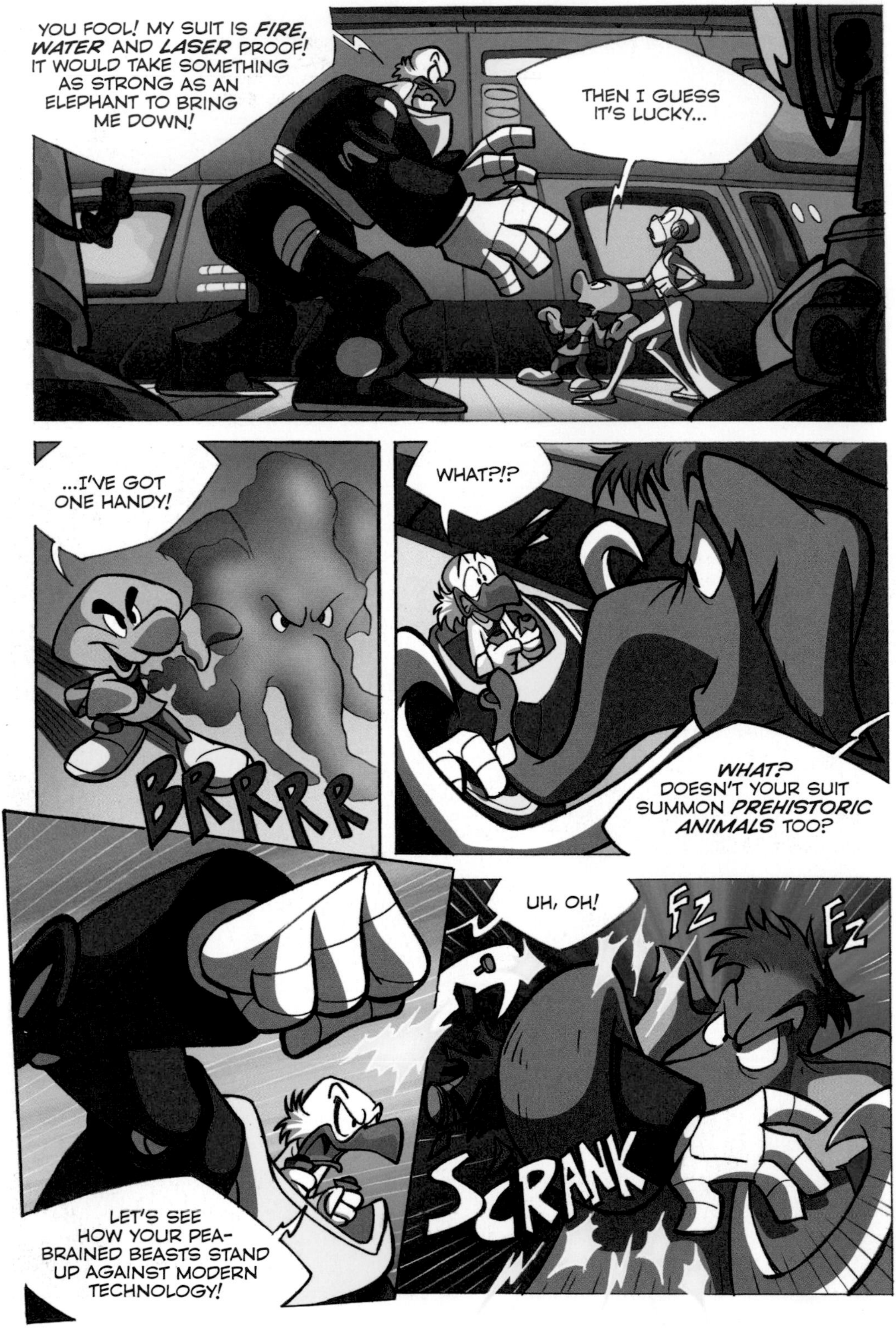
YOU FOOL! MY SUIT IS FIRE, WATER AND LASER PROOF! IT WOULD TAKE SOMETHING AS STRONG AS AN ELEPHANT TO BRING ME DOWN!
THEN I GUESS IT'S LUCKY...
...I'VE GOT ONE HANDY!
BRRRRR
WHAT?!?
WHAT? DOESN'T YOUR SUIT SUMMON PREHISTORIC ANIMALS TOO?
LET'S SEE HOW YOUR PEA-BRAINED BEASTS STAND UP AGAINST MODERN TECHNOLOGY!
UH, OH!
FZ
FZ
SCRANK

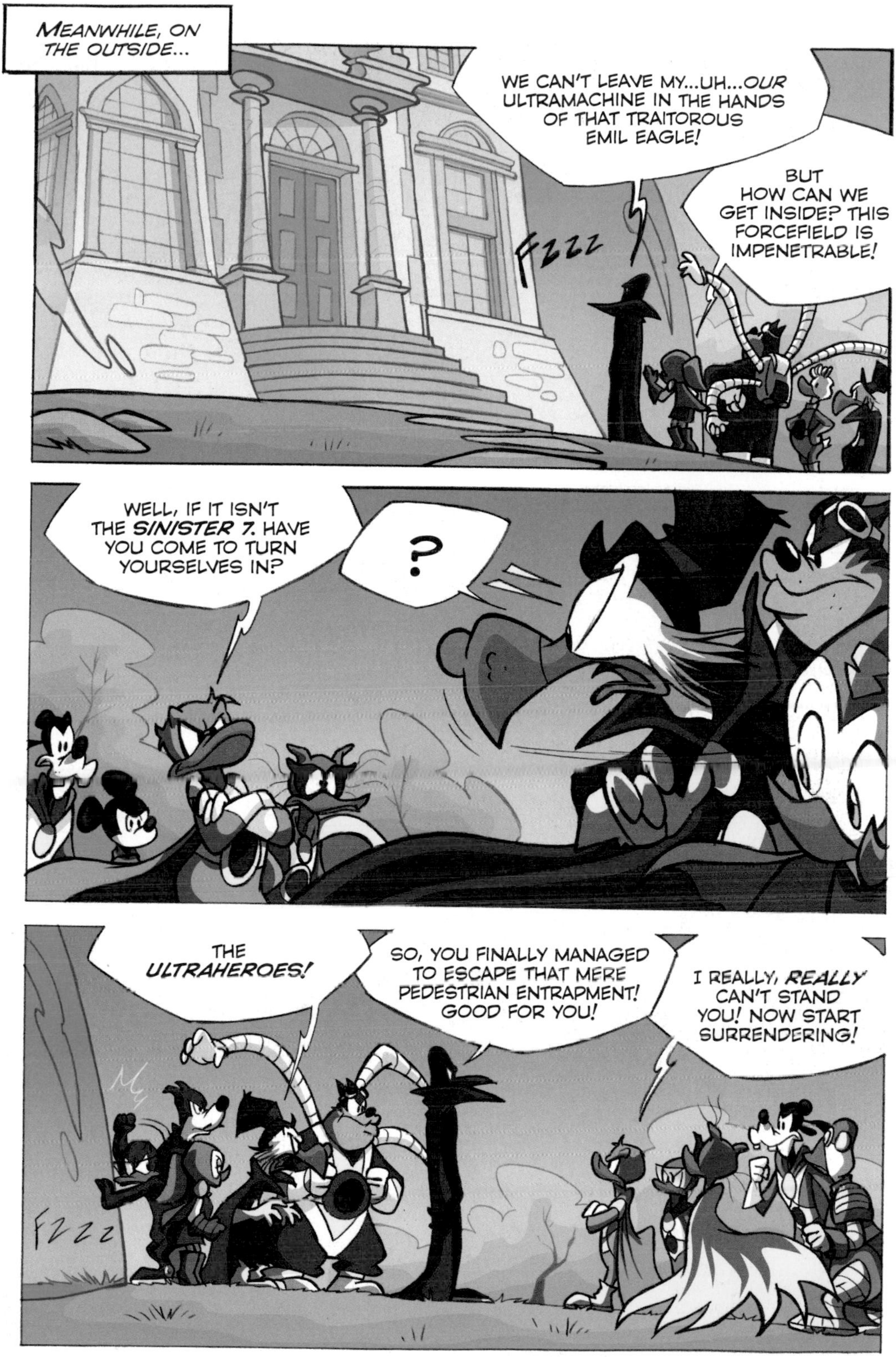
MEANWHILE, ON THE OUTSIDE...
WE CAN'T LEAVE MY...UH...OUR ULTRAMACHINE IN THE HANDS OF THAT TRAITOROUS EMIL EAGLE!
FZZZ
BUT HOW CAN WE GET INSIDE? THIS FORCEFIELD IS IMPENETRABLE!
WELL, IF IT ISN'T THE SINISTER 7. HAVE YOU COME TO TURN YOURSELVES IN?
?
THE ULTRAHEROES!
SO, YOU FINALLY MANAGED TO ESCAPE THAT MERE PEDESTRIAN ENTRAPMENT! GOOD FOR YOU!
I REALLY, REALLY CAN'T STAND YOU! NOW START SURRENDERING!
FZZZ

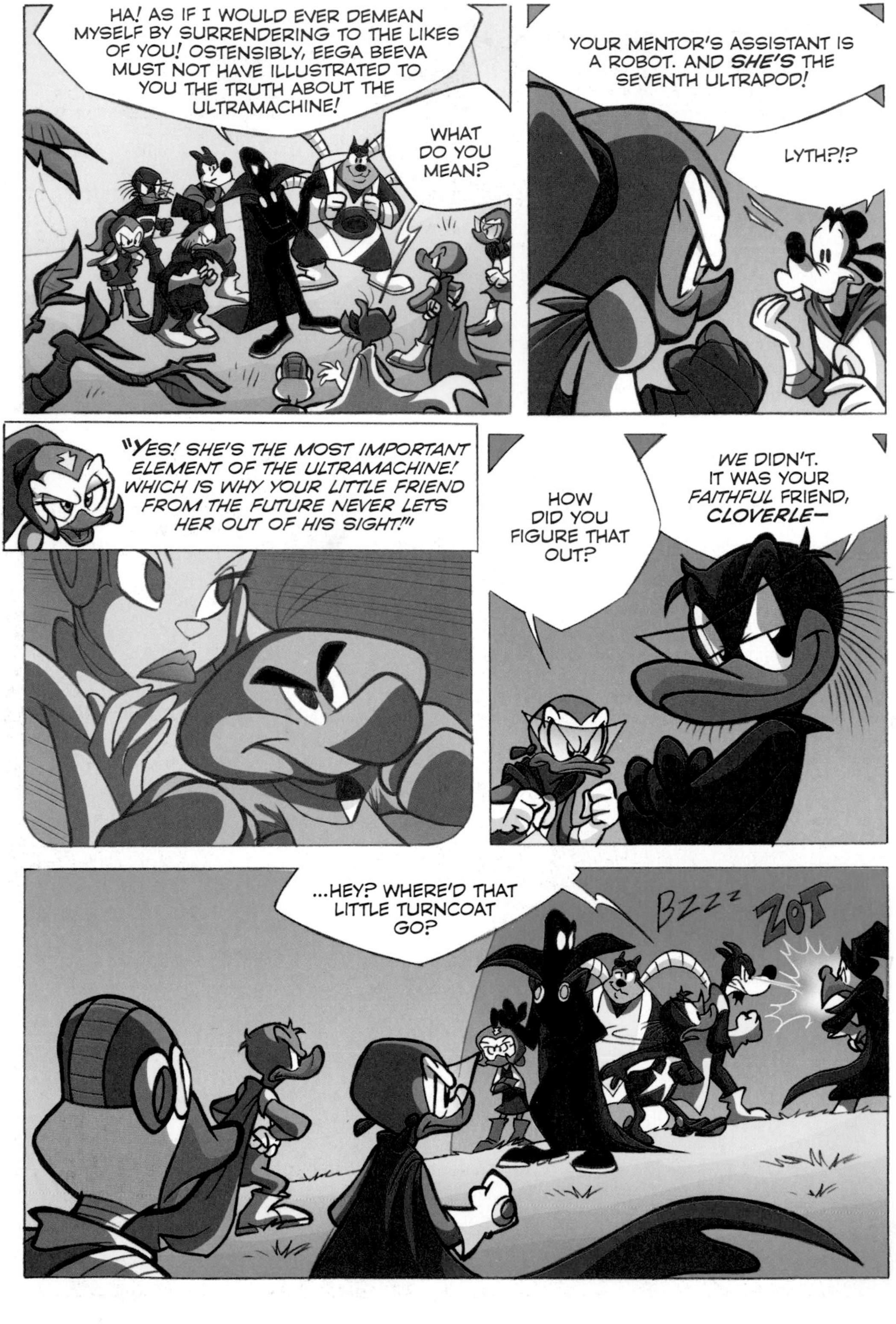
HA! AS IF I WOULD EVER DEMEAN MYSELF BY SURRENDERING TO THE LIKES OF YOU! OSTENSIBLY, EEGA BEEVA MUST NOT HAVE ILLUSTRATED TO YOU THE TRUTH ABOUT THE ULTRAMACHINE!
WHAT DO YOU MEAN?
YOUR MENTOR'S ASSISTANT IS A ROBOT. AND SHE'S THE SEVENTH ULTRAPOD!
LYTH?!?
"YES! SHE'S THE MOST IMPORTANT ELEMENT OF THE ULTRAMACHINE! WHICH IS WHY YOUR LITTLE FRIEND FROM THE FUTURE NEVER LETS HER OUT OF HIS SIGHT!"
HOW DID YOU FIGURE THAT OUT?
WE DIDN'T. IT WAS YOUR FAITHFUL FRIEND, CLOVERLE—
...HEY? WHERE'D THAT LITTLE TURNCOAT GO?
BZZZ
ZOT

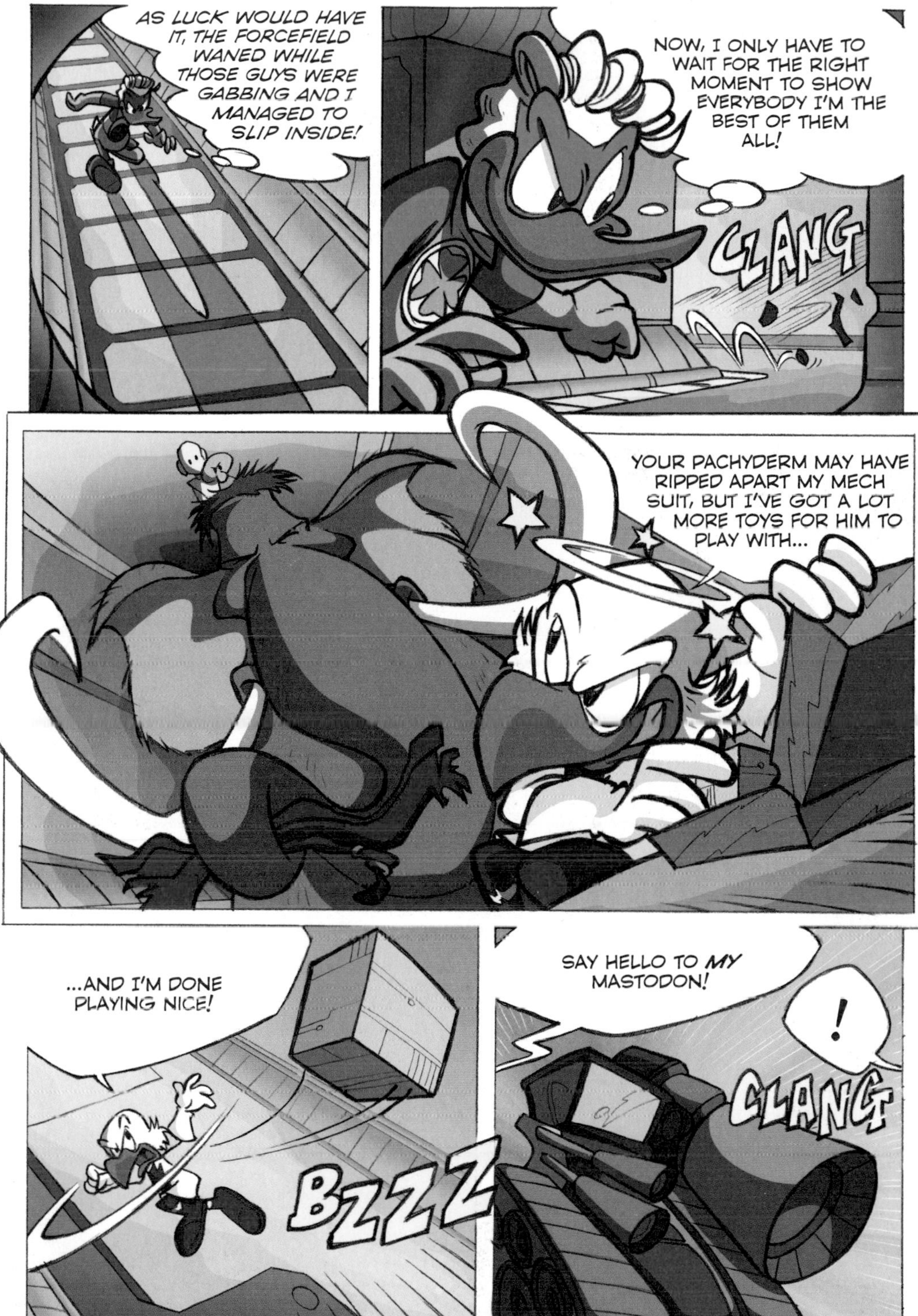

AS LUCK WOULD HAVE IT, THE FORCEFIELD WANED WHILE THOSE GUYS WERE GABBING AND I MANAGED TO SLIP INSIDE!
NOW, I ONLY HAVE TO WAIT FOR THE RIGHT MOMENT TO SHOW EVERYBODY I'M THE BEST OF THEM ALL!
CLANG
YOUR PACHYDERM MAY HAVE RIPPED APART MY MECH SUIT, BUT I'VE GOT A LOT MORE TOYS FOR HIM TO PLAY WITH...
...AND I'M DONE PLAYING NICE!
BZZZ
SAY HELLO TO MY MASTODON!
!
CLANG

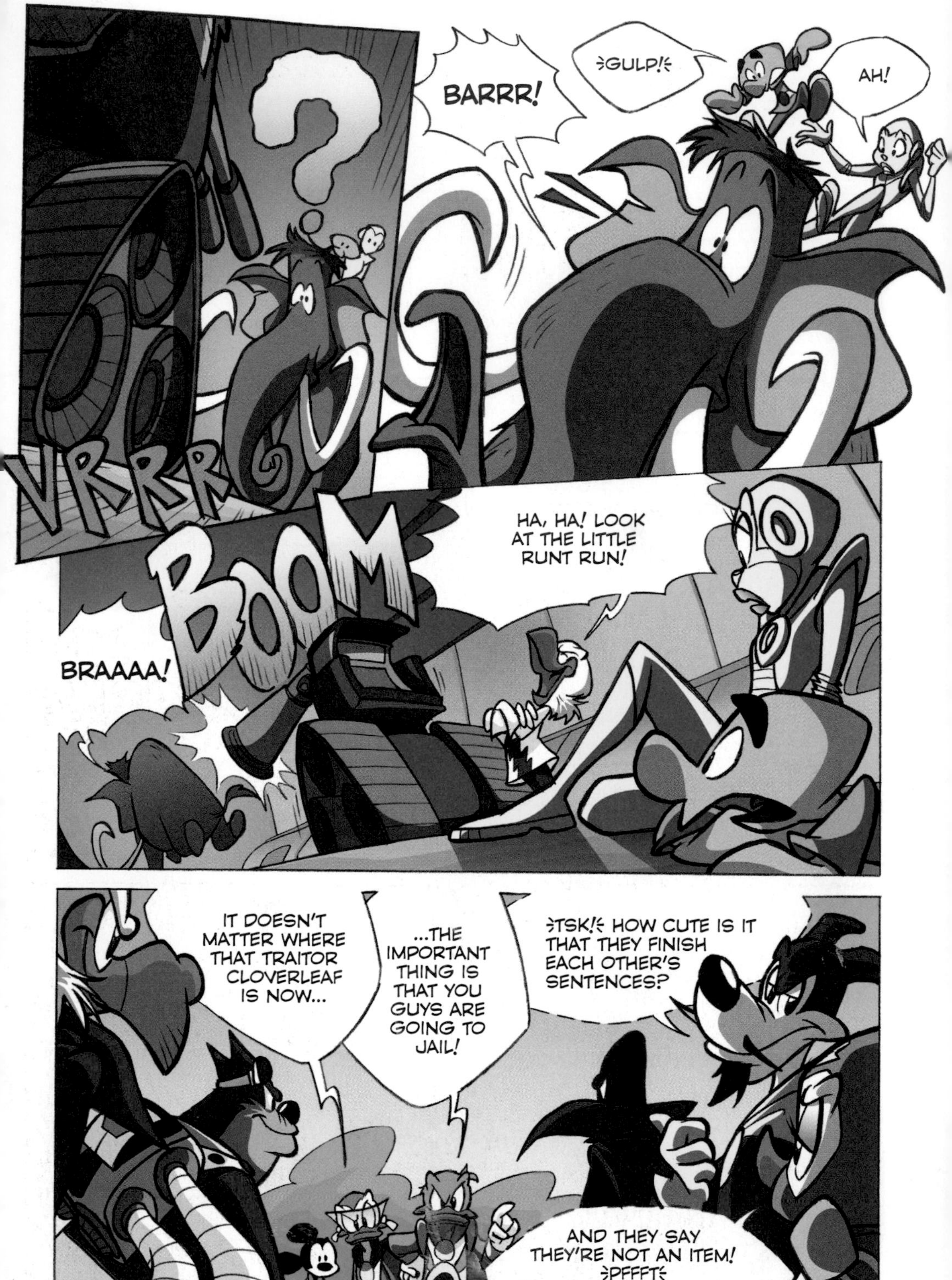
BARRR!
⊰GULP!⊱
AH!
VRRRGU
BOOM
BRAAAA!
HA, HA! LOOK AT THE LITTLE RUNT RUN!
IT DOESN'T MATTER WHERE THAT TRAITOR CLOVERLEAF IS NOW...
...THE IMPORTANT THING IS THAT YOU GUYS ARE GOING TO JAIL!
⊰TSK!⊱ HOW CUTE IS IT THAT THEY FINISH EACH OTHER'S SENTENCES?
AND THEY SAY THEY'RE NOT AN ITEM! ⊰PFFFT⊱

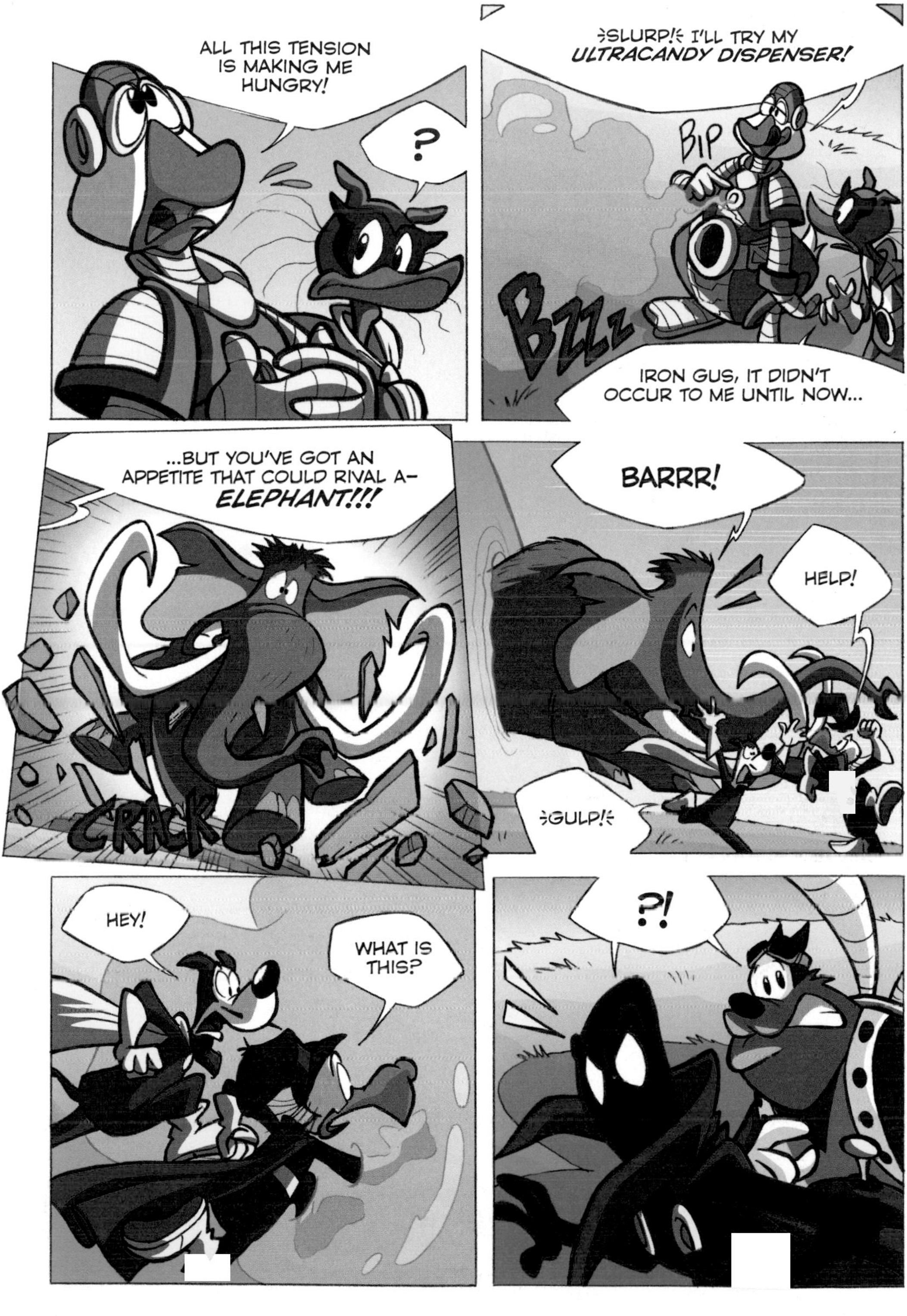
ALL THIS TENSION IS MAKING ME HUNGRY!
?
SLURP! I'LL TRY MY *ULTRACANDY DISPENSER!*
BIP
BZZZ
IRON GUS, IT DIDN'T OCCUR TO ME UNTIL NOW...
...BUT YOU'VE GOT AN APPETITE THAT COULD RIVAL A— *ELEPHANT!!!*
CRACK
BARRR!
HELP!
GULP!
HEY!
WHAT IS THIS?
?!

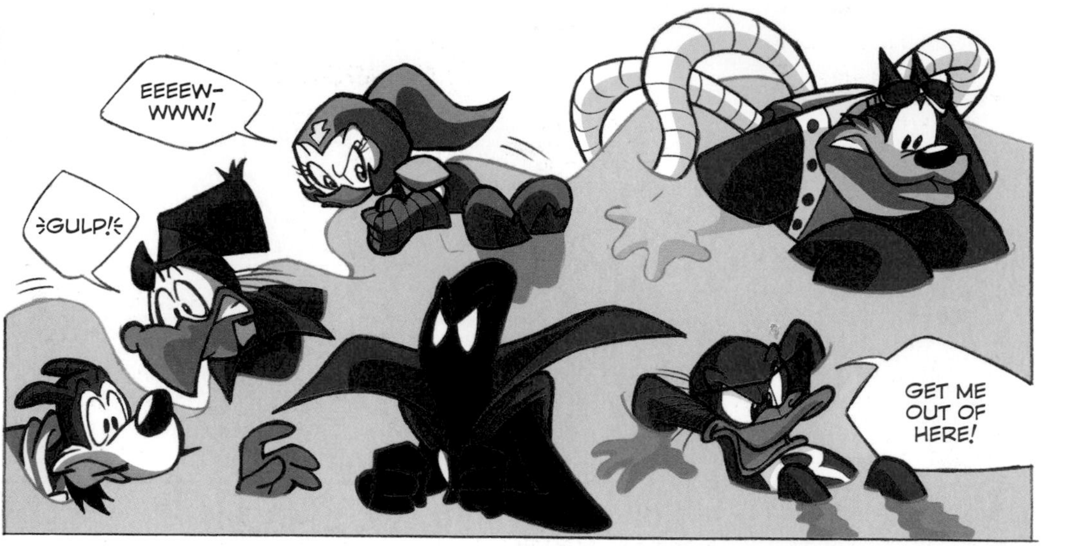
EEEEW-WWW!
GULP!
GET ME OUT OF HERE!

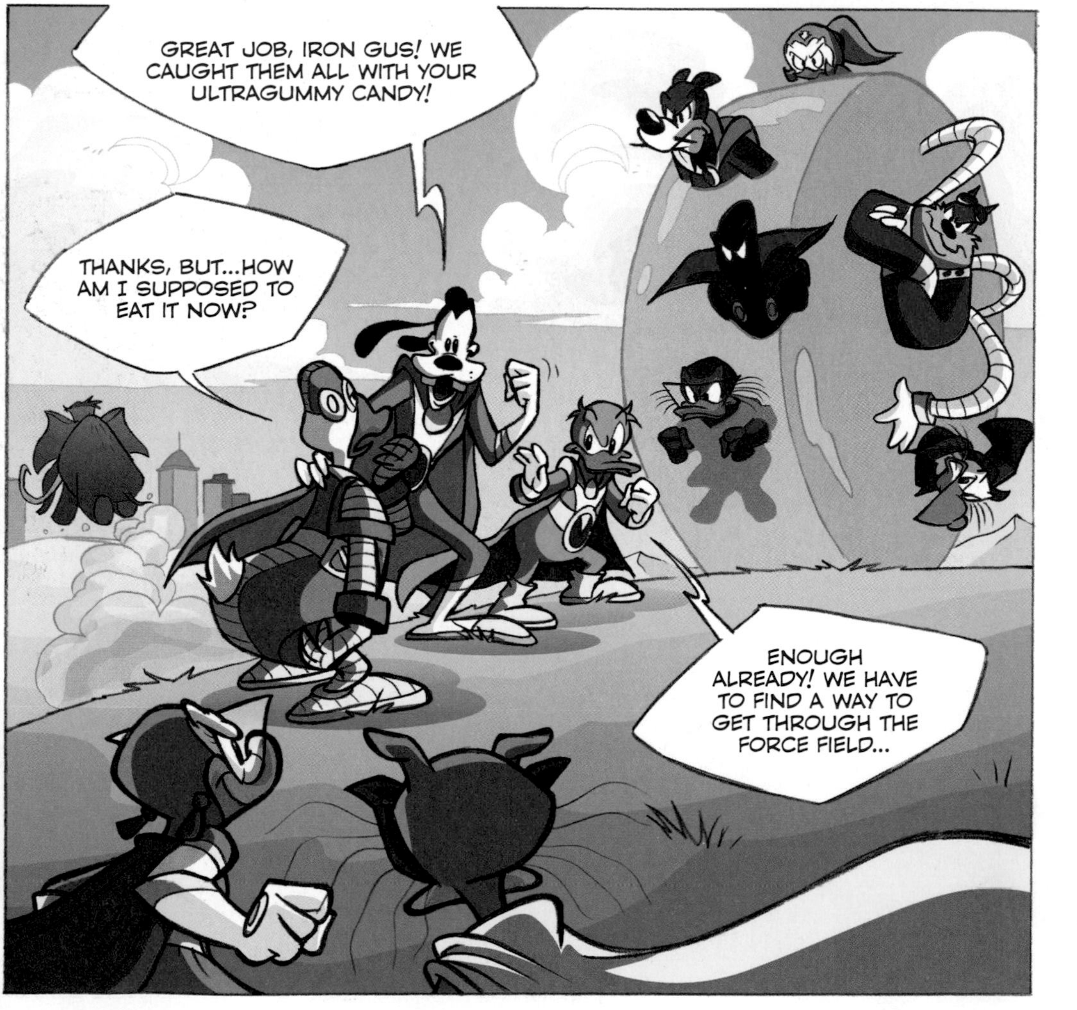
GREAT JOB, IRON GUS! WE CAUGHT THEM ALL WITH YOUR ULTRAGUMMY CANDY!
THANKS, BUT...HOW AM I SUPPOSED TO EAT IT NOW?
ENOUGH ALREADY! WE HAVE TO FIND A WAY TO GET THROUGH THE FORCE FIELD...

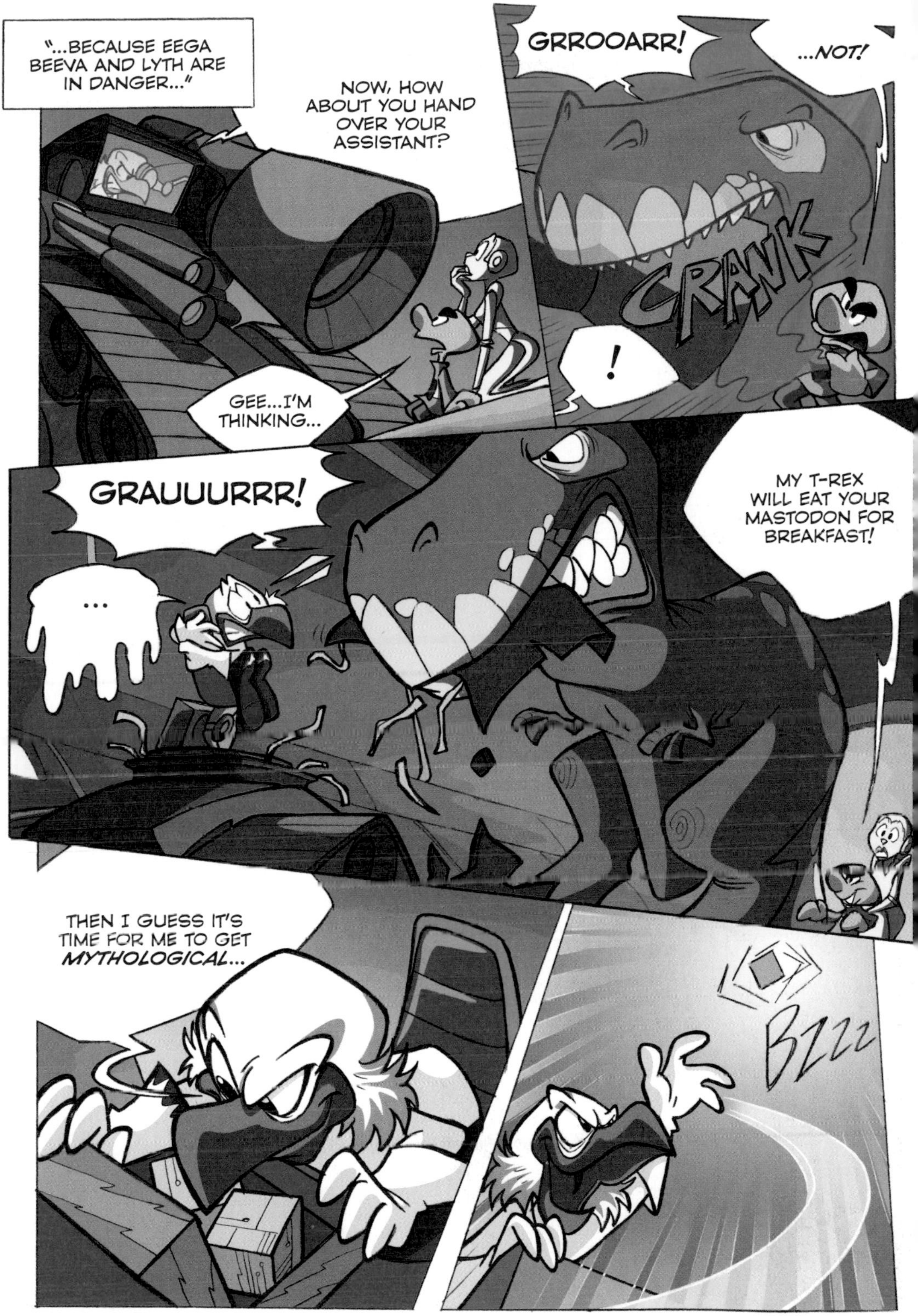
"...BECAUSE EEGA BEEVA AND LYTH ARE IN DANGER..."
NOW, HOW ABOUT YOU HAND OVER YOUR ASSISTANT?
GEE...I'M THINKING...
GRROOARR!
...NOT!
CRANK
!
GRAUUURRR!
MY T-REX WILL EAT YOUR MASTODON FOR BREAKFAST!
...
THEN I GUESS IT'S TIME FOR ME TO GET MYTHOLOGICAL...
BZZZ

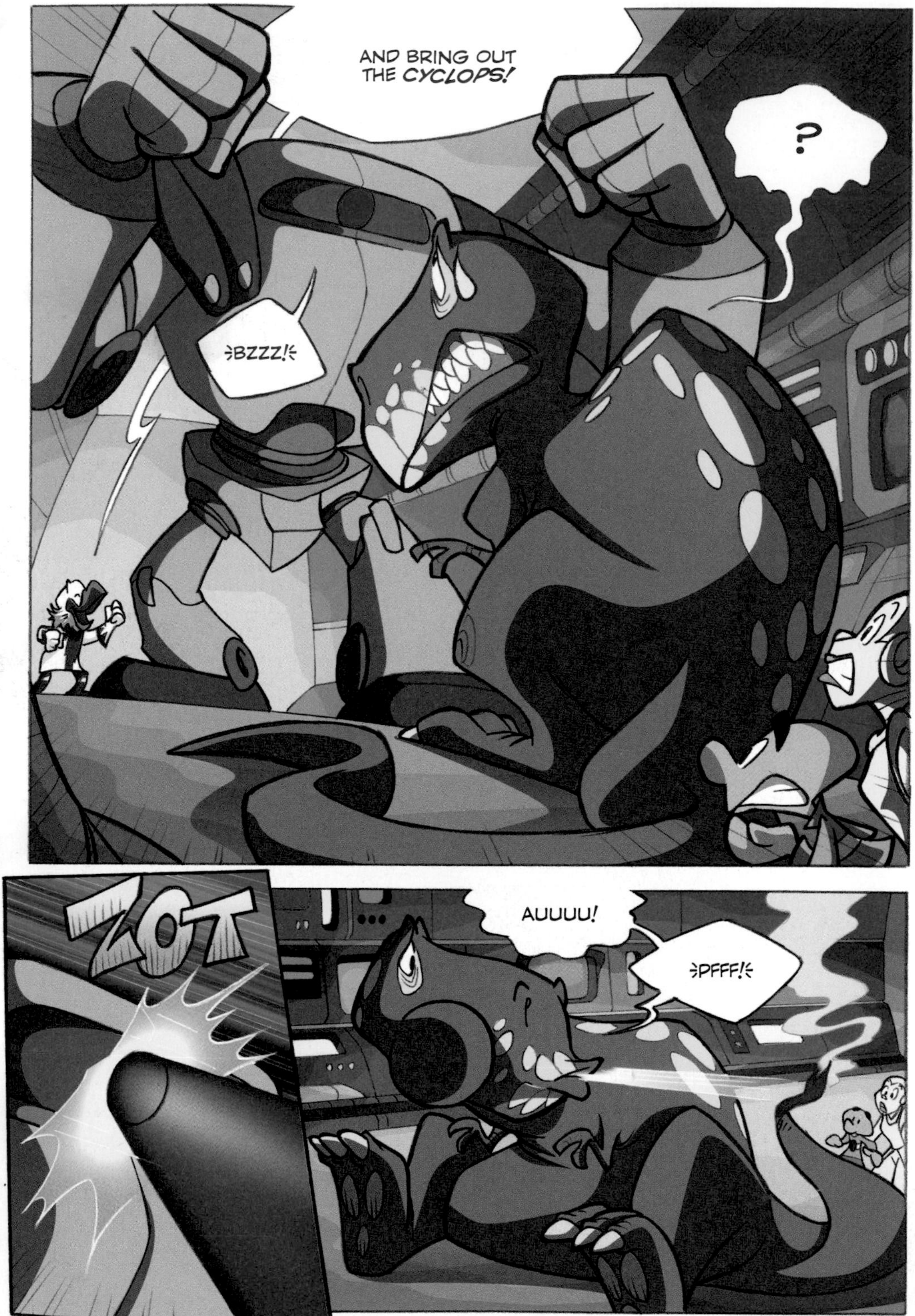
AND BRING OUT THE *CYCLOPS!*
?
BZZZ!
ZOT
AUUUU!
PFFF!

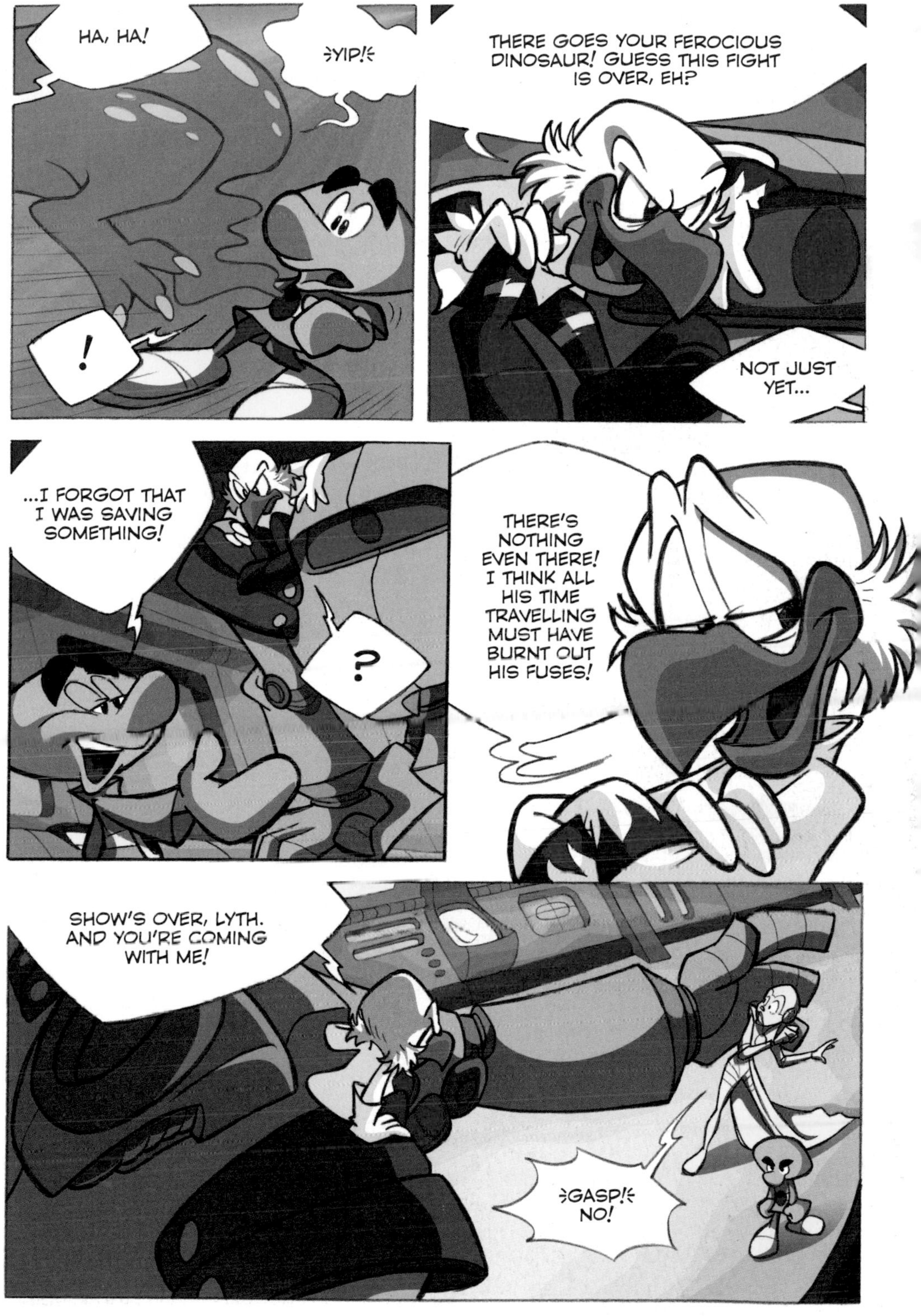
HA, HA!
≽YIP!≼
!
THERE GOES YOUR FEROCIOUS DINOSAUR! GUESS THIS FIGHT IS OVER, EH?
NOT JUST YET...
...I FORGOT THAT I WAS SAVING SOMETHING!
?
THERE'S NOTHING EVEN THERE! I THINK ALL HIS TIME TRAVELLING MUST HAVE BURNT OUT HIS FUSES!
SHOW'S OVER, LYTH. AND YOU'RE COMING WITH ME!
≽GASP!≼ NO!

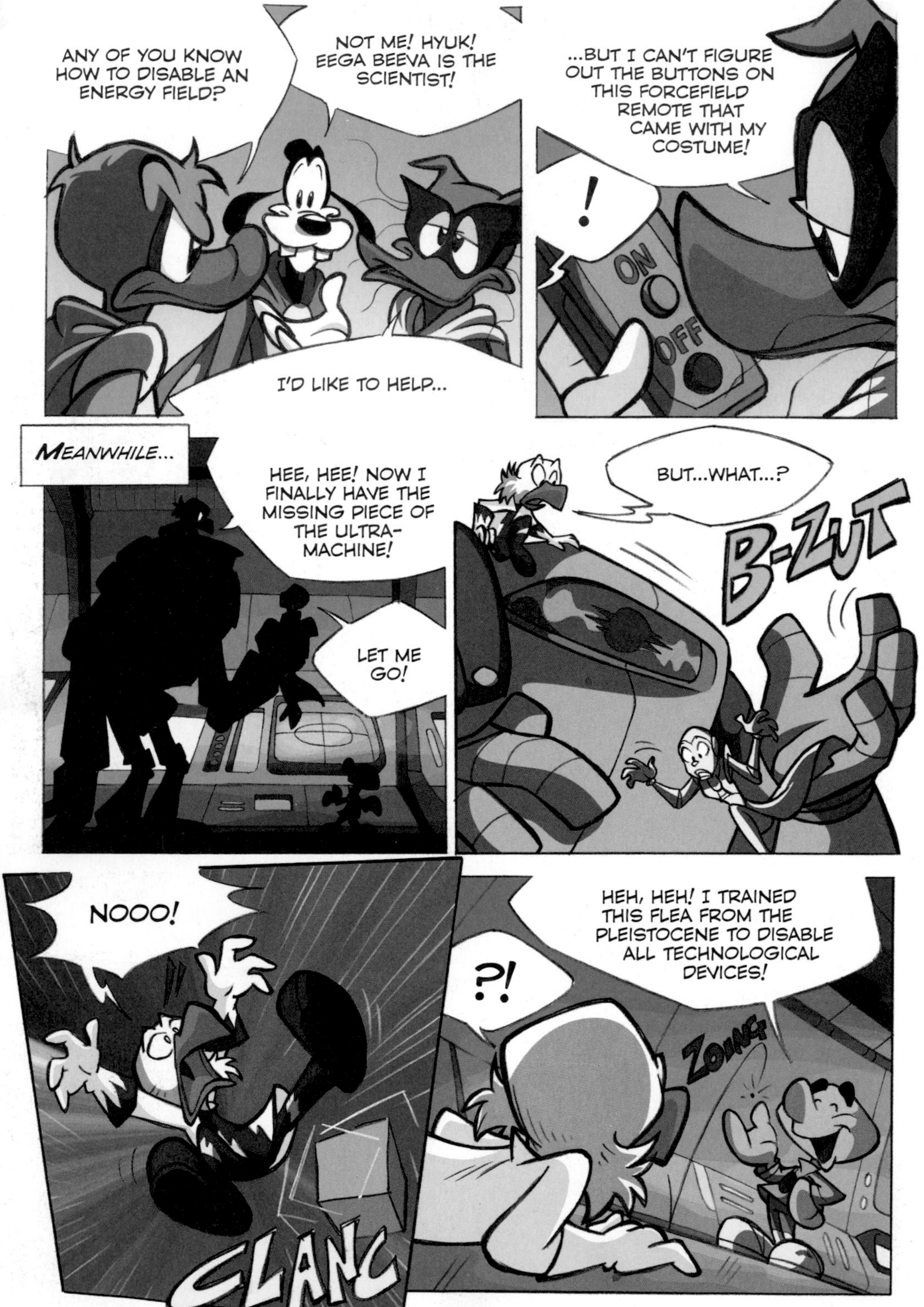
ANY OF YOU KNOW HOW TO DISABLE AN ENERGY FIELD?
NOT ME! HYUK! EEGA BEEVA IS THE SCIENTIST!
I'D LIKE TO HELP...
...BUT I CAN'T FIGURE OUT THE BUTTONS ON THIS FORCEFIELD REMOTE THAT CAME WITH MY COSTUME!
!
ON
OFF
MEANWHILE...
HEE, HEE! NOW I FINALLY HAVE THE MISSING PIECE OF THE ULTRA-MACHINE!
LET ME GO!
BUT...WHAT...?
B-ZUT
NOOO!
CLANC
HEH, HEH! I TRAINED THIS FLEA FROM THE PLEISTOCENE TO DISABLE ALL TECHNOLOGICAL DEVICES!
?!
ZOING

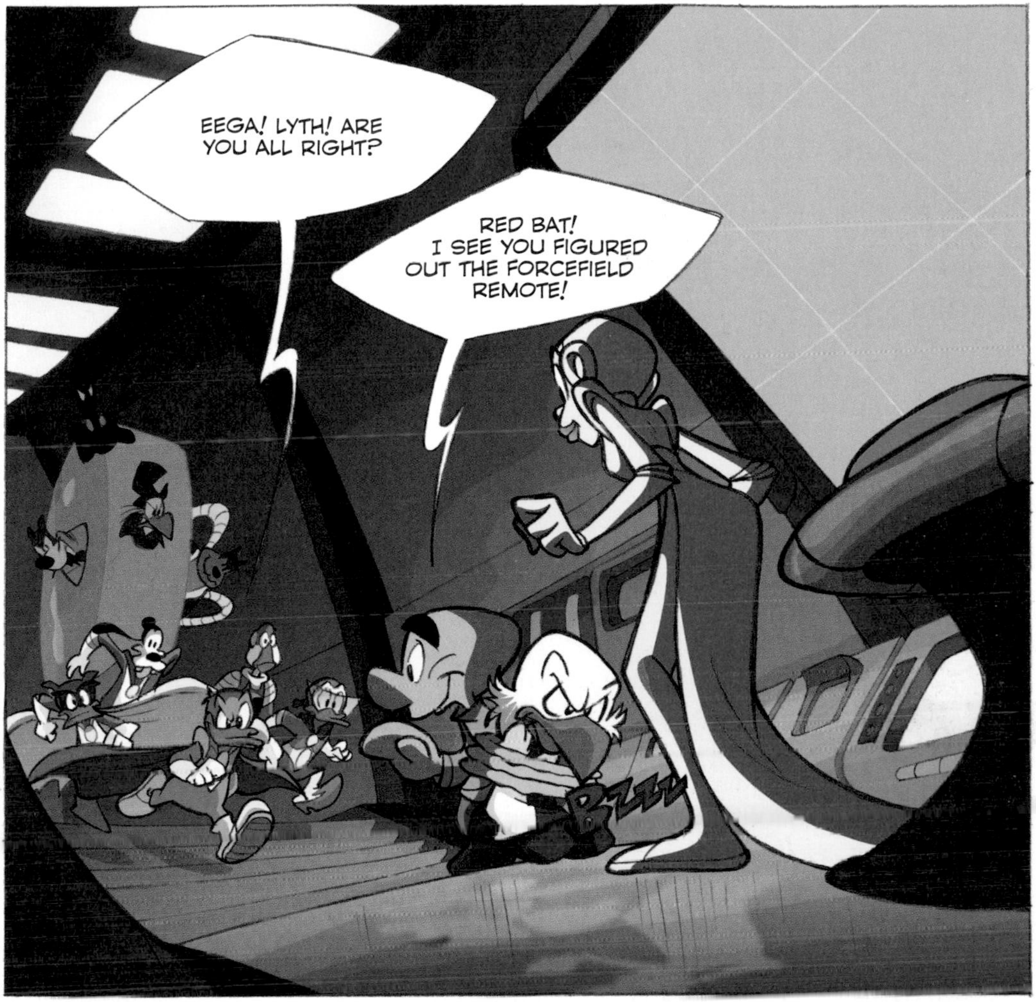
EEGA! LYTH! ARE YOU ALL RIGHT?
RED BAT! I SEE YOU FIGURED OUT THE FORCEFIELD REMOTE!
BZZZ

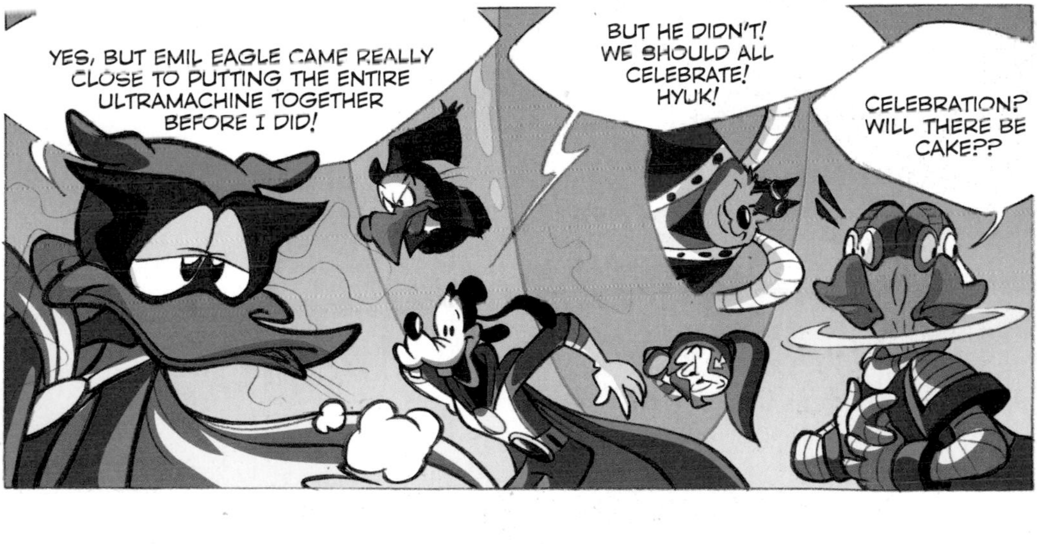
YES, BUT EMIL EAGLE CAME REALLY CLOSE TO PUTTING THE ENTIRE ULTRAMACHINE TOGETHER BEFORE I DID!
BUT HE DIDN'T! WE SHOULD ALL CELEBRATE! HYUK!
CELEBRATION? WILL THERE BE CAKE??

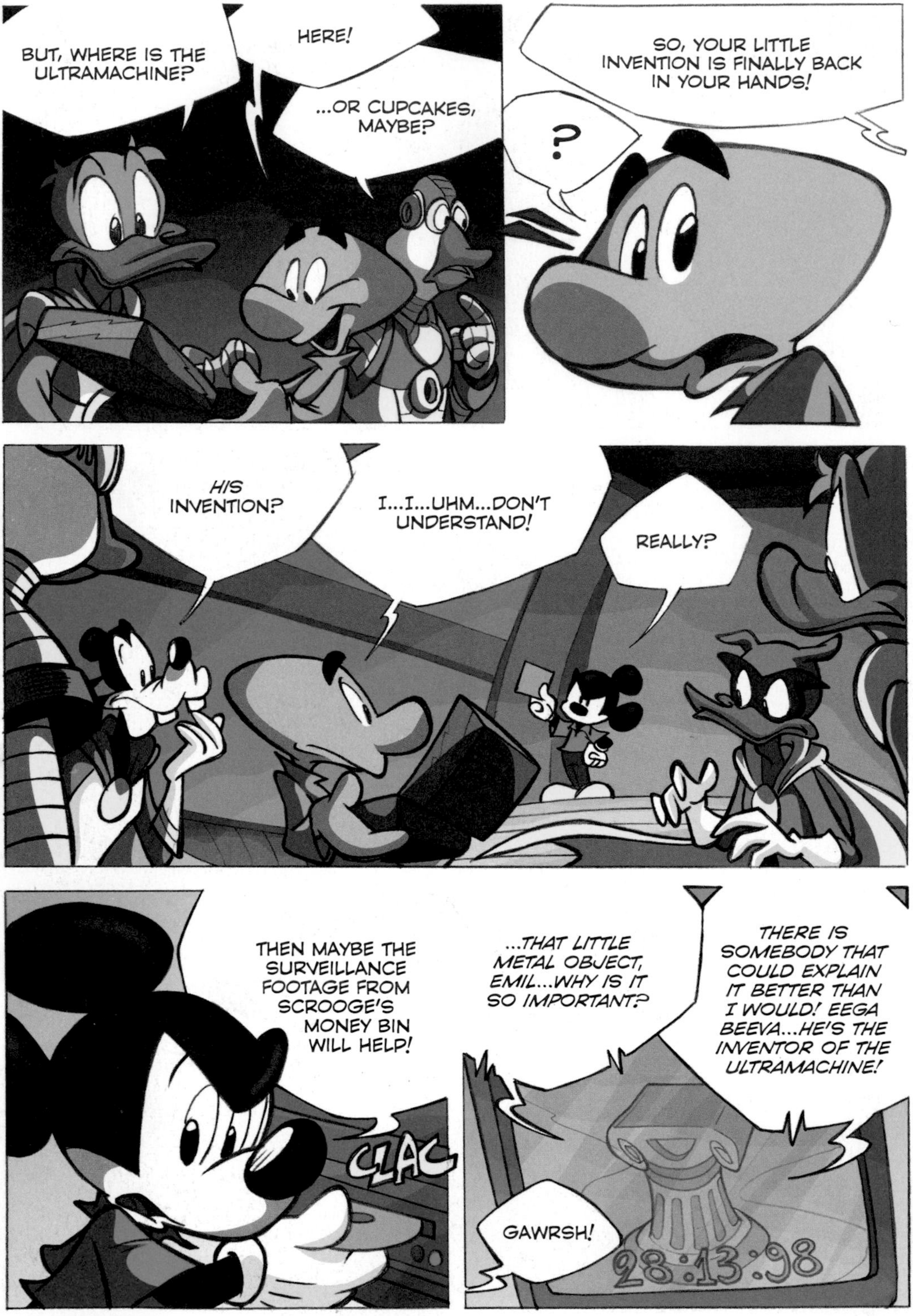
BUT, WHERE IS THE ULTRAMACHINE?
HERE!
...OR CUPCAKES, MAYBE?
SO, YOUR LITTLE INVENTION IS FINALLY BACK IN YOUR HANDS!
?
HIS INVENTION?
I...I...UHM...DON'T UNDERSTAND!
REALLY?
THEN MAYBE THE SURVEILLANCE FOOTAGE FROM SCROOGE'S MONEY BIN WILL HELP!
CLAC
...THAT LITTLE METAL OBJECT, EMIL...WHY IS IT SO IMPORTANT?
THERE IS SOMEBODY THAT COULD EXPLAIN IT BETTER THAN I WOULD! EEGA BEEVA...HE'S THE INVENTOR OF THE ULTRAMACHINE!
GAWRSH!
28:13:98

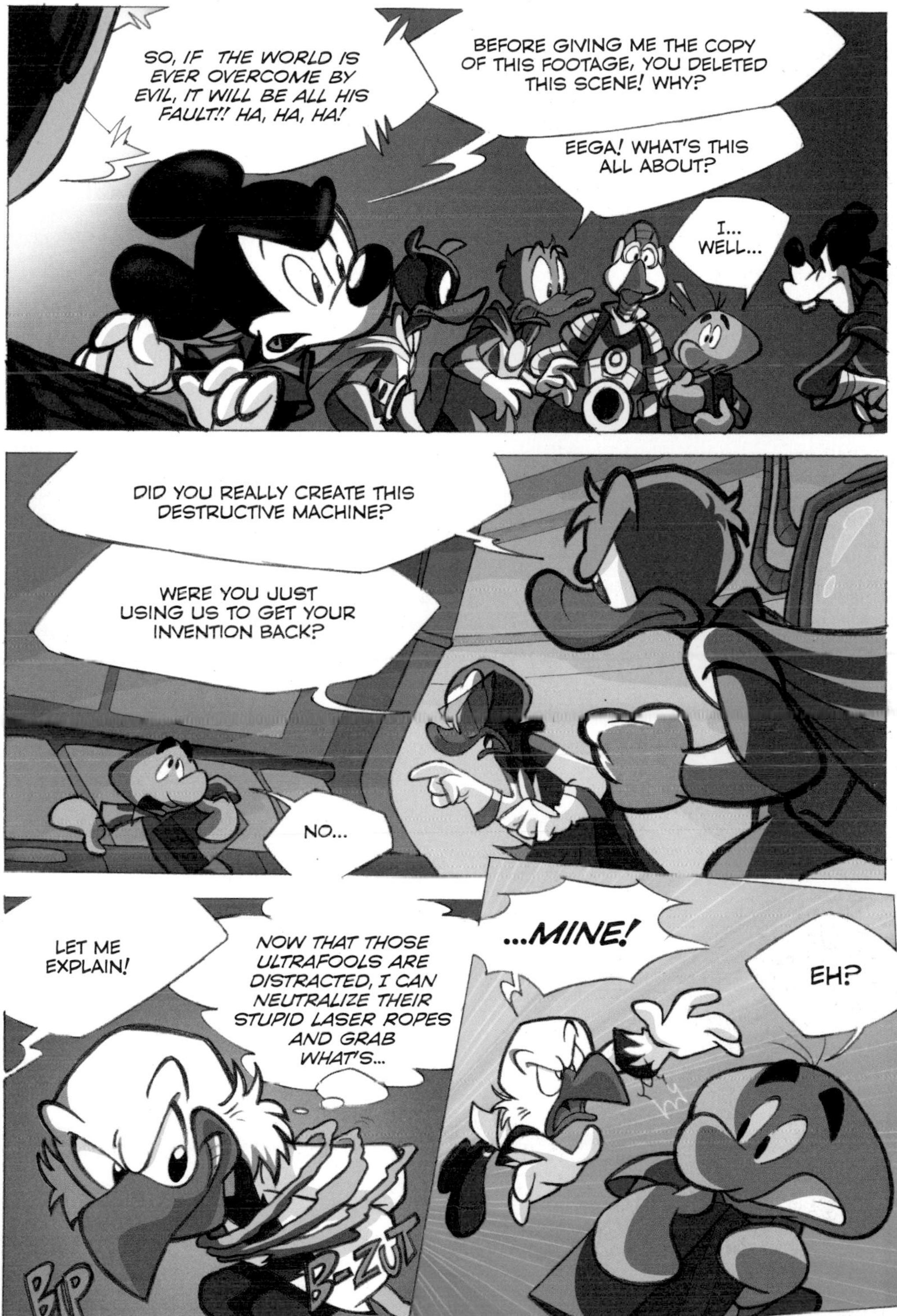
SO, IF THE WORLD IS EVER OVERCOME BY EVIL, IT WILL BE ALL HIS FAULT!! HA, HA, HA!
BEFORE GIVING ME THE COPY OF THIS FOOTAGE, YOU DELETED THIS SCENE! WHY?
EEGA! WHAT'S THIS ALL ABOUT?
I... WELL...
DID YOU REALLY CREATE THIS DESTRUCTIVE MACHINE?
WERE YOU JUST USING US TO GET YOUR INVENTION BACK?
NO...
LET ME EXPLAIN!
NOW THAT THOSE ULTRAFOOLS ARE DISTRACTED, I CAN NEUTRALIZE THEIR STUPID LASER ROPES AND GRAB WHAT'S...
BIP
B-ZUT
...MINE!
EH?

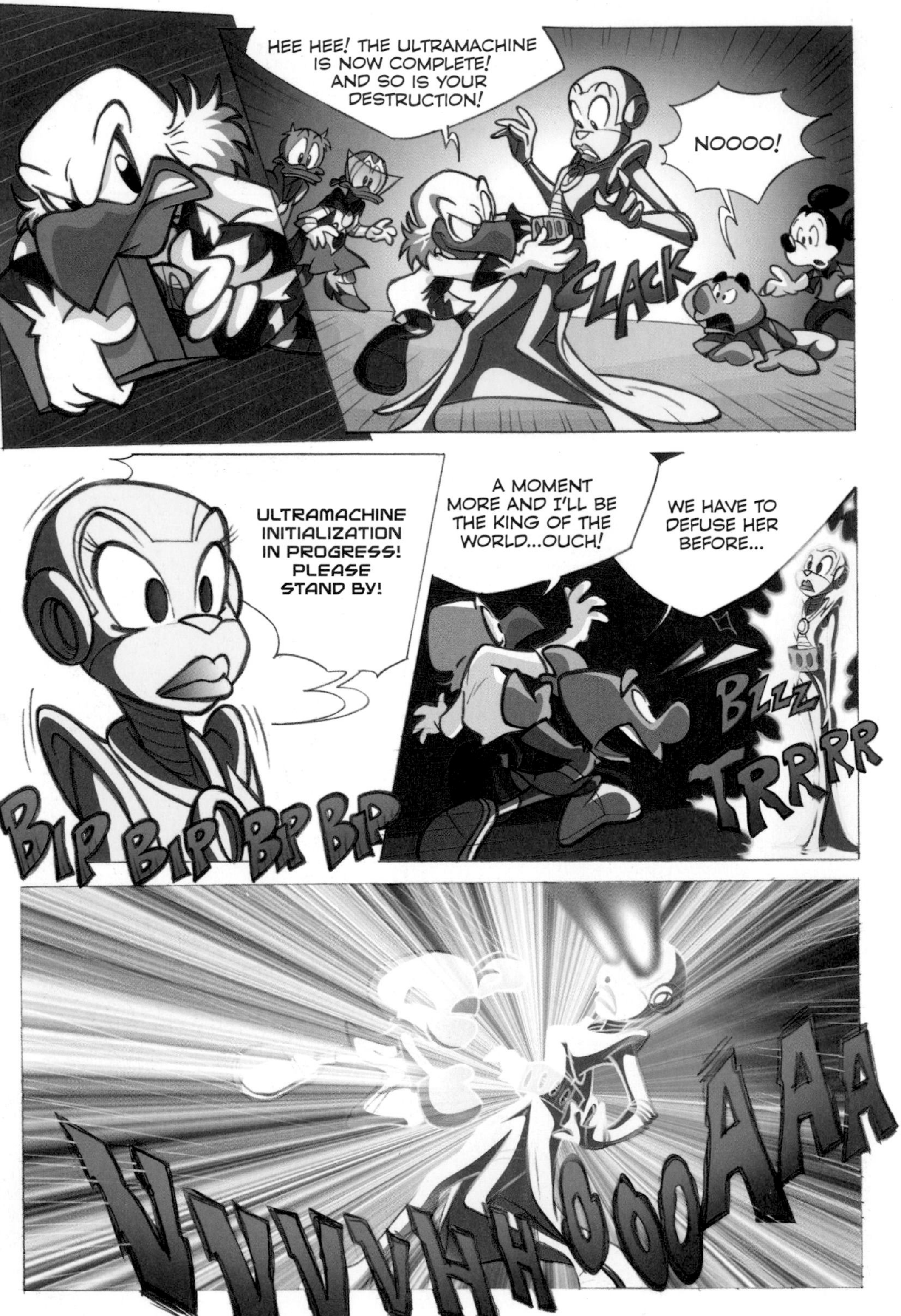
HEE HEE! THE ULTRAMACHINE IS NOW COMPLETE! AND SO IS YOUR DESTRUCTION!
NOOOO!
CLACK
ULTRAMACHINE INITIALIZATION IN PROGRESS! PLEASE STAND BY!
BIP BIP BIP BIP
A MOMENT MORE AND I'LL BE THE KING OF THE WORLD...OUCH!
WE HAVE TO DEFUSE HER BEFORE...
BZZZ
TRRRR
VVVVHH-OOOAAA

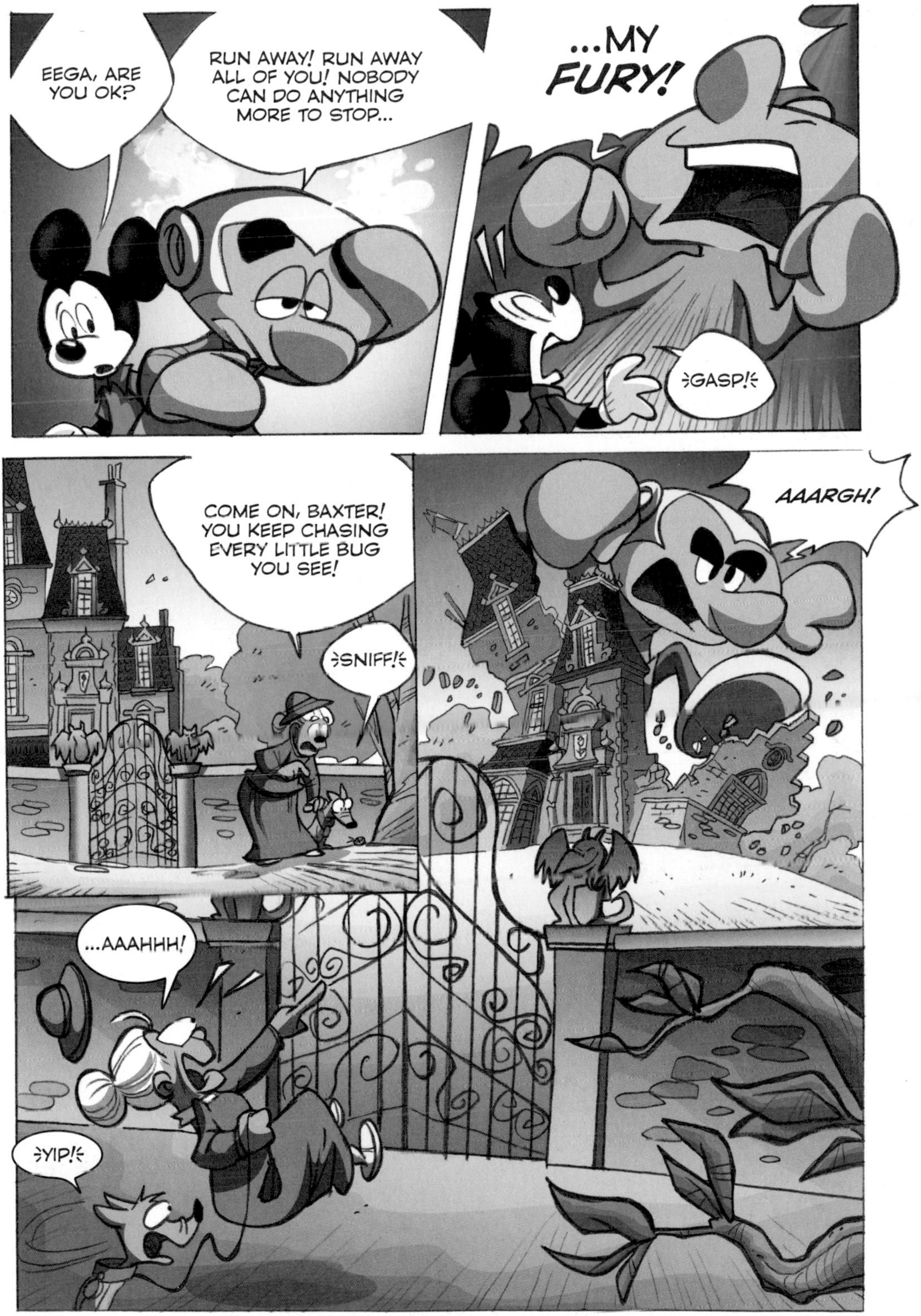
EEGA, ARE YOU OK?
RUN AWAY! RUN AWAY ALL OF YOU! NOBODY CAN DO ANYTHING MORE TO STOP...
...MY FURY!
GASP!
COME ON, BAXTER! YOU KEEP CHASING EVERY LITTLE BUG YOU SEE!
SNIFF!
AAARGH!
...AAAHHH!
YIP!

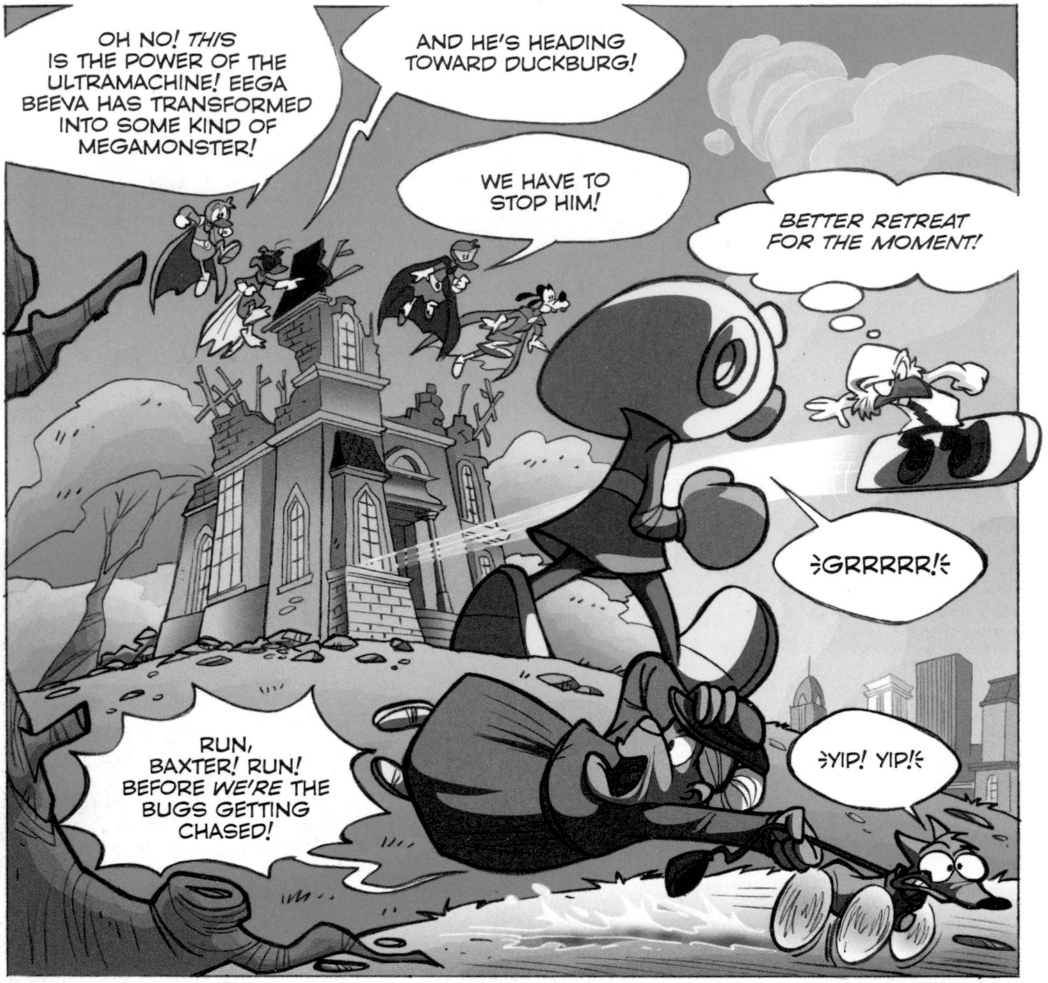
OH NO! *THIS* IS THE POWER OF THE ULTRAMACHINE! EEGA BEEVA HAS TRANSFORMED INTO SOME KIND OF MEGAMONSTER!
AND HE'S HEADING TOWARD DUCKBURG!
WE HAVE TO STOP HIM!
BETTER RETREAT FOR THE MOMENT!
GRRRRR!
RUN, BAXTER! RUN! BEFORE *WE'RE* THE BUGS GETTING CHASED!
YIP! YIP!

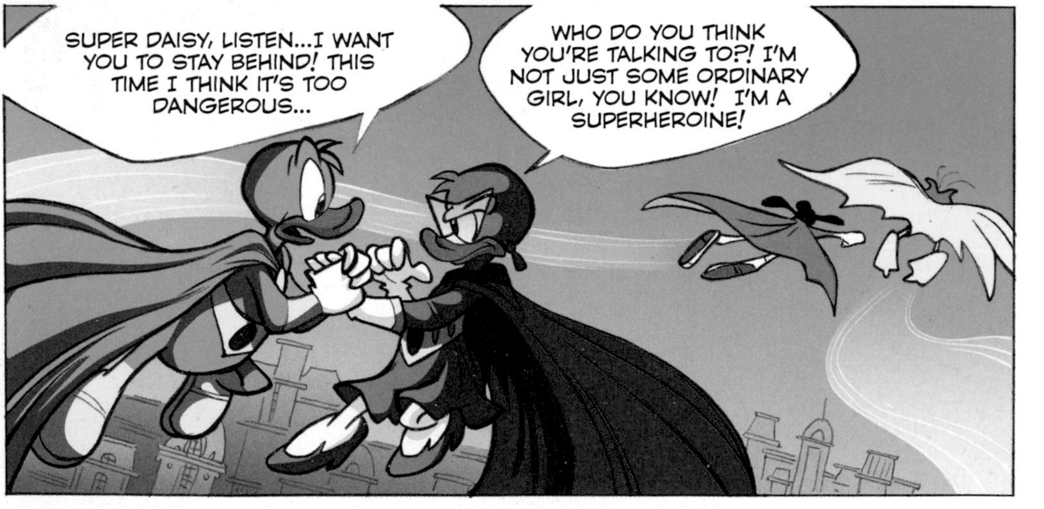
SUPER DAISY, LISTEN...I WANT YOU TO STAY BEHIND! THIS TIME I THINK IT'S TOO DANGEROUS...
WHO DO YOU THINK YOU'RE TALKING TO?! I'M NOT JUST SOME ORDINARY GIRL, YOU KNOW! I'M A SUPERHEROINE!

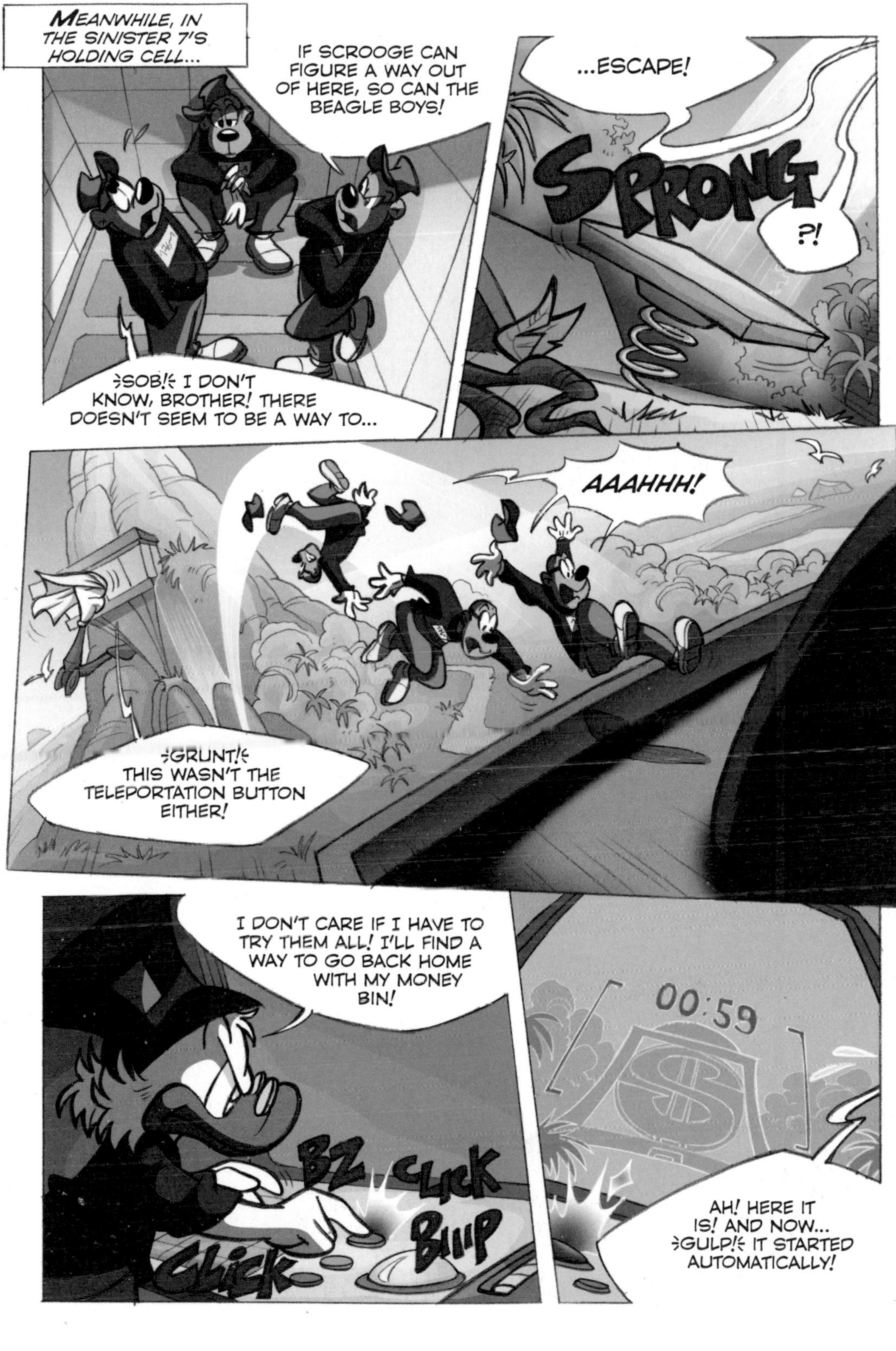
MEANWHILE, IN THE SINISTER 7'S HOLDING CELL...
IF SCROOGE CAN FIGURE A WAY OUT OF HERE, SO CAN THE BEAGLE BOYS!
SOB! I DON'T KNOW, BROTHER! THERE DOESN'T SEEM TO BE A WAY TO...
...ESCAPE!
SPRONG
?!
AAAHHH!
GRUNT! THIS WASN'T THE TELEPORTATION BUTTON EITHER!
I DON'T CARE IF I HAVE TO TRY THEM ALL! I'LL FIND A WAY TO GO BACK HOME WITH MY MONEY BIN!
BZ
CLICK
BLIIP
CLICK
00:59
AH! HERE IT IS! AND NOW... GULP! IT STARTED AUTOMATICALLY!

FIFTY-SEVEN SECONDS TO TELEPORTATION!

I'VE GOT TO HURRY! I HAVE LESS THEN A MINUTE TO REACH THE MONEY BIN!

THIRTY SECONDS!

UH? WHAT'S HAPPENING?

TEN, NINE, EIGHT...

§PUFF!§ JUST IN TIME!

...TWO, ONE... CONTACT!

SSSHAAAA

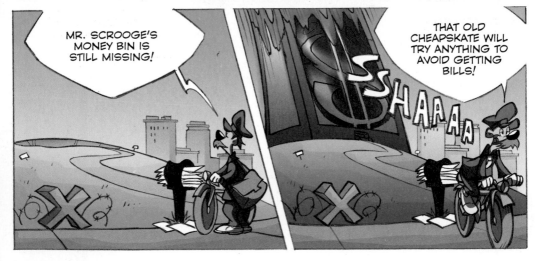

MR. SCROOGE'S MONEY BIN IS STILL MISSING!

THAT OLD CHEAPSKATE WILL TRY ANYTHING TO AVOID GETTING BILLS!

SSHAAAA

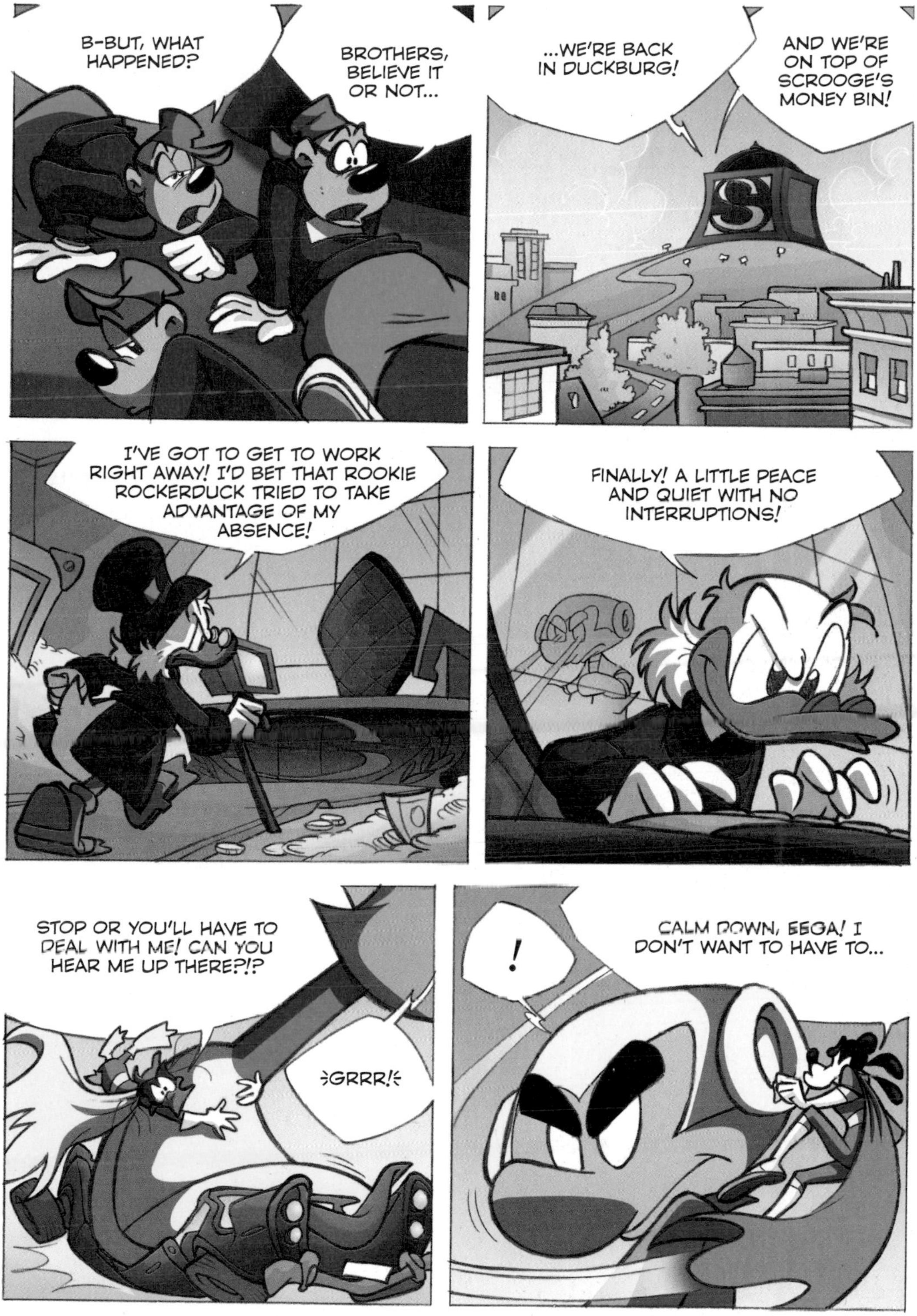
B-BUT, WHAT HAPPENED?
BROTHERS, BELIEVE IT OR NOT...
...WE'RE BACK IN DUCKBURG!
AND WE'RE ON TOP OF SCROOGE'S MONEY BIN!
I'VE GOT TO GET TO WORK RIGHT AWAY! I'D BET THAT ROOKIE ROCKERDUCK TRIED TO TAKE ADVANTAGE OF MY ABSENCE!
FINALLY! A LITTLE PEACE AND QUIET WITH NO INTERRUPTIONS!
STOP OR YOU'LL HAVE TO DEAL WITH ME! CAN YOU HEAR ME UP THERE?!?
GRRR!
!
CALM DOWN, EEGA! I DON'T WANT TO HAVE TO...

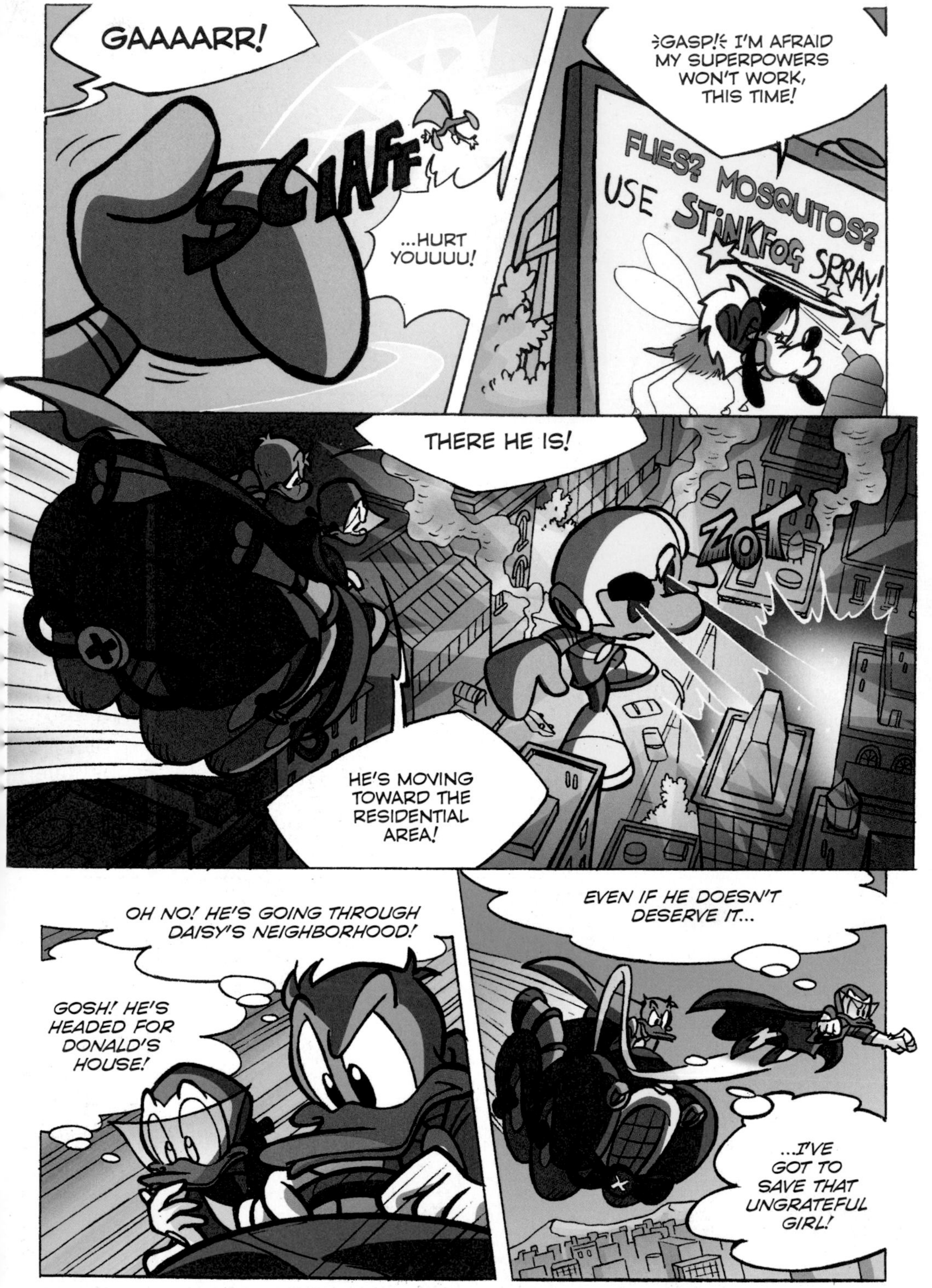
GAAAARR!
SCIAFF
...HURT YOUUUU!
GASP! I'M AFRAID MY SUPERPOWERS WON'T WORK, THIS TIME!
FLIES? MOSQUITOS? USE STINKFOG SPRAY!
THERE HE IS!
ZOT
HE'S MOVING TOWARD THE RESIDENTIAL AREA!
OH NO! HE'S GOING THROUGH DAISY'S NEIGHBORHOOD!
GOSH! HE'S HEADED FOR DONALD'S HOUSE!
EVEN IF HE DOESN'T DESERVE IT...
...I'VE GOT TO SAVE THAT UNGRATEFUL GIRL!

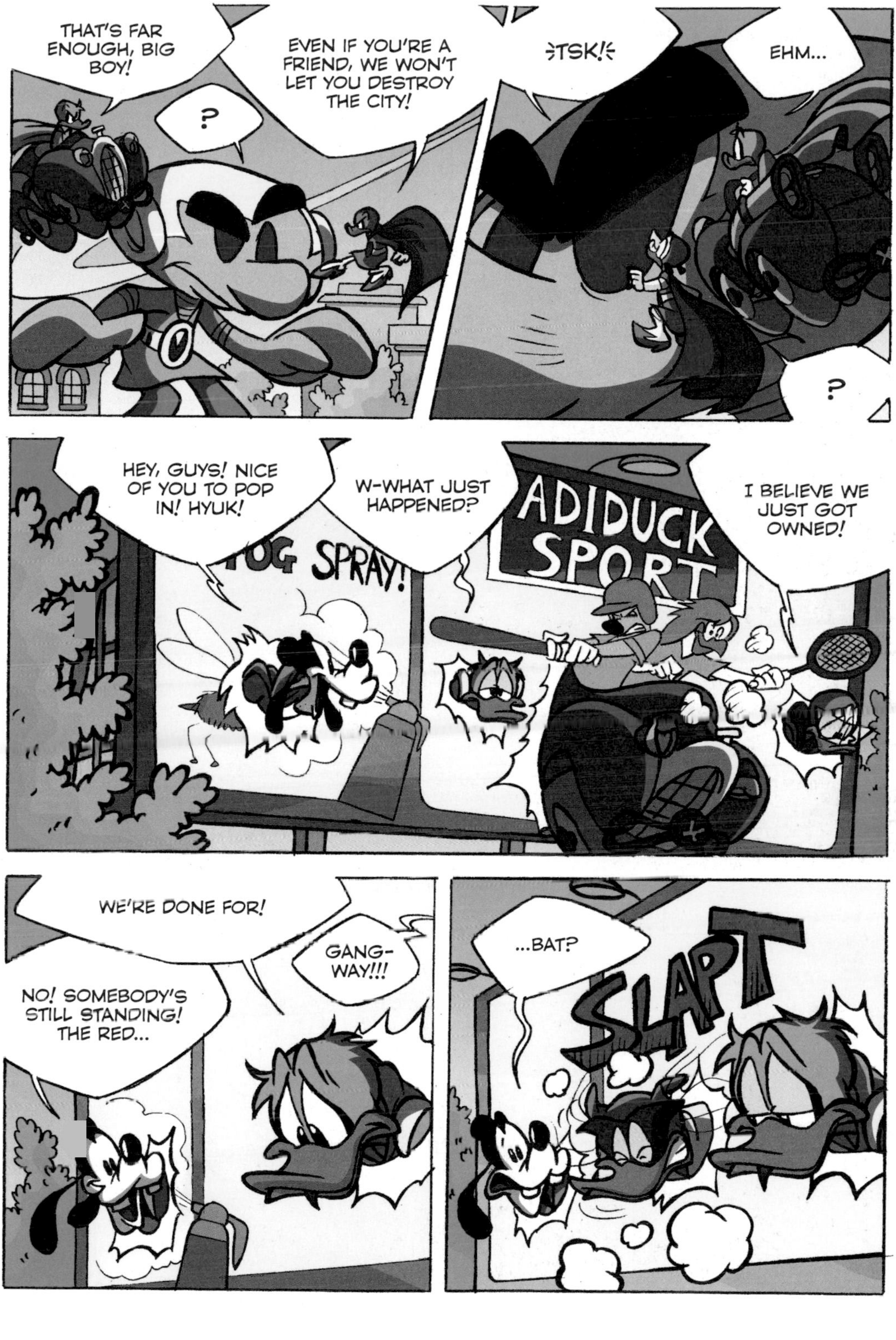
THAT'S FAR ENOUGH, BIG BOY!
?
EVEN IF YOU'RE A FRIEND, WE WON'T LET YOU DESTROY THE CITY!
TSK!
EHM...
?
HEY, GUYS! NICE OF YOU TO POP IN! HYUK!
W-WHAT JUST HAPPENED?
ADIDUCK SPORT
I BELIEVE WE JUST GOT OWNED!
WE'RE DONE FOR!
NO! SOMEBODY'S STILL STANDING! THE RED...
GANG-WAY!!!
...BAT?
SLAPT

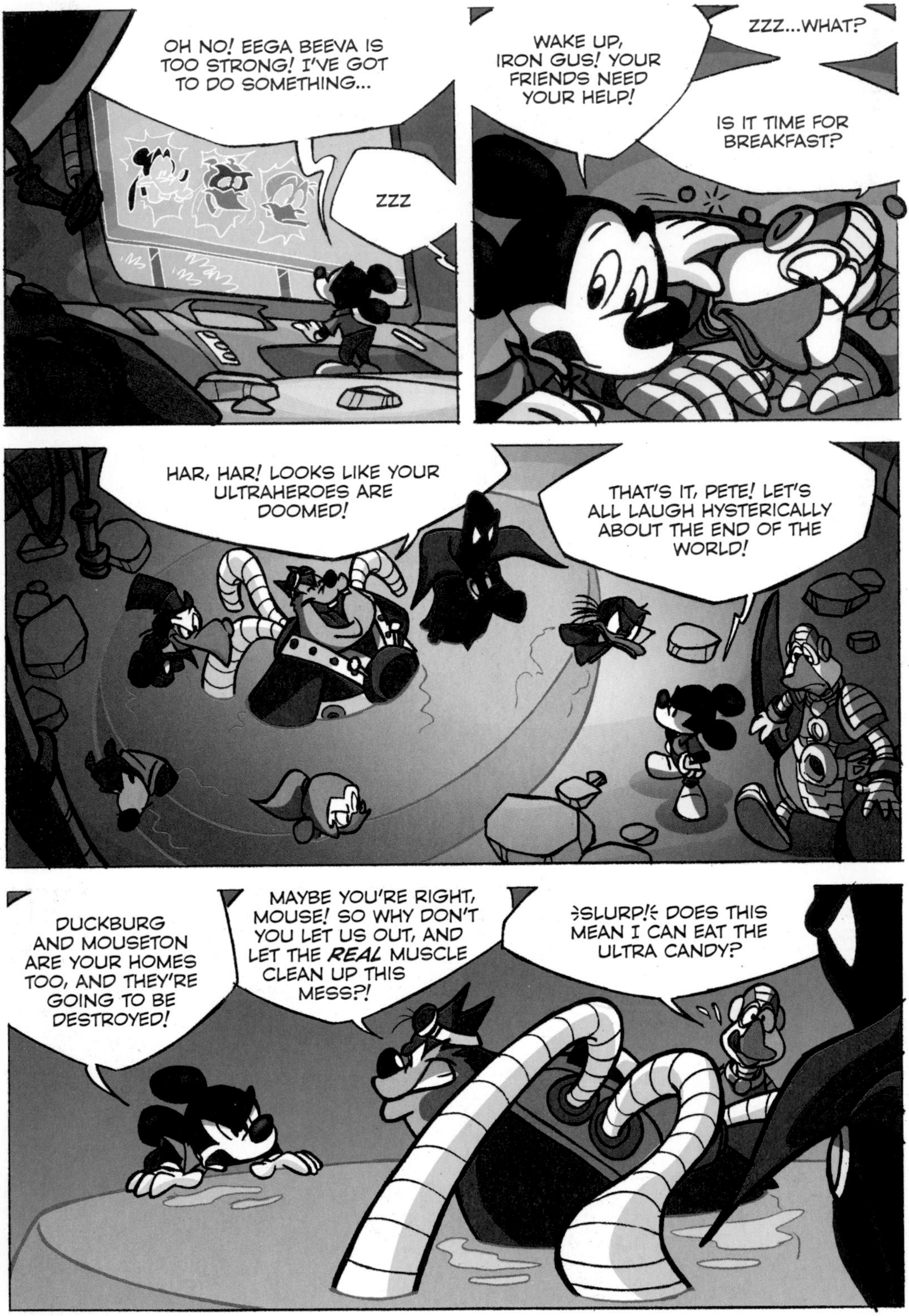
OH NO! EEGA BEEVA IS TOO STRONG! I'VE GOT TO DO SOMETHING...
ZZZ
WAKE UP, IRON GUS! YOUR FRIENDS NEED YOUR HELP!
ZZZ...WHAT?
IS IT TIME FOR BREAKFAST?
HAR, HAR! LOOKS LIKE YOUR ULTRAHEROES ARE DOOMED!
THAT'S IT, PETE! LET'S ALL LAUGH HYSTERICALLY ABOUT THE END OF THE WORLD!
DUCKBURG AND MOUSETON ARE YOUR HOMES TOO, AND THEY'RE GOING TO BE DESTROYED!
MAYBE YOU'RE RIGHT, MOUSE! SO WHY DON'T YOU LET US OUT, AND LET THE REAL MUSCLE CLEAN UP THIS MESS?!
SLURP! DOES THIS MEAN I CAN EAT THE ULTRA CANDY?

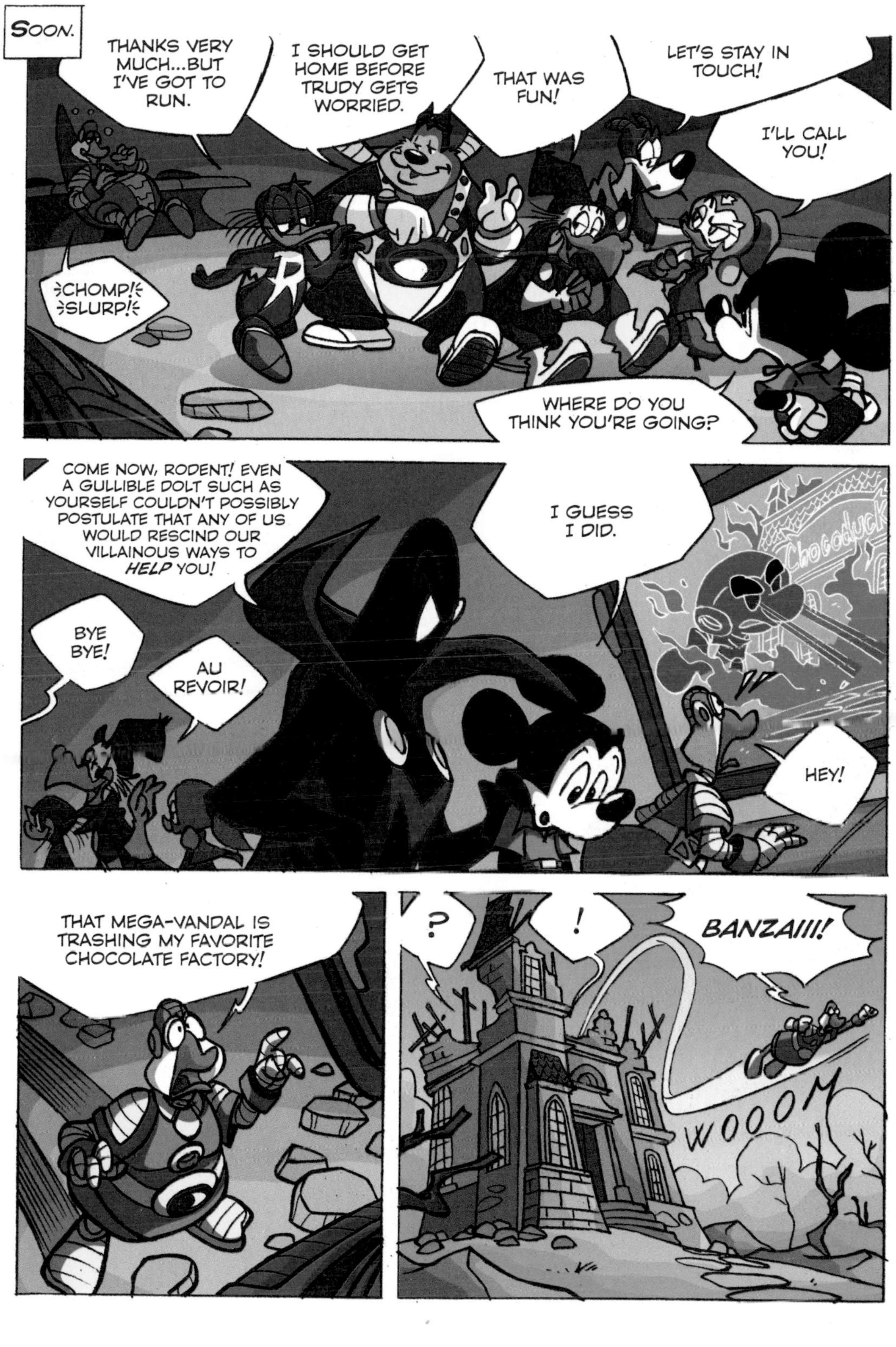
SOON.
THANKS VERY MUCH...BUT I'VE GOT TO RUN.
I SHOULD GET HOME BEFORE TRUDY GETS WORRIED.
THAT WAS FUN!
LET'S STAY IN TOUCH!
I'LL CALL YOU!
CHOMP! SLURP!
WHERE DO YOU THINK YOU'RE GOING?
COME NOW, RODENT! EVEN A GULLIBLE DOLT SUCH AS YOURSELF COULDN'T POSSIBLY POSTULATE THAT ANY OF US WOULD RESCIND OUR VILLAINOUS WAYS TO *HELP* YOU!
I GUESS I DID.
Chocoduck
BYE BYE!
AU REVOIR!
HEY!
THAT MEGA-VANDAL IS TRASHING MY FAVORITE CHOCOLATE FACTORY!
?
!
BANZAIII!
WOOOM

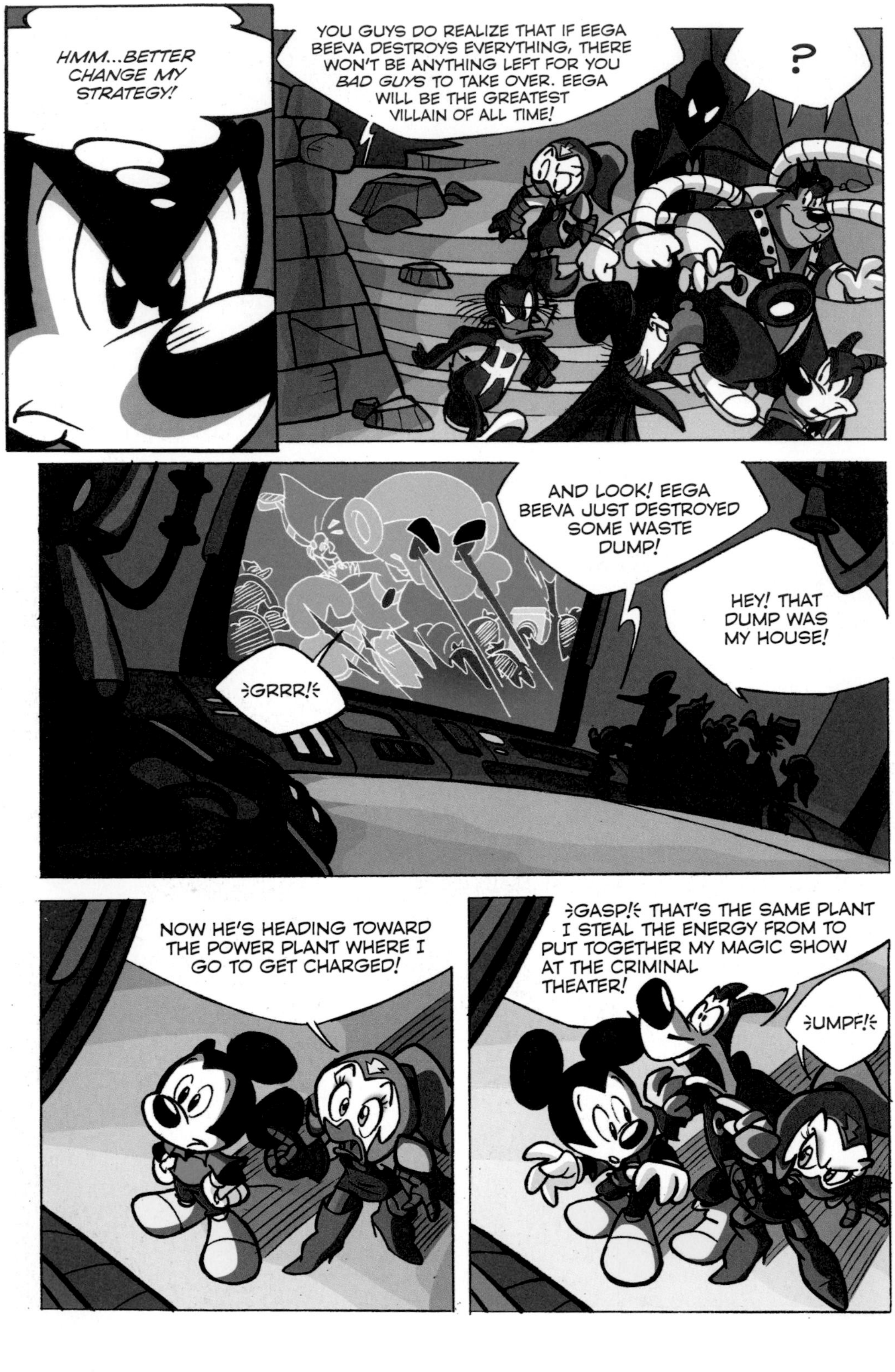
HMM...BETTER CHANGE MY STRATEGY!
YOU GUYS DO REALIZE THAT IF EEGA BEEVA DESTROYS EVERYTHING, THERE WON'T BE ANYTHING LEFT FOR YOU BAD GUYS TO TAKE OVER. EEGA WILL BE THE GREATEST VILLAIN OF ALL TIME!
?
AND LOOK! EEGA BEEVA JUST DESTROYED SOME WASTE DUMP!
HEY! THAT DUMP WAS MY HOUSE!
GRRR!
NOW HE'S HEADING TOWARD THE POWER PLANT WHERE I GO TO GET CHARGED!
GASP! THAT'S THE SAME PLANT I STEAL THE ENERGY FROM TO PUT TOGETHER MY MAGIC SHOW AT THE CRIMINAL THEATER!
UMPF!

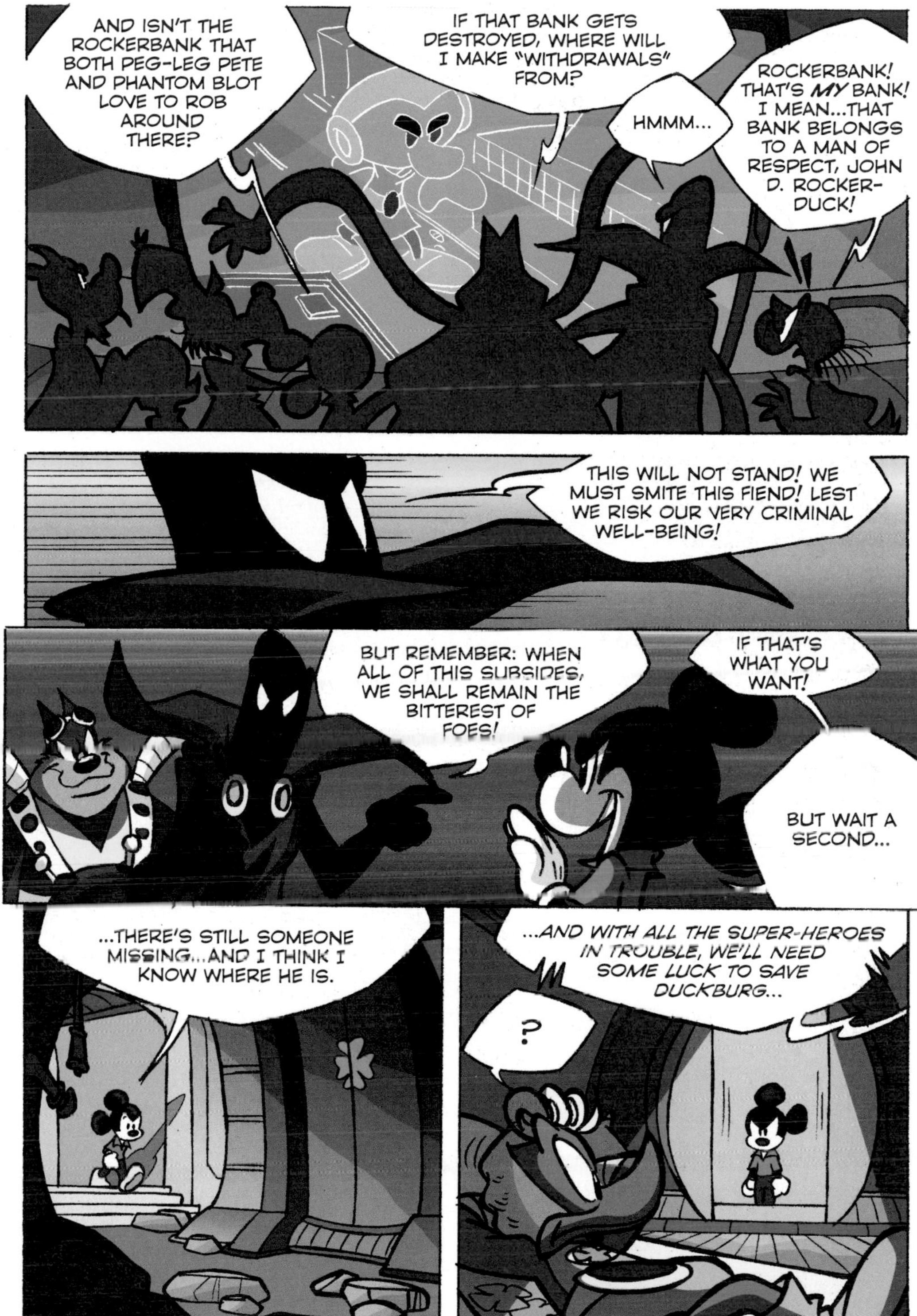
AND ISN'T THE ROCKERBANK THAT BOTH PEG-LEG PETE AND PHANTOM BLOT LOVE TO ROB AROUND THERE?
IF THAT BANK GETS DESTROYED, WHERE WILL I MAKE "WITHDRAWALS" FROM?
HMMM...
ROCKERBANK! THAT'S MY BANK! I MEAN...THAT BANK BELONGS TO A MAN OF RESPECT, JOHN D. ROCKER-DUCK!
THIS WILL NOT STAND! WE MUST SMITE THIS FIEND! LEST WE RISK OUR VERY CRIMINAL WELL-BEING!
BUT REMEMBER: WHEN ALL OF THIS SUBSIDES, WE SHALL REMAIN THE BITTEREST OF FOES!
IF THAT'S WHAT YOU WANT!
BUT WAIT A SECOND...
...THERE'S STILL SOMEONE MISSING...AND I THINK I KNOW WHERE HE IS.
...AND WITH ALL THE SUPER-HEROES IN TROUBLE, WE'LL NEED SOME LUCK TO SAVE DUCKBURG...
?

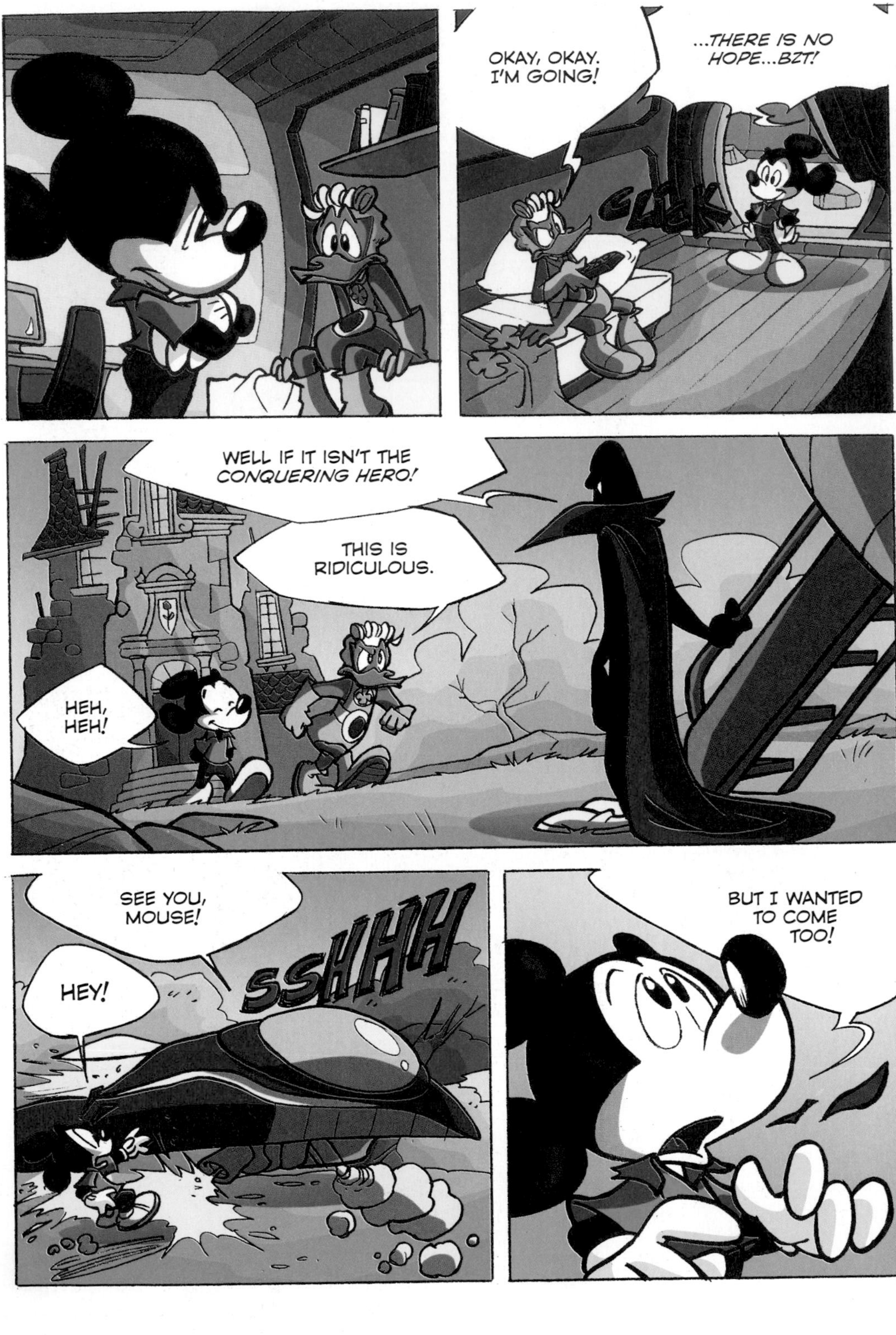
OKAY, OKAY. I'M GOING!
...THERE IS NO HOPE...BZT!
CLICK
WELL IF IT ISN'T THE *CONQUERING HERO!*
THIS IS RIDICULOUS.
HEH, HEH!
SEE YOU, MOUSE!
HEY!
SSHHH
BUT I WANTED TO COME *TOO!*

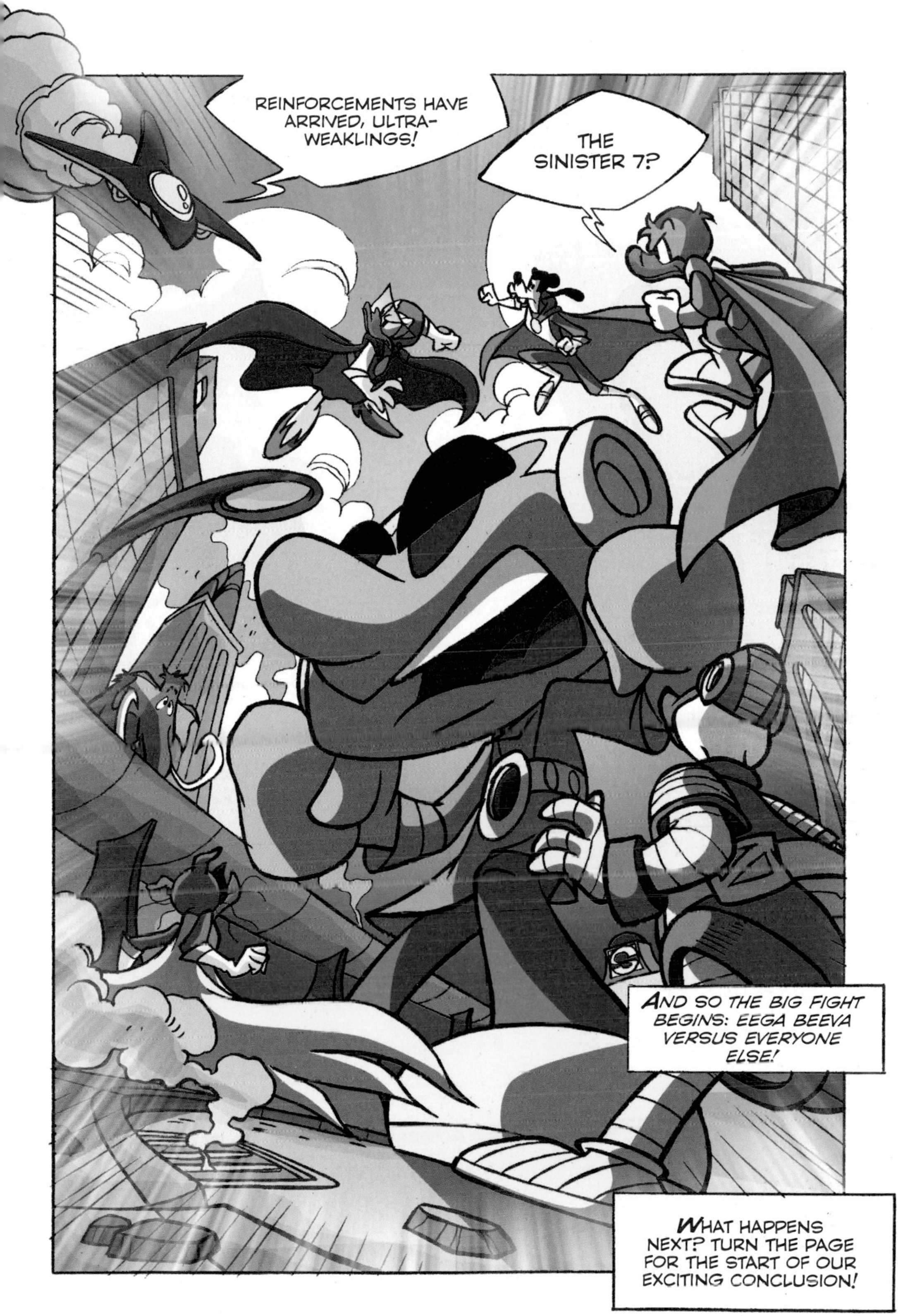
REINFORCEMENTS HAVE ARRIVED, ULTRA-WEAKLINGS!
THE SINISTER 7?
AND SO THE BIG FIGHT BEGINS: EEGA BEEVA VERSUS EVERYONE ELSE!
WHAT HAPPENS NEXT? TURN THE PAGE FOR THE START OF OUR EXCITING CONCLUSION!

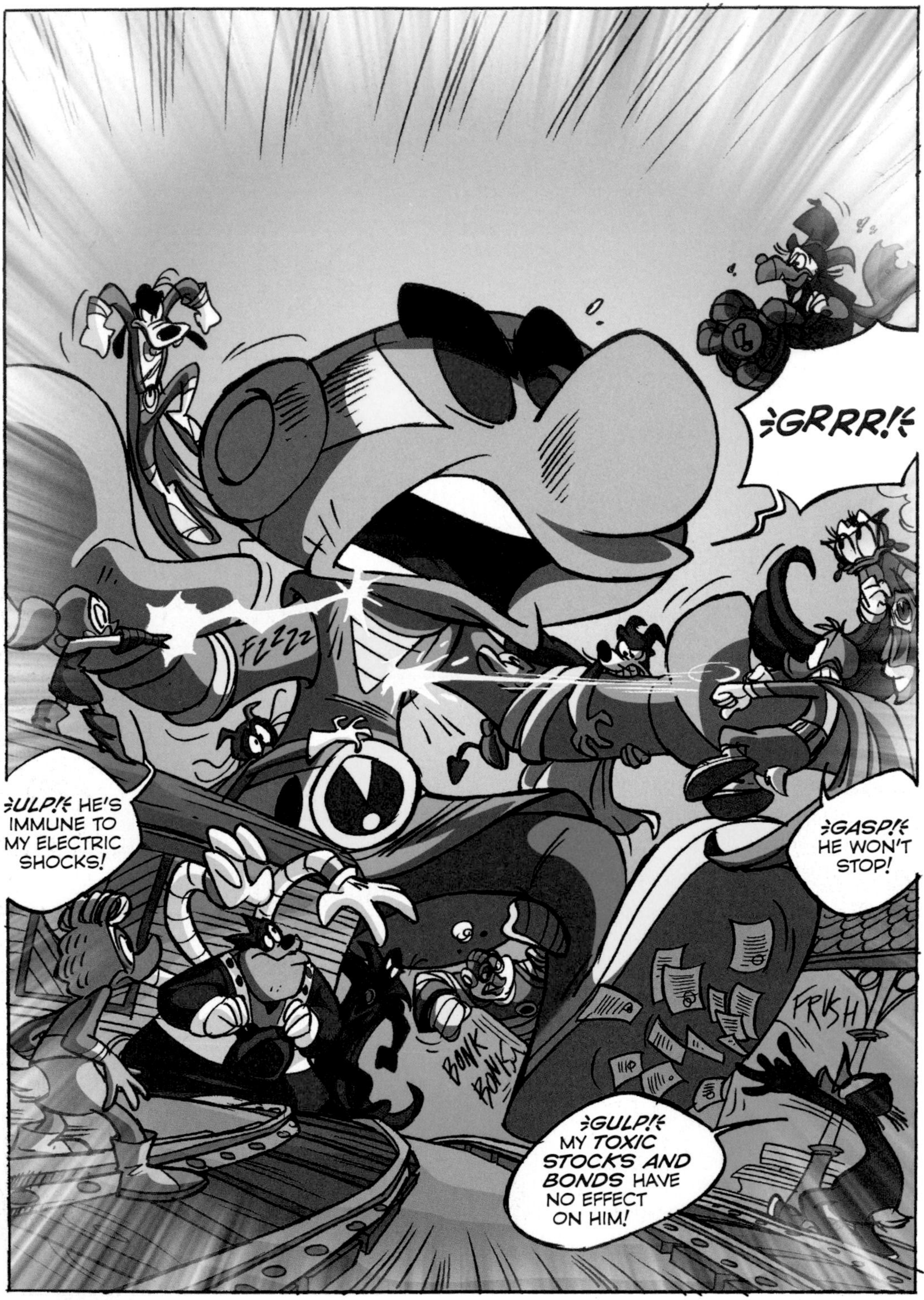
GRRR!
ULP! HE'S IMMUNE TO MY ELECTRIC SHOCKS!
GASP! HE WON'T STOP!
GULP! MY TOXIC STOCKS AND BONDS HAVE NO EFFECT ON HIM!
FZZZZ
BONK BONK
FRISH

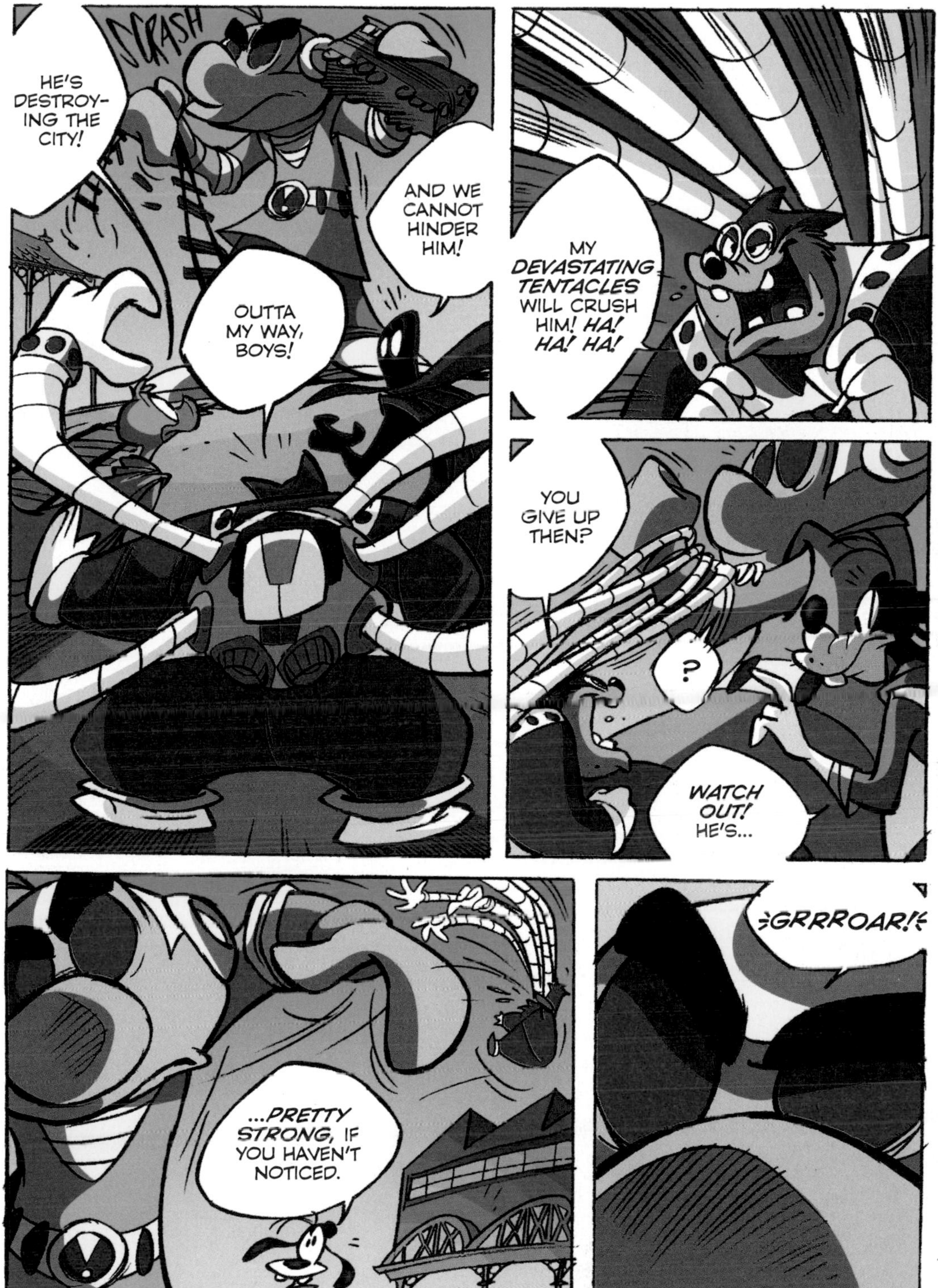
SCRASH
HE'S DESTROYING THE CITY!
AND WE CANNOT HINDER HIM!
OUTTA MY WAY, BOYS!
MY *DEVASTATING TENTACLES* WILL CRUSH HIM! *HA! HA! HA!*
YOU GIVE UP THEN?
?
WATCH OUT! HE'S...
...*PRETTY STRONG,* IF YOU HAVEN'T NOTICED.
GRRROAR!

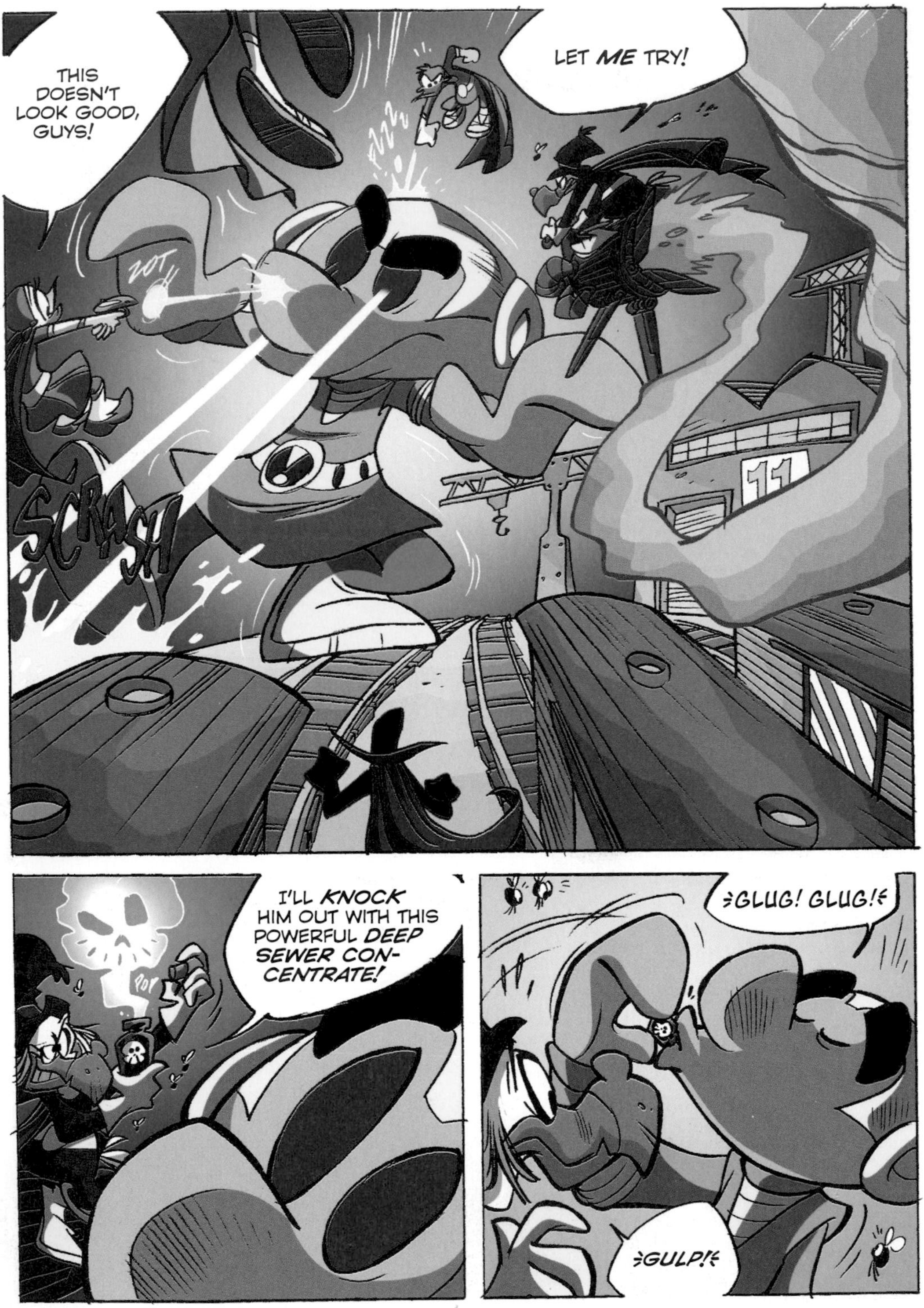
THIS DOESN'T LOOK GOOD, GUYS!
LET *ME* TRY!
ZOT
SCRASH
I'LL *KNOCK* HIM OUT WITH THIS POWERFUL *DEEP SEWER CONCENTRATE!*
GLUG! GLUG!
GULP!

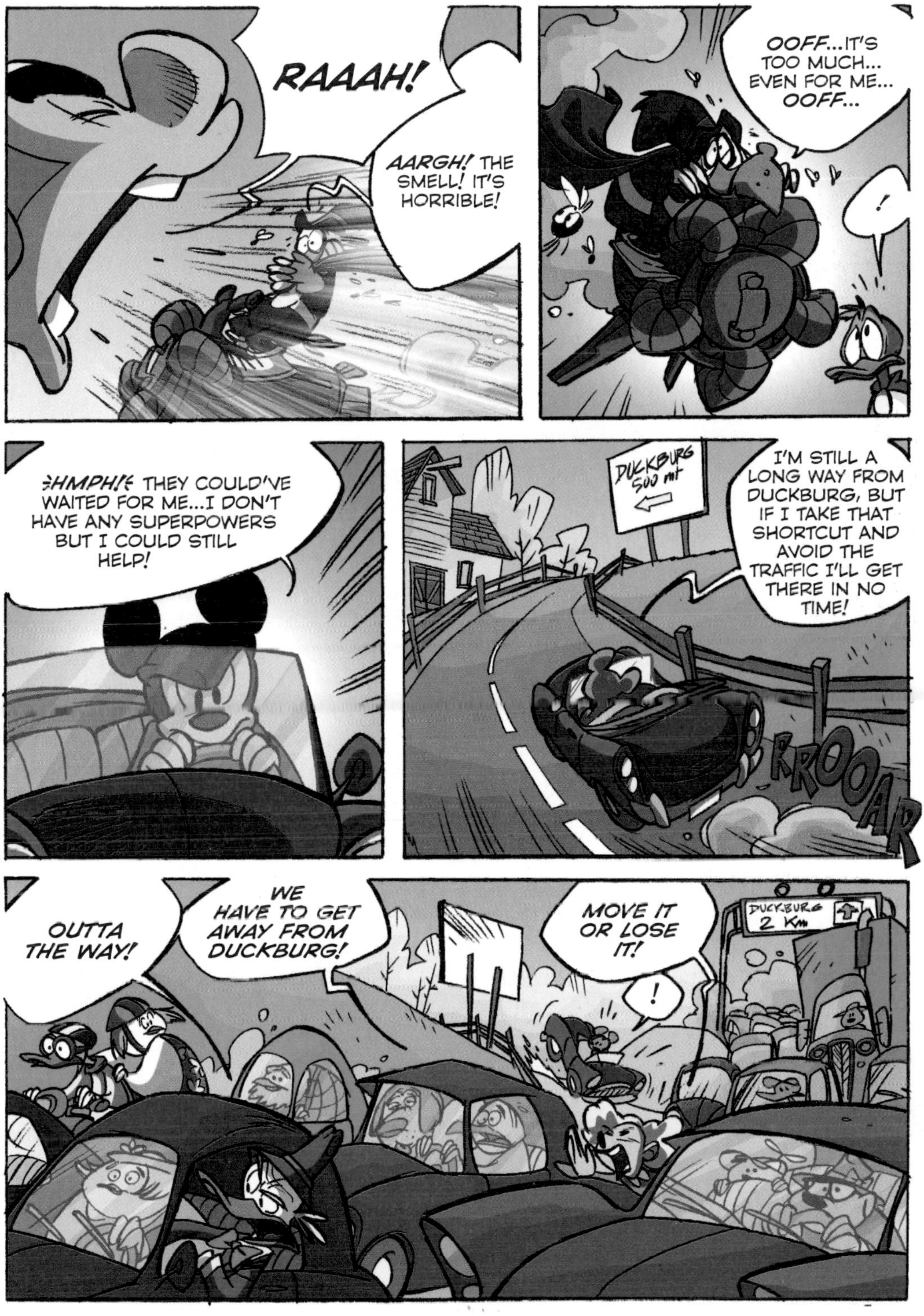
RAAAH!
AARGH! THE SMELL! IT'S HORRIBLE!
OOFF...IT'S TOO MUCH... EVEN FOR ME... OOFF...
!
HMPH! THEY COULD'VE WAITED FOR ME...I DON'T HAVE ANY SUPERPOWERS BUT I COULD STILL HELP!
DUCKBURG 500 mt
I'M STILL A LONG WAY FROM DUCKBURG, BUT IF I TAKE THAT SHORTCUT AND AVOID THE TRAFFIC I'LL GET THERE IN NO TIME!
RROOAR
OUTTA THE WAY!
WE HAVE TO GET AWAY FROM DUCKBURG!
MOVE IT OR LOSE IT!
DUCKBURG 2 Km
!

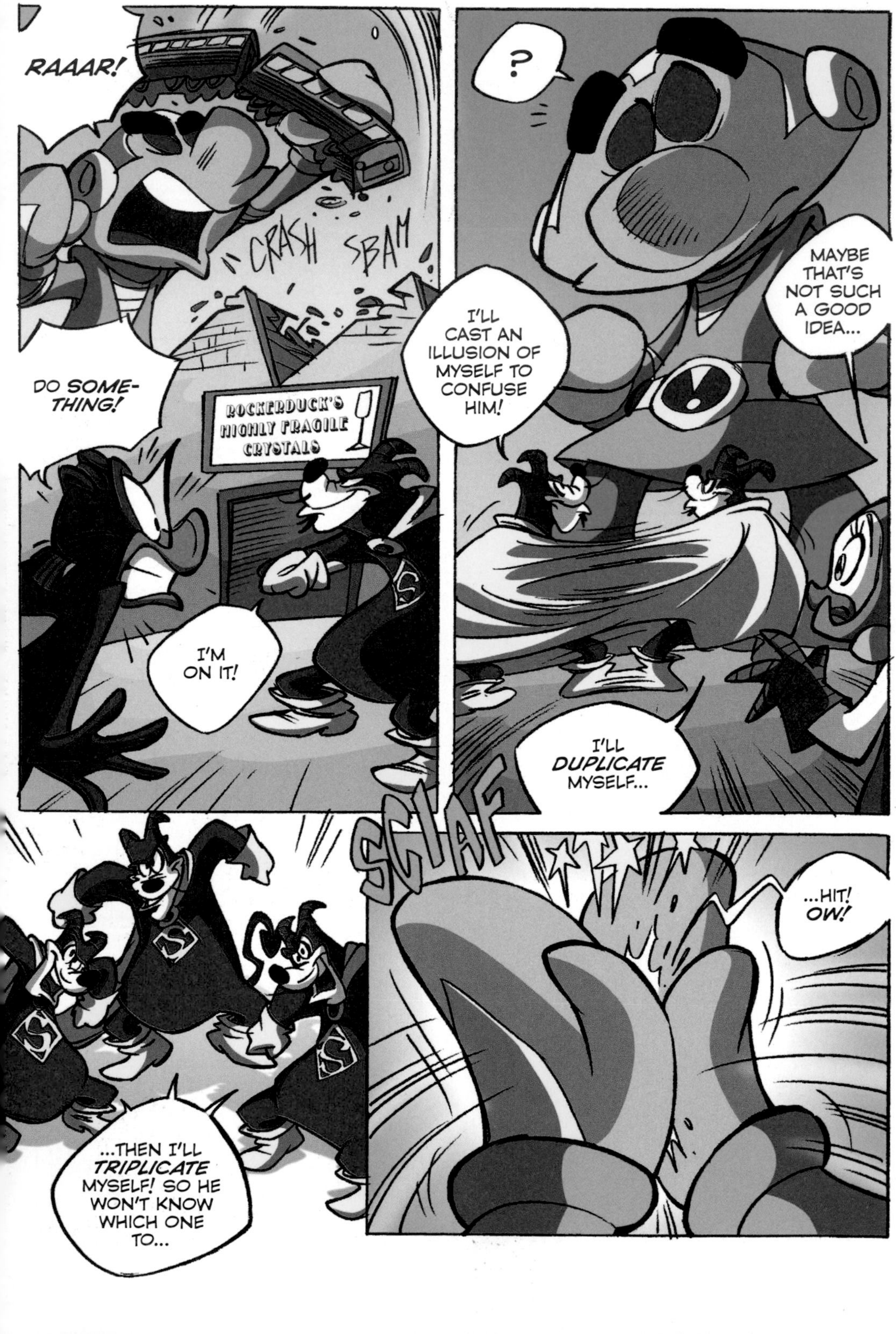
RAAAR!
CRASH SBAM
DO SOME-THING!
ROCKERDUCK'S HIGHLY FRAGILE CRYSTALS
I'M ON IT!
?
I'LL CAST AN ILLUSION OF MYSELF TO CONFUSE HIM!
MAYBE THAT'S NOT SUCH A GOOD IDEA...
I'LL *DUPLICATE* MYSELF...
...THEN I'LL *TRIPLICATE* MYSELF! SO HE WON'T KNOW WHICH ONE TO...
SCIAF
...HIT! *OW!*

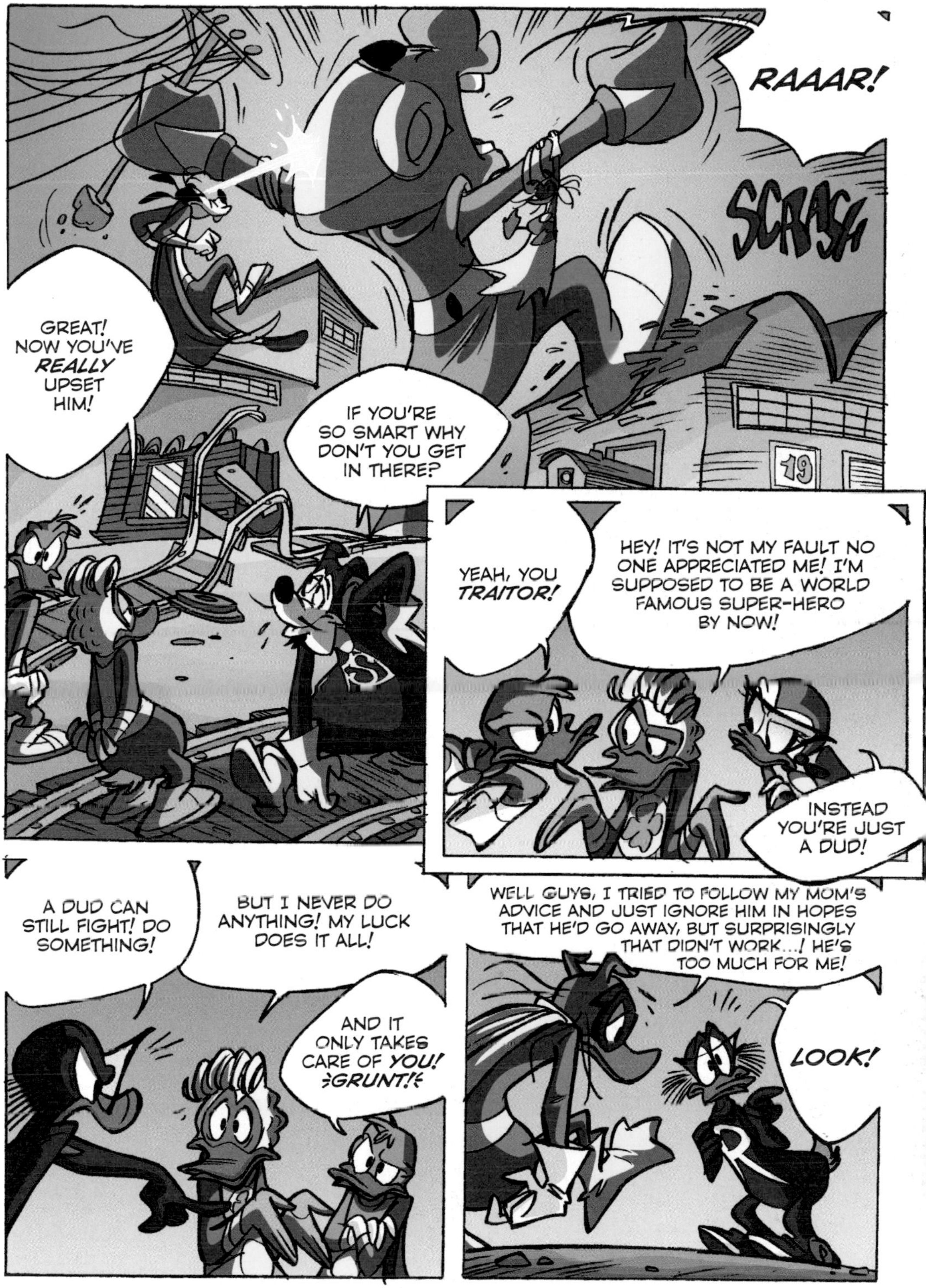
RAAAR!
SCRASH
GREAT! NOW YOU'VE *REALLY* UPSET HIM!
IF YOU'RE SO SMART WHY DON'T YOU GET IN THERE?
YEAH, YOU *TRAITOR!*
HEY! IT'S NOT MY FAULT NO ONE APPRECIATED ME! I'M SUPPOSED TO BE A WORLD FAMOUS SUPER-HERO BY NOW!
INSTEAD YOU'RE JUST A DUD!
A DUD CAN STILL FIGHT! DO SOMETHING!
BUT I NEVER DO ANYTHING! MY LUCK DOES IT ALL!
AND IT ONLY TAKES CARE OF *YOU!* *GRUNT!*
WELL GUYS, I TRIED TO FOLLOW MY MOM'S ADVICE AND JUST IGNORE HIM IN HOPES THAT HE'D GO AWAY, BUT SURPRISINGLY THAT DIDN'T WORK...! HE'S TOO MUCH FOR ME!
LOOK!

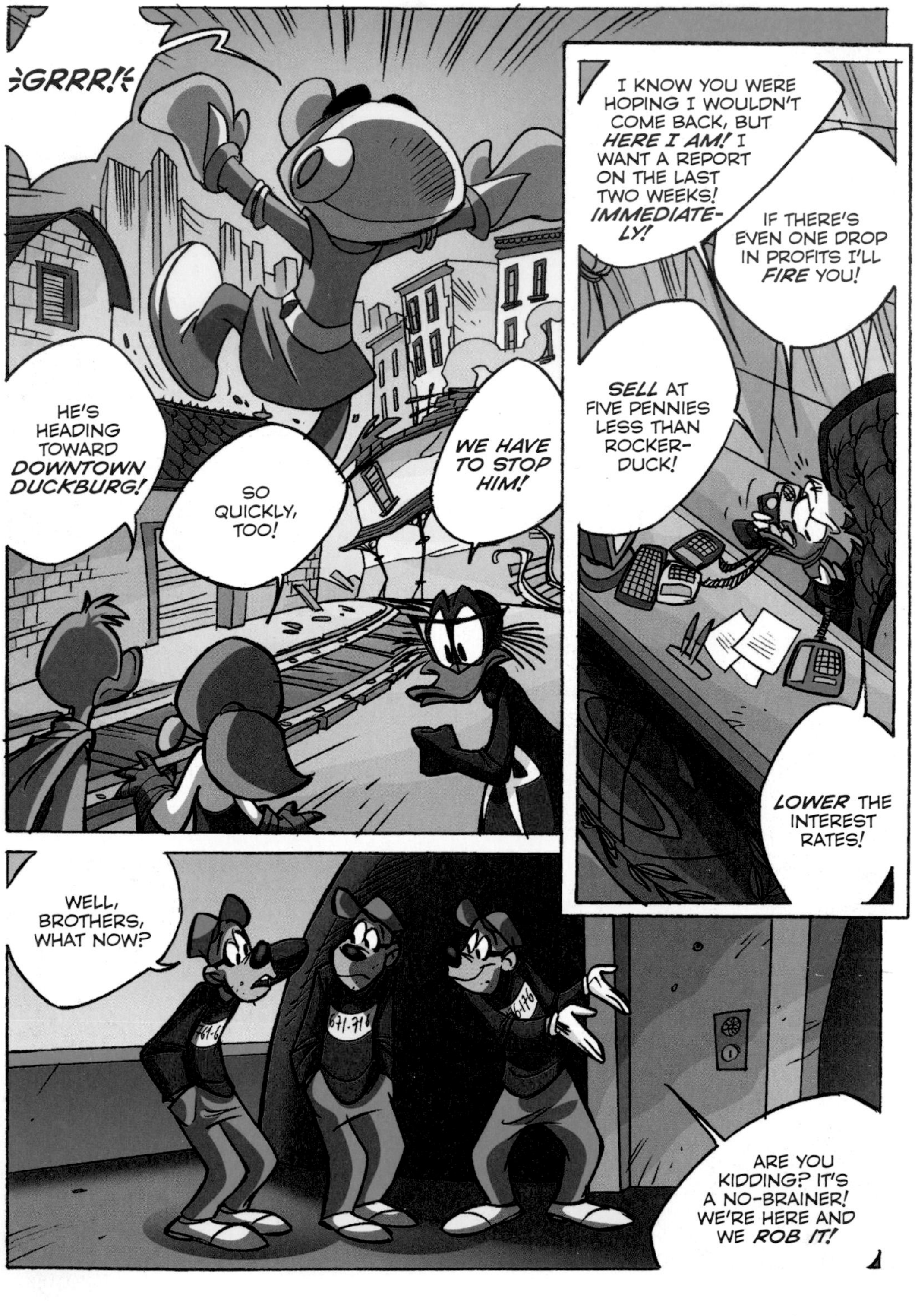
GRRR!
HE'S HEADING TOWARD DOWNTOWN DUCKBURG!
SO QUICKLY, TOO!
WE HAVE TO STOP HIM!
I KNOW YOU WERE HOPING I WOULDN'T COME BACK, BUT HERE I AM! I WANT A REPORT ON THE LAST TWO WEEKS! IMMEDIATE-LY!
IF THERE'S EVEN ONE DROP IN PROFITS I'LL FIRE YOU!
SELL AT FIVE PENNIES LESS THAN ROCKER-DUCK!
LOWER THE INTEREST RATES!
WELL, BROTHERS, WHAT NOW?
ARE YOU KIDDING? IT'S A NO-BRAINER! WE'RE HERE AND WE ROB IT!

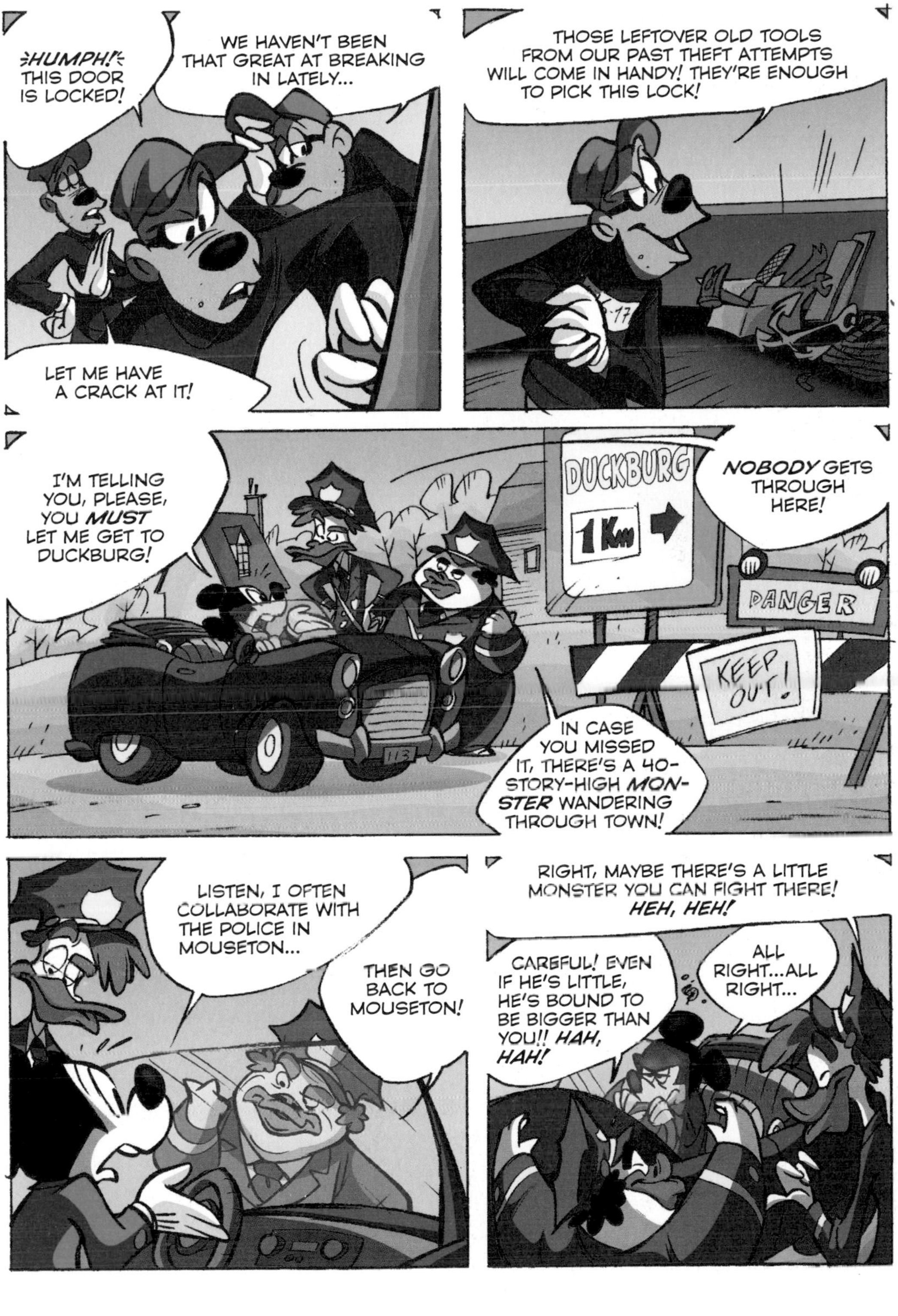
HUMPH! THIS DOOR IS LOCKED!
WE HAVEN'T BEEN THAT GREAT AT BREAKING IN LATELY...
LET ME HAVE A CRACK AT IT!
THOSE LEFTOVER OLD TOOLS FROM OUR PAST THEFT ATTEMPTS WILL COME IN HANDY! THEY'RE ENOUGH TO PICK THIS LOCK!
I'M TELLING YOU, PLEASE, YOU MUST LET ME GET TO DUCKBURG!
DUCKBURG
1 KM
NOBODY GETS THROUGH HERE!
DANGER
KEEP OUT!
IN CASE YOU MISSED IT, THERE'S A 40-STORY-HIGH MONSTER WANDERING THROUGH TOWN!
LISTEN, I OFTEN COLLABORATE WITH THE POLICE IN MOUSETON...
THEN GO BACK TO MOUSETON!
RIGHT, MAYBE THERE'S A LITTLE MONSTER YOU CAN FIGHT THERE! HEH, HEH!
CAREFUL! EVEN IF HE'S LITTLE, HE'S BOUND TO BE BIGGER THAN YOU!! HAH, HAH!
ALL RIGHT...ALL RIGHT...

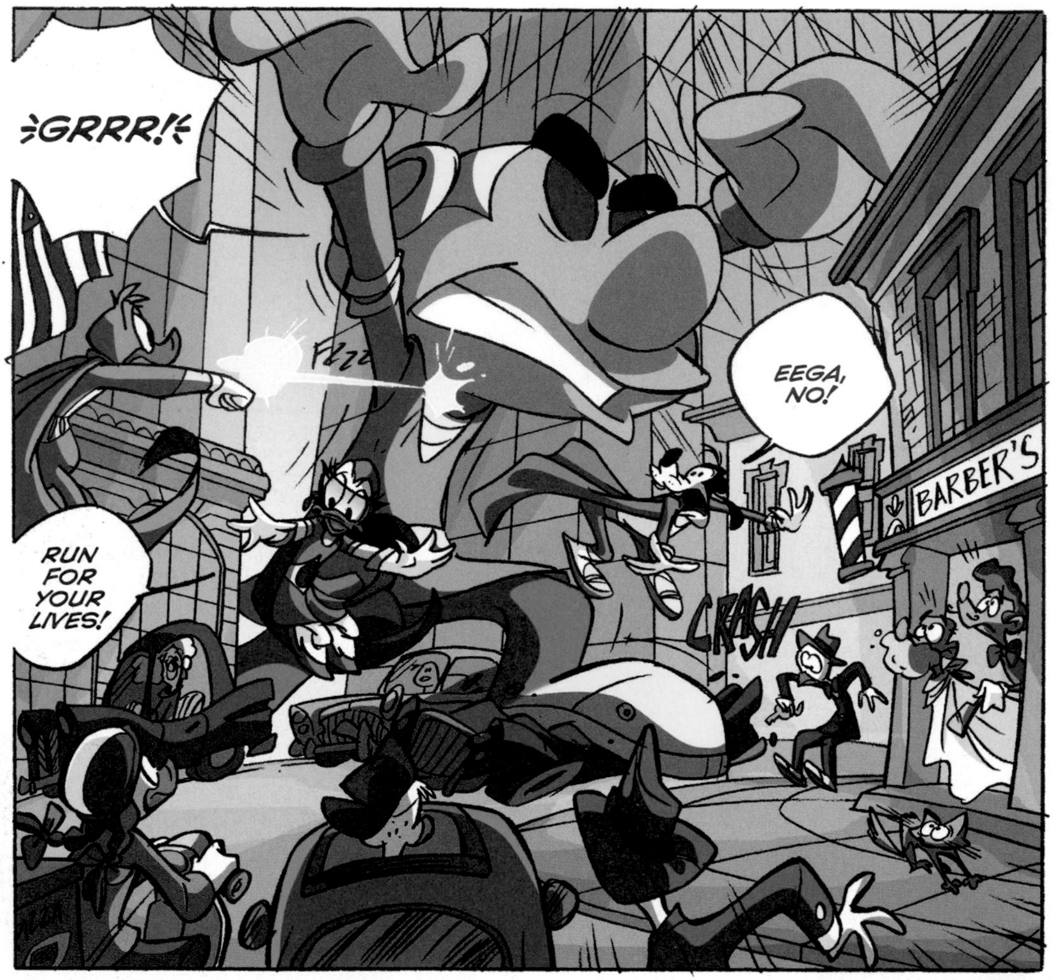
GRRR!
FZZZ
EEGA, NO!
BARBER'S
RUN FOR YOUR LIVES!
CRASH

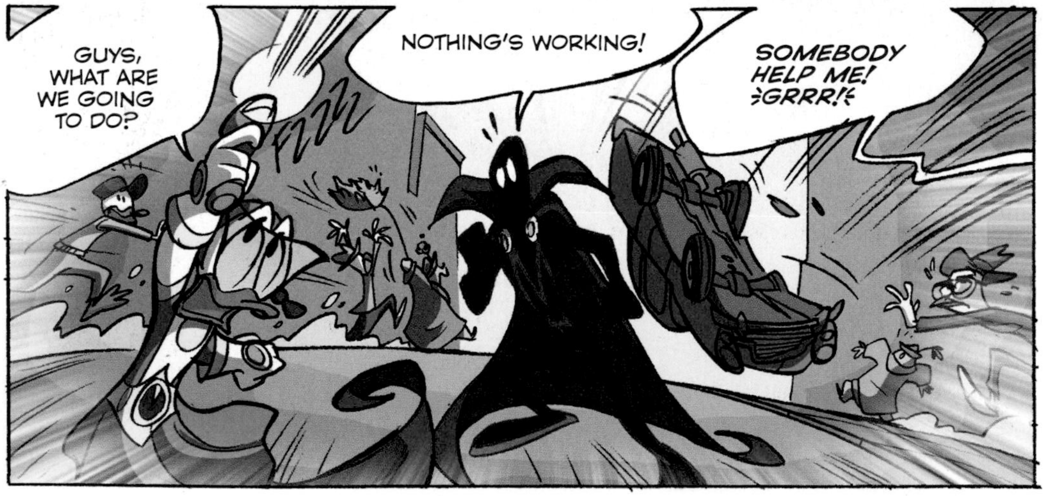
GUYS, WHAT ARE WE GOING TO DO?
NOTHING'S WORKING!
SOMEBODY HELP ME! GRRR!
FZZZZ

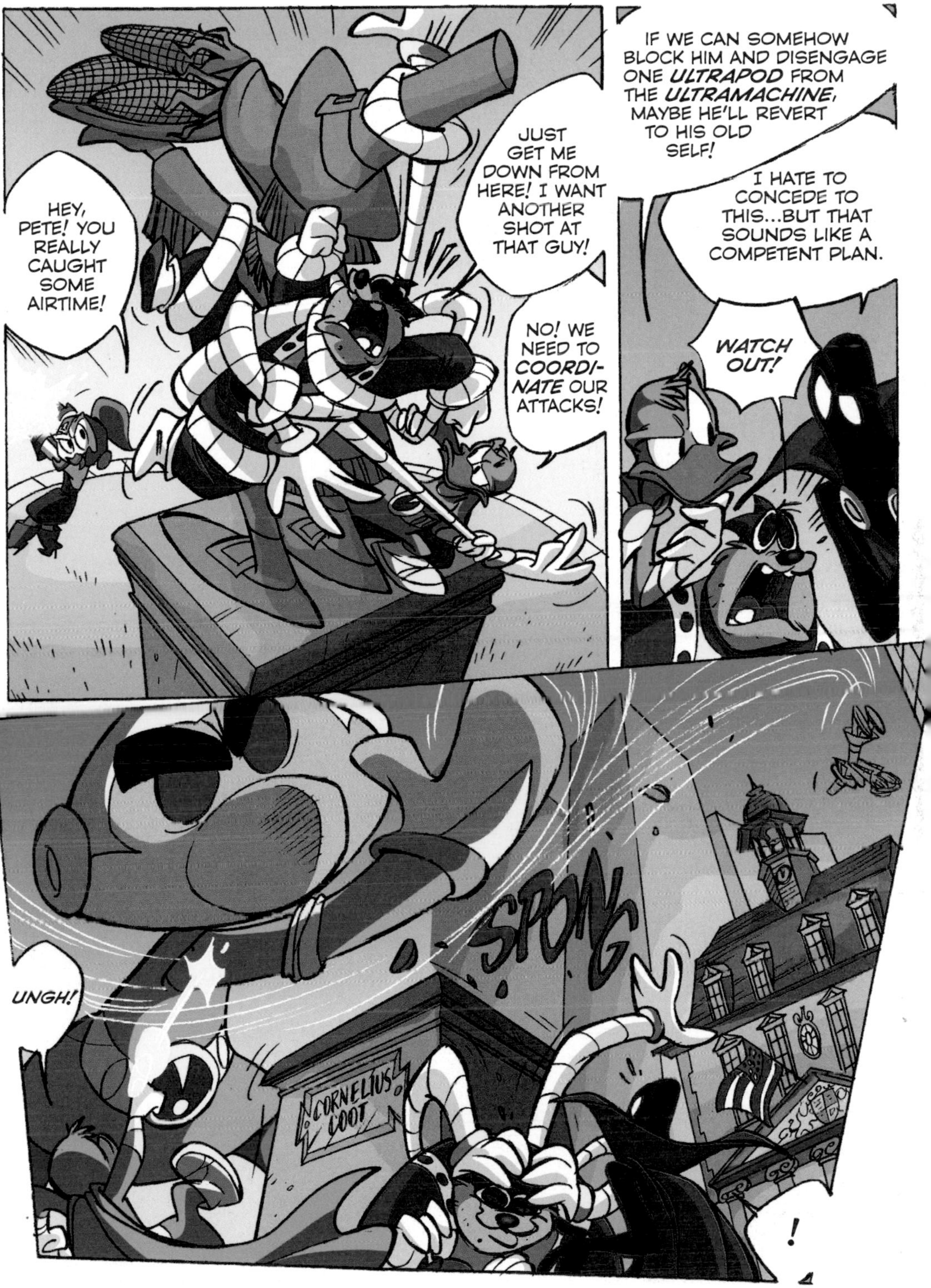
HEY, PETE! YOU REALLY CAUGHT SOME AIRTIME!
JUST GET ME DOWN FROM HERE! I WANT ANOTHER SHOT AT THAT GUY!
NO! WE NEED TO COORDI-NATE OUR ATTACKS!
IF WE CAN SOMEHOW BLOCK HIM AND DISENGAGE ONE ULTRAPOD FROM THE ULTRAMACHINE, MAYBE HE'LL REVERT TO HIS OLD SELF!
I HATE TO CONCEDE TO THIS...BUT THAT SOUNDS LIKE A COMPETENT PLAN.
WATCH OUT!
SPONG
UNGH!
CORNELIUS COOT
!

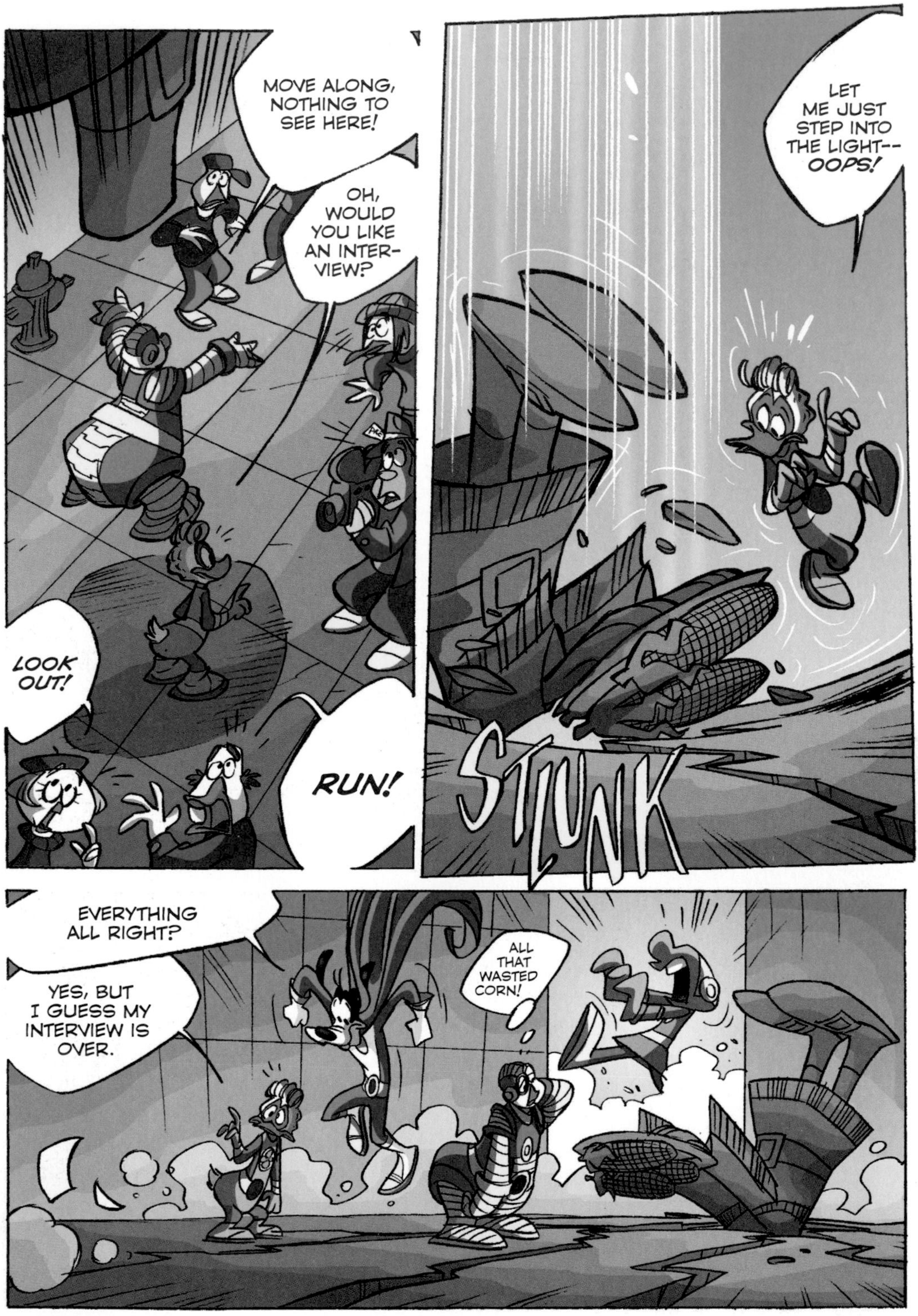
MOVE ALONG, NOTHING TO SEE HERE!
OH, WOULD YOU LIKE AN INTER-VIEW?
LOOK OUT!
RUN!
LET ME JUST STEP INTO THE LIGHT-- OOPS!
STLUNK
EVERYTHING ALL RIGHT?
YES, BUT I GUESS MY INTERVIEW IS OVER.
ALL THAT WASTED CORN!

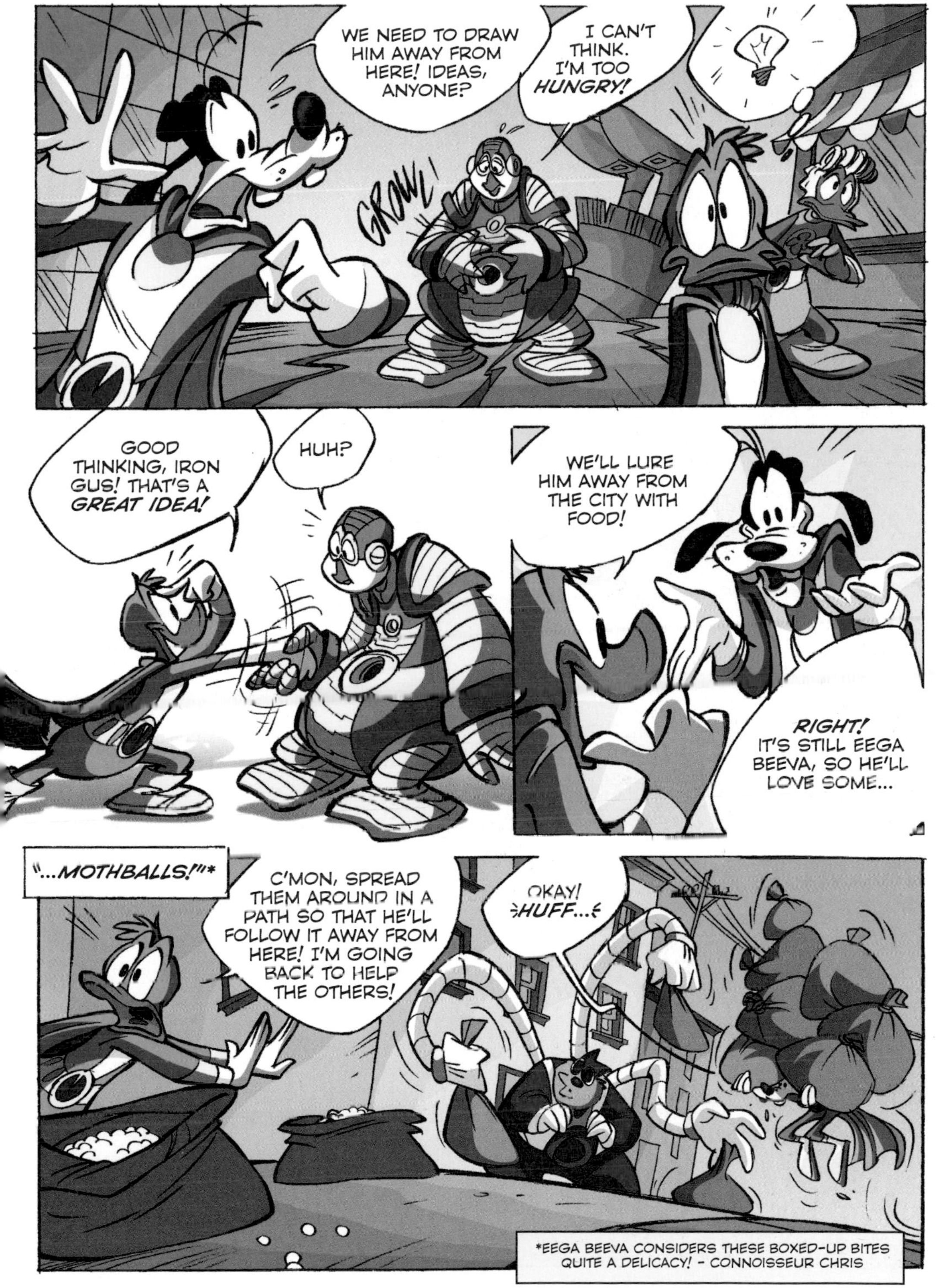
WE NEED TO DRAW HIM AWAY FROM HERE! IDEAS, ANYONE?
I CAN'T THINK. I'M TOO HUNGRY!
GROWL!
GOOD THINKING, IRON GUS! THAT'S A GREAT IDEA!
HUH?
WE'LL LURE HIM AWAY FROM THE CITY WITH FOOD!
RIGHT! IT'S STILL EEGA BEEVA, SO HE'LL LOVE SOME...
"...MOTHBALLS!"*
C'MON, SPREAD THEM AROUND IN A PATH SO THAT HE'LL FOLLOW IT AWAY FROM HERE! I'M GOING BACK TO HELP THE OTHERS!
OKAY! HUFF...
*EEGA BEEVA CONSIDERS THESE BOXED-UP BITES QUITE A DELICACY! - CONNOISSEUR CHRIS

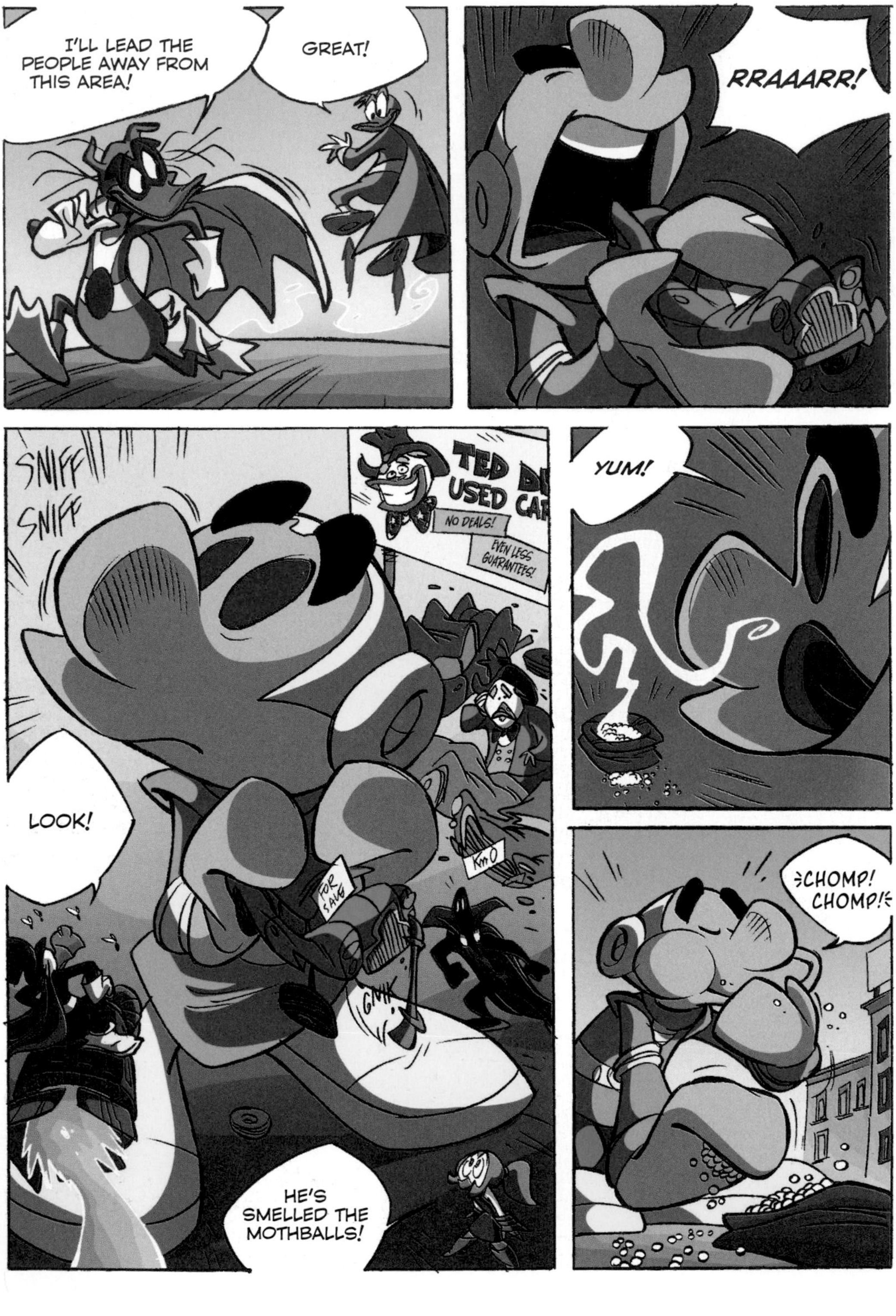
I'LL LEAD THE PEOPLE AWAY FROM THIS AREA!
GREAT!
RRAAARR!
SNIFF
SNIFF
TED D
USED CA
NO DEALS!
EVEN LESS GUARANTEES!
FOR SALE
LOOK!
HE'S SMELLED THE MOTHBALLS!
YUM!
CHOMP! CHOMP!

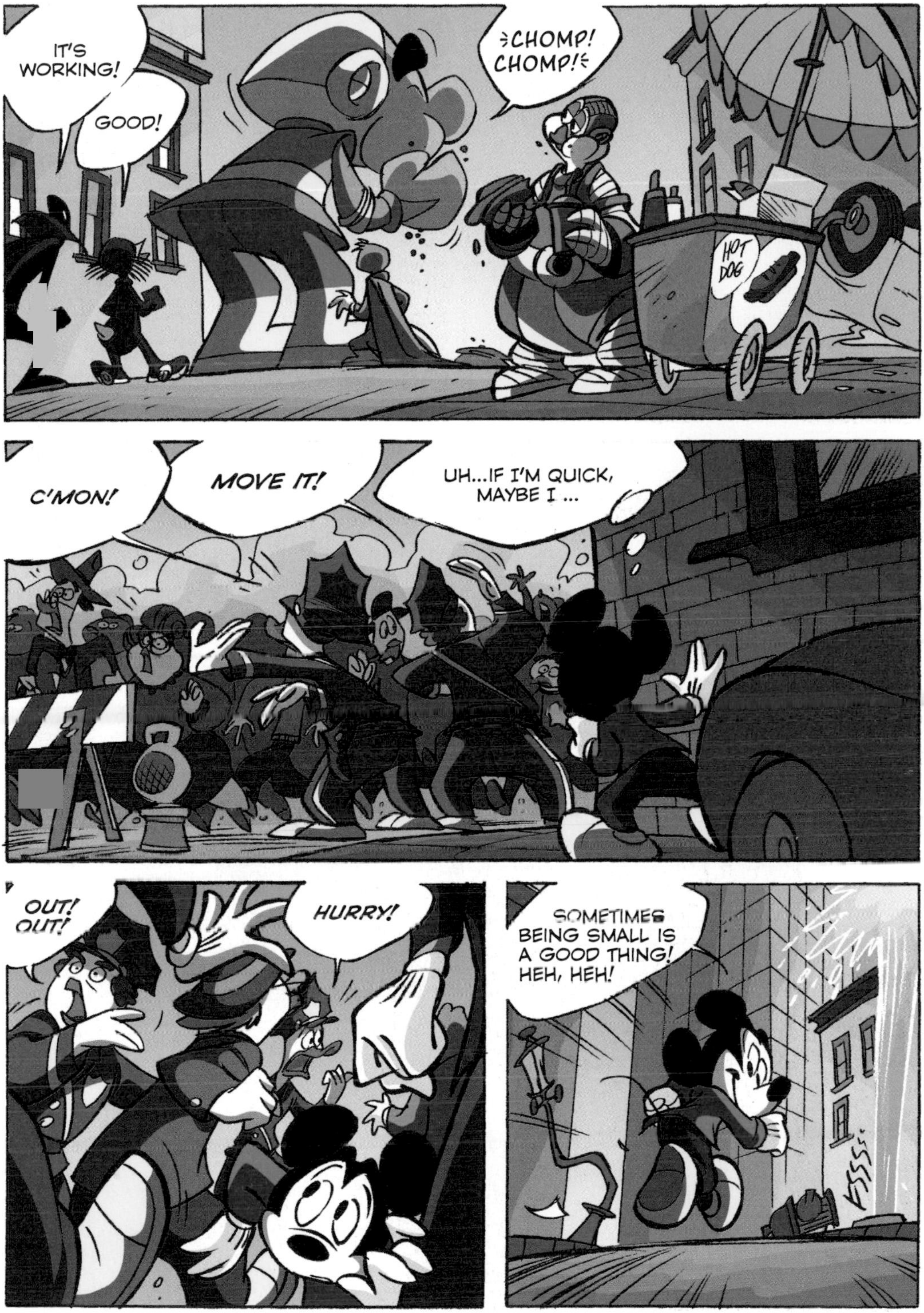
IT'S WORKING!
GOOD!
CHOMP! CHOMP!
HOT DOG
C'MON!
MOVE IT!
UH...IF I'M QUICK, MAYBE I ...
OUT! OUT!
HURRY!
SOMETIMES BEING SMALL IS A GOOD THING! HEH, HEH!
FSSS

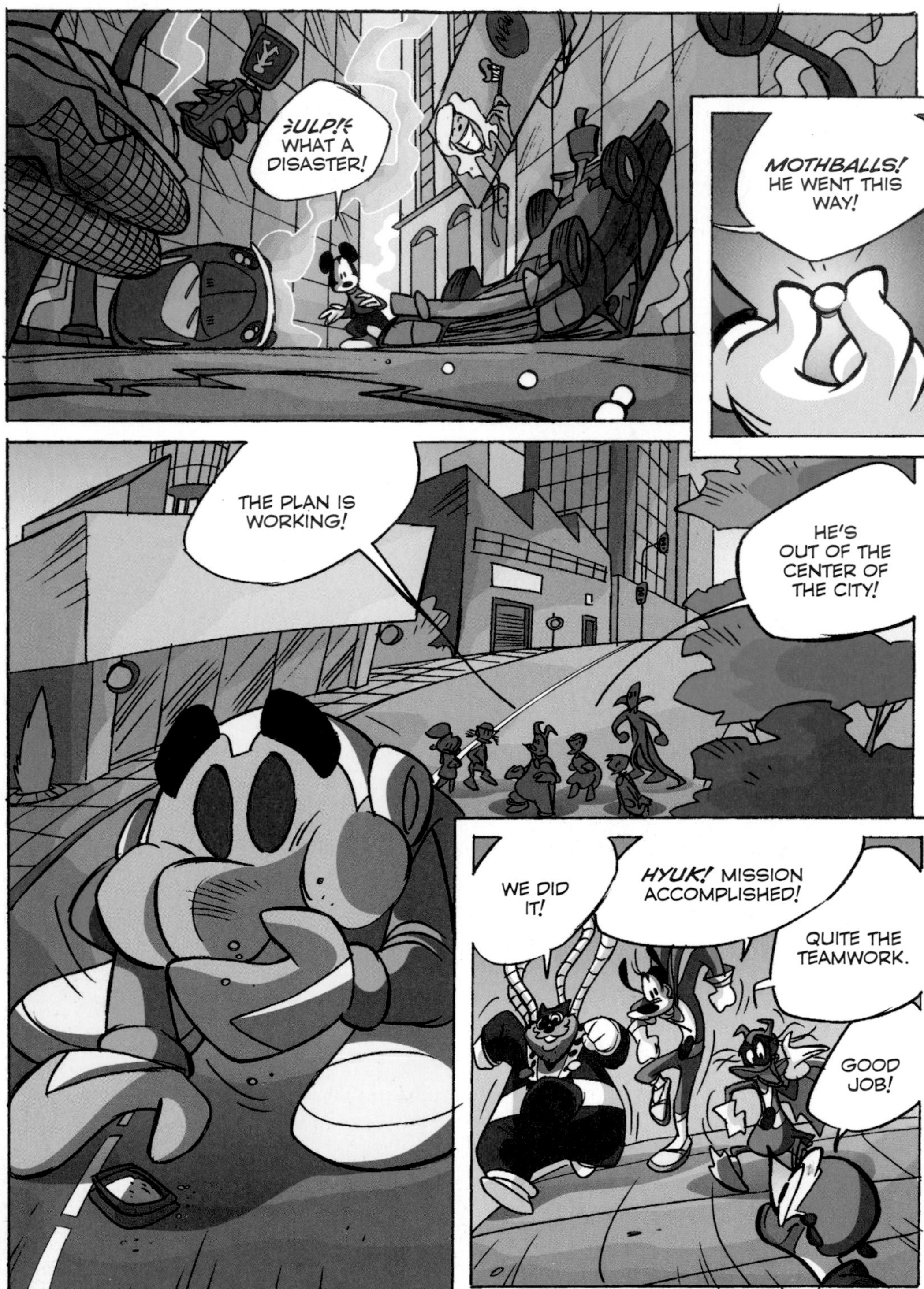

⚡ULP!⚡ WHAT A DISASTER!
MOTHBALLS! HE WENT THIS WAY!
THE PLAN IS WORKING!
HE'S OUT OF THE CENTER OF THE CITY!
WE DID IT!
HYUK! MISSION ACCOMPLISHED!
QUITE THE TEAMWORK.
GOOD JOB!

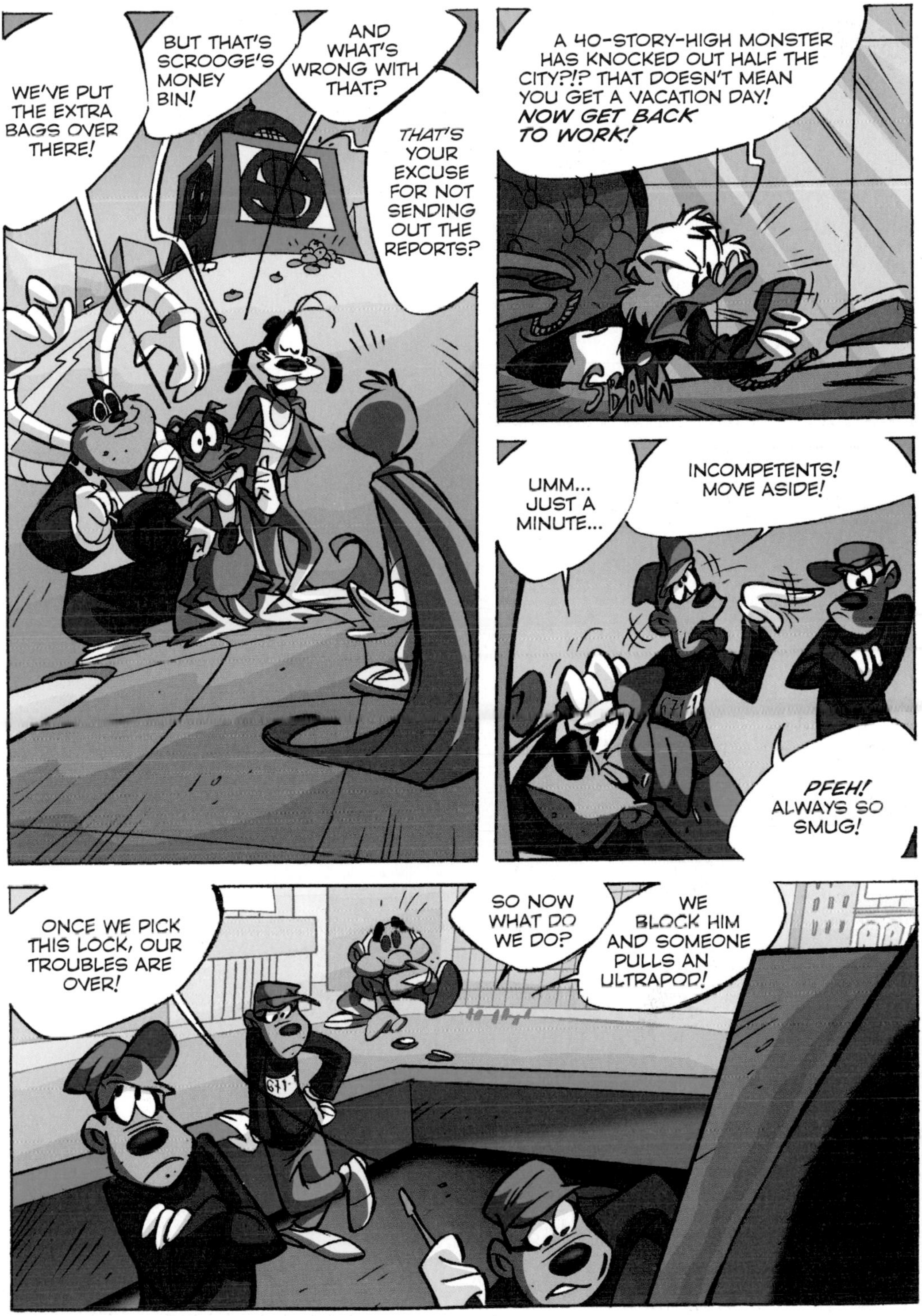

WE'VE PUT THE EXTRA BAGS OVER THERE!
BUT THAT'S SCROOGE'S MONEY BIN!
AND WHAT'S WRONG WITH THAT?
THAT'S YOUR EXCUSE FOR NOT SENDING OUT THE REPORTS?
A 40-STORY-HIGH MONSTER HAS KNOCKED OUT HALF THE CITY?!? THAT DOESN'T MEAN YOU GET A VACATION DAY! NOW GET BACK TO WORK!
SBAM
UMM... JUST A MINUTE...
INCOMPETENTS! MOVE ASIDE!
PFEH! ALWAYS SO SMUG!
ONCE WE PICK THIS LOCK, OUR TROUBLES ARE OVER!
SO NOW WHAT DO WE DO?
WE BLOCK HIM AND SOMEONE PULLS AN ULTRAPOD!

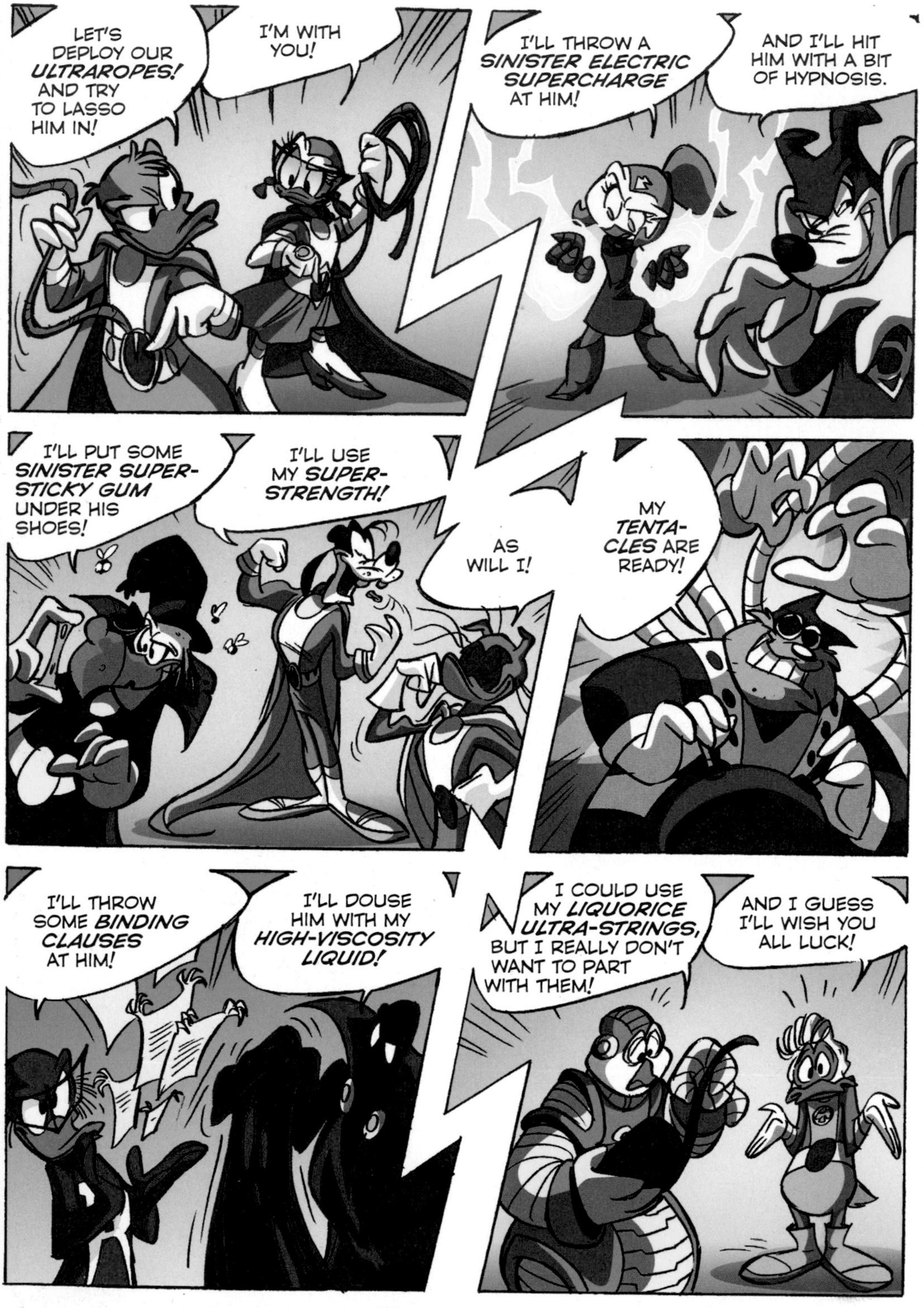

LET'S DEPLOY OUR ULTRAROPES! AND TRY TO LASSO HIM IN!
I'M WITH YOU!
I'LL THROW A SINISTER ELECTRIC SUPERCHARGE AT HIM!
AND I'LL HIT HIM WITH A BIT OF HYPNOSIS.
I'LL PUT SOME SINISTER SUPER-STICKY GUM UNDER HIS SHOES!
I'LL USE MY SUPER-STRENGTH!
AS WILL I!
MY TENTA-CLES ARE READY!
I'LL THROW SOME BINDING CLAUSES AT HIM!
I'LL DOUSE HIM WITH MY HIGH-VISCOSITY LIQUID!
I COULD USE MY LIQUORICE ULTRA-STRINGS, BUT I REALLY DON'T WANT TO PART WITH THEM!
AND I GUESS I'LL WISH YOU ALL LUCK!

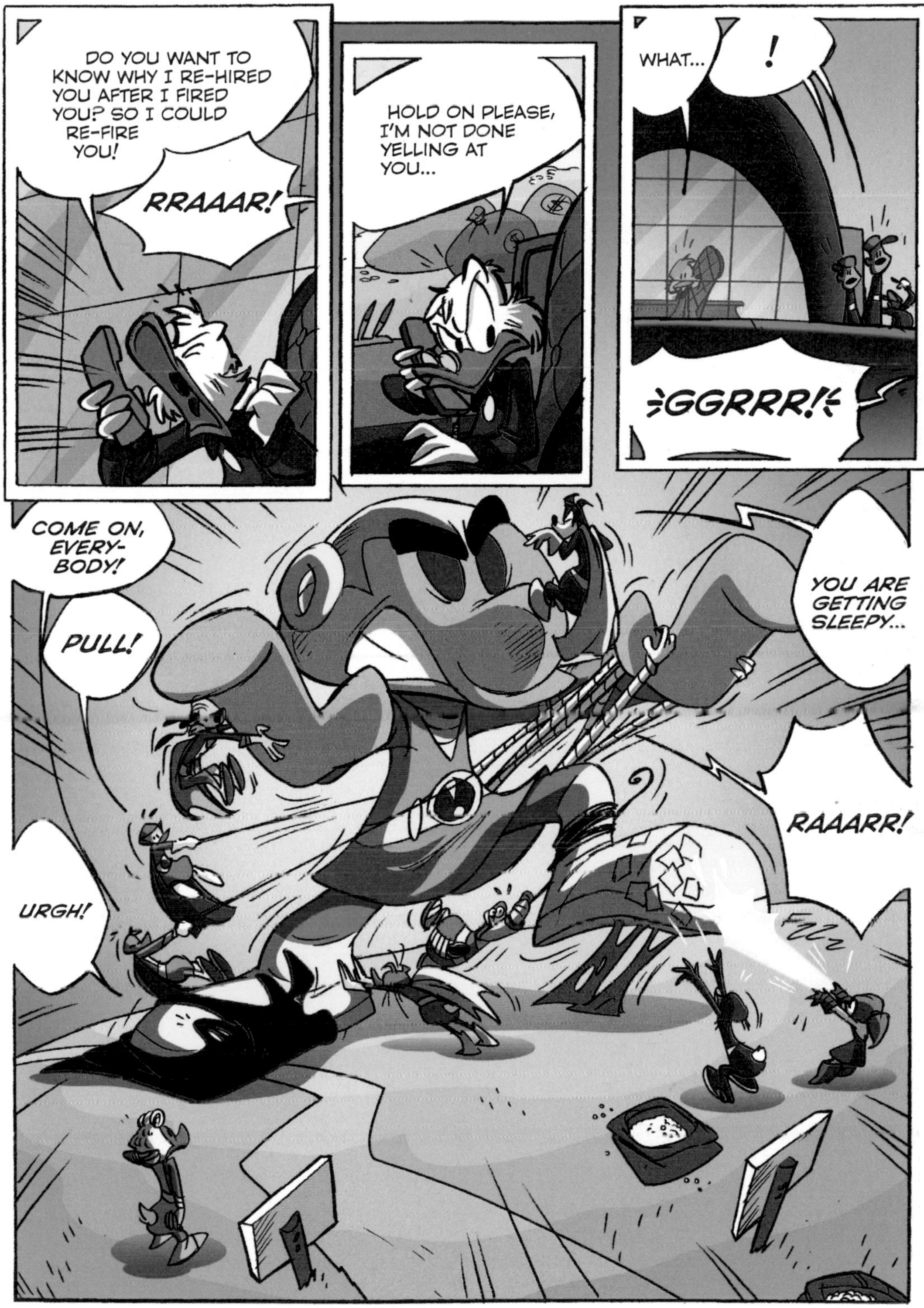
DO YOU WANT TO KNOW WHY I RE-HIRED YOU AFTER I FIRED YOU? SO I COULD RE-FIRE YOU!
RRAAAR!
HOLD ON PLEASE, I'M NOT DONE YELLING AT YOU...
WHAT...
!
GGRRR!
COME ON, EVERY-BODY!
PULL!
YOU ARE GETTING SLEEPY...
RAAARR!
URGH!

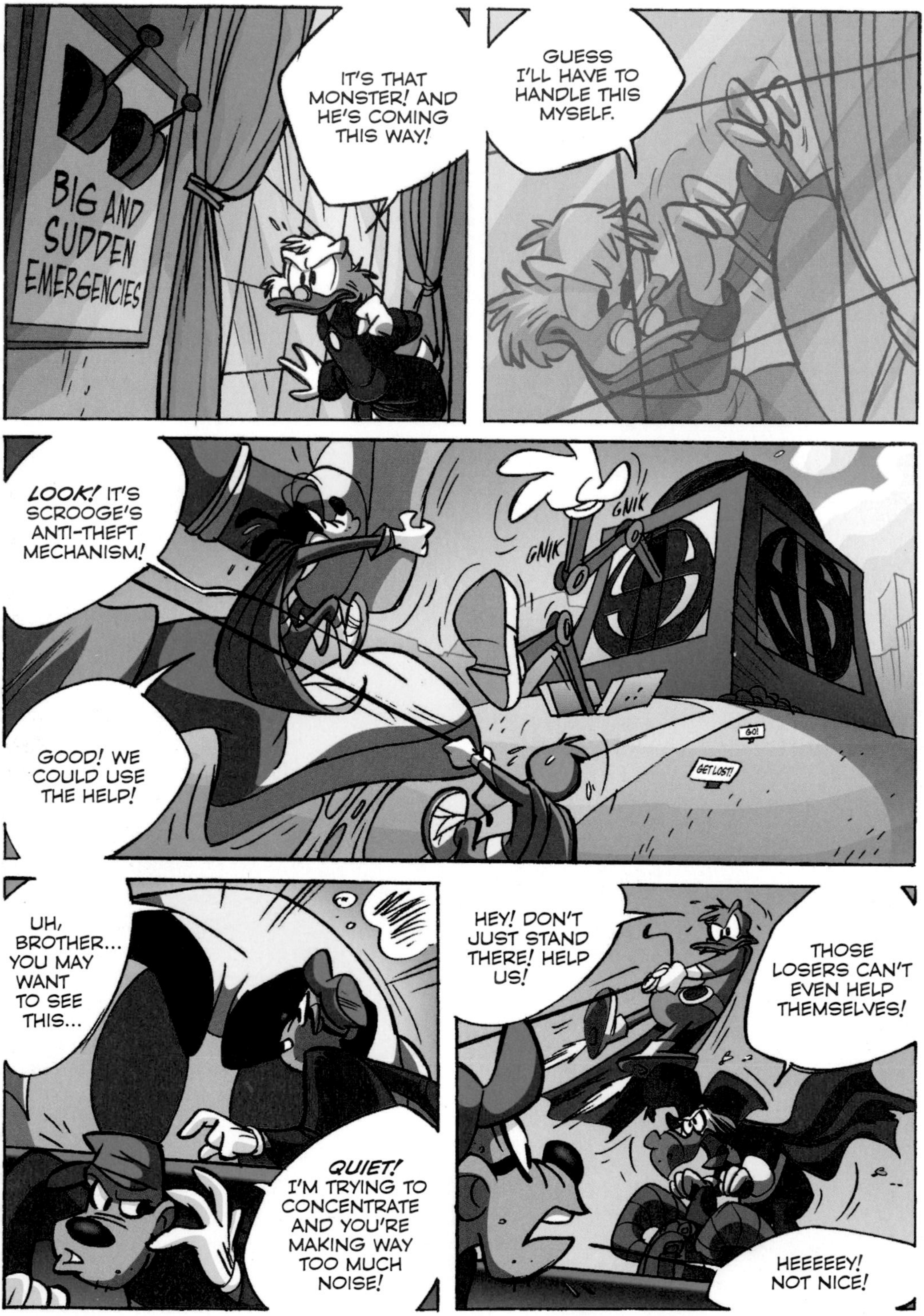
BIG AND SUDDEN EMERGENCIES
IT'S THAT MONSTER! AND HE'S COMING THIS WAY!
GUESS I'LL HAVE TO HANDLE THIS MYSELF.
LOOK! IT'S SCROOGE'S ANTI-THEFT MECHANISM!
GNIK
GNIK
GOOD! WE COULD USE THE HELP!
GO!
GET LOST!
UH, BROTHER... YOU MAY WANT TO SEE THIS...
QUIET! I'M TRYING TO CONCENTRATE AND YOU'RE MAKING WAY TOO MUCH NOISE!
HEY! DON'T JUST STAND THERE! HELP US!
THOSE LOSERS CAN'T EVEN HELP THEMSELVES!
HEEEEEY! NOT NICE!

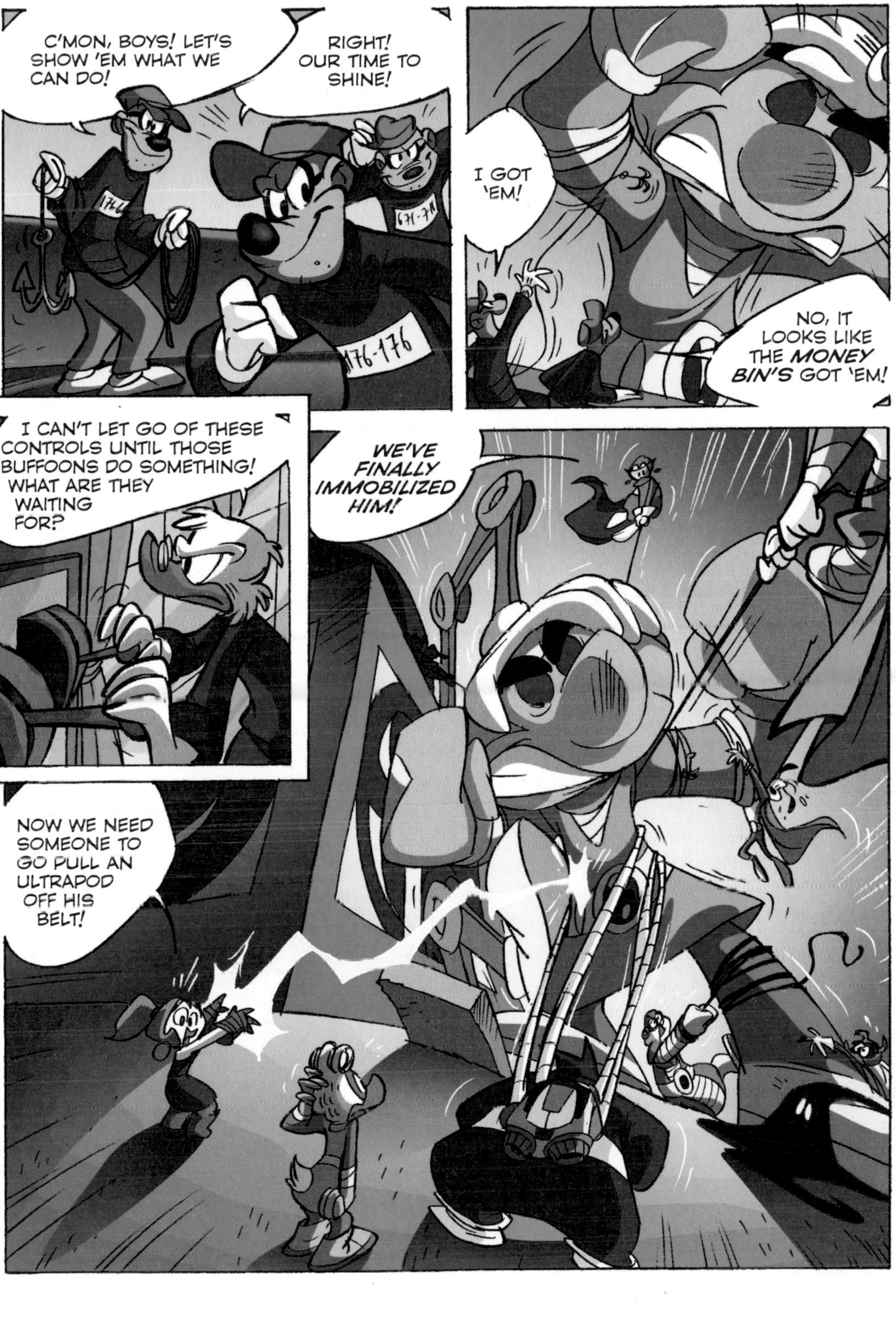
C'MON, BOYS! LET'S SHOW 'EM WHAT WE CAN DO!
RIGHT! OUR TIME TO SHINE!
I GOT 'EM!
NO, IT LOOKS LIKE THE ***MONEY BIN'S*** GOT 'EM!
I CAN'T LET GO OF THESE CONTROLS UNTIL THOSE BUFFOONS DO SOMETHING! WHAT ARE THEY WAITING FOR?
WE'VE FINALLY IMMOBILIZED HIM!
NOW WE NEED SOMEONE TO GO PULL AN ULTRAPOD OFF HIS BELT!

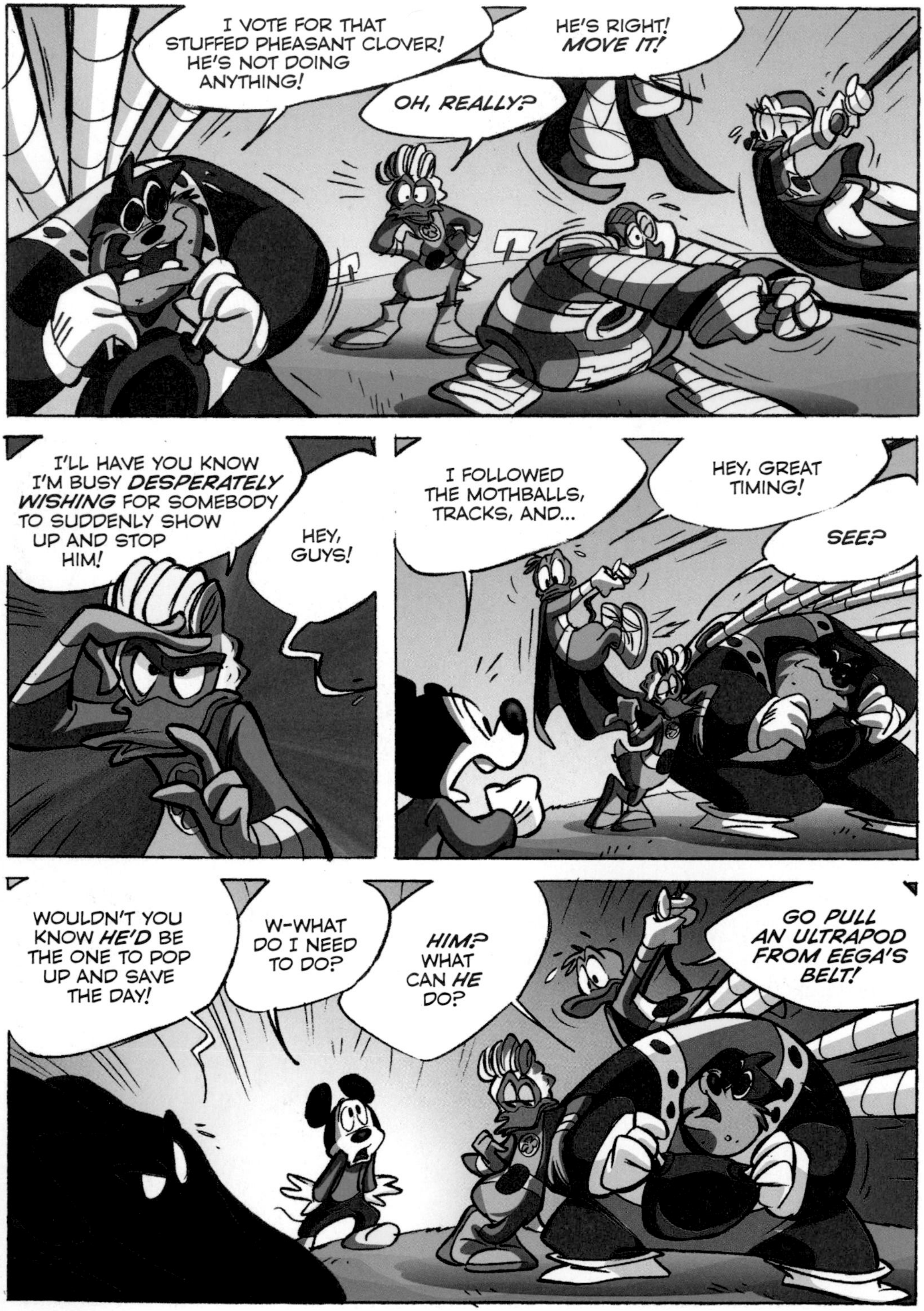
I VOTE FOR THAT STUFFED PHEASANT CLOVER! HE'S NOT DOING ANYTHING!
HE'S RIGHT! MOVE IT!
OH, REALLY?
I'LL HAVE YOU KNOW I'M BUSY DESPERATELY WISHING FOR SOMEBODY TO SUDDENLY SHOW UP AND STOP HIM!
HEY, GUYS!
I FOLLOWED THE MOTHBALLS, TRACKS, AND...
HEY, GREAT TIMING!
SEE?
WOULDN'T YOU KNOW HE'D BE THE ONE TO POP UP AND SAVE THE DAY!
W-WHAT DO I NEED TO DO?
HIM? WHAT CAN HE DO?
GO PULL AN ULTRAPOD FROM EEGA'S BELT!

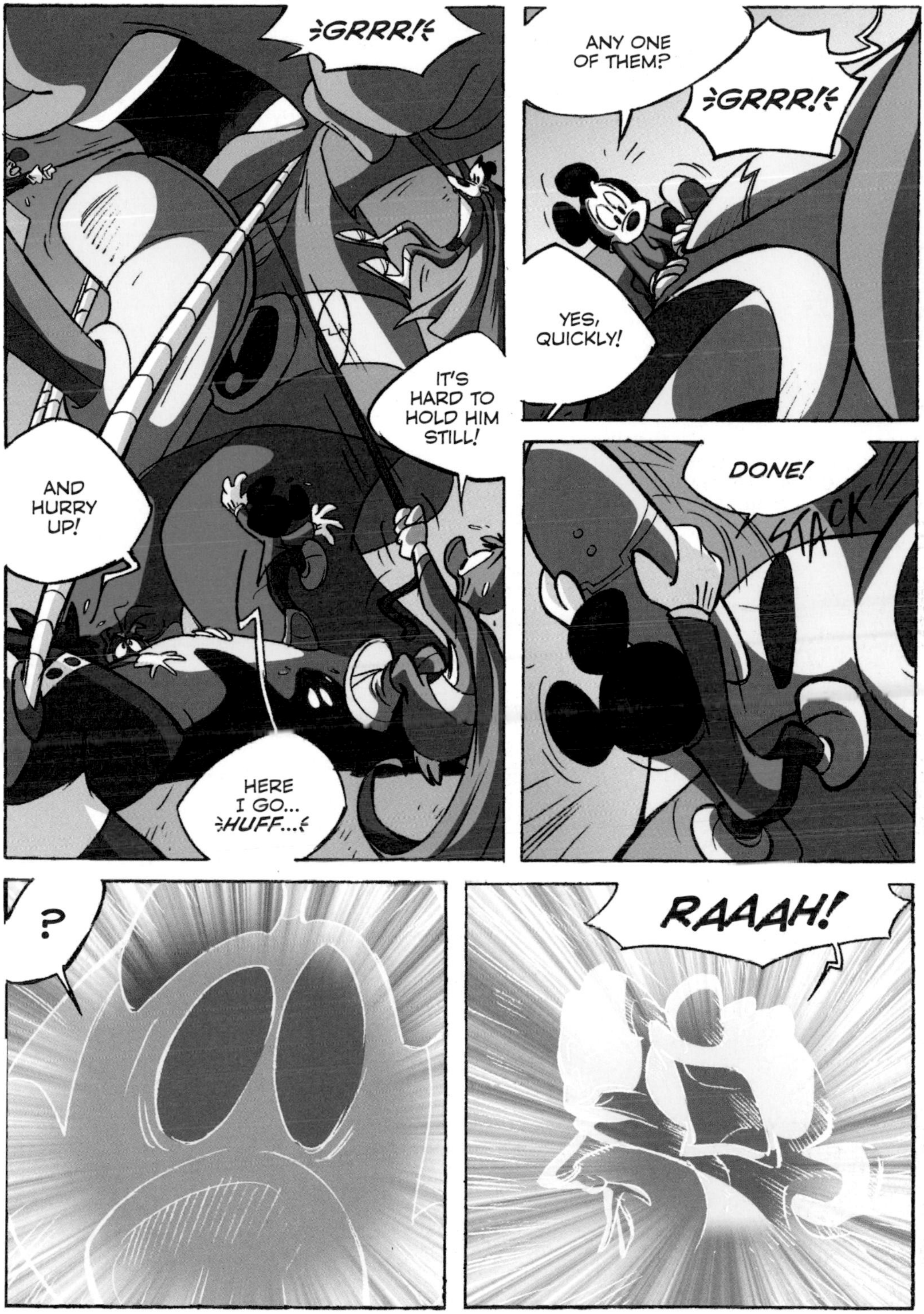

¡GRRR!¡
IT'S HARD TO HOLD HIM STILL!
AND HURRY UP!
HERE I GO... ¡HUFF...¡
ANY ONE OF THEM?
¡GRRR!¡
YES, QUICKLY!
DONE!
STACK
?
RAAAH!

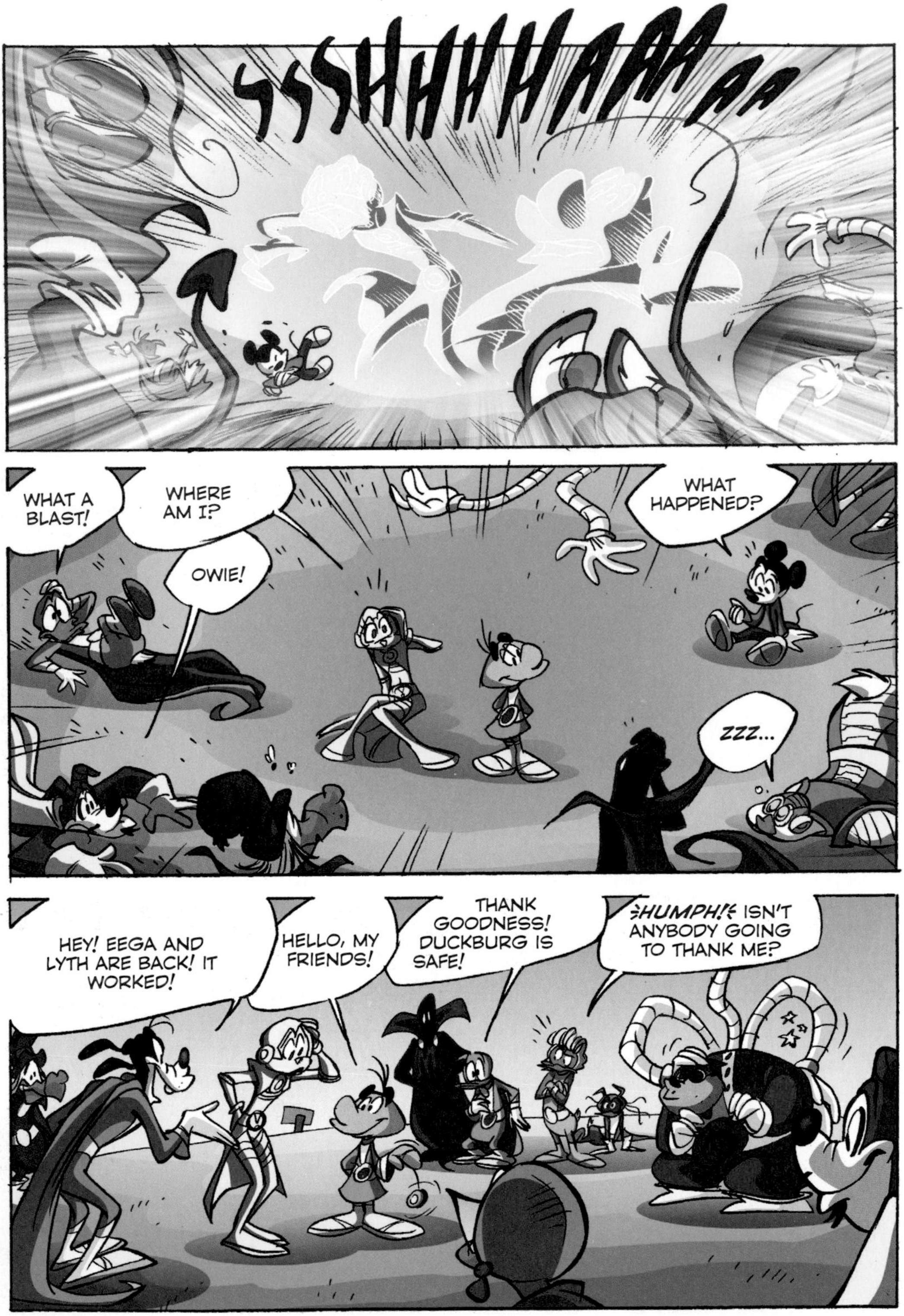
SSSHHHHHAAAAAA
WHAT A BLAST!
WHERE AM I?
OWIE!
WHAT HAPPENED?
ZZZ...
HEY! EEGA AND LYTH ARE BACK! IT WORKED!
HELLO, MY FRIENDS!
THANK GOODNESS! DUCKBURG IS SAFE!
HUMPH! ISN'T ANYBODY GOING TO THANK ME?

I TOLD YOU THE ULTRA-MACHINE WAS DANGEROUS! ARE YOU ALRIGHT, LYTH?

YES! TAKE THIS!

IF IT WEREN'T *INDESTRUCTIBLE*, I'D SUGGEST *DESTROYING* IT!

NO! I MEAN... FOR SCIENCE'S SAKE... WE SHOULDN'T DESTROY SUCH A TECHNOLOGICAL ACHIEVEMENT...

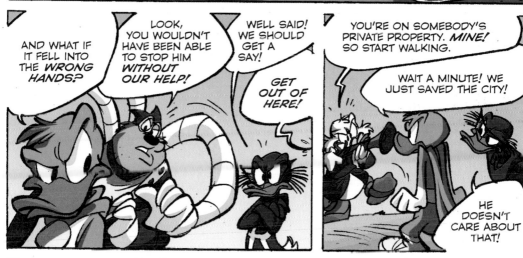

AND WHAT IF IT FELL INTO THE *WRONG HANDS?*

LOOK, YOU WOULDN'T HAVE BEEN ABLE TO STOP HIM *WITHOUT OUR HELP!*

WELL SAID! WE SHOULD GET A SAY!

GET OUT OF HERE!

YOU'RE ON SOMEBODY'S PRIVATE PROPERTY. *MINE!* SO START WALKING.

WAIT A MINUTE! WE JUST SAVED THE CITY!

HE DOESN'T CARE ABOUT THAT!

I DON'T KNOW WHO YOU ARE BUT I ALREADY *LIKE* YOU *LESS* THAN THE OTHERS!

FEELING'S MUTUAL!

AND I DON'T KNOW WHY YOU'RE HERE, BUT IF YOU DON'T SCRAM YOU'LL BE THE FIRST ONES TO--

EXCUSE ME, MISTER MCDUCK...

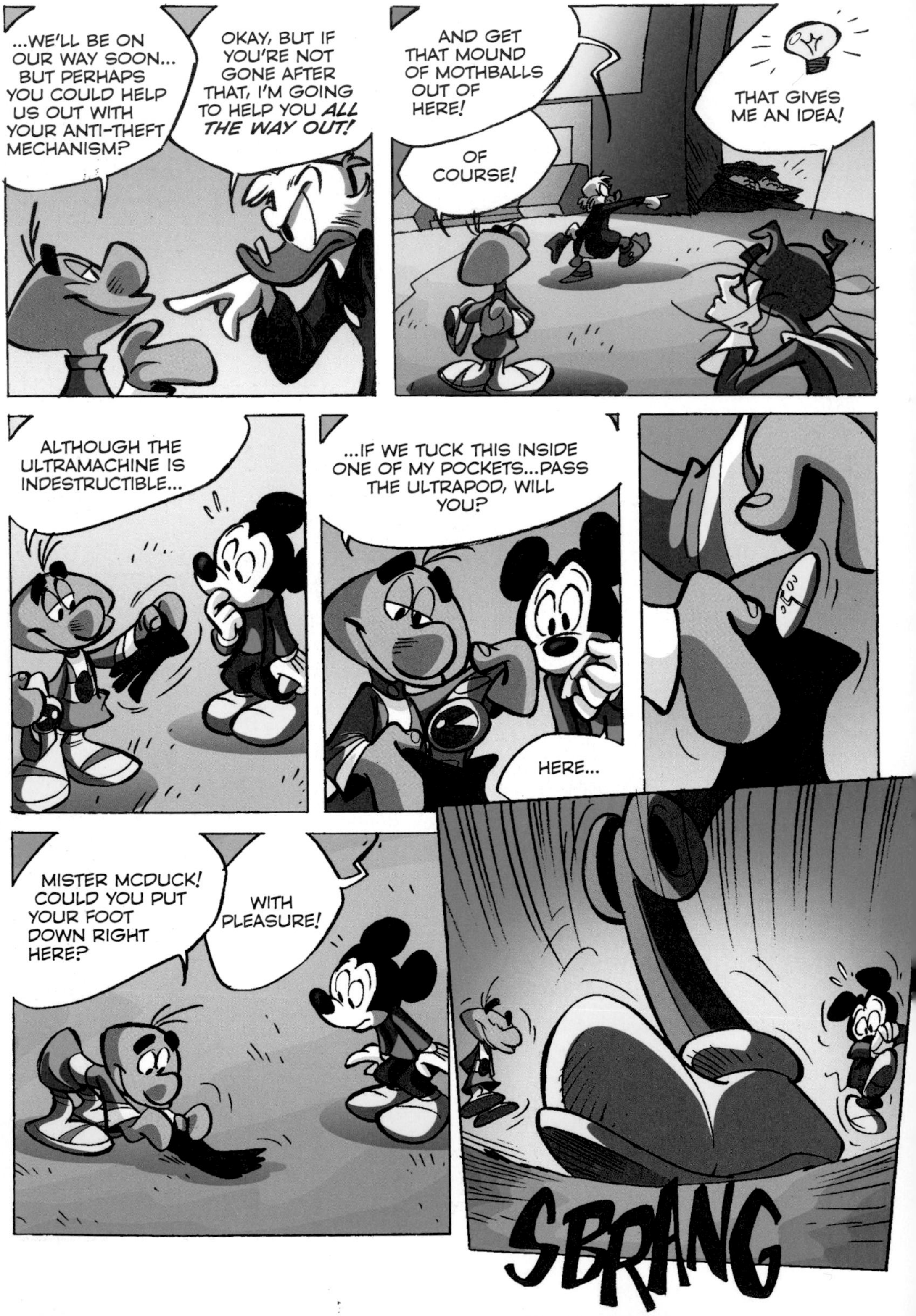
...WE'LL BE ON OUR WAY SOON... BUT PERHAPS YOU COULD HELP US OUT WITH YOUR ANTI-THEFT MECHANISM?
OKAY, BUT IF YOU'RE NOT GONE AFTER THAT, I'M GOING TO HELP YOU *ALL THE WAY OUT!*
AND GET THAT MOUND OF MOTHBALLS OUT OF HERE!
OF COURSE!
THAT GIVES ME AN IDEA!
ALTHOUGH THE ULTRAMACHINE IS INDESTRUCTIBLE...
...IF WE TUCK THIS INSIDE ONE OF MY POCKETS...PASS THE ULTRAPOD, WILL YOU?
HERE...
MISTER MCDUCK! COULD YOU PUT YOUR FOOT DOWN RIGHT HERE?
WITH PLEASURE!
SBRANG

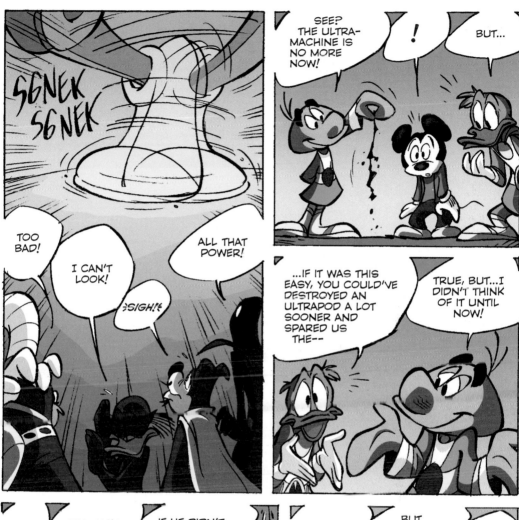

SGNEK SGNEK

SEE? THE ULTRA-MACHINE IS NO MORE NOW!

!

BUT...

TOO BAD!

I CAN'T LOOK!

ALL THAT POWER!

¡SIGH!¿

...IF IT WAS THIS EASY, YOU COULD'VE DESTROYED AN ULTRAPOD A LOT SOONER AND SPARED US THE--

TRUE, BUT...I DIDN'T THINK OF IT UNTIL NOW!

I...I...

WELL, HE'S RIGHT!

IF HE DIDN'T THINK OF IT...

NEXT THING THIS FOOT SQUASHES IS ALL OF *YOU!*

TIME TO GO...

BUT WHERE?

I NEED TO STOP BY VILLA ROSE...

LET'S ALL MEET UP THERE!

GO!

NO TRESPASSING!

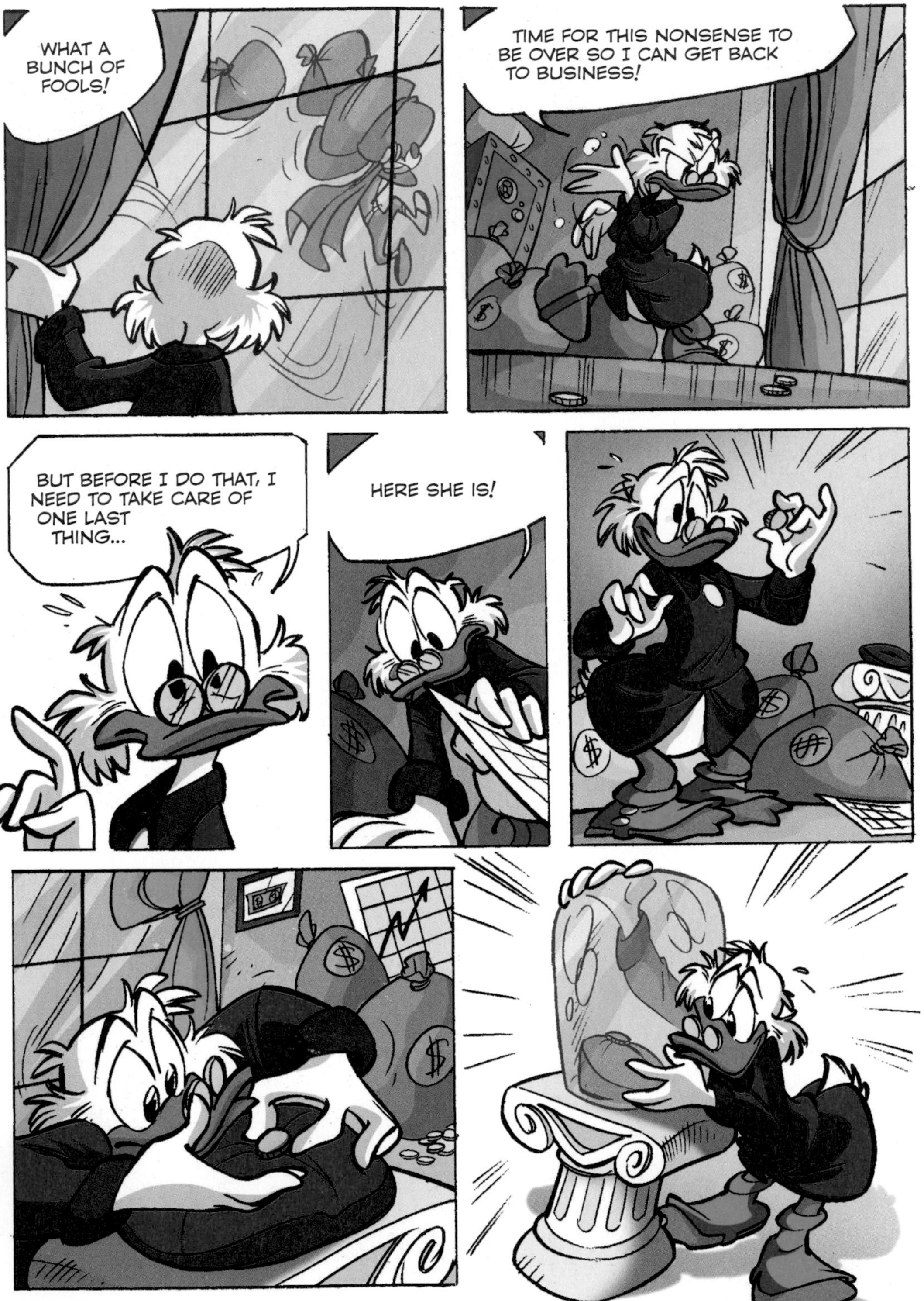
WHAT A BUNCH OF FOOLS!
TIME FOR THIS NONSENSE TO BE OVER SO I CAN GET BACK TO BUSINESS!
BUT BEFORE I DO THAT, I NEED TO TAKE CARE OF ONE LAST THING...
HERE SHE IS!

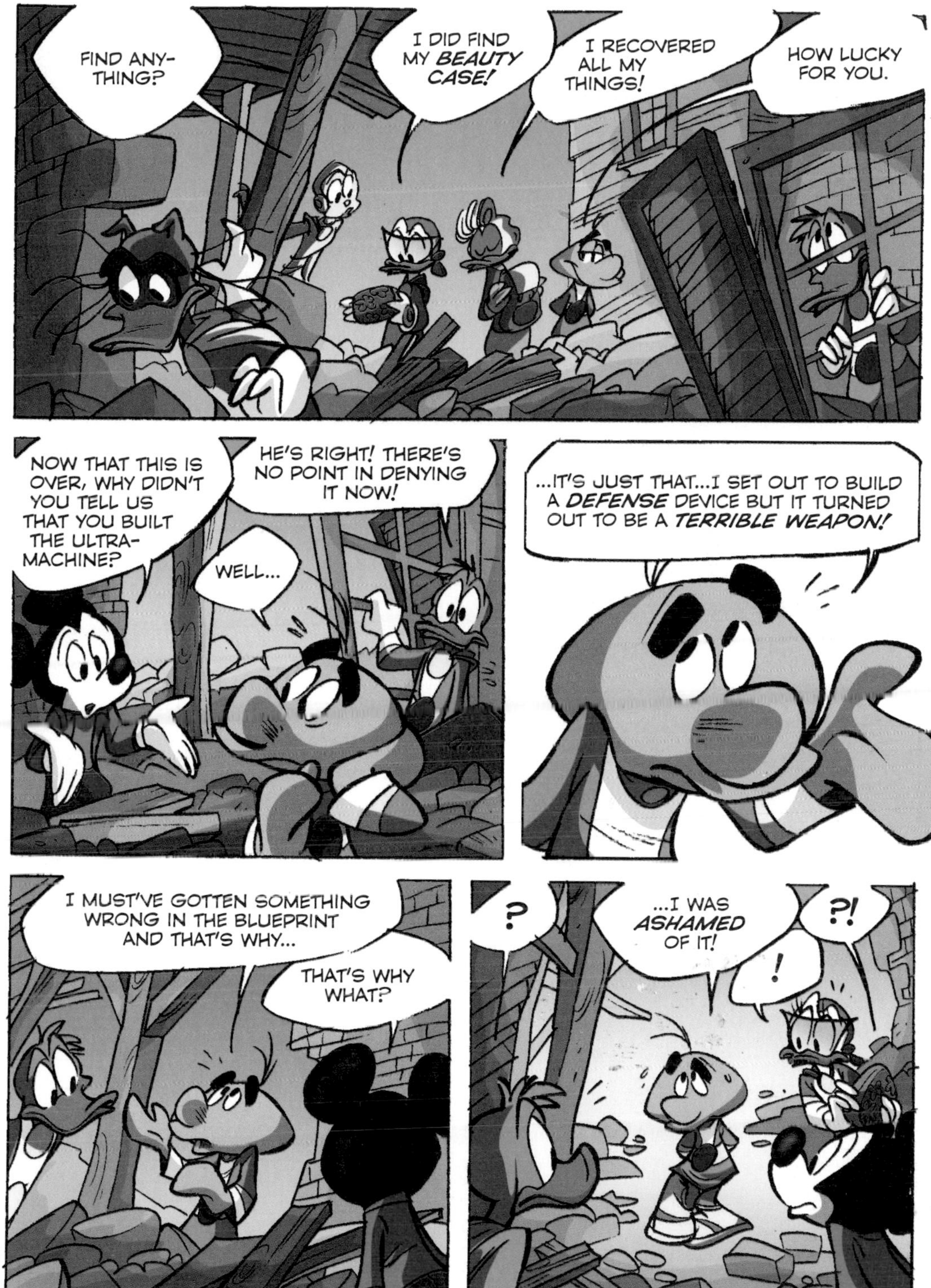
FIND ANY-THING?
I DID FIND MY BEAUTY CASE!
I RECOVERED ALL MY THINGS!
HOW LUCKY FOR YOU.
NOW THAT THIS IS OVER, WHY DIDN'T YOU TELL US THAT YOU BUILT THE ULTRA-MACHINE?
HE'S RIGHT! THERE'S NO POINT IN DENYING IT NOW!
WELL...
...IT'S JUST THAT...I SET OUT TO BUILD A DEFENSE DEVICE BUT IT TURNED OUT TO BE A TERRIBLE WEAPON!
I MUST'VE GOTTEN SOMETHING WRONG IN THE BLUEPRINT AND THAT'S WHY...
THAT'S WHY WHAT?
?
...I WAS ASHAMED OF IT!
!
?!

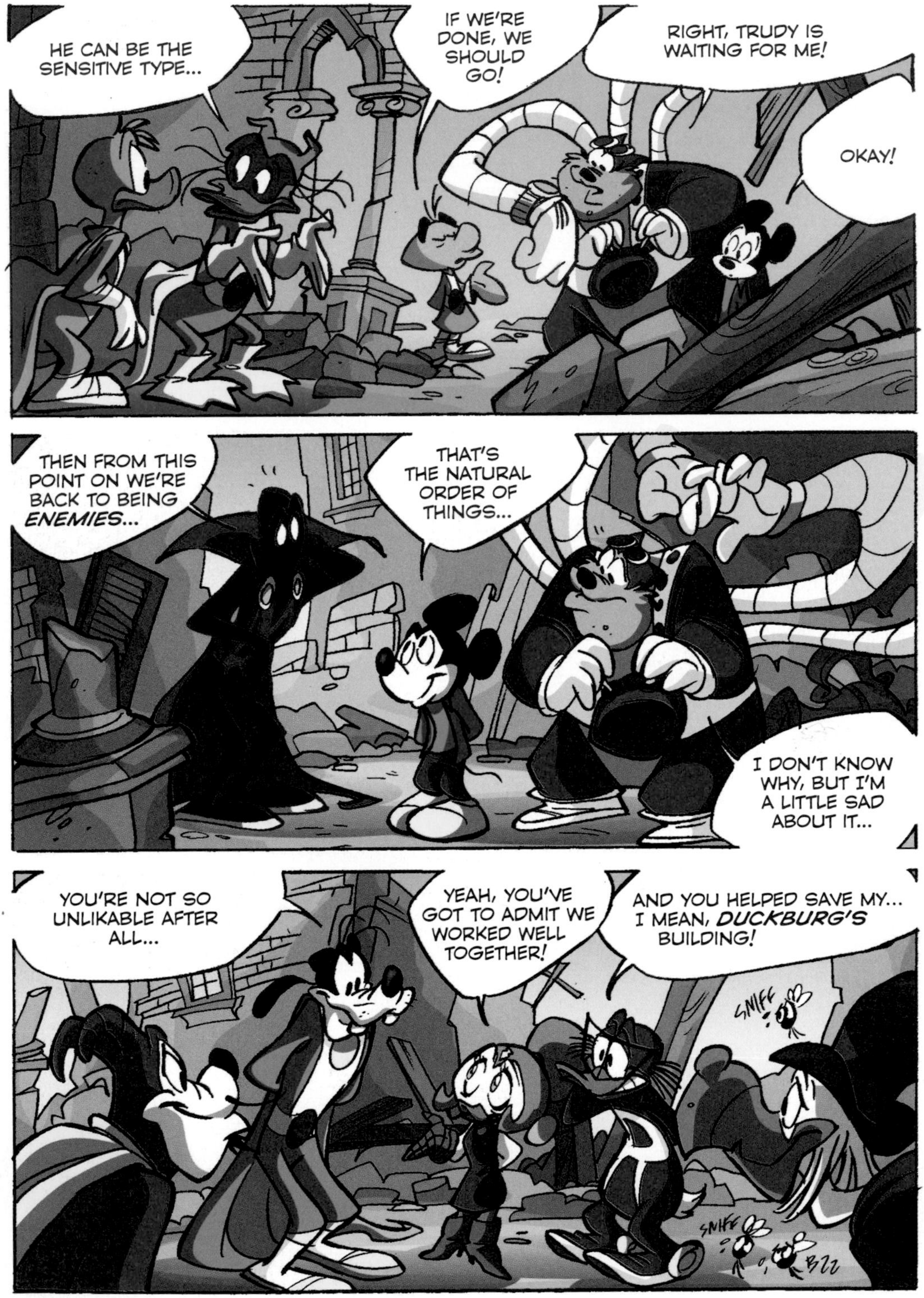
HE CAN BE THE SENSITIVE TYPE...
IF WE'RE DONE, WE SHOULD GO!
RIGHT, TRUDY IS WAITING FOR ME!
OKAY!
THEN FROM THIS POINT ON WE'RE BACK TO BEING *ENEMIES*...
THAT'S THE NATURAL ORDER OF THINGS...
I DON'T KNOW WHY, BUT I'M A LITTLE SAD ABOUT IT...
YOU'RE NOT SO UNLIKABLE AFTER ALL...
YEAH, YOU'VE GOT TO ADMIT WE WORKED WELL TOGETHER!
AND YOU HELPED SAVE MY... I MEAN, *DUCKBURG'S* BUILDING!
SNIFF
SNIFF
BZZ

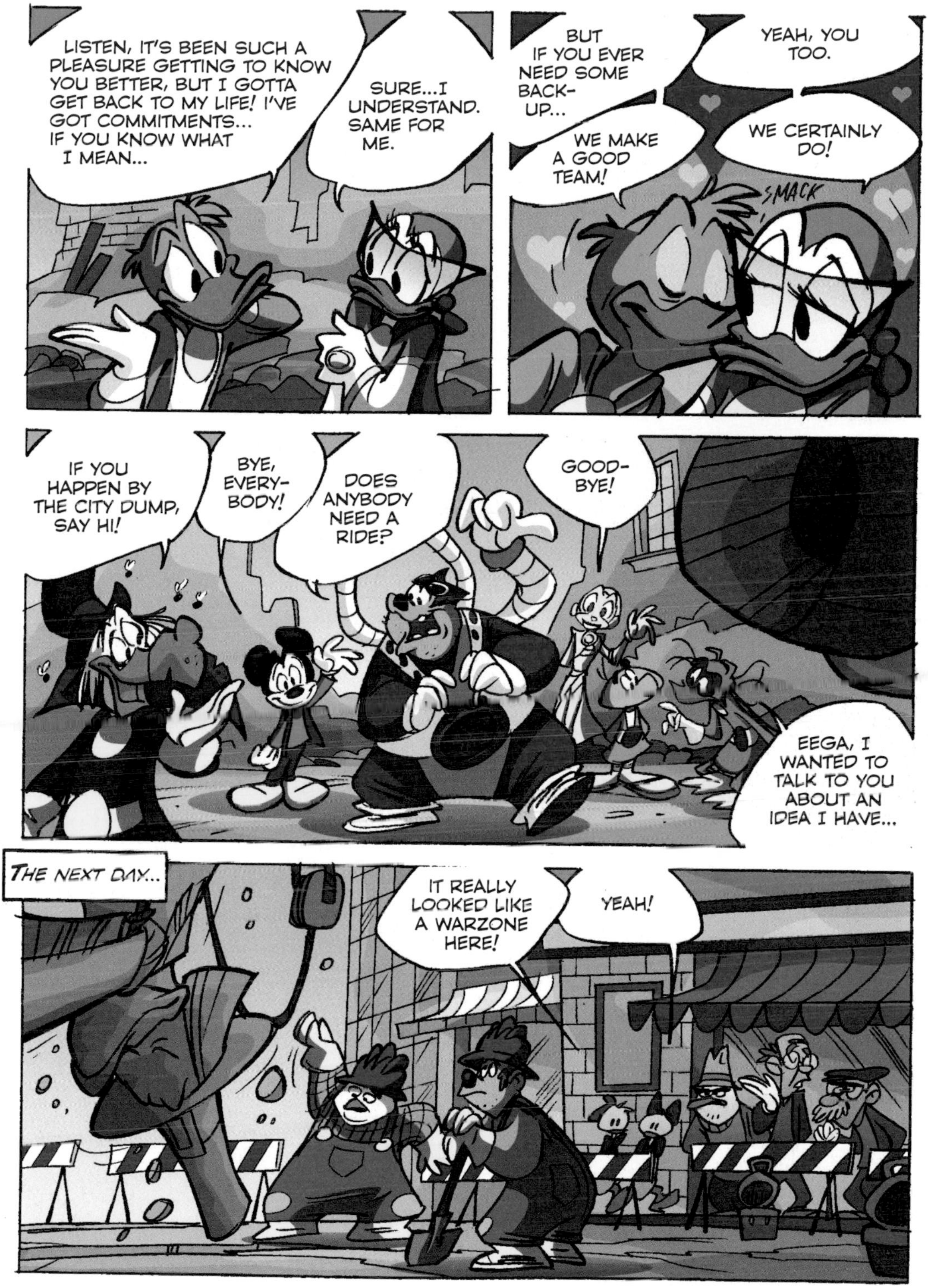

LISTEN, IT'S BEEN SUCH A PLEASURE GETTING TO KNOW YOU BETTER, BUT I GOTTA GET BACK TO MY LIFE! I'VE GOT COMMITMENTS... IF YOU KNOW WHAT I MEAN...
SURE...I UNDERSTAND. SAME FOR ME.
BUT IF YOU EVER NEED SOME BACK-UP...
YEAH, YOU TOO.
WE MAKE A GOOD TEAM!
WE CERTAINLY DO!
SMACK
IF YOU HAPPEN BY THE CITY DUMP, SAY HI!
BYE, EVERY-BODY!
DOES ANYBODY NEED A RIDE?
GOOD-BYE!
EEGA, I WANTED TO TALK TO YOU ABOUT AN IDEA I HAVE...
THE NEXT DAY...
IT REALLY LOOKED LIKE A WARZONE HERE!
YEAH!

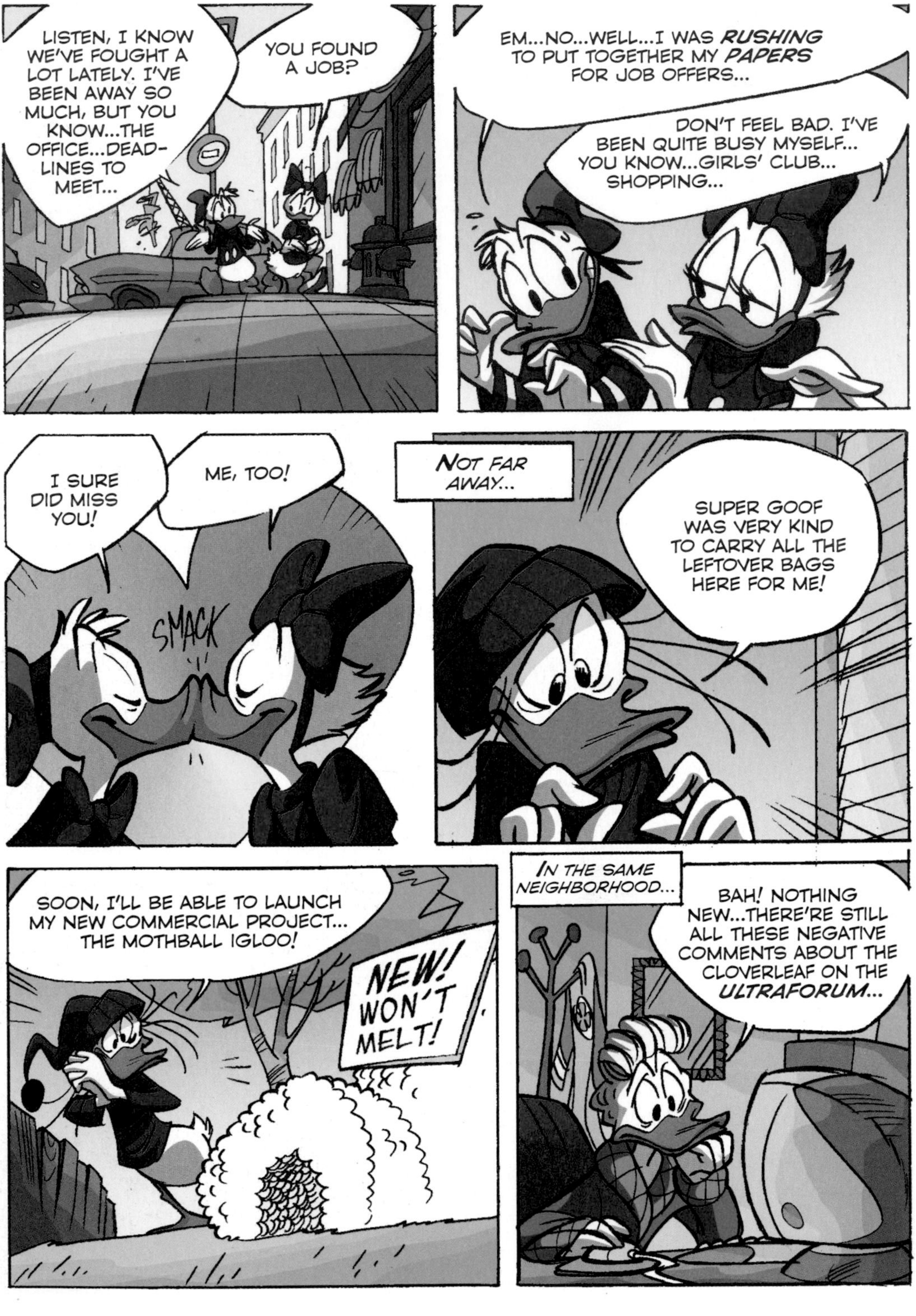
LISTEN, I KNOW WE'VE FOUGHT A LOT LATELY. I'VE BEEN AWAY SO MUCH, BUT YOU KNOW...THE OFFICE...DEAD-LINES TO MEET...
YOU FOUND A JOB?
EM...NO...WELL...I WAS RUSHING TO PUT TOGETHER MY PAPERS FOR JOB OFFERS...
DON'T FEEL BAD. I'VE BEEN QUITE BUSY MYSELF... YOU KNOW...GIRLS' CLUB... SHOPPING...
I SURE DID MISS YOU!
ME, TOO!
SMACK
NOT FAR AWAY...
SUPER GOOF WAS VERY KIND TO CARRY ALL THE LEFTOVER BAGS HERE FOR ME!
SOON, I'LL BE ABLE TO LAUNCH MY NEW COMMERCIAL PROJECT... THE MOTHBALL IGLOO!
NEW! WON'T MELT!
IN THE SAME NEIGHBORHOOD...
BAH! NOTHING NEW...THERE'RE STILL ALL THESE NEGATIVE COMMENTS ABOUT THE CLOVERLEAF ON THE ULTRAFORUM...

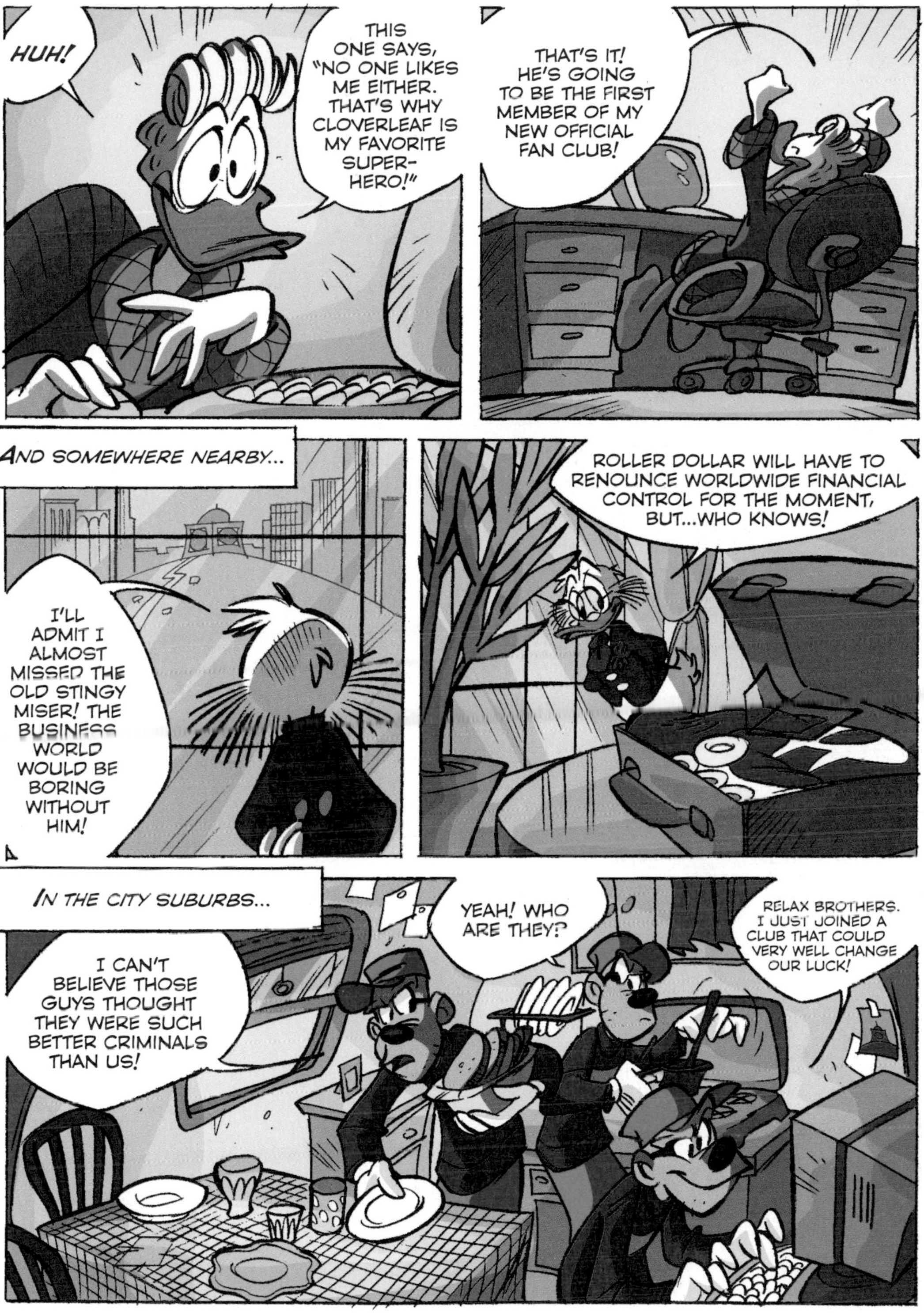
HUH!
THIS ONE SAYS, "NO ONE LIKES ME EITHER. THAT'S WHY CLOVERLEAF IS MY FAVORITE SUPER-HERO!"
THAT'S IT! HE'S GOING TO BE THE FIRST MEMBER OF MY NEW OFFICIAL FAN CLUB!
AND SOMEWHERE NEARBY...
I'LL ADMIT I ALMOST MISSED THE OLD STINGY MISER! THE BUSINESS WORLD WOULD BE BORING WITHOUT HIM!
ROLLER DOLLAR WILL HAVE TO RENOUNCE WORLDWIDE FINANCIAL CONTROL FOR THE MOMENT, BUT...WHO KNOWS!
IN THE CITY SUBURBS...
I CAN'T BELIEVE THOSE GUYS THOUGHT THEY WERE SUCH BETTER CRIMINALS THAN US!
YEAH! WHO ARE THEY?
RELAX BROTHERS. I JUST JOINED A CLUB THAT COULD VERY WELL CHANGE OUR LUCK!

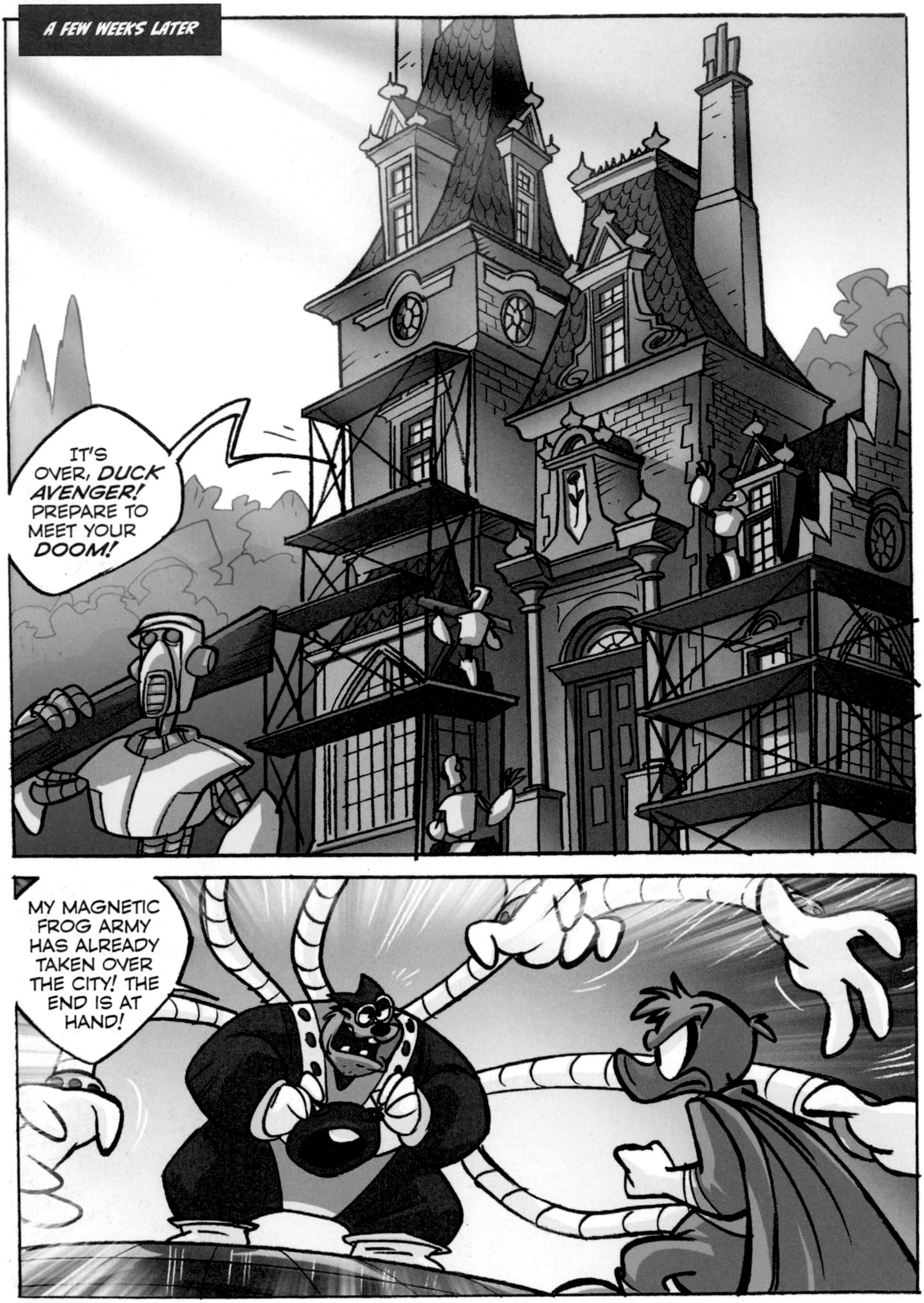
A FEW WEEKS LATER
IT'S OVER, DUCK AVENGER! PREPARE TO MEET YOUR DOOM!
MY MAGNETIC FROG ARMY HAS ALREADY TAKEN OVER THE CITY! THE END IS AT HAND!

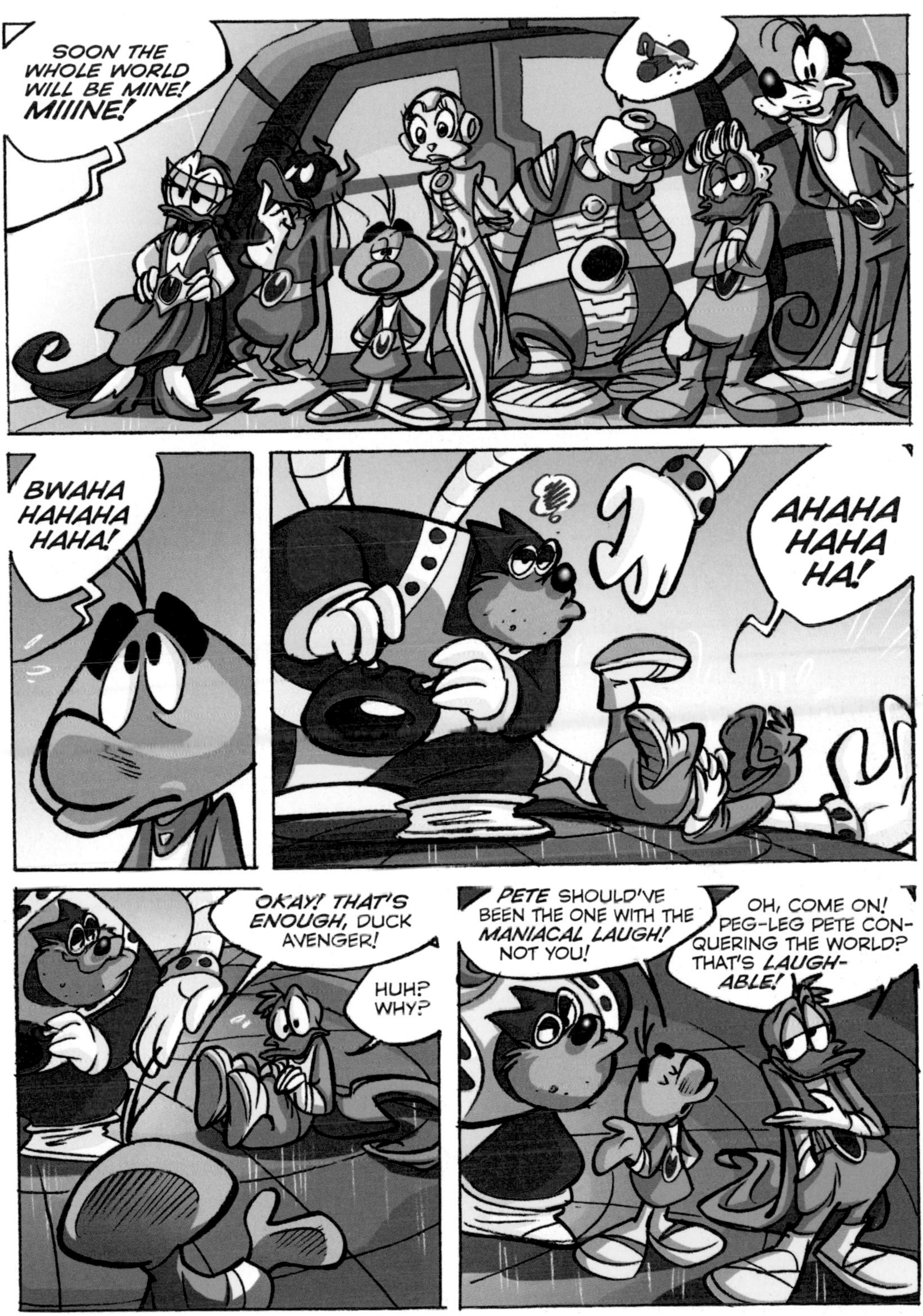
SOON THE WHOLE WORLD WILL BE MINE! MIIINE!
BWAHA HAHAHA HAHA!
AHAHA HAHA HA!
OKAY! THAT'S ENOUGH, DUCK AVENGER!
HUH? WHY?
PETE SHOULD'VE BEEN THE ONE WITH THE MANIACAL LAUGH! NOT YOU!
OH, COME ON! PEG-LEG PETE CONQUERING THE WORLD? THAT'S LAUGHABLE!

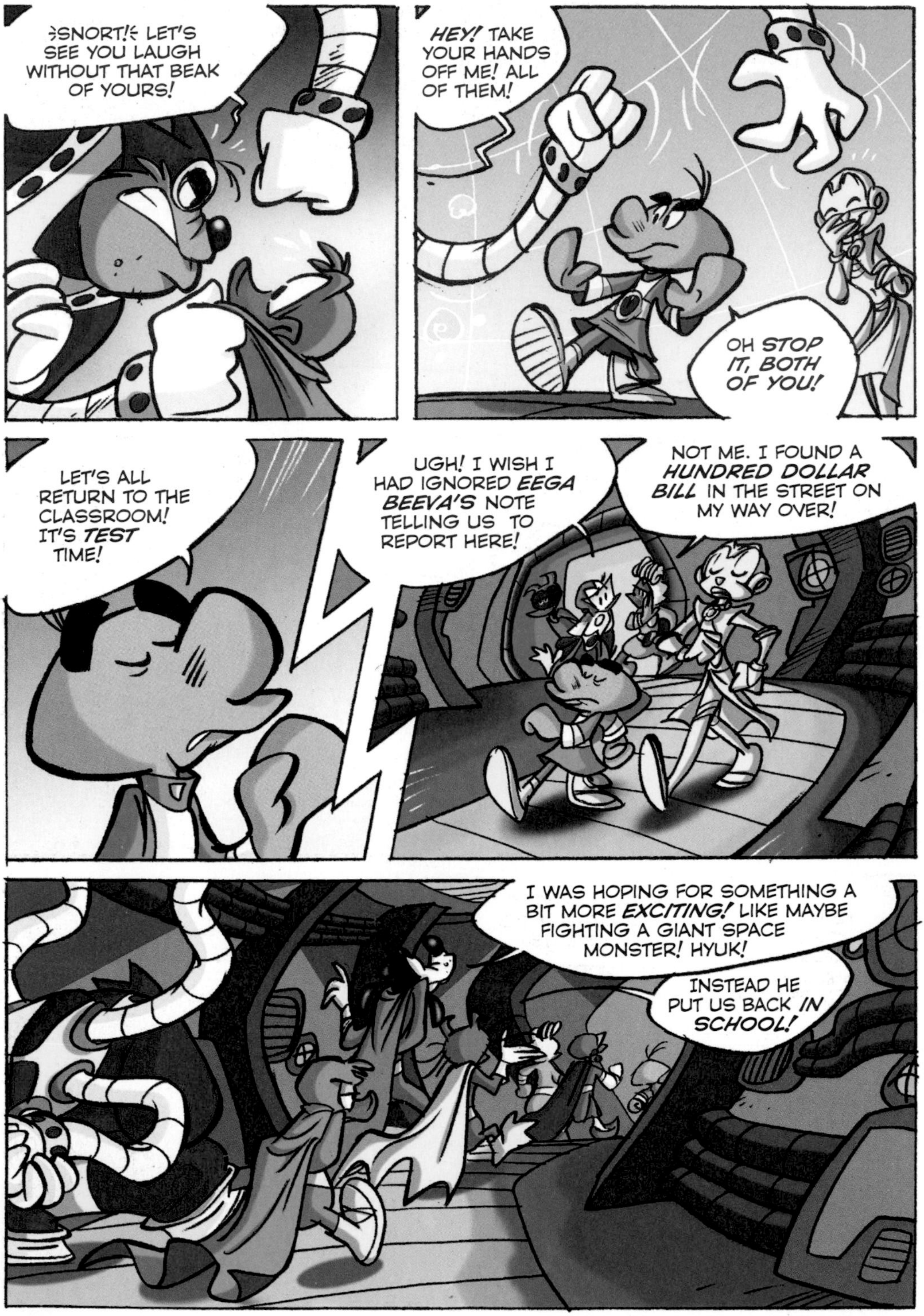

SNORT! LET'S SEE YOU LAUGH WITHOUT THAT BEAK OF YOURS!
HEY! TAKE YOUR HANDS OFF ME! ALL OF THEM!
OH STOP IT, BOTH OF YOU!
LET'S ALL RETURN TO THE CLASSROOM! IT'S TEST TIME!
UGH! I WISH I HAD IGNORED EEGA BEEVA'S NOTE TELLING US TO REPORT HERE!
NOT ME. I FOUND A HUNDRED DOLLAR BILL IN THE STREET ON MY WAY OVER!
I WAS HOPING FOR SOMETHING A BIT MORE EXCITING! LIKE MAYBE FIGHTING A GIANT SPACE MONSTER! HYUK!
INSTEAD HE PUT US BACK IN SCHOOL!

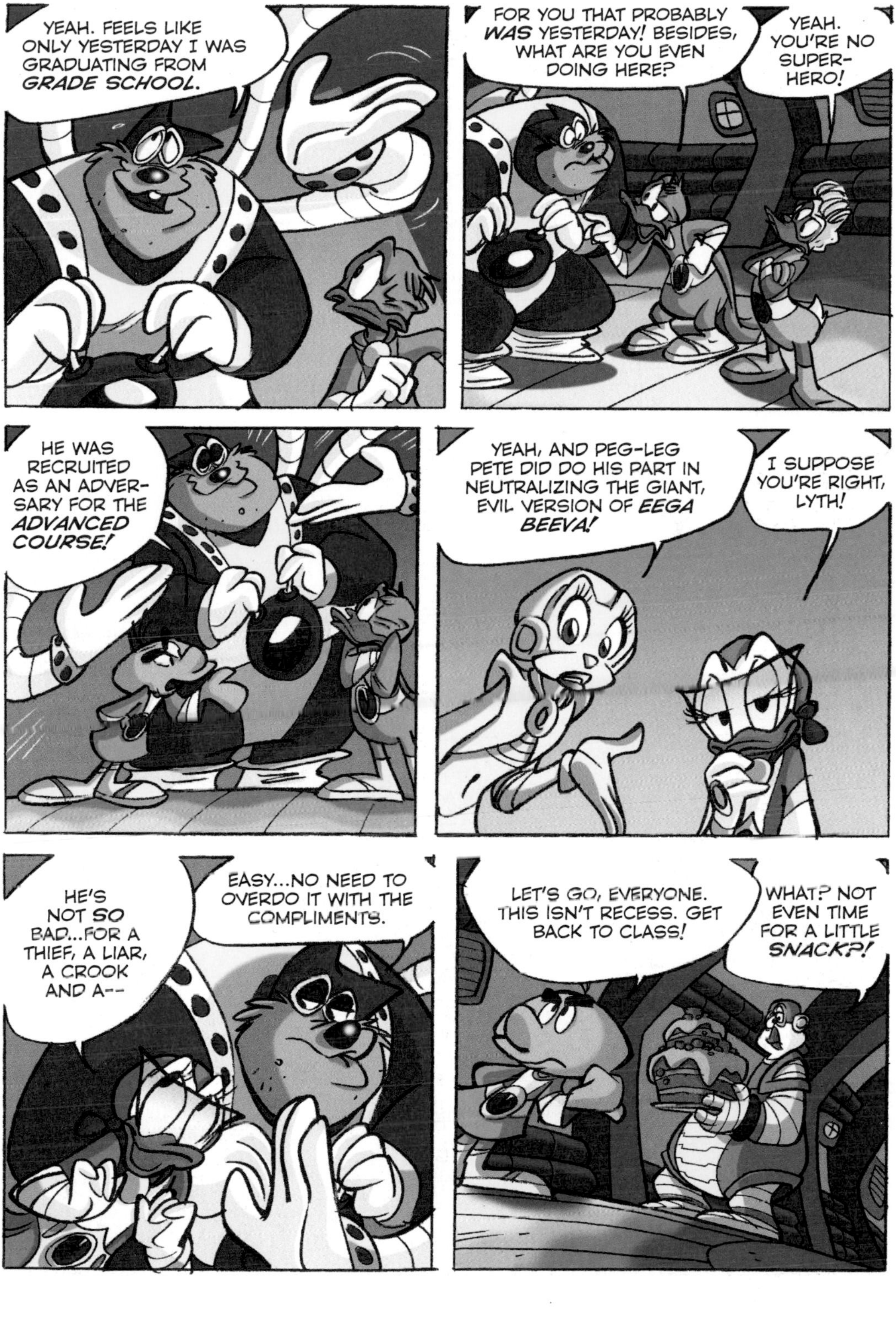
YEAH. FEELS LIKE ONLY YESTERDAY I WAS GRADUATING FROM GRADE SCHOOL.
FOR YOU THAT PROBABLY WAS YESTERDAY! BESIDES, WHAT ARE YOU EVEN DOING HERE?
YEAH. YOU'RE NO SUPER-HERO!
HE WAS RECRUITED AS AN ADVER-SARY FOR THE ADVANCED COURSE!
YEAH, AND PEG-LEG PETE DID DO HIS PART IN NEUTRALIZING THE GIANT, EVIL VERSION OF EEGA BEEVA!
I SUPPOSE YOU'RE RIGHT, LYTH!
HE'S NOT SO BAD...FOR A THIEF, A LIAR, A CROOK AND A--
EASY...NO NEED TO OVERDO IT WITH THE COMPLIMENTS.
LET'S GO, EVERYONE. THIS ISN'T RECESS. GET BACK TO CLASS!
WHAT? NOT EVEN TIME FOR A LITTLE SNACK?!

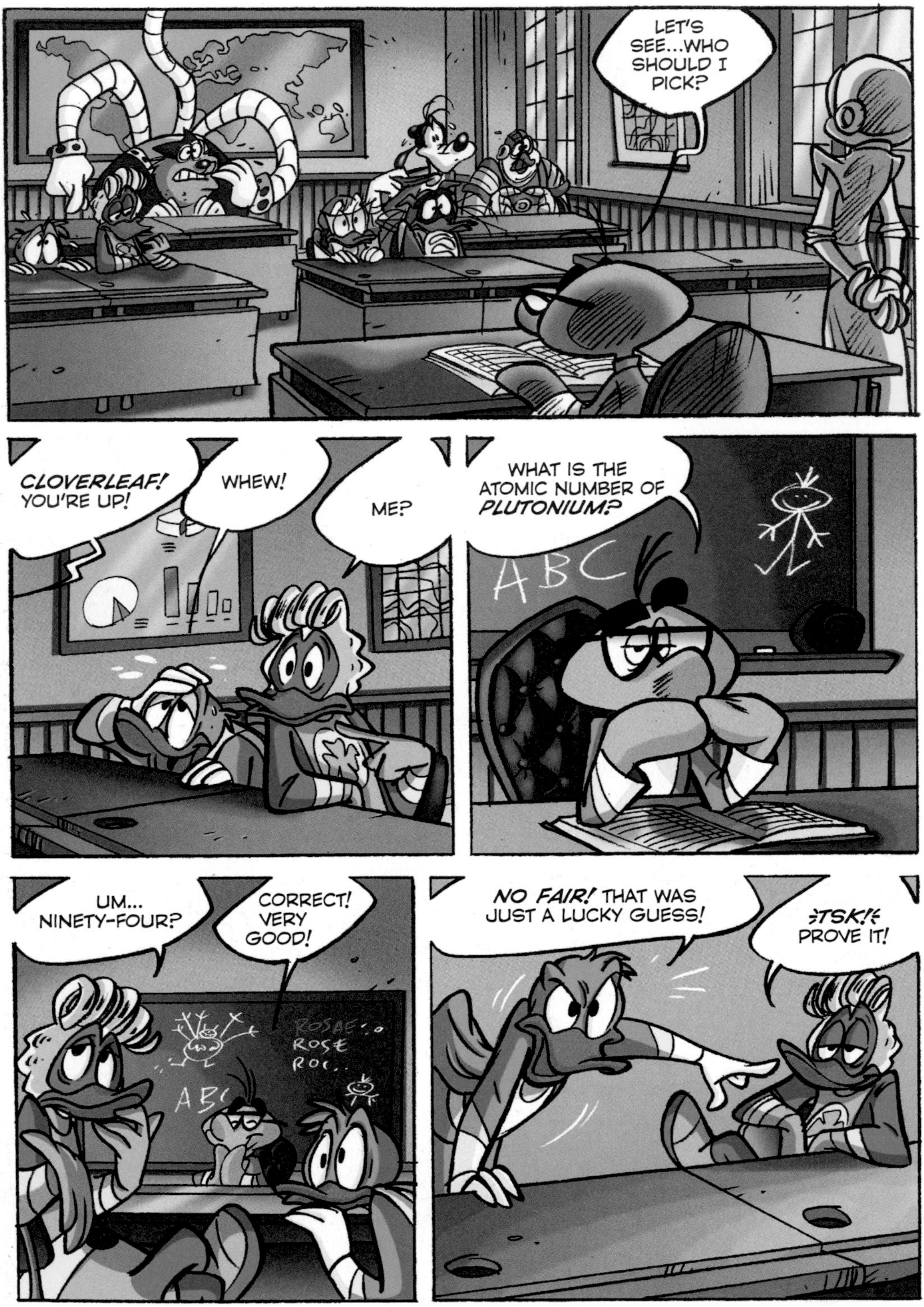
LET'S SEE...WHO SHOULD I PICK?
CLOVERLEAF! YOU'RE UP!
WHEW!
ME?
WHAT IS THE ATOMIC NUMBER OF PLUTONIUM?
UM... NINETY-FOUR?
CORRECT! VERY GOOD!
ROSAE
ROSE
ROC...
NO FAIR! THAT WAS JUST A LUCKY GUESS!
TSK! PROVE IT!

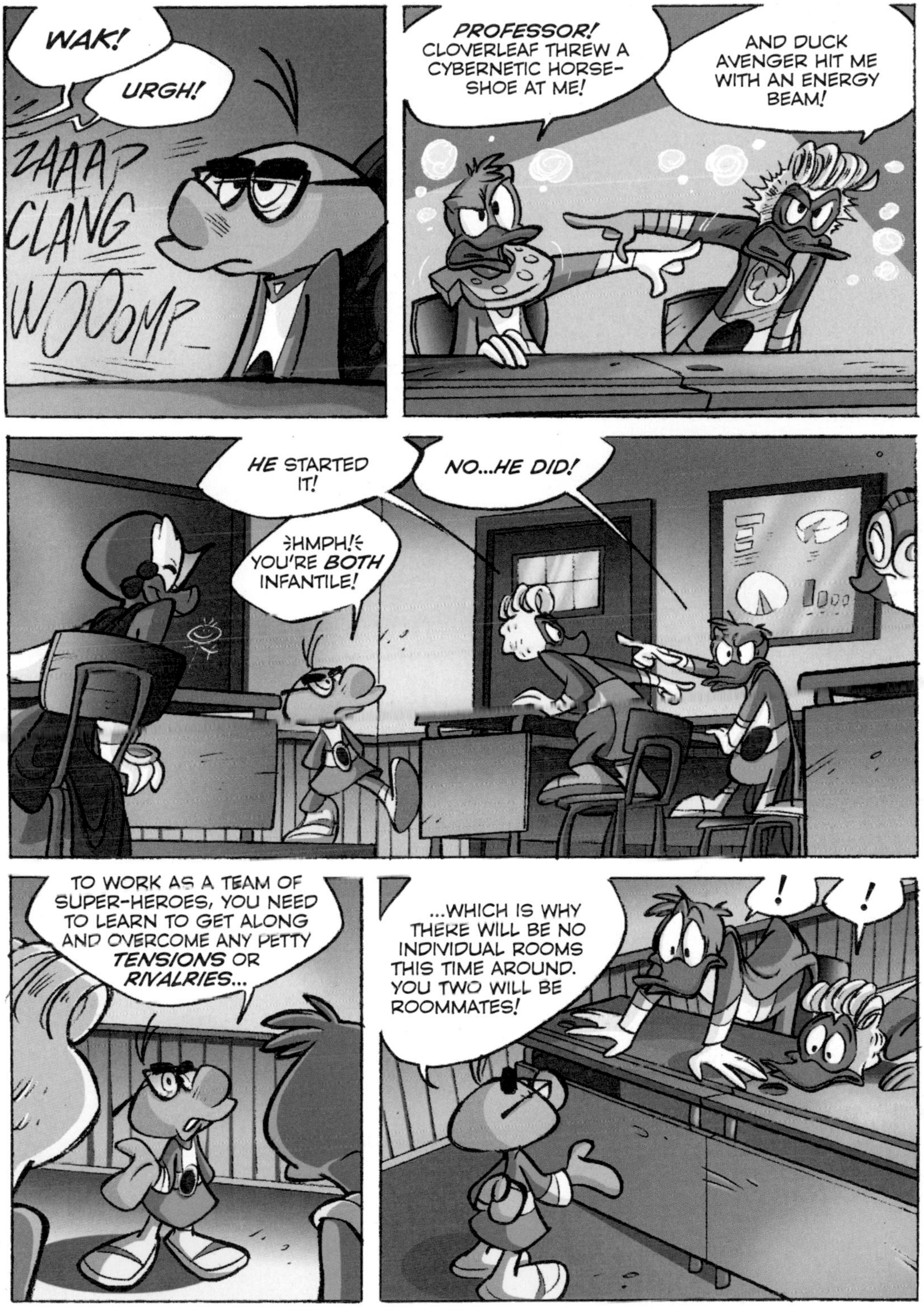
WAK!
URGH!
ZAAAP
CLANG
WOOOMP
PROFESSOR! CLOVERLEAF THREW A CYBERNETIC HORSE-SHOE AT ME!
AND DUCK AVENGER HIT ME WITH AN ENERGY BEAM!
HE STARTED IT!
NO...HE DID!
HMPH! YOU'RE BOTH INFANTILE!
TO WORK AS A TEAM OF SUPER-HEROES, YOU NEED TO LEARN TO GET ALONG AND OVERCOME ANY PETTY TENSIONS OR RIVALRIES...
...WHICH IS WHY THERE WILL BE NO INDIVIDUAL ROOMS THIS TIME AROUND. YOU TWO WILL BE ROOMMATES!
!
!

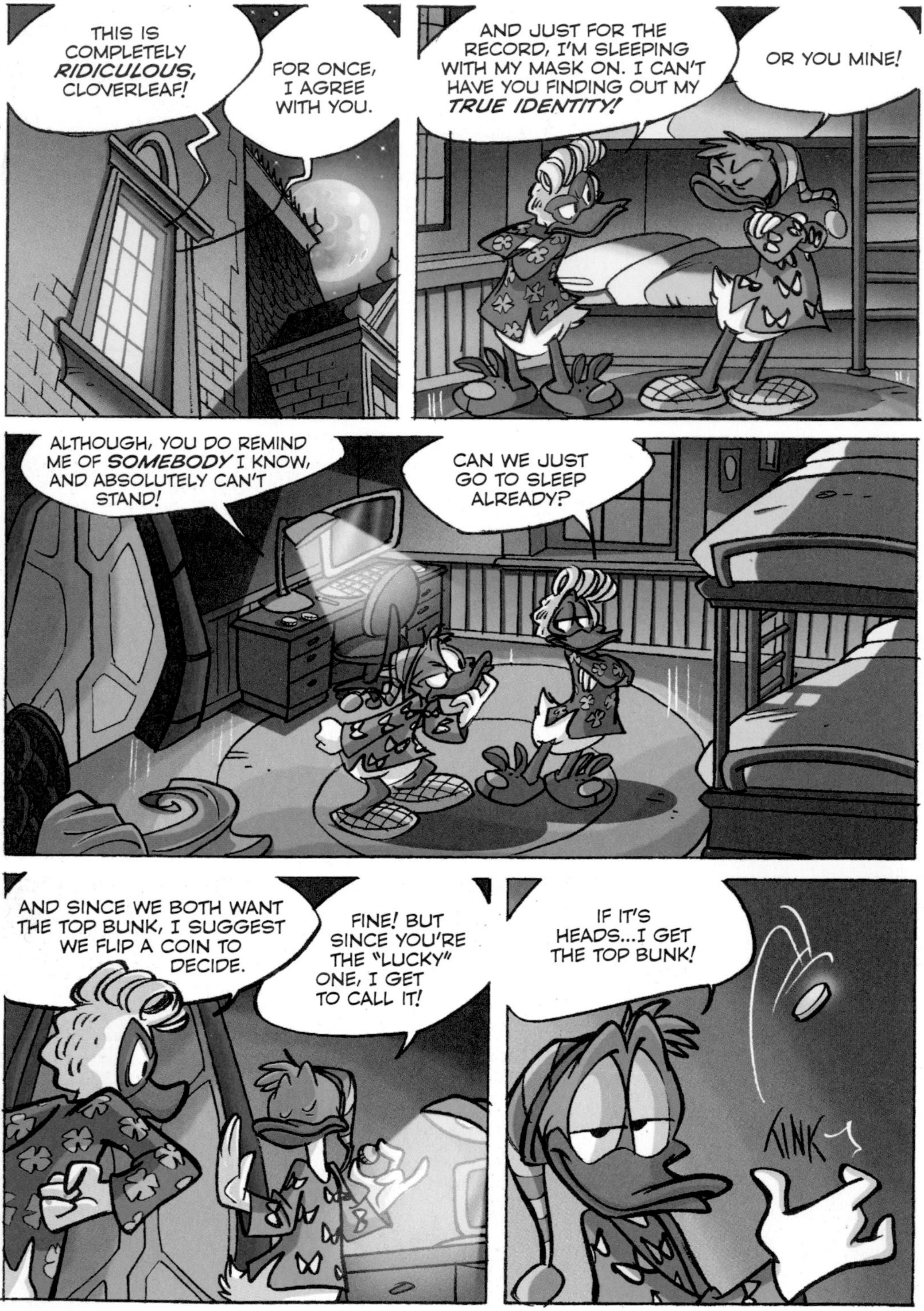
THIS IS COMPLETELY *RIDICULOUS*, CLOVERLEAF!
FOR ONCE, I AGREE WITH YOU.
AND JUST FOR THE RECORD, I'M SLEEPING WITH MY MASK ON. I CAN'T HAVE YOU FINDING OUT MY *TRUE IDENTITY!*
OR YOU MINE!
ALTHOUGH, YOU DO REMIND ME OF *SOMEBODY* I KNOW, AND ABSOLUTELY CAN'T STAND!
CAN WE JUST GO TO SLEEP ALREADY?
AND SINCE WE BOTH WANT THE TOP BUNK, I SUGGEST WE FLIP A COIN TO DECIDE.
FINE! BUT SINCE YOU'RE THE "LUCKY" ONE, I GET TO CALL IT!
IF IT'S HEADS...I GET THE TOP BUNK!
KINK

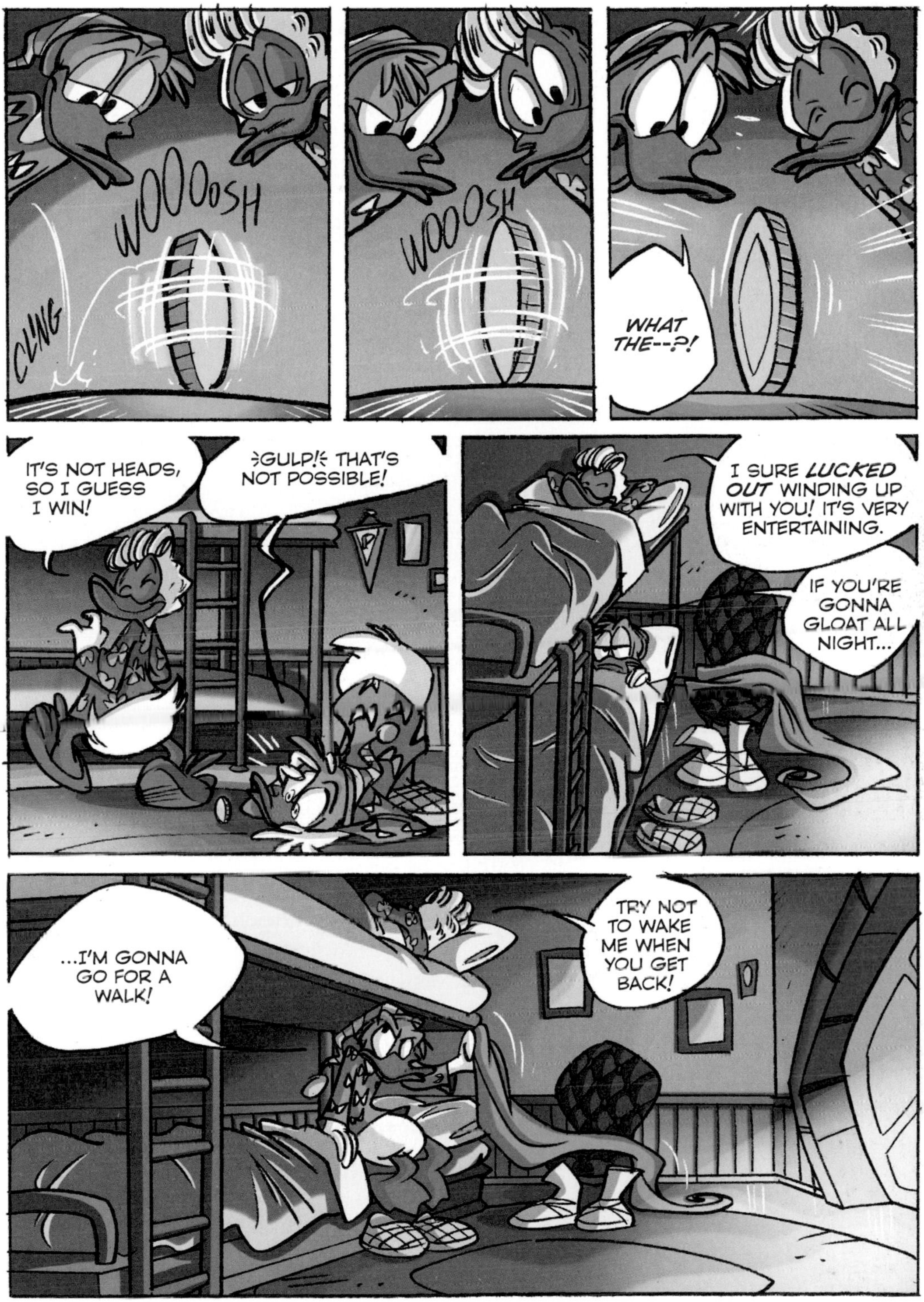
WOOOoosH
CLING
WOOOSH
WHAT THE--?!
IT'S NOT HEADS, SO I GUESS I WIN!
GULP! THAT'S NOT POSSIBLE!
I SURE *LUCKED OUT* WINDING UP WITH YOU! IT'S VERY ENTERTAINING.
IF YOU'RE GONNA GLOAT ALL NIGHT...
...I'M GONNA GO FOR A WALK!
TRY NOT TO WAKE ME WHEN YOU GET BACK!

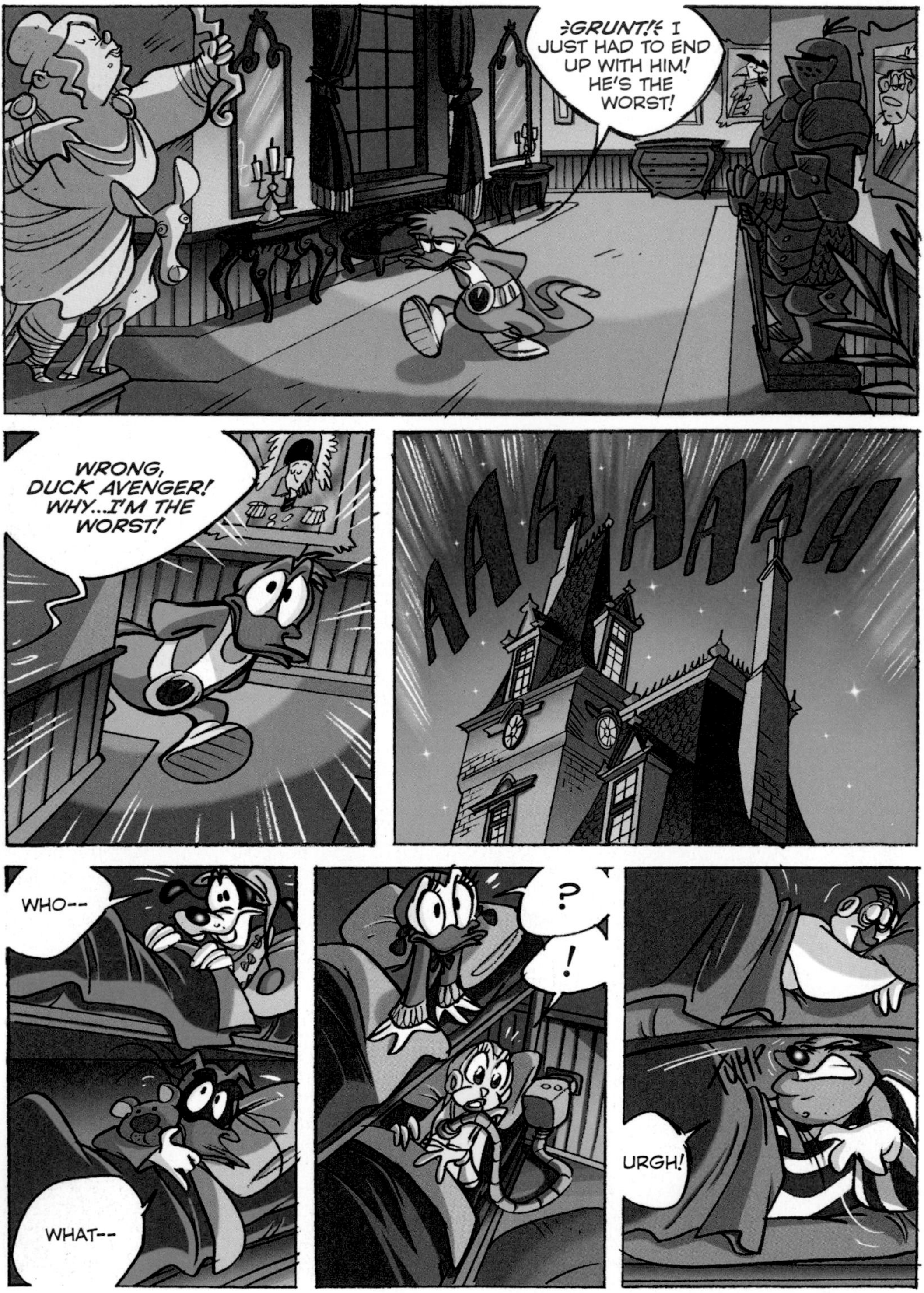
GRUNT! I JUST HAD TO END UP WITH HIM! HE'S THE WORST!
WRONG, DUCK AVENGER! WHY...I'M THE WORST!
AAAAAAAH
WHO--
WHAT--
?
!
YUMP
URGH!

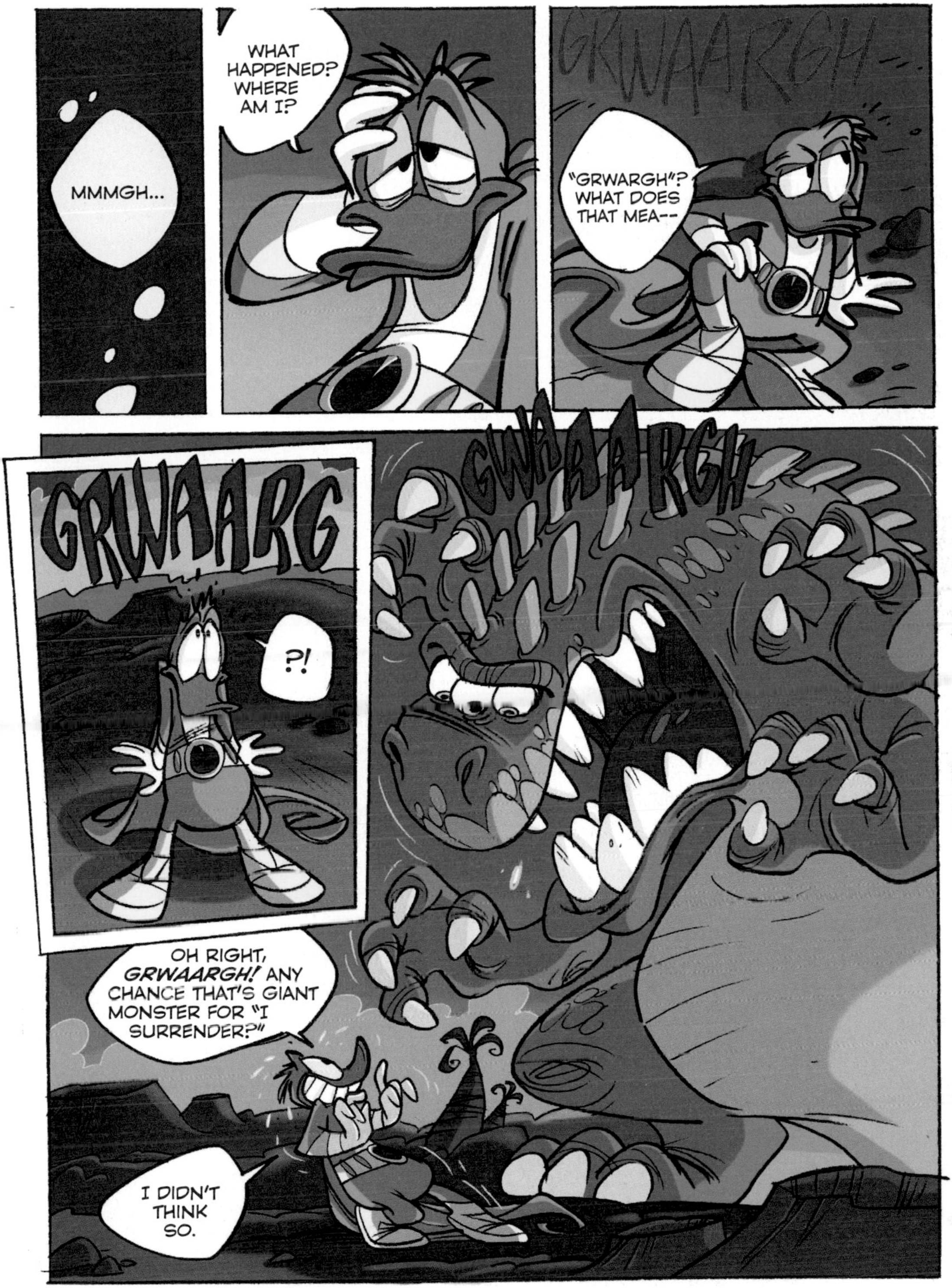
MMMGH...
WHAT HAPPENED? WHERE AM I?
GRWAARGH
"GRWARGH"? WHAT DOES THAT MEA--
GRWAARG
?!
GWAAARGH
OH RIGHT, *GRWAARGH!* ANY CHANCE THAT'S GIANT MONSTER FOR "I SURRENDER?"
I DIDN'T THINK SO.

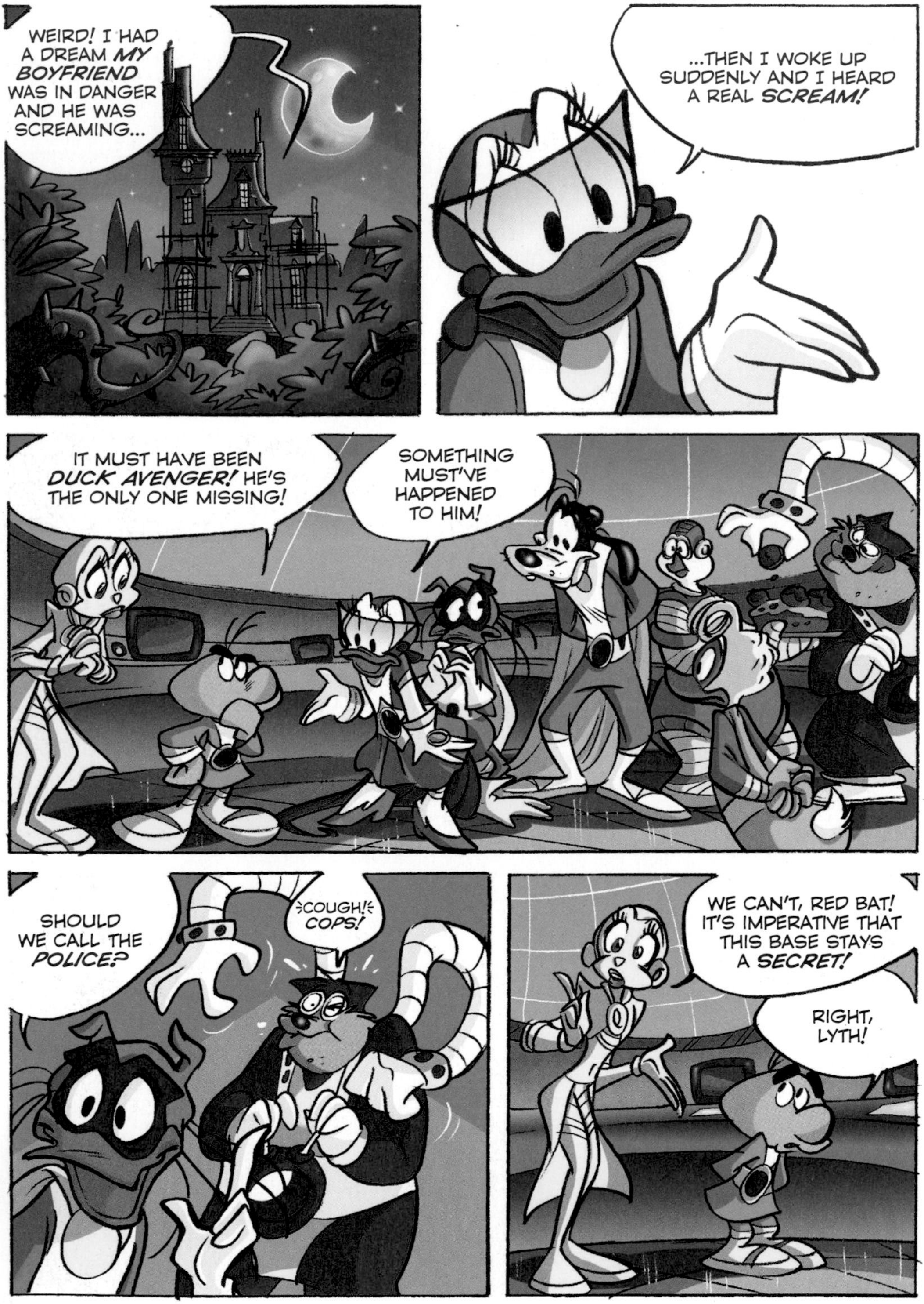
WEIRD! I HAD A DREAM MY BOYFRIEND WAS IN DANGER AND HE WAS SCREAMING...
...THEN I WOKE UP SUDDENLY AND I HEARD A REAL SCREAM!
IT MUST HAVE BEEN DUCK AVENGER! HE'S THE ONLY ONE MISSING!
SOMETHING MUST'VE HAPPENED TO HIM!
SHOULD WE CALL THE POLICE?
COUGH! COPS!
WE CAN'T, RED BAT! IT'S IMPERATIVE THAT THIS BASE STAYS A SECRET!
RIGHT, LYTH!

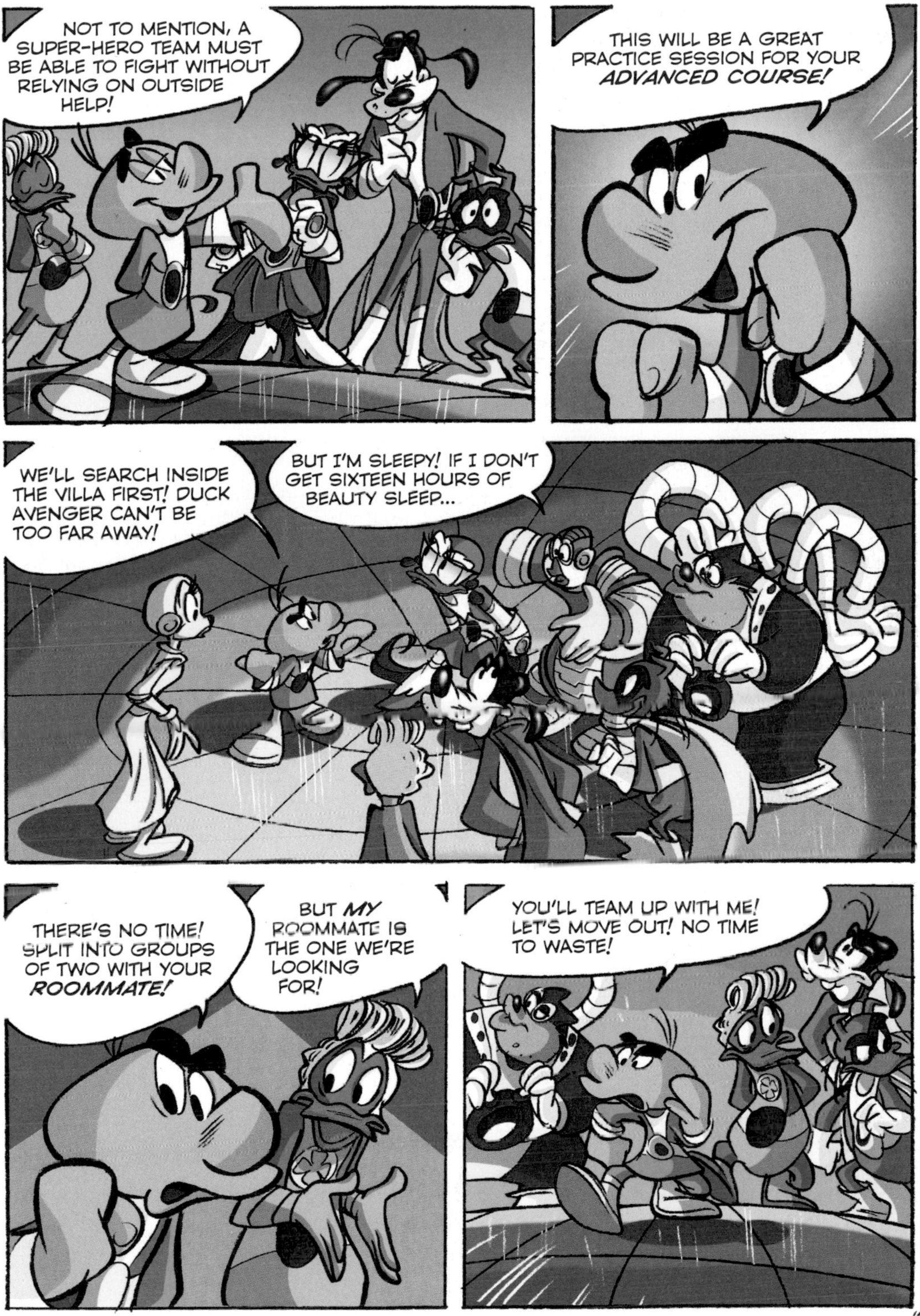
NOT TO MENTION, A SUPER-HERO TEAM MUST BE ABLE TO FIGHT WITHOUT RELYING ON OUTSIDE HELP!
THIS WILL BE A GREAT PRACTICE SESSION FOR YOUR ADVANCED COURSE!
WE'LL SEARCH INSIDE THE VILLA FIRST! DUCK AVENGER CAN'T BE TOO FAR AWAY!
BUT I'M SLEEPY! IF I DON'T GET SIXTEEN HOURS OF BEAUTY SLEEP...
THERE'S NO TIME! SPLIT INTO GROUPS OF TWO WITH YOUR ROOMMATE!
BUT MY ROOMMATE IS THE ONE WE'RE LOOKING FOR!
YOU'LL TEAM UP WITH ME! LET'S MOVE OUT! NO TIME TO WASTE!

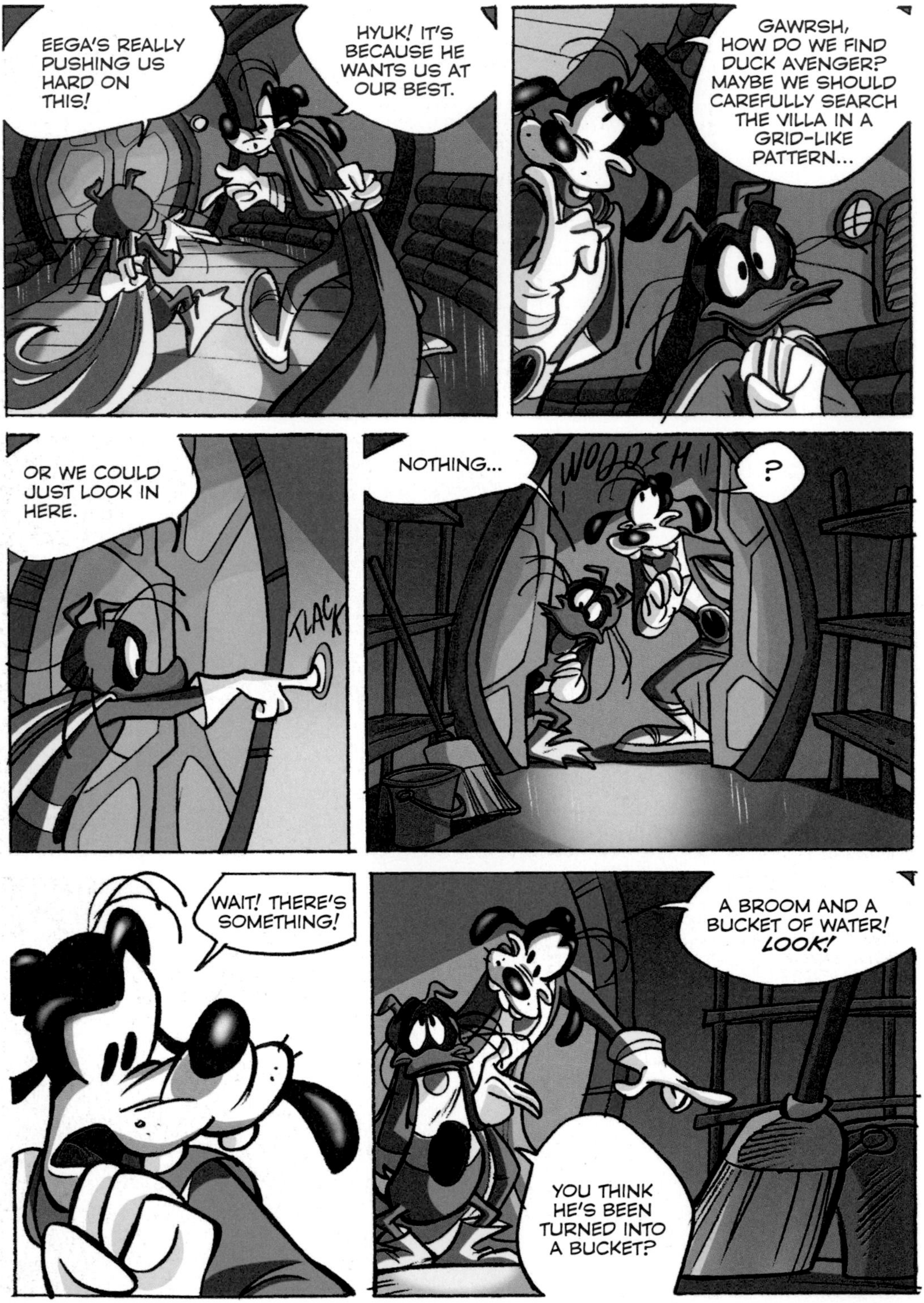
EEGA'S REALLY PUSHING US HARD ON THIS!
HYUK! IT'S BECAUSE HE WANTS US AT OUR BEST.
GAWRSH, HOW DO WE FIND DUCK AVENGER? MAYBE WE SHOULD CAREFULLY SEARCH THE VILLA IN A GRID-LIKE PATTERN...
OR WE COULD JUST LOOK IN HERE.
TLACK
NOTHING...
WOOOSH!!
?
WAIT! THERE'S SOMETHING!
A BROOM AND A BUCKET OF WATER! LOOK!
YOU THINK HE'S BEEN TURNED INTO A BUCKET?

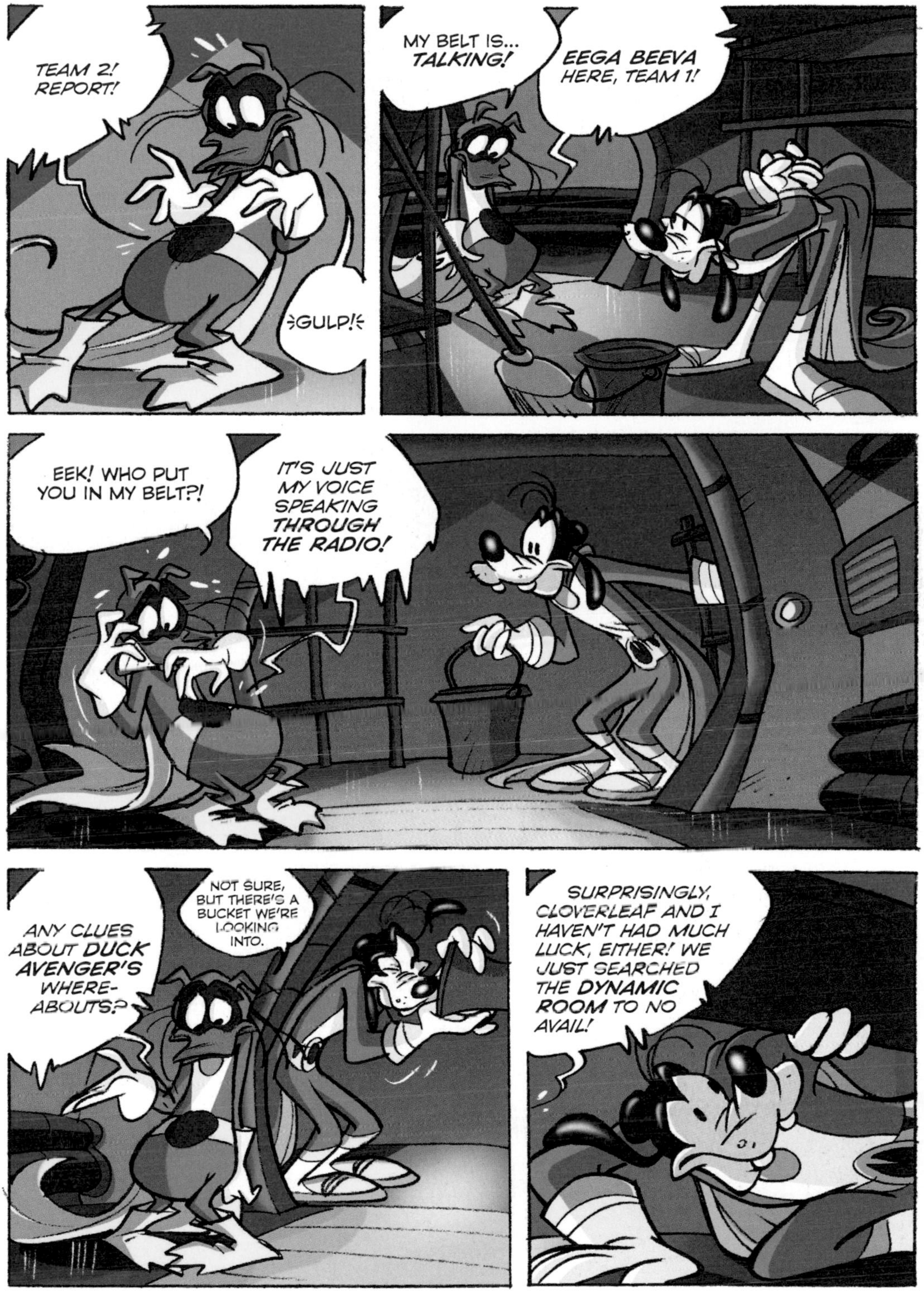
TEAM 2! REPORT!
GULP!
MY BELT IS... TALKING!
EEGA BEEVA HERE, TEAM 1!
EEK! WHO PUT YOU IN MY BELT?!
IT'S JUST MY VOICE SPEAKING THROUGH THE RADIO!
ANY CLUES ABOUT DUCK AVENGER'S WHEREABOUTS?
NOT SURE, BUT THERE'S A BUCKET WE'RE LOOKING INTO.
SURPRISINGLY, CLOVERLEAF AND I HAVEN'T HAD MUCH LUCK, EITHER! WE JUST SEARCHED THE DYNAMIC ROOM TO NO AVAIL!

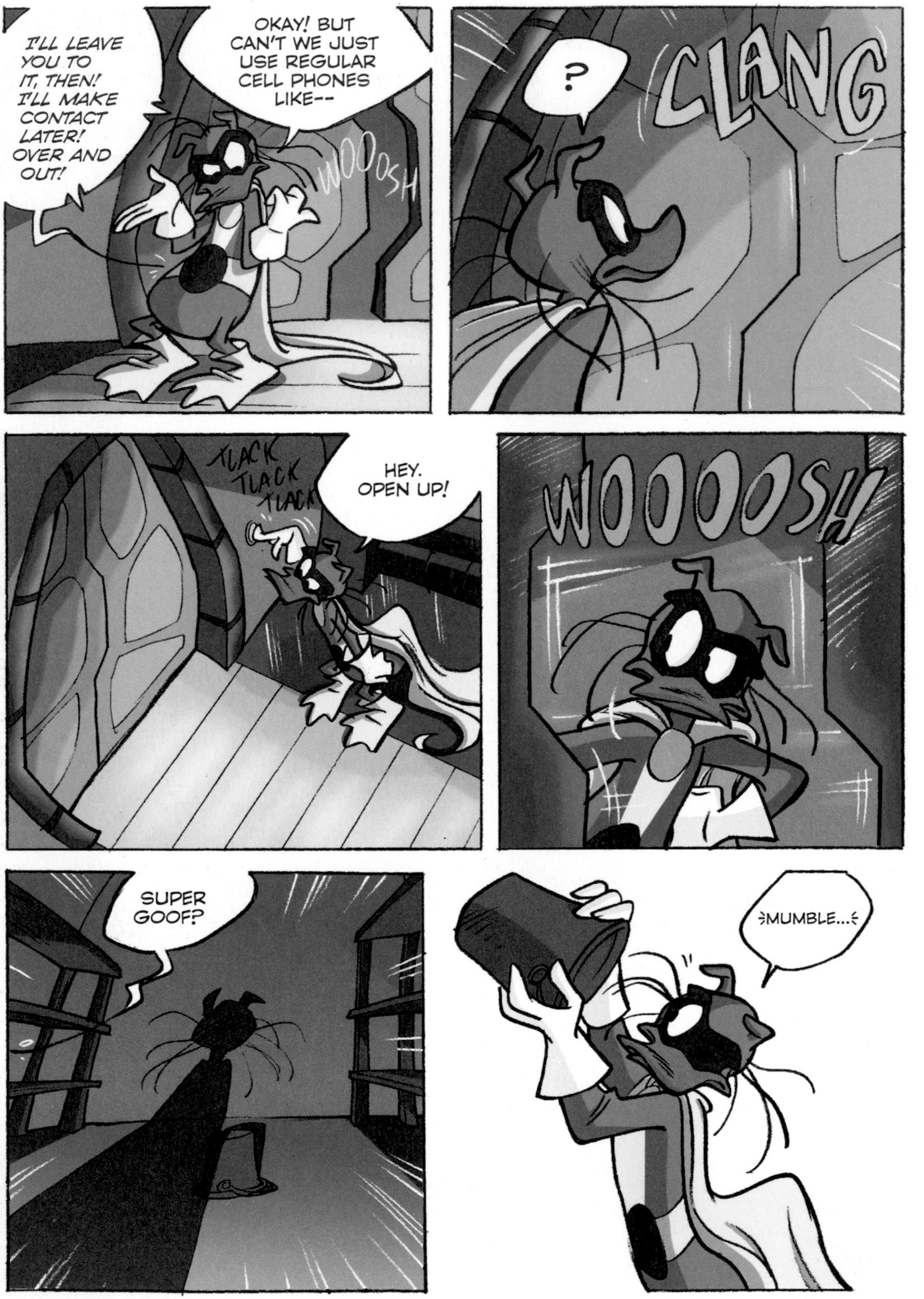
I'LL LEAVE YOU TO IT, THEN! I'LL MAKE CONTACT LATER! OVER AND OUT!
OKAY! BUT CAN'T WE JUST USE REGULAR CELL PHONES LIKE--
WOOOOSH
?
CLANG
TLACK TLACK TLACK
HEY. OPEN UP!
WOOOOSH
SUPER GOOF?
MUMBLE...

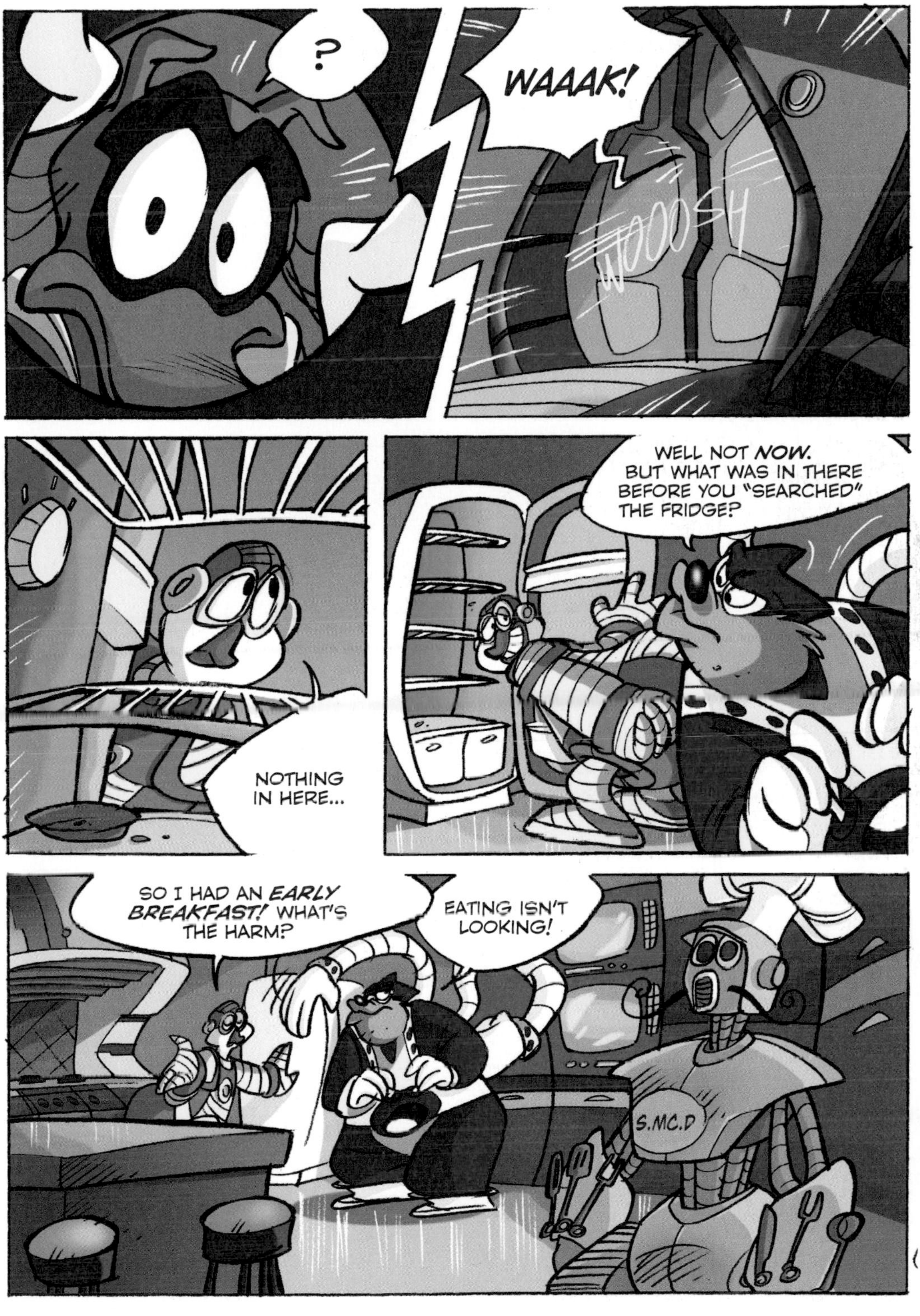
?
WAAAK!
WOOOSH
NOTHING IN HERE...
WELL NOT NOW. BUT WHAT WAS IN THERE BEFORE YOU "SEARCHED" THE FRIDGE?
SO I HAD AN EARLY BREAKFAST! WHAT'S THE HARM?
EATING ISN'T LOOKING!
S.MC.D

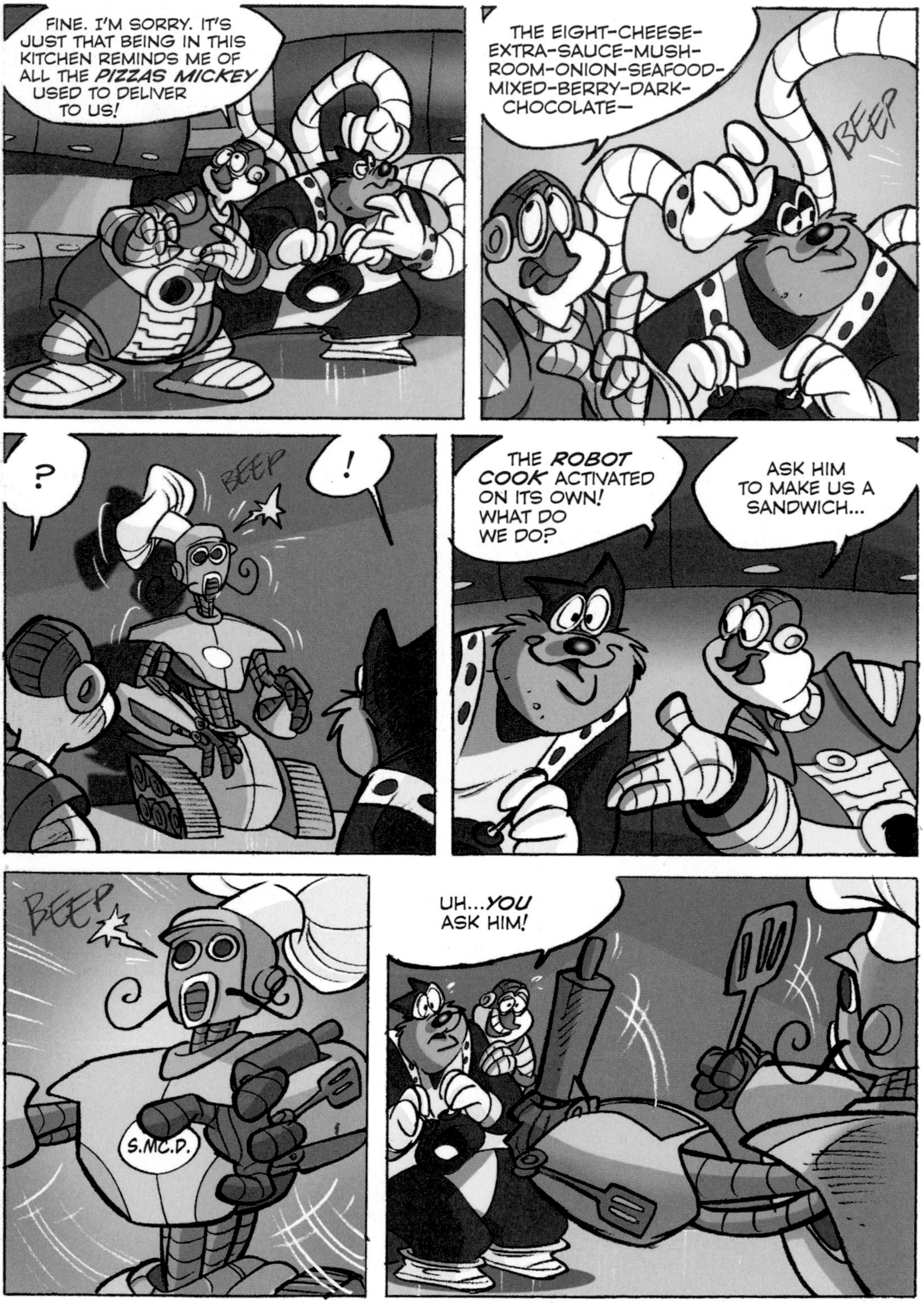
FINE. I'M SORRY. IT'S JUST THAT BEING IN THIS KITCHEN REMINDS ME OF ALL THE *PIZZAS MICKEY* USED TO DELIVER TO US!
THE EIGHT-CHEESE-EXTRA-SAUCE-MUSH-ROOM-ONION-SEAFOOD-MIXED-BERRY-DARK-CHOCOLATE—
BEEP
?
BEEP
!
THE *ROBOT COOK* ACTIVATED ON ITS OWN! WHAT DO WE DO?
ASK HIM TO MAKE US A SANDWICH...
BEEP
S.MC.D.
UH...*YOU* ASK HIM!

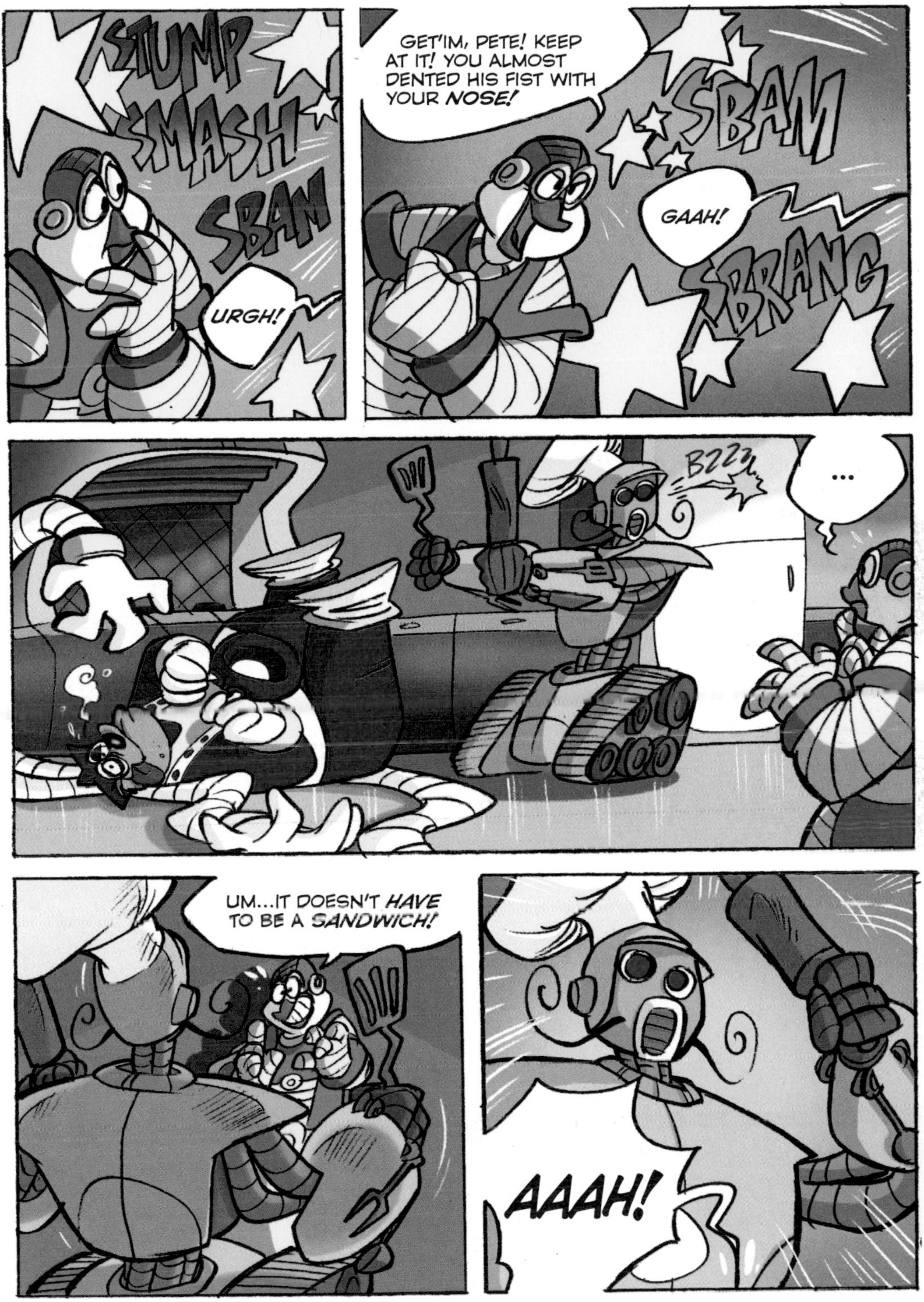
STUMP
SMASH
SBAM
URGH!
GET'IM, PETE! KEEP AT IT! YOU ALMOST DENTED HIS FIST WITH YOUR *NOSE!*
SBAM
GAAH!
SBRANG
BZZZ
...
UM...IT DOESN'T *HAVE* TO BE A *SANDWICH!*
AAAH!

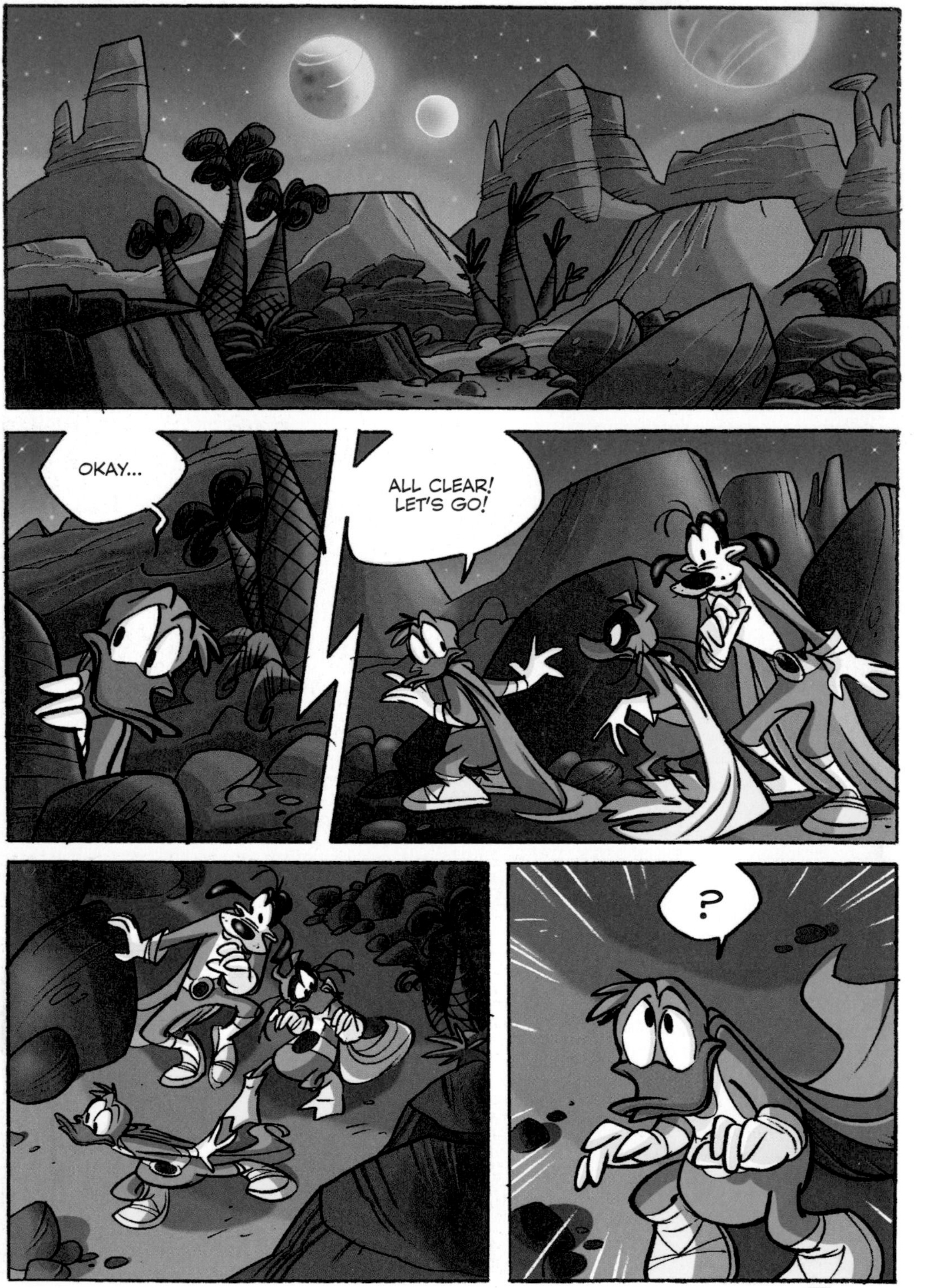
OKAY...
ALL CLEAR! LET'S GO!
?

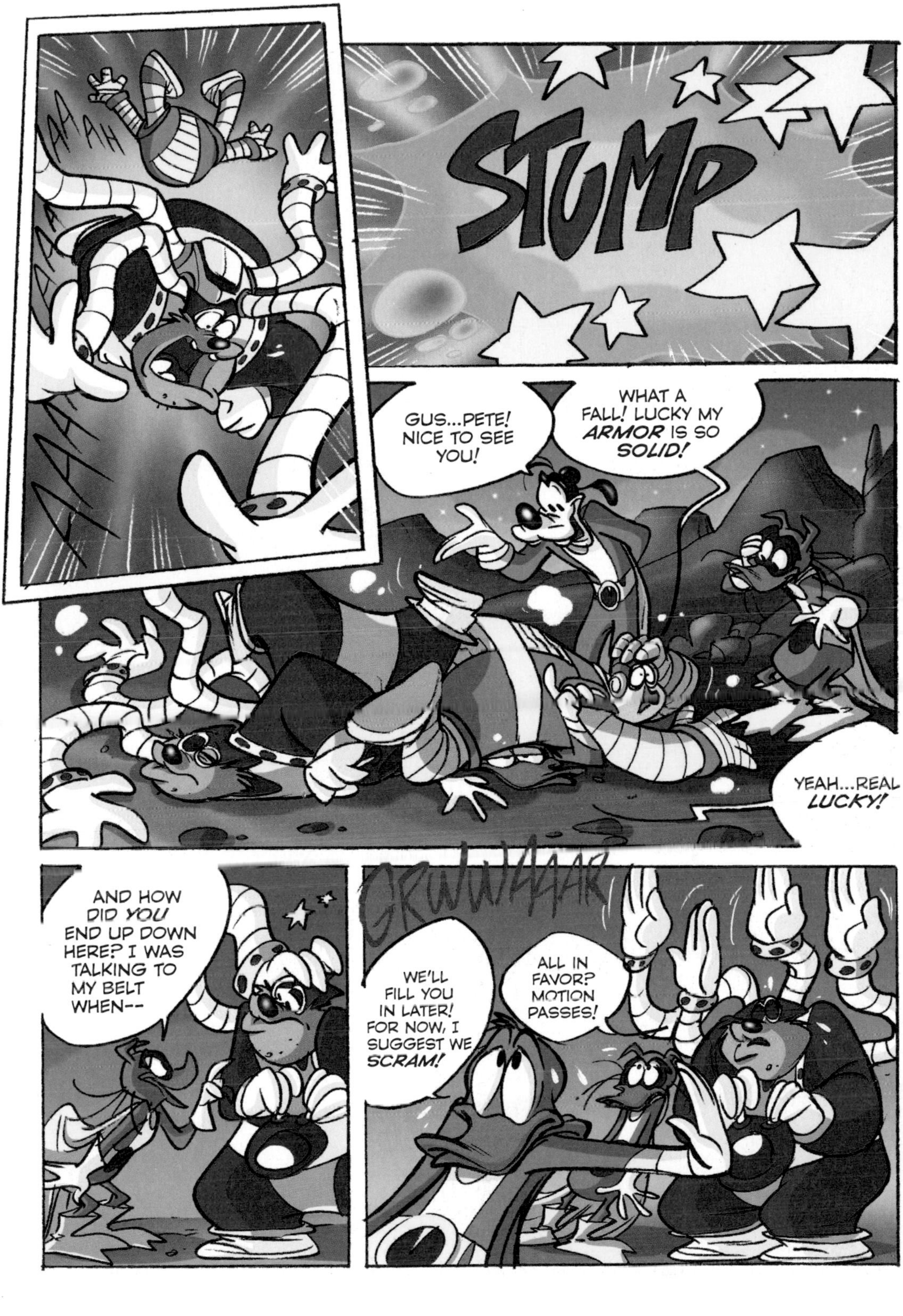
AAAHHH
STUMP
GUS...PETE! NICE TO SEE YOU!
WHAT A FALL! LUCKY MY ARMOR IS SO SOLID!
YEAH...REAL LUCKY!
AND HOW DID YOU END UP DOWN HERE? I WAS TALKING TO MY BELT WHEN--
GRWWAAAR
WE'LL FILL YOU IN LATER! FOR NOW, I SUGGEST WE SCRAM!
ALL IN FAVOR? MOTION PASSES!

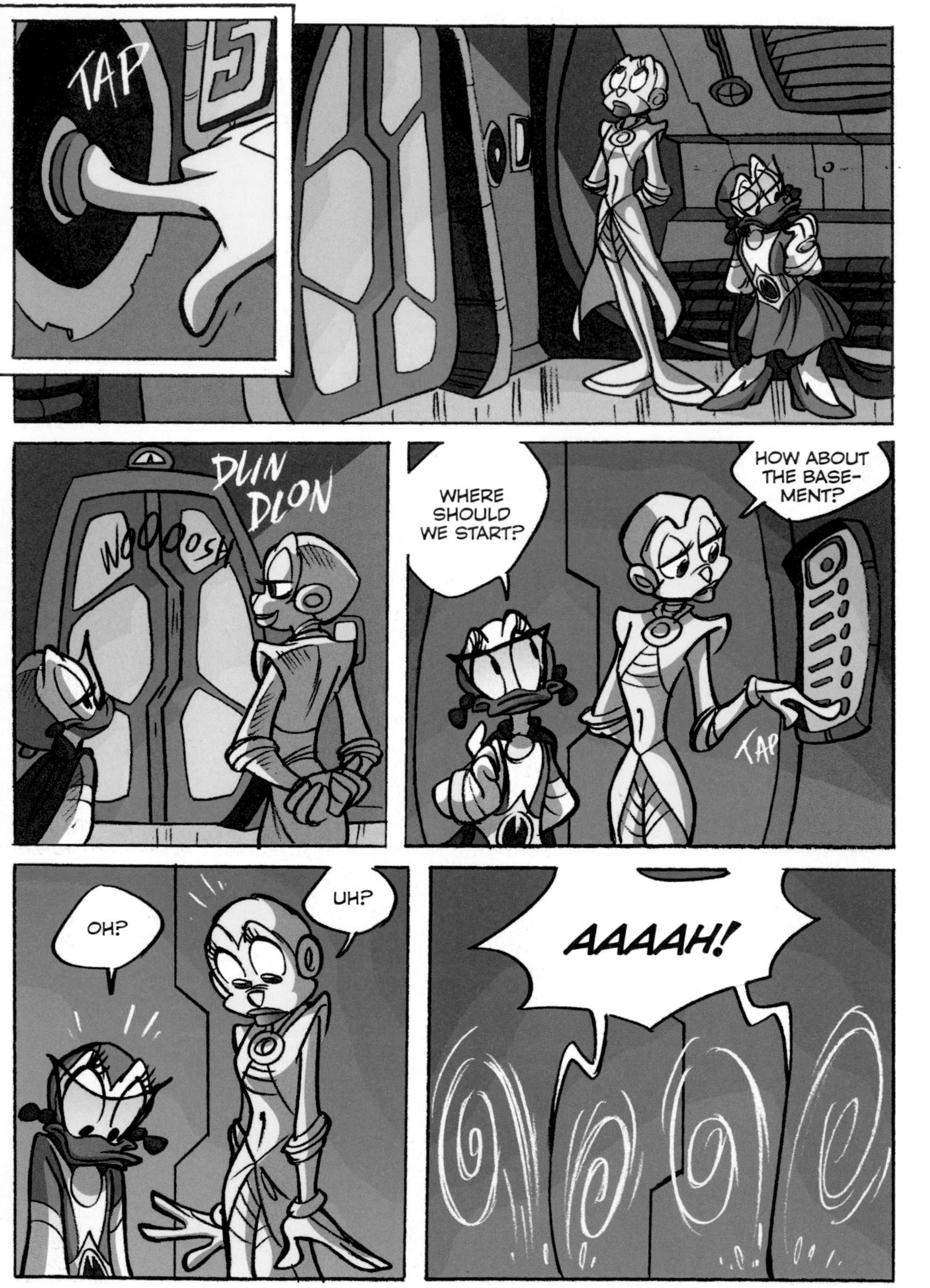
TAP
DLIN DLON
WOOOOSH
WHERE SHOULD WE START?
HOW ABOUT THE BASE- MENT?
TAP
OH?
UH?
AAAAH!

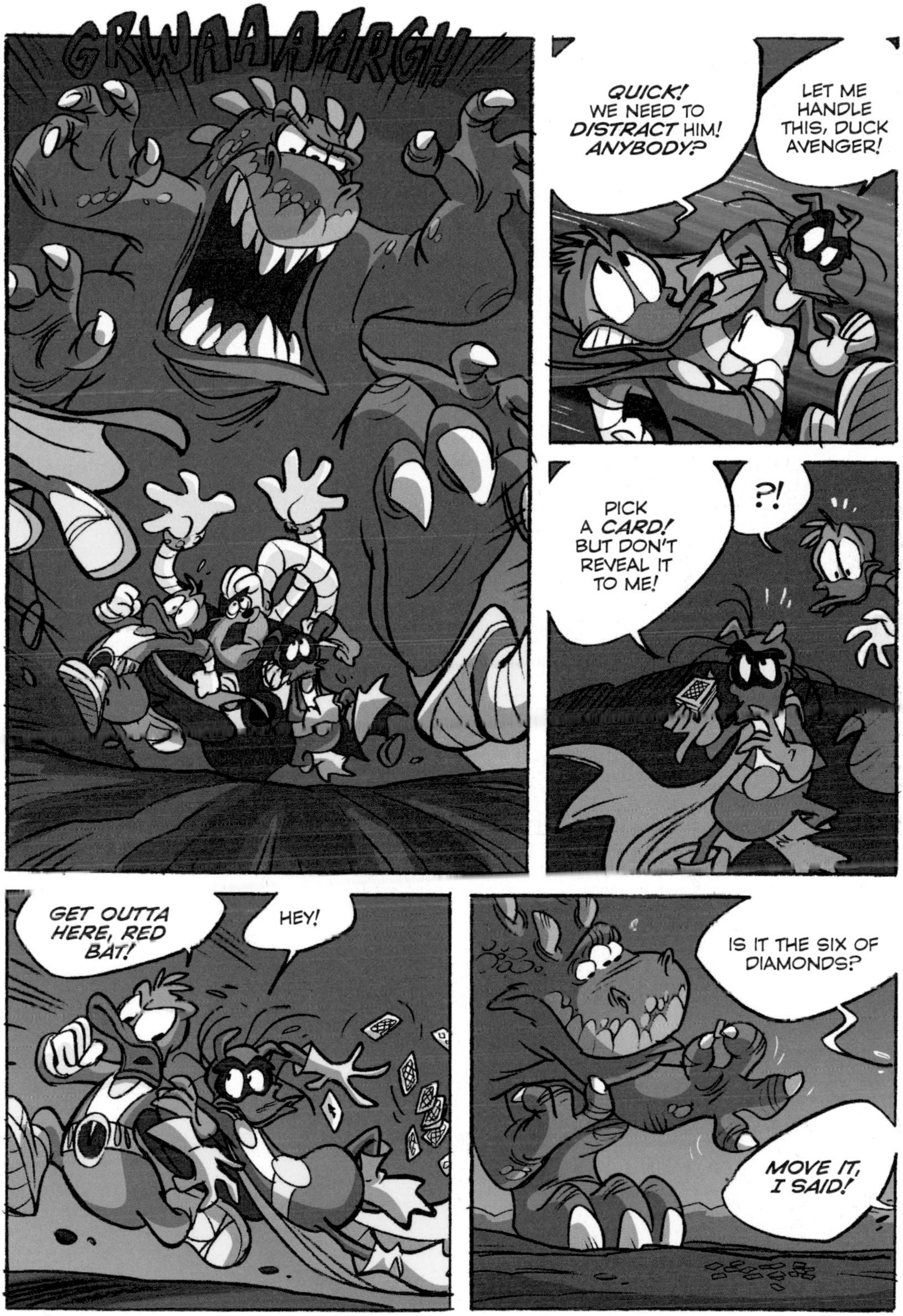
GRWAAAAARGH
QUICK! WE NEED TO DISTRACT HIM! ANYBODY?
LET ME HANDLE THIS, DUCK AVENGER!
PICK A CARD! BUT DON'T REVEAL IT TO ME!
?!
GET OUTTA HERE, RED BAT!
HEY!
IS IT THE SIX OF DIAMONDS?
MOVE IT, I SAID!

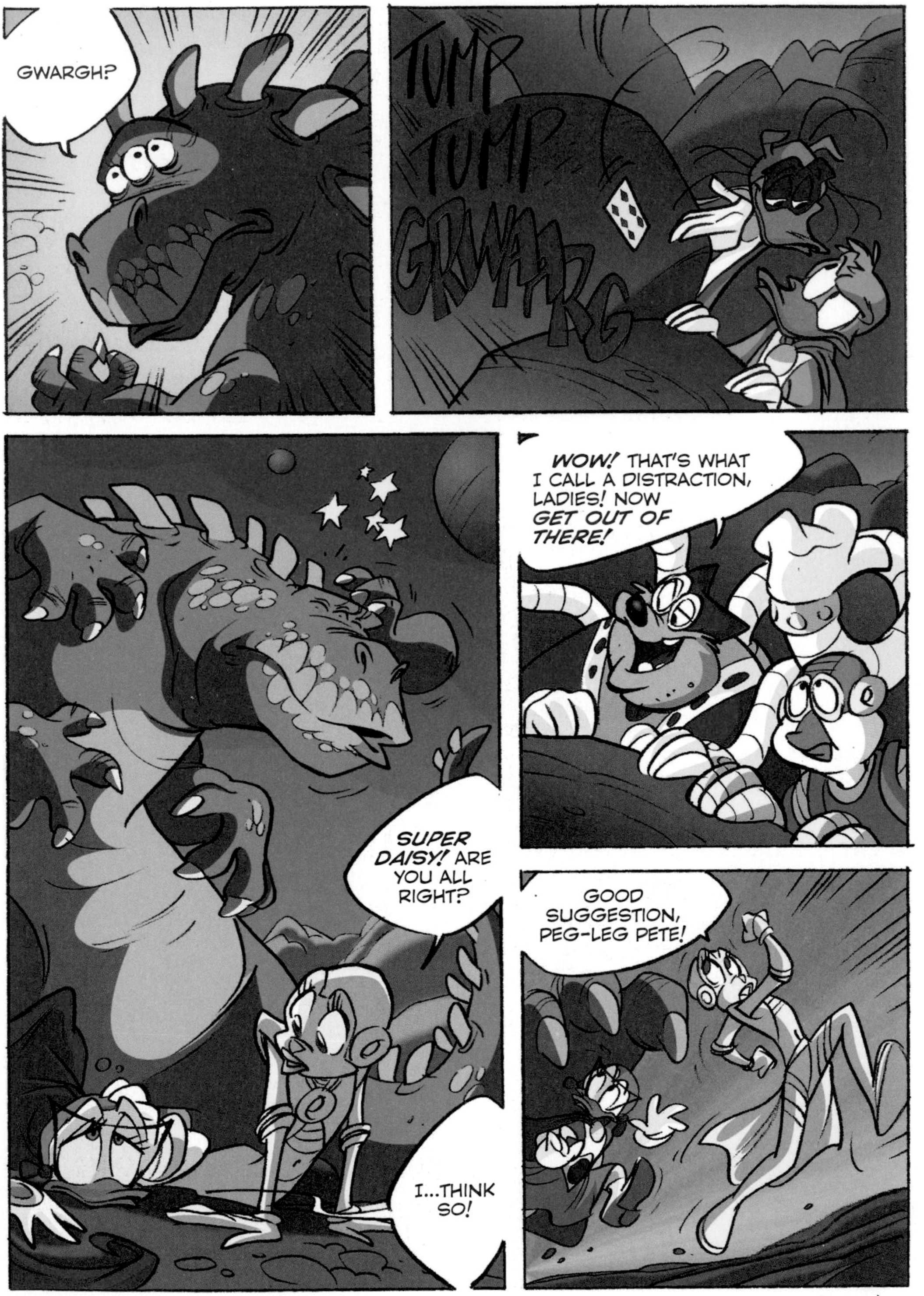
GWARGH?
TUMP
TUMP
GRWAARG
WOW! THAT'S WHAT I CALL A DISTRACTION, LADIES! NOW GET OUT OF THERE!
SUPER DAISY! ARE YOU ALL RIGHT?
I...THINK SO!
GOOD SUGGESTION, PEG-LEG PETE!

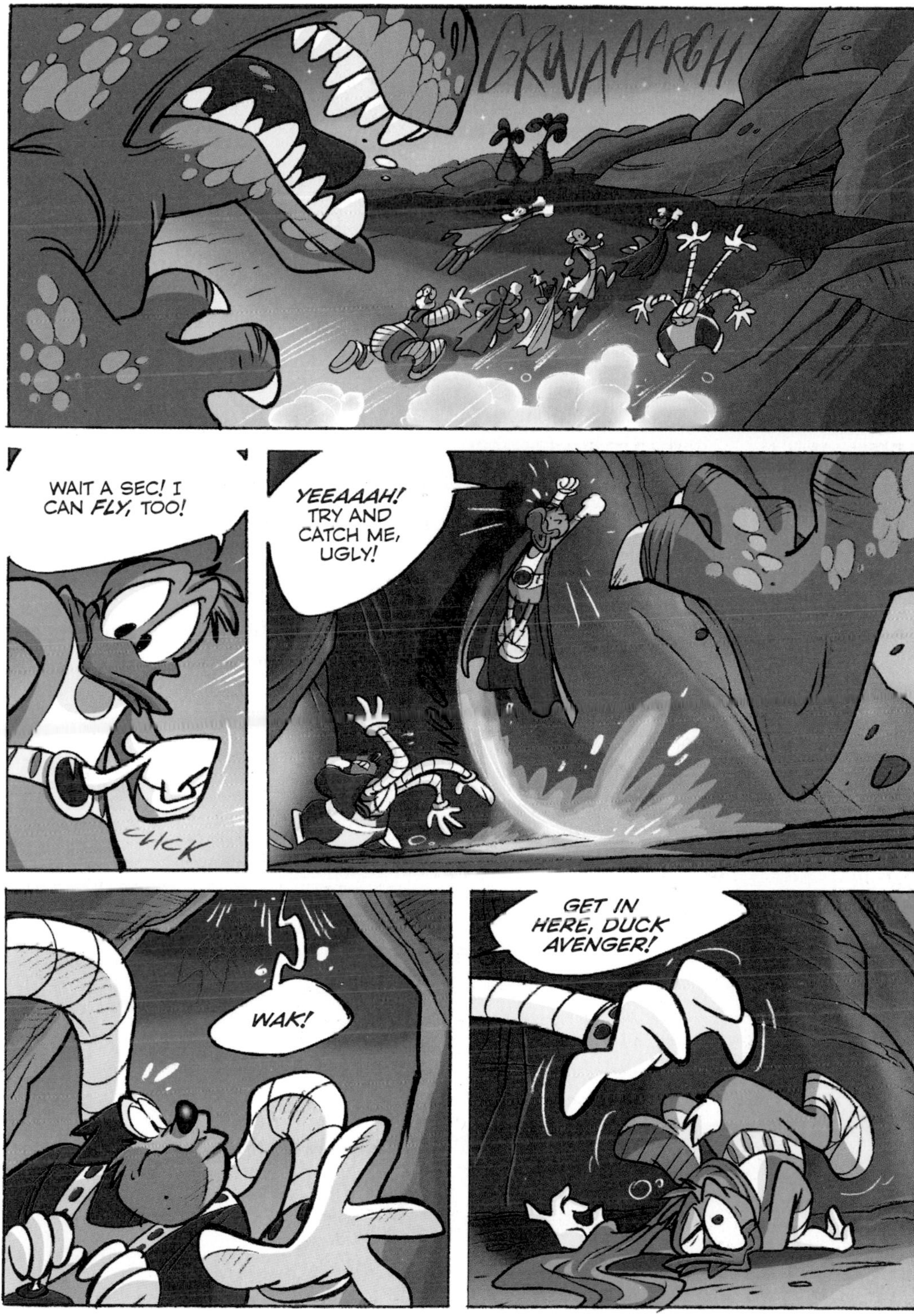
GRWAAARGH
WAIT A SEC! I CAN FLY, TOO!
CLICK
YEEAAAH! TRY AND CATCH ME, UGLY!
WAK!
GET IN HERE, DUCK AVENGER!

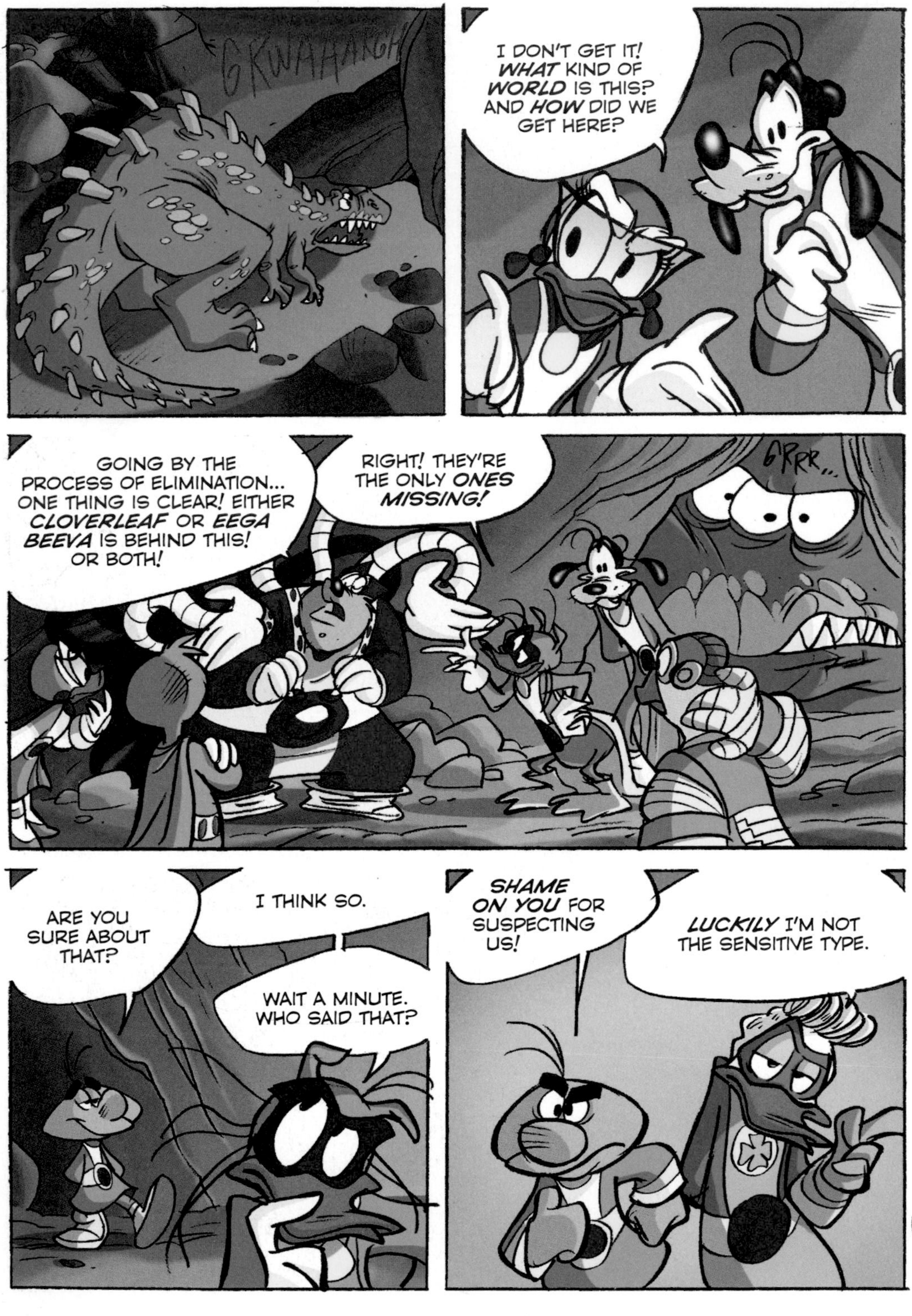
GKWAAHAAGH
I DON'T GET IT! WHAT KIND OF WORLD IS THIS? AND HOW DID WE GET HERE?
GOING BY THE PROCESS OF ELIMINATION... ONE THING IS CLEAR! EITHER CLOVERLEAF OR EEGA BEEVA IS BEHIND THIS! OR BOTH!
RIGHT! THEY'RE THE ONLY ONES MISSING!
GRRR...
ARE YOU SURE ABOUT THAT?
I THINK SO.
WAIT A MINUTE. WHO SAID THAT?
SHAME ON YOU FOR SUSPECTING US!
LUCKILY I'M NOT THE SENSITIVE TYPE.

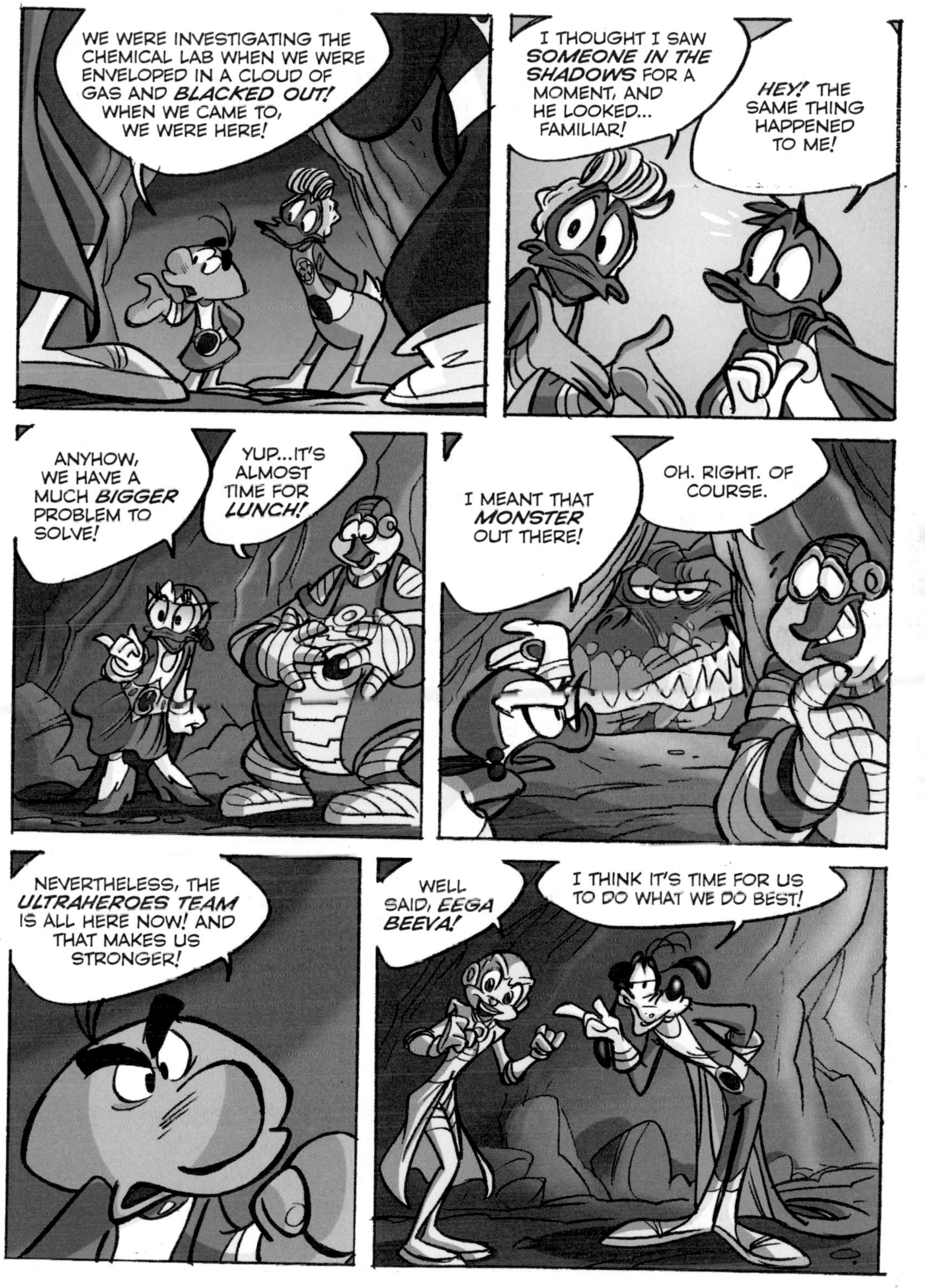
WE WERE INVESTIGATING THE CHEMICAL LAB WHEN WE WERE ENVELOPED IN A CLOUD OF GAS AND BLACKED OUT! WHEN WE CAME TO, WE WERE HERE!
I THOUGHT I SAW SOMEONE IN THE SHADOWS FOR A MOMENT, AND HE LOOKED... FAMILIAR!
HEY! THE SAME THING HAPPENED TO ME!
ANYHOW, WE HAVE A MUCH BIGGER PROBLEM TO SOLVE!
YUP...IT'S ALMOST TIME FOR LUNCH!
I MEANT THAT MONSTER OUT THERE!
OH. RIGHT. OF COURSE.
NEVERTHELESS, THE ULTRAHEROES TEAM IS ALL HERE NOW! AND THAT MAKES US STRONGER!
WELL SAID, EEGA BEEVA!
I THINK IT'S TIME FOR US TO DO WHAT WE DO BEST!

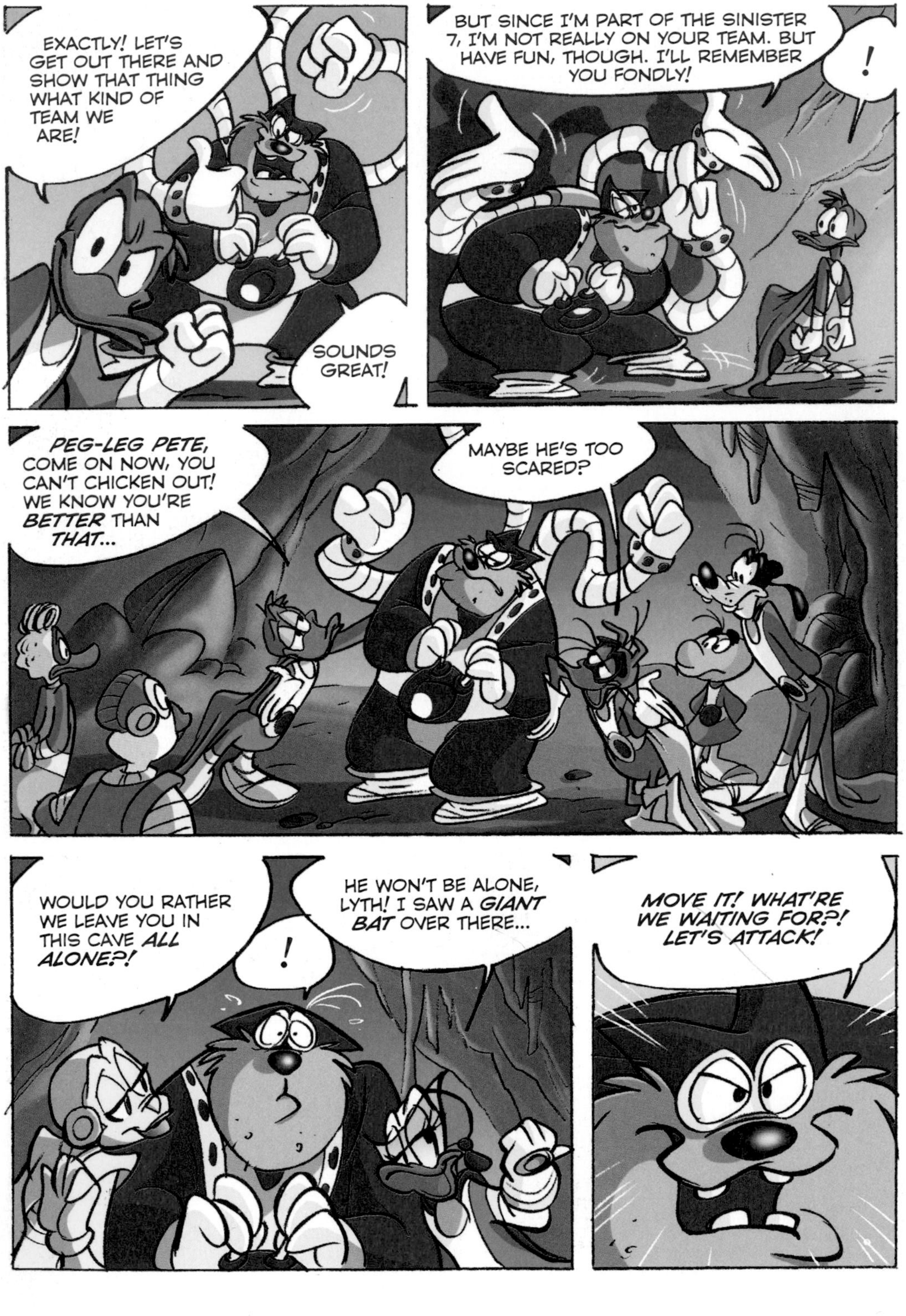
EXACTLY! LET'S GET OUT THERE AND SHOW THAT THING WHAT KIND OF TEAM WE ARE!
SOUNDS GREAT!
BUT SINCE I'M PART OF THE SINISTER 7, I'M NOT REALLY ON YOUR TEAM. BUT HAVE FUN, THOUGH. I'LL REMEMBER YOU FONDLY!
!
PEG-LEG PETE, COME ON NOW, YOU CAN'T CHICKEN OUT! WE KNOW YOU'RE BETTER THAN THAT...
MAYBE HE'S TOO SCARED?
WOULD YOU RATHER WE LEAVE YOU IN THIS CAVE ALL ALONE?!
HE WON'T BE ALONE, LYTH! I SAW A GIANT BAT OVER THERE...
!
MOVE IT! WHAT'RE WE WAITING FOR?! LET'S ATTACK!

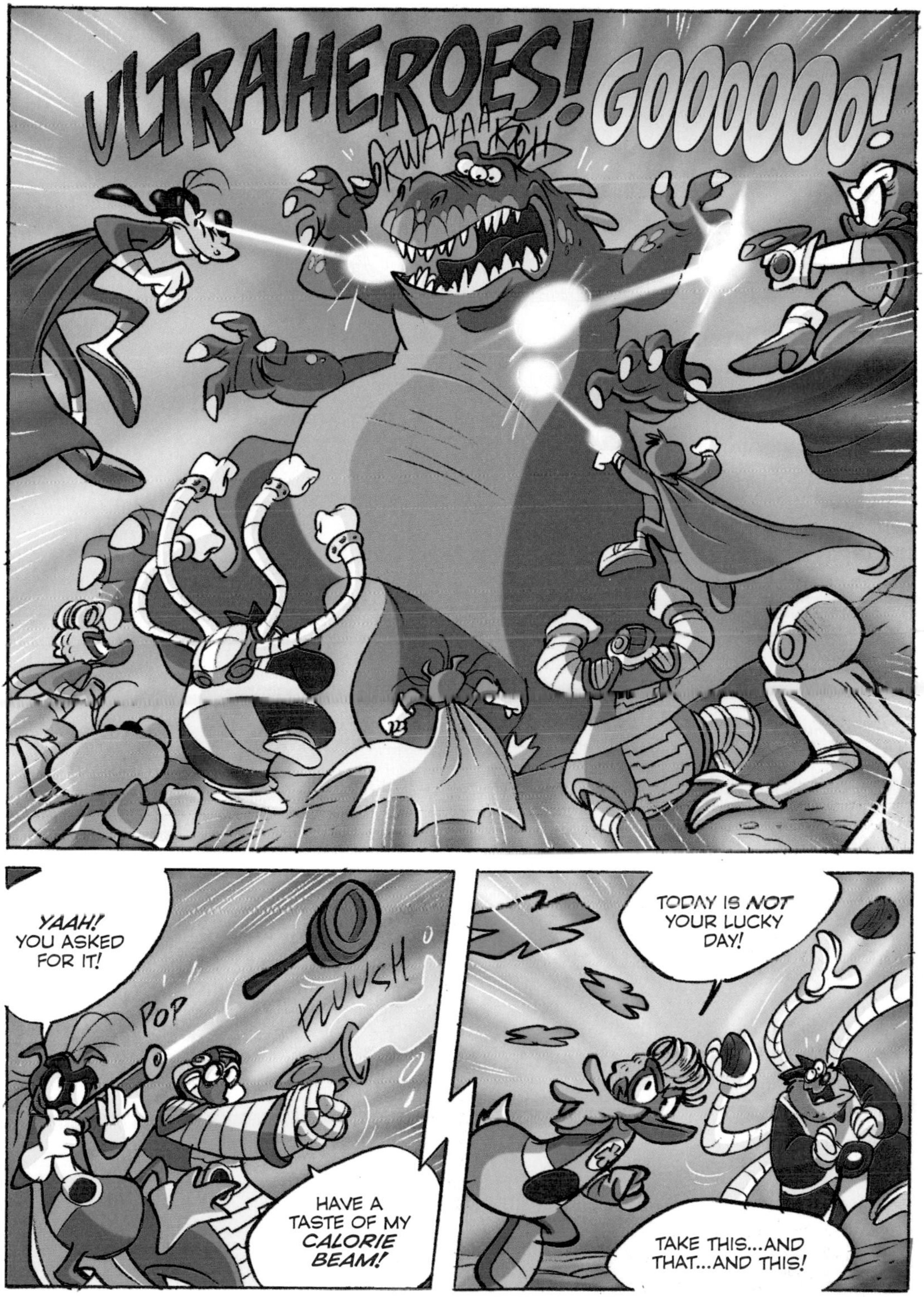
ULTRAHEROES! GOOOOOO!
GRWAAAARGH
YAAH! YOU ASKED FOR IT!
POP
FLUUSH
HAVE A TASTE OF MY CALORIE BEAM!
TODAY IS NOT YOUR LUCKY DAY!
TAKE THIS...AND THAT...AND THIS!

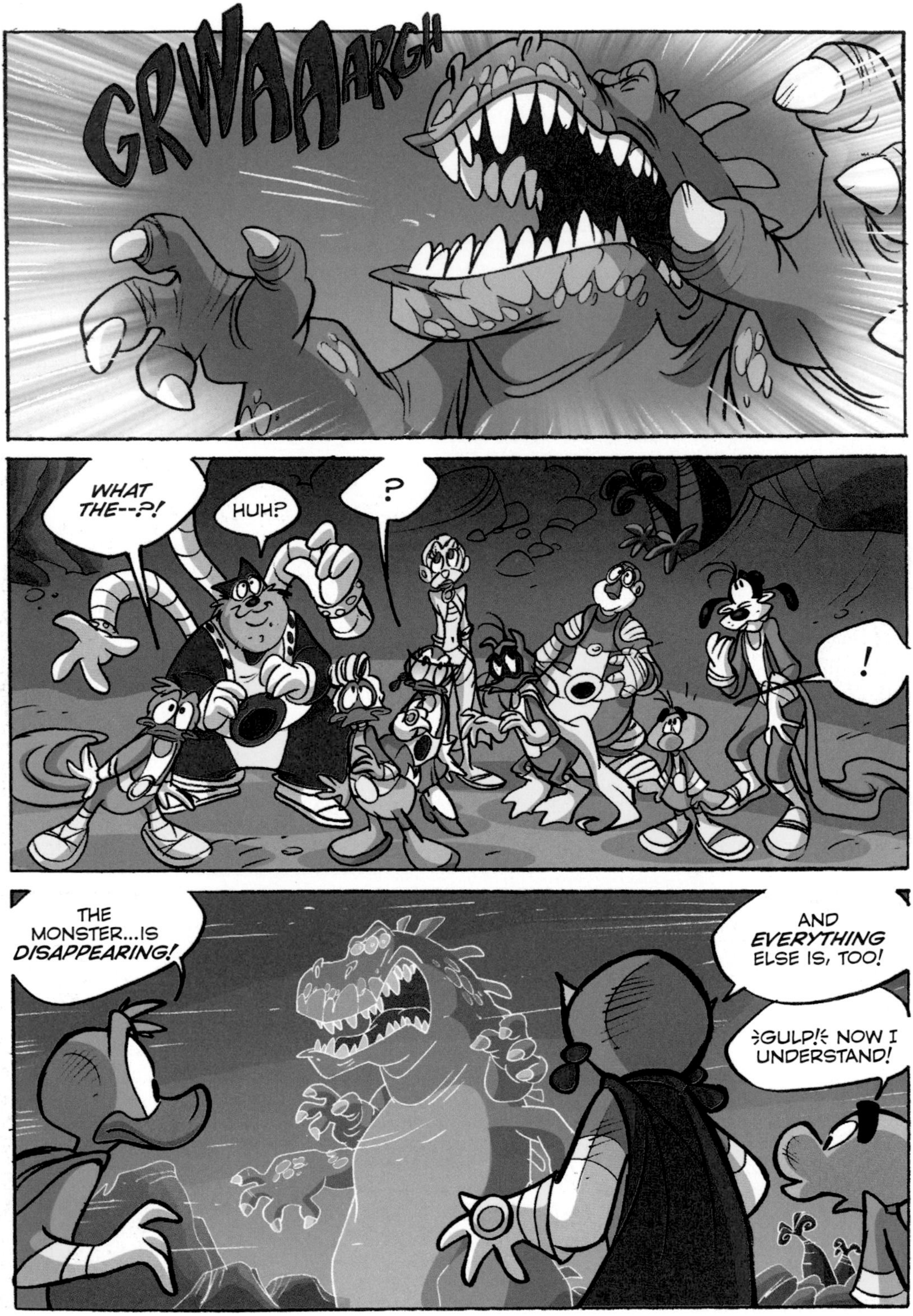
GRWAAARGH
WHAT THE--?!
HUH?
?
!
THE MONSTER...IS DISAPPEARING!
AND EVERYTHING ELSE IS, TOO!
GULP! NOW I UNDERSTAND!

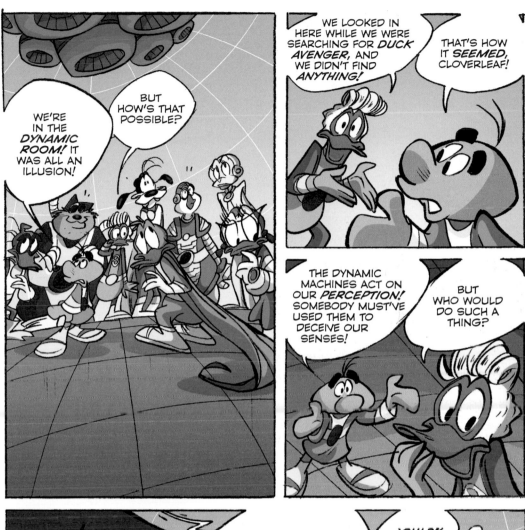

WE'RE IN THE *DYNAMIC ROOM!* IT WAS ALL AN ILLUSION!

BUT HOW'S THAT POSSIBLE?

WE LOOKED IN HERE WHILE WE WERE SEARCHING FOR *DUCK AVENGER,* AND WE DIDN'T FIND *ANYTHING!*

THAT'S HOW IT *SEEMED,* CLOVERLEAF!

THE DYNAMIC MACHINES ACT ON OUR *PERCEPTION!* SOMEBODY MUST'VE USED THEM TO DECEIVE OUR SENSES!

BUT WHO WOULD DO SUCH A THING?

I THINK I CAN ANSWER THAT!

HUH?!

⇒GULP!⇐

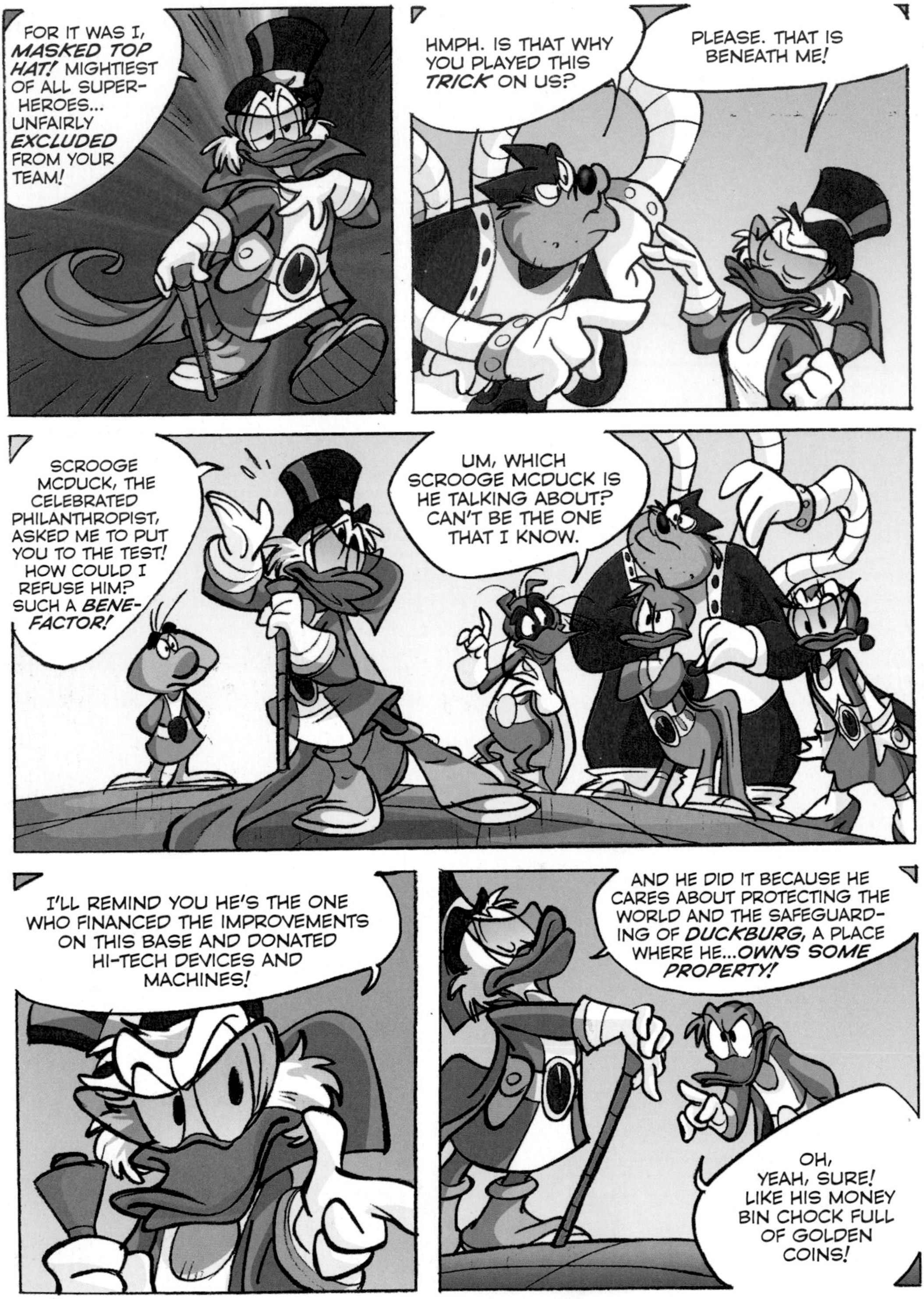
FOR IT WAS I, MASKED TOP HAT! MIGHTIEST OF ALL SUPER-HEROES... UNFAIRLY EXCLUDED FROM YOUR TEAM!
HMPH. IS THAT WHY YOU PLAYED THIS TRICK ON US?
PLEASE. THAT IS BENEATH ME!
SCROOGE MCDUCK, THE CELEBRATED PHILANTHROPIST, ASKED ME TO PUT YOU TO THE TEST! HOW COULD I REFUSE HIM? SUCH A BENE-FACTOR!
UM, WHICH SCROOGE MCDUCK IS HE TALKING ABOUT? CAN'T BE THE ONE THAT I KNOW.
I'LL REMIND YOU HE'S THE ONE WHO FINANCED THE IMPROVEMENTS ON THIS BASE AND DONATED HI-TECH DEVICES AND MACHINES!
AND HE DID IT BECAUSE HE CARES ABOUT PROTECTING THE WORLD AND THE SAFEGUARDING OF DUCKBURG, A PLACE WHERE HE...OWNS SOME PROPERTY!
OH, YEAH, SURE! LIKE HIS MONEY BIN CHOCK FULL OF GOLDEN COINS!

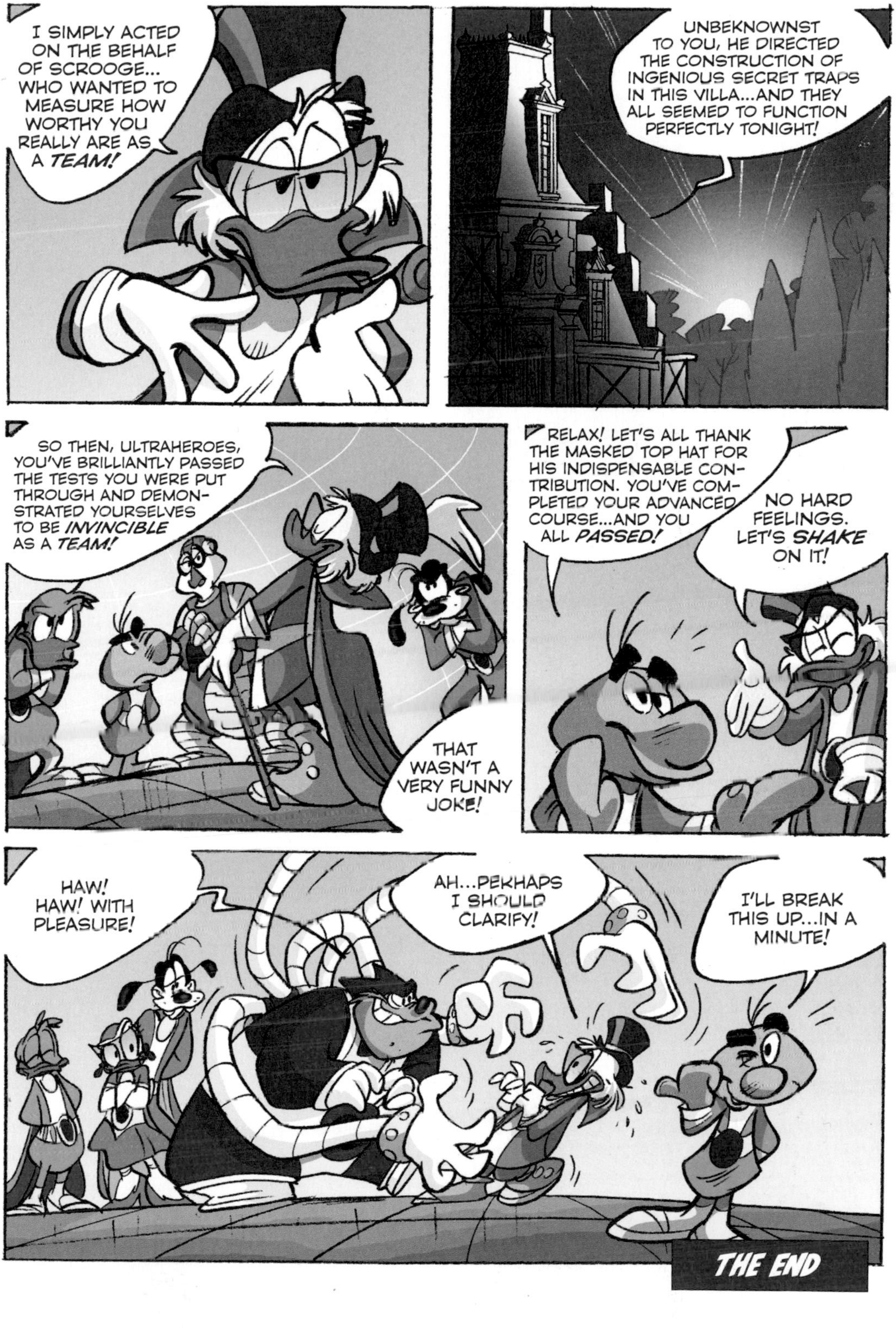
I SIMPLY ACTED ON THE BEHALF OF SCROOGE... WHO WANTED TO MEASURE HOW WORTHY YOU REALLY ARE AS A *TEAM!*
UNBEKNOWNST TO YOU, HE DIRECTED THE CONSTRUCTION OF INGENIOUS SECRET TRAPS IN THIS VILLA...AND THEY ALL SEEMED TO FUNCTION PERFECTLY TONIGHT!
SO THEN, ULTRAHEROES, YOU'VE BRILLIANTLY PASSED THE TESTS YOU WERE PUT THROUGH AND DEMONSTRATED YOURSELVES TO BE *INVINCIBLE* AS A *TEAM!*
THAT WASN'T A VERY FUNNY JOKE!
RELAX! LET'S ALL THANK THE MASKED TOP HAT FOR HIS INDISPENSABLE CONTRIBUTION. YOU'VE COMPLETED YOUR ADVANCED COURSE...AND YOU ALL *PASSED!*
NO HARD FEELINGS. LET'S *SHAKE* ON IT!
HAW! HAW! WITH PLEASURE!
AH...PERHAPS I SHOULD CLARIFY!
I'LL BREAK THIS UP...IN A MINUTE!
THE END

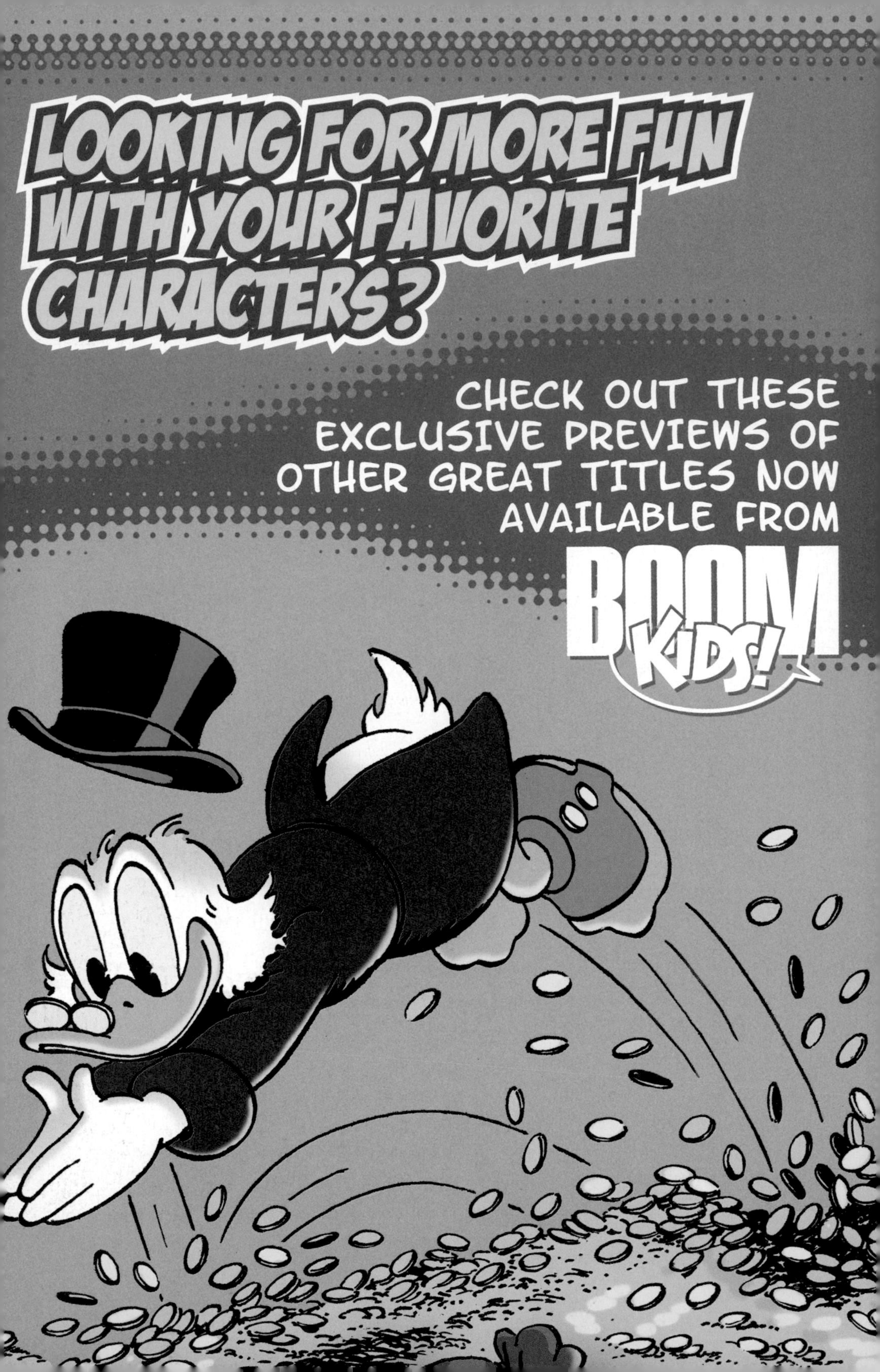
LOOKING FOR MORE FUN WITH YOUR FAVORITE CHARACTERS?
CHECK OUT THESE EXCLUSIVE PREVIEWS OF OTHER GREAT TITLES NOW AVAILABLE FROM
BOOM KIDS!

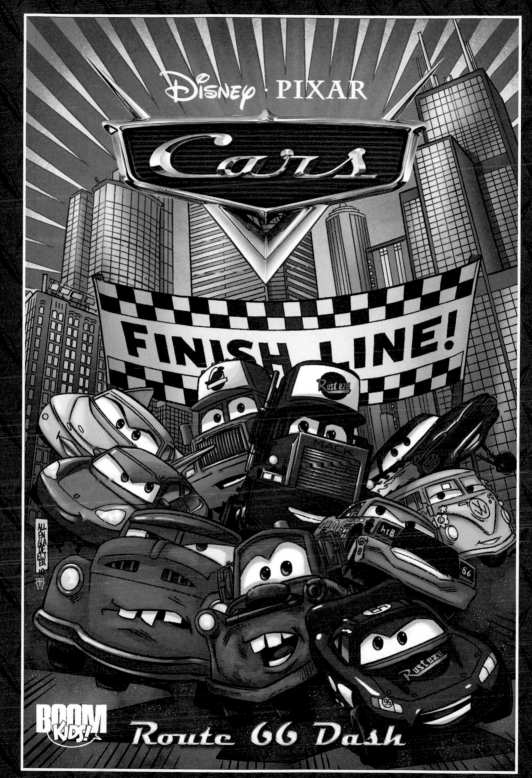

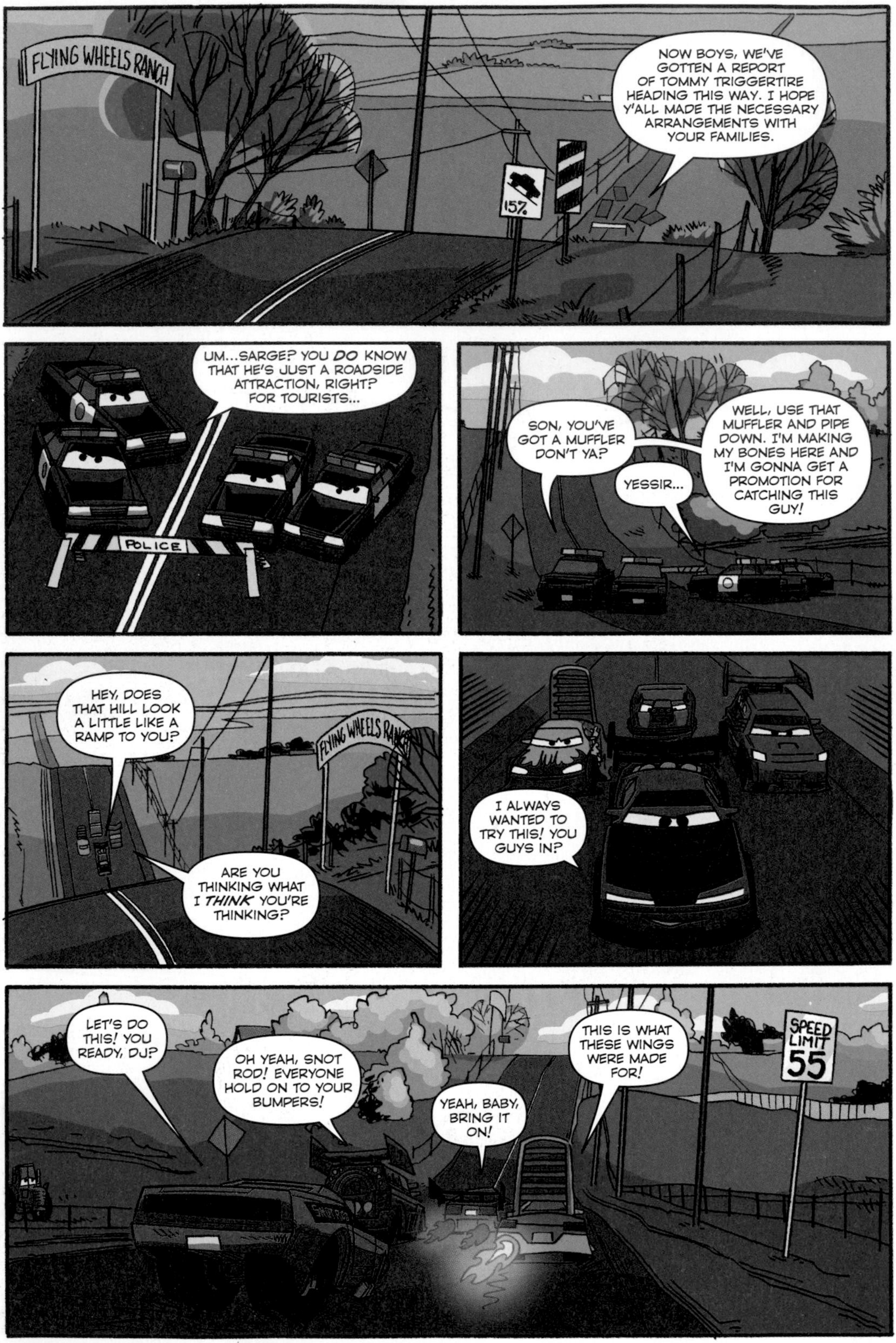
FLYING WHEELS RANCH
15%
NOW BOYS, WE'VE GOTTEN A REPORT OF TOMMY TRIGGERTIRE HEADING THIS WAY. I HOPE Y'ALL MADE THE NECESSARY ARRANGEMENTS WITH YOUR FAMILIES.
UM...SARGE? YOU DO KNOW THAT HE'S JUST A ROADSIDE ATTRACTION, RIGHT? FOR TOURISTS...
POLICE
SON, YOU'VE GOT A MUFFLER DON'T YA?
YESSIR...
WELL, USE THAT MUFFLER AND PIPE DOWN. I'M MAKING MY BONES HERE AND I'M GONNA GET A PROMOTION FOR CATCHING THIS GUY!
HEY, DOES THAT HILL LOOK A LITTLE LIKE A RAMP TO YOU?
FLYING WHEELS RANCH
ARE YOU THINKING WHAT I THINK YOU'RE THINKING?
I ALWAYS WANTED TO TRY THIS! YOU GUYS IN?
LET'S DO THIS! YOU READY, DJ?
OH YEAH, SNOT ROD! EVERYONE HOLD ON TO YOUR BUMPERS!
YEAH, BABY, BRING IT ON!
THIS IS WHAT THESE WINGS WERE MADE FOR!
SPEED LIMIT 55

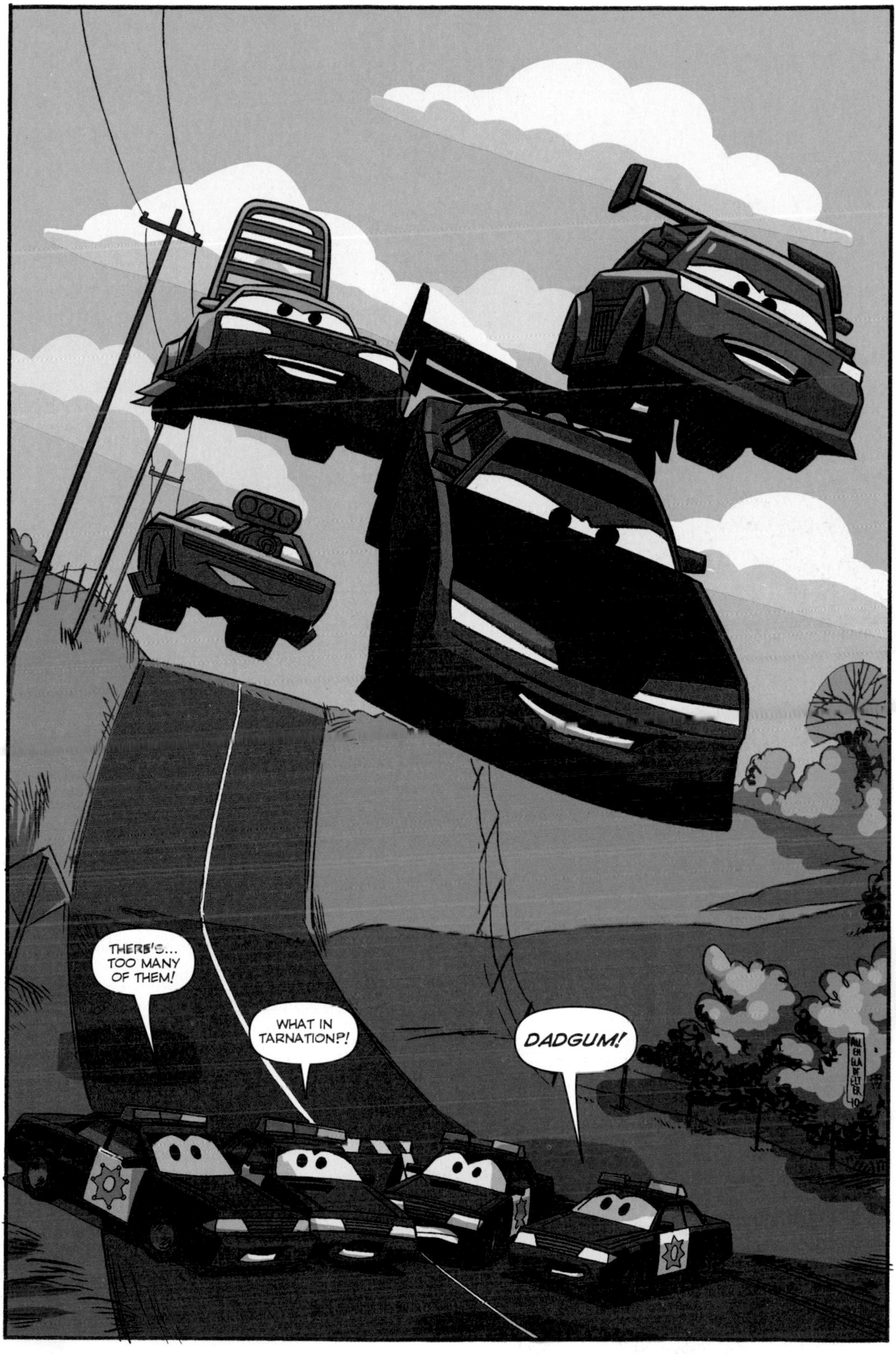
THERE'S... TOO MANY OF THEM!
WHAT IN TARNATION?!
DADGUM!

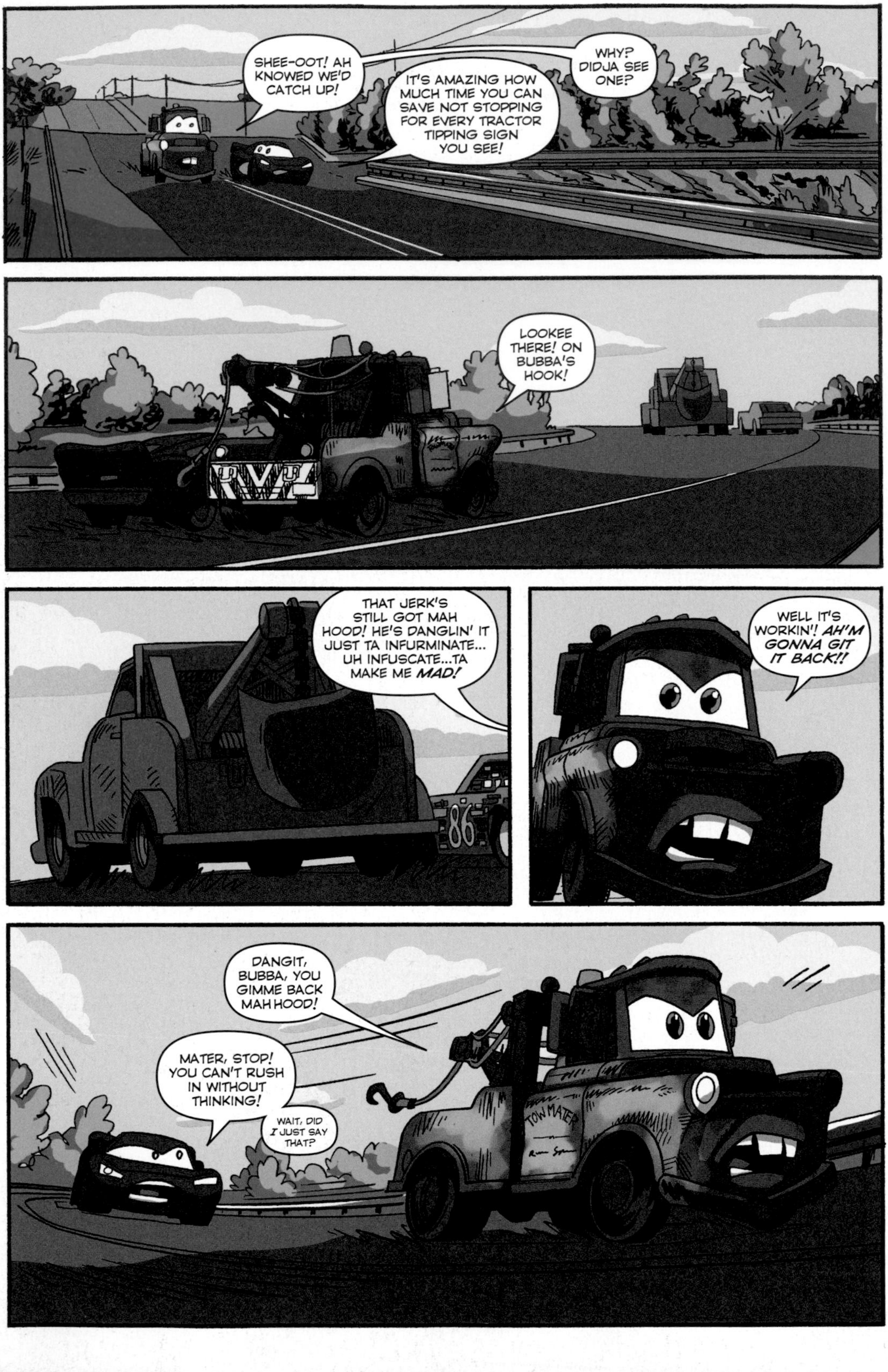
SHEE-OOT! AH KNOWED WE'D CATCH UP!
IT'S AMAZING HOW MUCH TIME YOU CAN SAVE NOT STOPPING FOR EVERY TRACTOR TIPPING SIGN YOU SEE!
WHY? DIDJA SEE ONE?
LOOKEE THERE! ON BUBBA'S HOOK!
THAT JERK'S STILL GOT MAH HOOD! HE'S DANGLIN' IT JUST TA INFURMINATE... UH INFUSCATE...TA MAKE ME MAD!
86
WELL IT'S WORKIN'! AH'M GONNA GIT IT BACK!!
DANGIT, BUBBA, YOU GIMME BACK MAH HOOD!
MATER, STOP! YOU CAN'T RUSH IN WITHOUT THINKING!
WAIT, DID I JUST SAY THAT?
TOW MATER

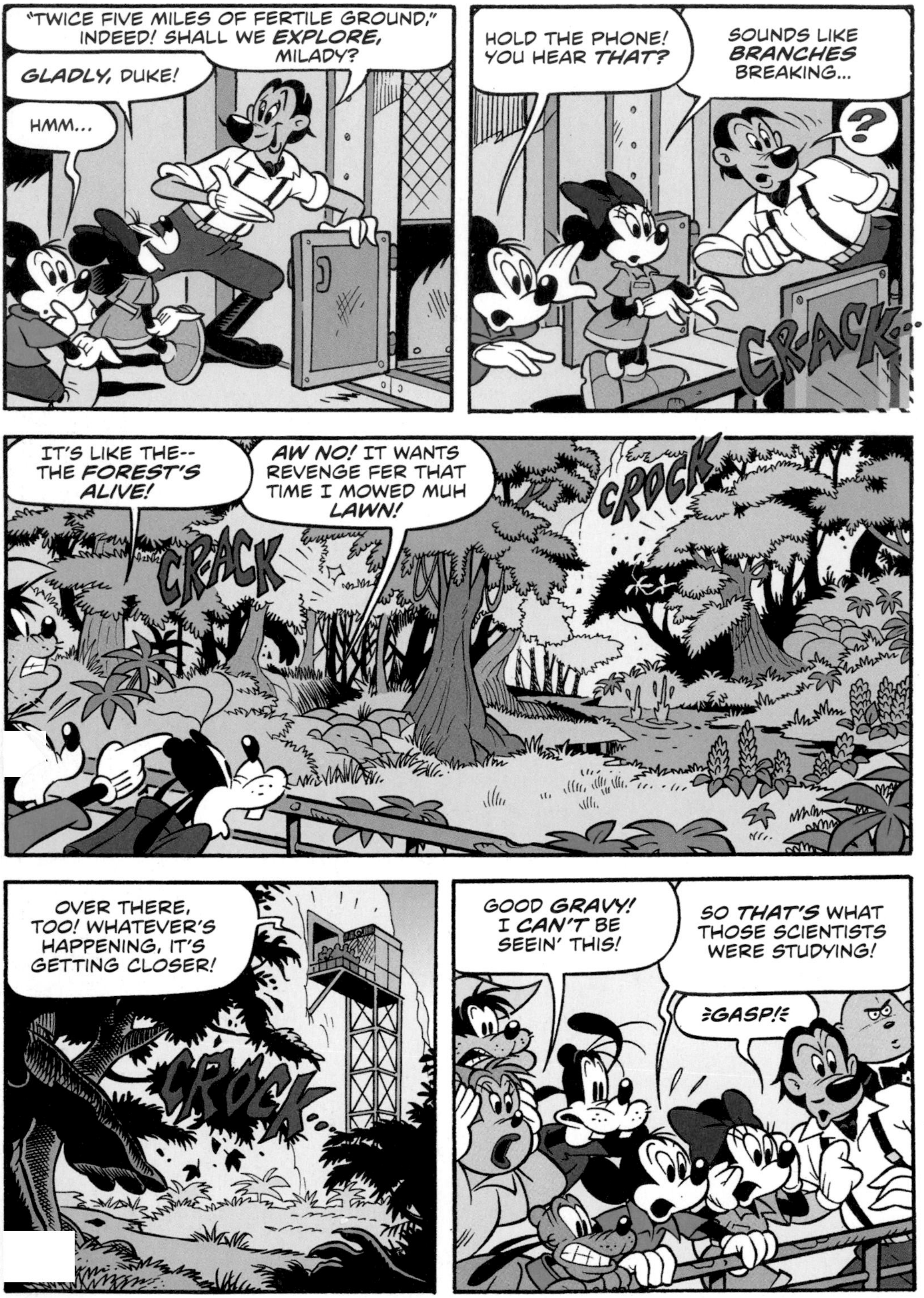
"TWICE FIVE MILES OF FERTILE GROUND," INDEED! SHALL WE EXPLORE, MILADY?
GLADLY, DUKE!
HMM...
HOLD THE PHONE! YOU HEAR THAT?
SOUNDS LIKE BRANCHES BREAKING...
?
CR-ACK...
IT'S LIKE THE-- THE FOREST'S ALIVE!
AW NO! IT WANTS REVENGE FER THAT TIME I MOWED MUH LAWN!
CRACK
CROCK
OVER THERE, TOO! WHATEVER'S HAPPENING, IT'S GETTING CLOSER!
CROCK...
GOOD GRAVY! I CAN'T BE SEEIN' THIS!
SO THAT'S WHAT THOSE SCIENTISTS WERE STUDYING!
GASP!

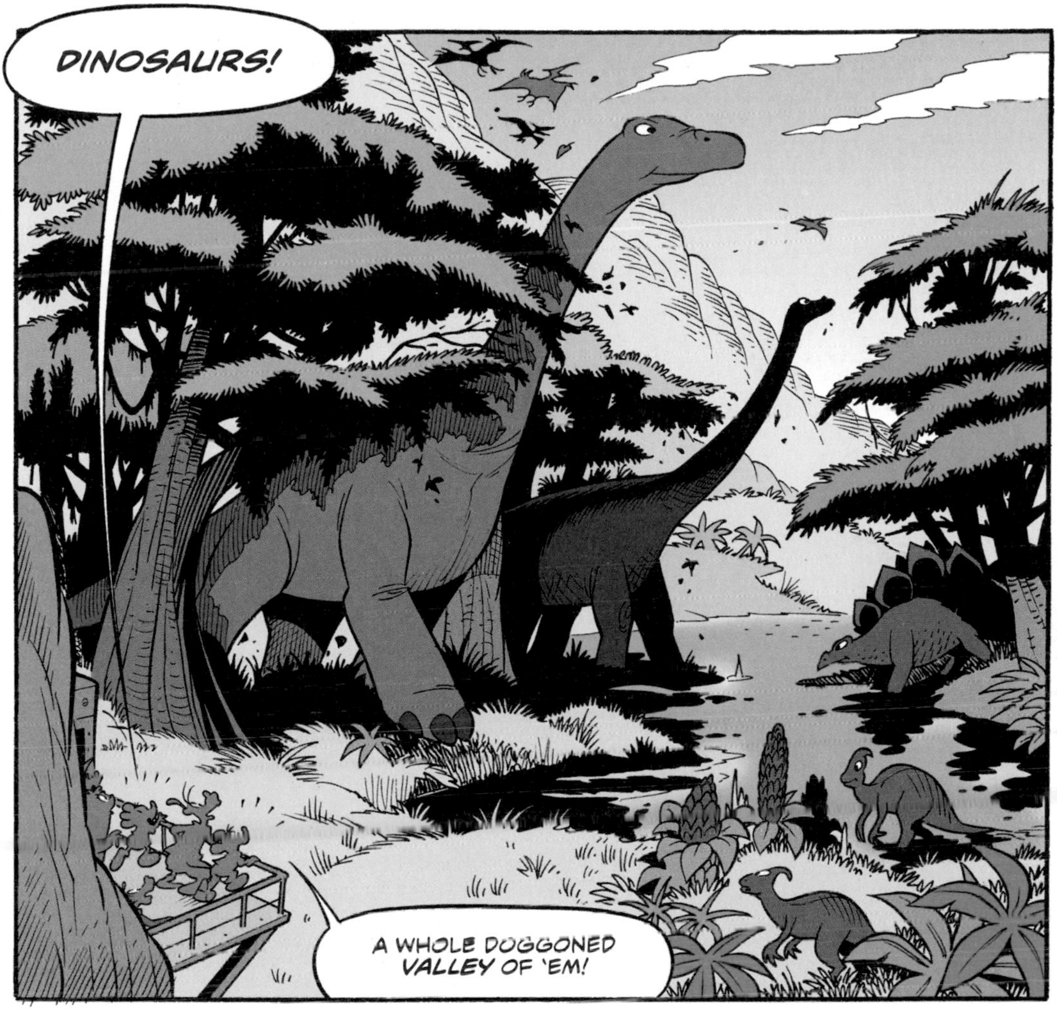
DINOSAURS!
A WHOLE DOGGONED VALLEY OF 'EM!

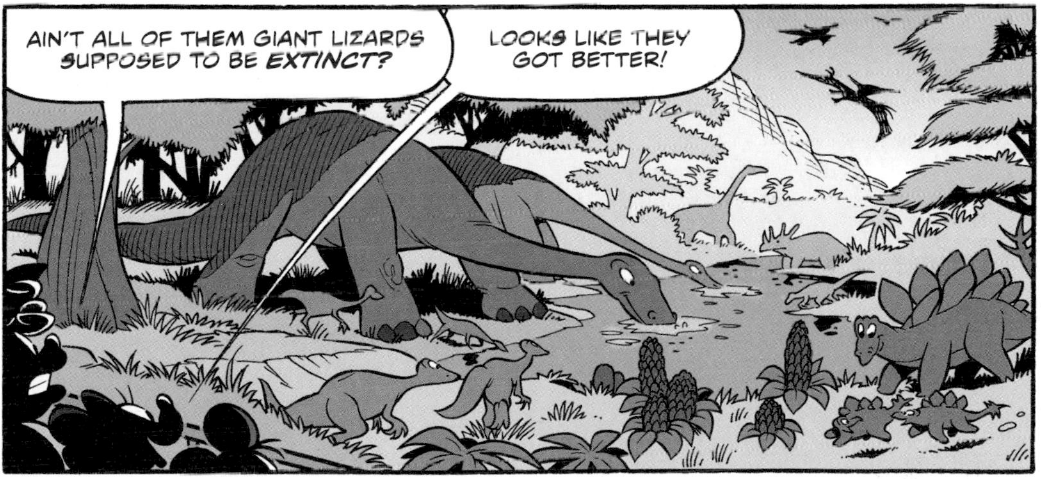
AIN'T ALL OF THEM GIANT LIZARDS SUPPOSED TO BE EXTINCT?
LOOKS LIKE THEY GOT BETTER!

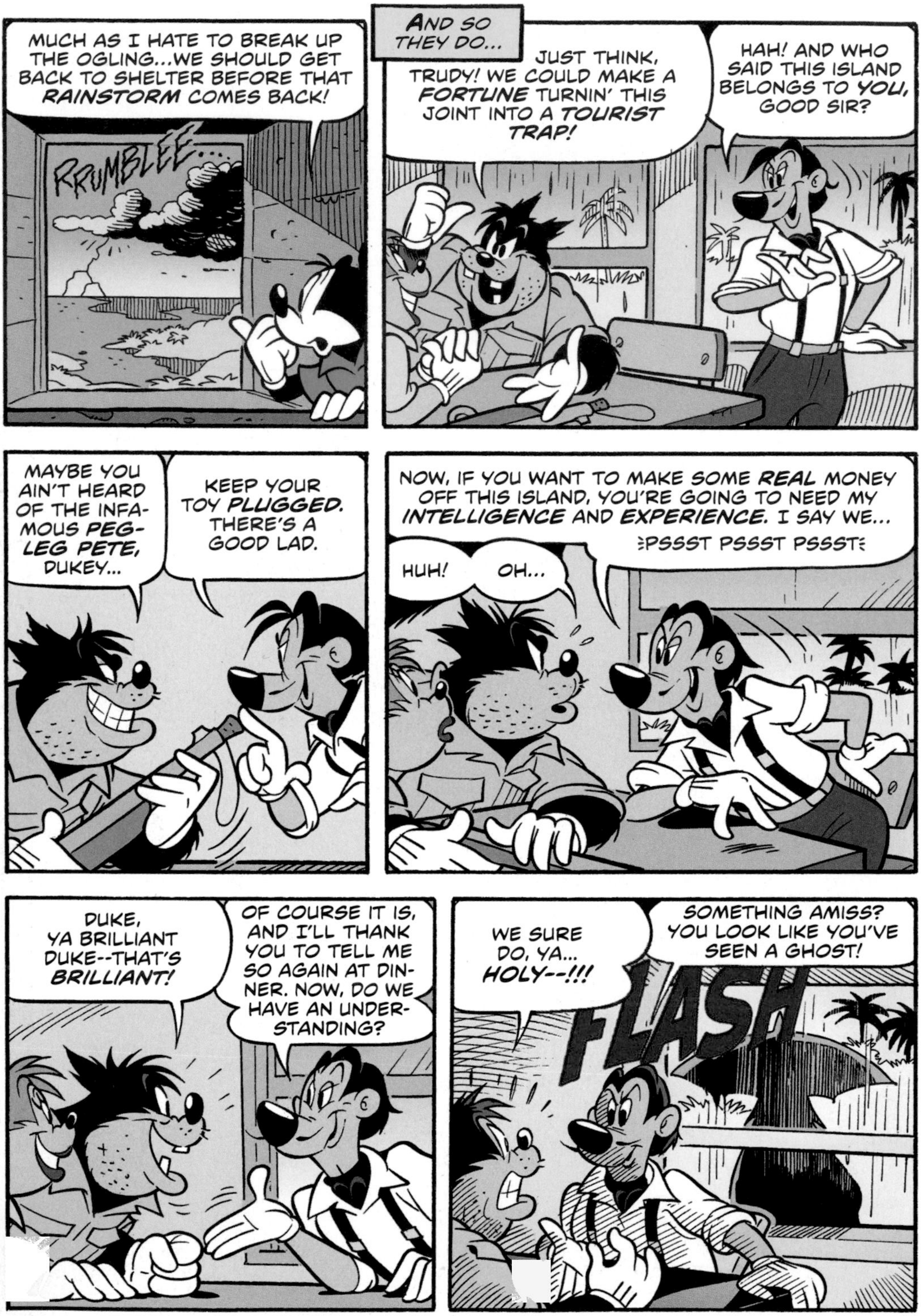
MUCH AS I HATE TO BREAK UP THE OGLING...WE SHOULD GET BACK TO SHELTER BEFORE THAT RAINSTORM COMES BACK!
RRUMBLEE...
AND SO THEY DO...
JUST THINK, TRUDY! WE COULD MAKE A FORTUNE TURNIN' THIS JOINT INTO A TOURIST TRAP!
HAH! AND WHO SAID THIS ISLAND BELONGS TO YOU, GOOD SIR?
MAYBE YOU AIN'T HEARD OF THE INFAMOUS PEG-LEG PETE, DUKEY...
KEEP YOUR TOY PLUGGED. THERE'S A GOOD LAD.
NOW, IF YOU WANT TO MAKE SOME REAL MONEY OFF THIS ISLAND, YOU'RE GOING TO NEED MY INTELLIGENCE AND EXPERIENCE. I SAY WE...
PSSST PSSST PSSST
HUH!
OH...
DUKE, YA BRILLIANT DUKE--THAT'S BRILLIANT!
OF COURSE IT IS, AND I'LL THANK YOU TO TELL ME SO AGAIN AT DINNER. NOW, DO WE HAVE AN UNDERSTANDING?
WE SURE DO, YA... HOLY--!!!
SOMETHING AMISS? YOU LOOK LIKE YOU'VE SEEN A GHOST!
FLASH

DISNEY · PIXAR
THE INCREDIBLES

SECRETS & LIES

BOOM KIDS!

When the Eiffel Tower explodes, only Mrs. Incredible can save the day! Meanwhile, Mr. Incredible, Dash and Violet track down a mysterious thief — and uncover a secret that could tear the family apart!

THE INCREDIBLES: SECRETS AND LIES
DIAMOND CODE: MAY100883
SC $9.99 ISBN 9781608865833

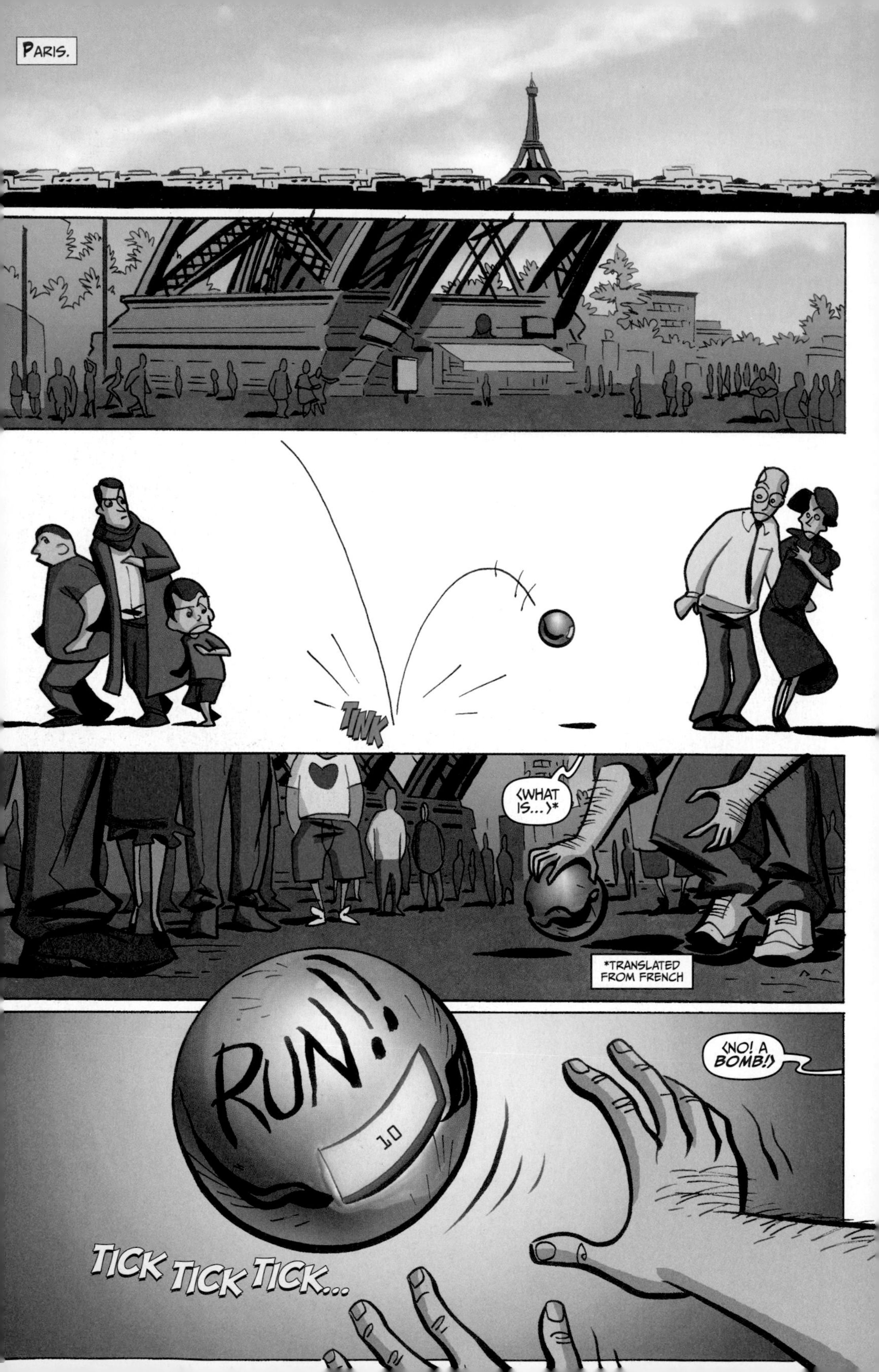

PARIS.
TINK
‹WHAT IS...›*
*TRANSLATED FROM FRENCH
RUN!
10
‹NO! A BOMB!›
TICK TICK TICK...

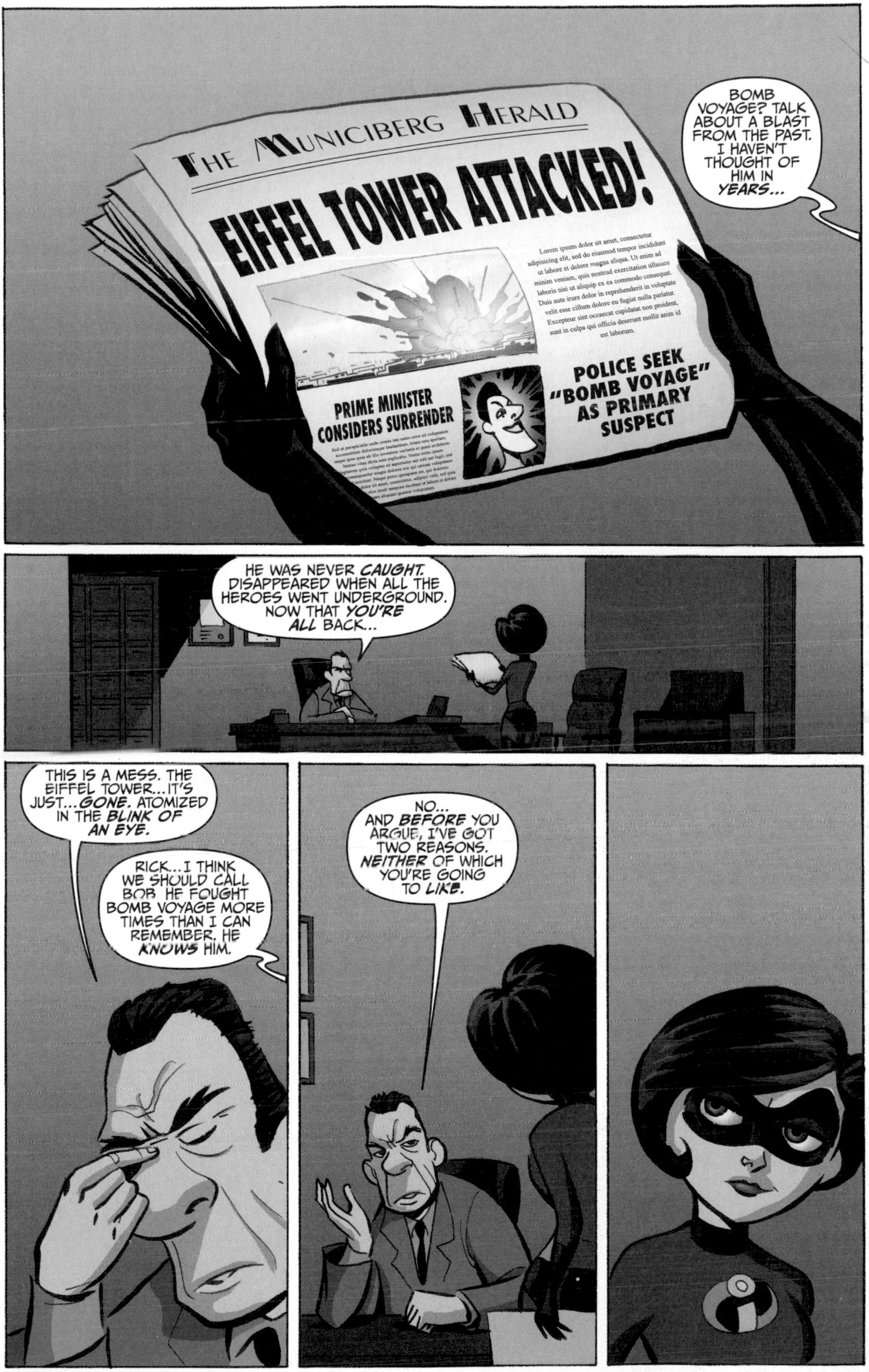
THE MUNICIBERG HERALD
EIFFEL TOWER ATTACKED!
Lorem ipsum dolor sit amet, consectetur adipisicing elit, sed do eiusmod tempor incididunt ut labore et dolore magna aliqua. Ut enim ad minim veniam, quis nostrud exercitation ullamco laboris nisi ut aliquip ex ea commodo consequat. Duis aute irure dolor in reprehenderit in voluptate velit esse cillum dolore eu fugiat nulla pariatur. Excepteur sint occaecat cupidatat non proident, sunt in culpa qui officia deserunt mollit anim id est laborum.
PRIME MINISTER CONSIDERS SURRENDER
POLICE SEEK "BOMB VOYAGE" AS PRIMARY SUSPECT
BOMB VOYAGE? TALK ABOUT A BLAST FROM THE PAST. I HAVEN'T THOUGHT OF HIM IN YEARS...
HE WAS NEVER CAUGHT. DISAPPEARED WHEN ALL THE HEROES WENT UNDERGROUND. NOW THAT YOU'RE ALL BACK...
THIS IS A MESS. THE EIFFEL TOWER...IT'S JUST...GONE. ATOMIZED IN THE BLINK OF AN EYE.
RICK...I THINK WE SHOULD CALL BOB. HE FOUGHT BOMB VOYAGE MORE TIMES THAN I CAN REMEMBER. HE KNOWS HIM.
NO... AND BEFORE YOU ARGUE, I'VE GOT TWO REASONS. NEITHER OF WHICH YOU'RE GOING TO LIKE.

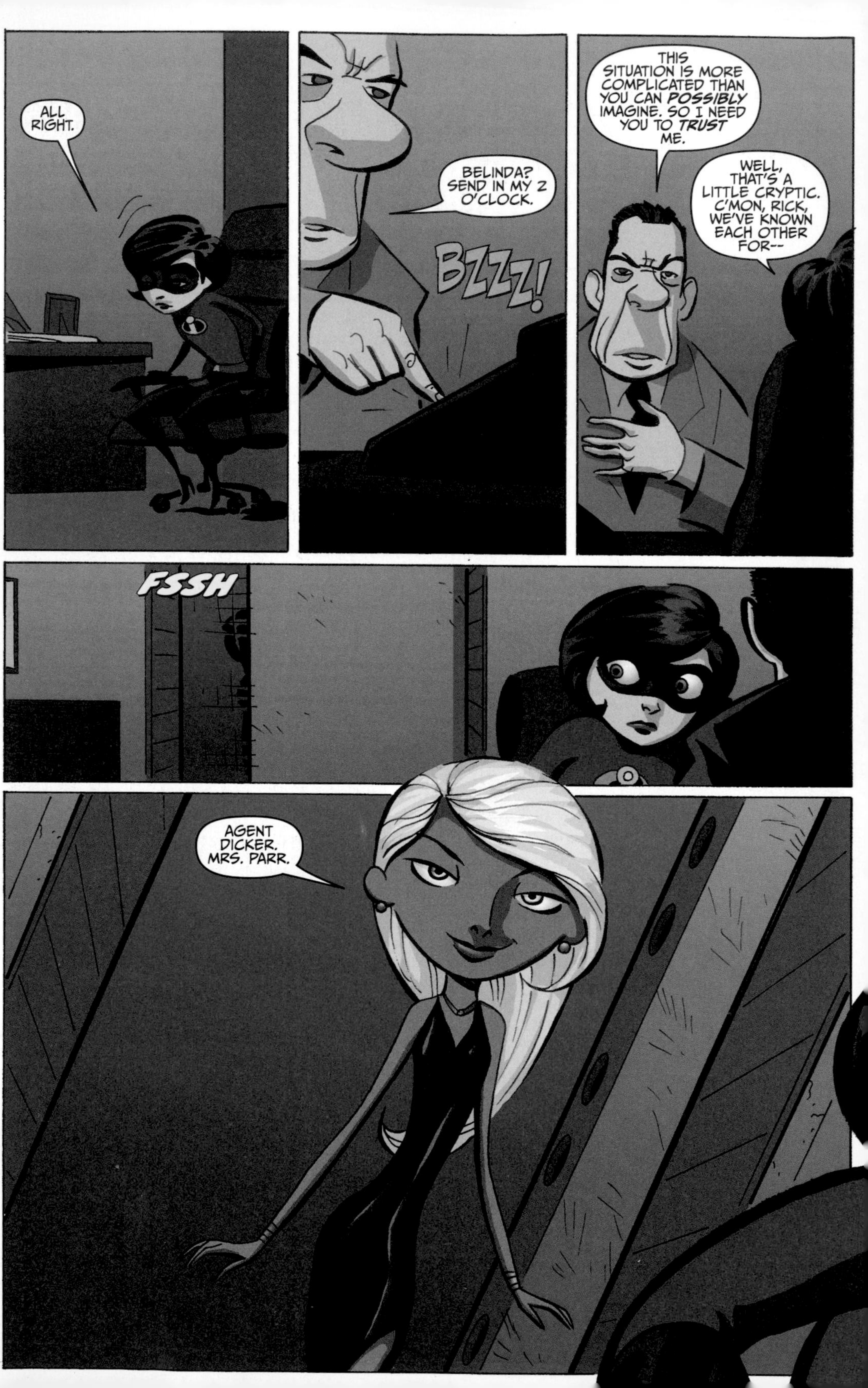
ALL RIGHT.
BELINDA? SEND IN MY 2 O'CLOCK.
BZZZ!
THIS SITUATION IS MORE COMPLICATED THAN YOU CAN POSSIBLY IMAGINE. SO I NEED YOU TO TRUST ME.
WELL, THAT'S A LITTLE CRYPTIC. C'MON, RICK, WE'VE KNOWN EACH OTHER FOR--
FSSH
AGENT DICKER. MRS. PARR.

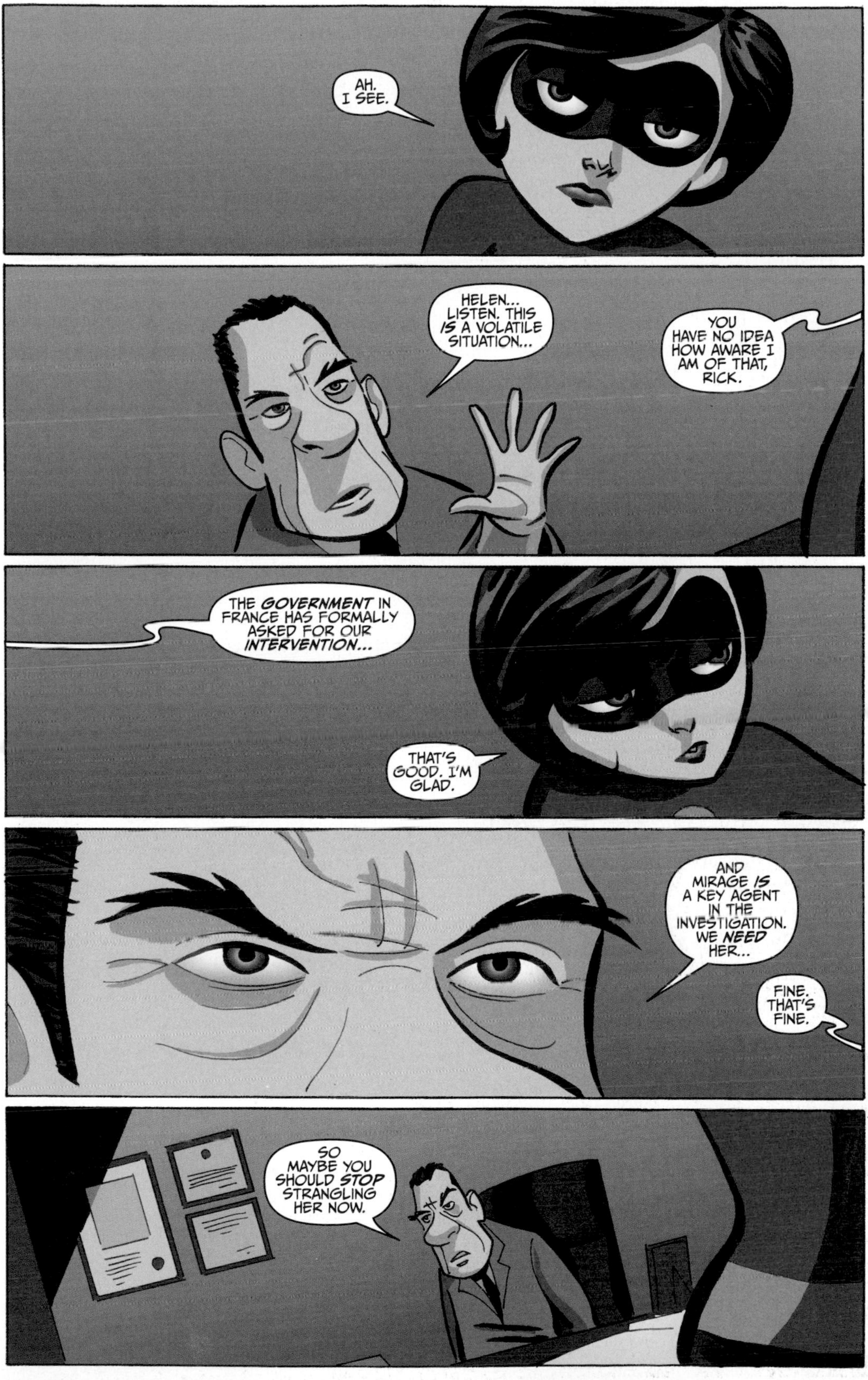
AH. I SEE.
HELEN... LISTEN. THIS *IS* A VOLATILE SITUATION...
YOU HAVE NO IDEA HOW AWARE I AM OF THAT, RICK.
THE ***GOVERNMENT*** IN FRANCE HAS FORMALLY ASKED FOR OUR ***INTERVENTION...***
THAT'S GOOD. I'M GLAD.
AND MIRAGE *IS* A KEY AGENT IN THE INVESTIGATION. WE ***NEED*** HER...
FINE. THAT'S FINE.
SO MAYBE YOU SHOULD ***STOP*** STRANGLING HER NOW.

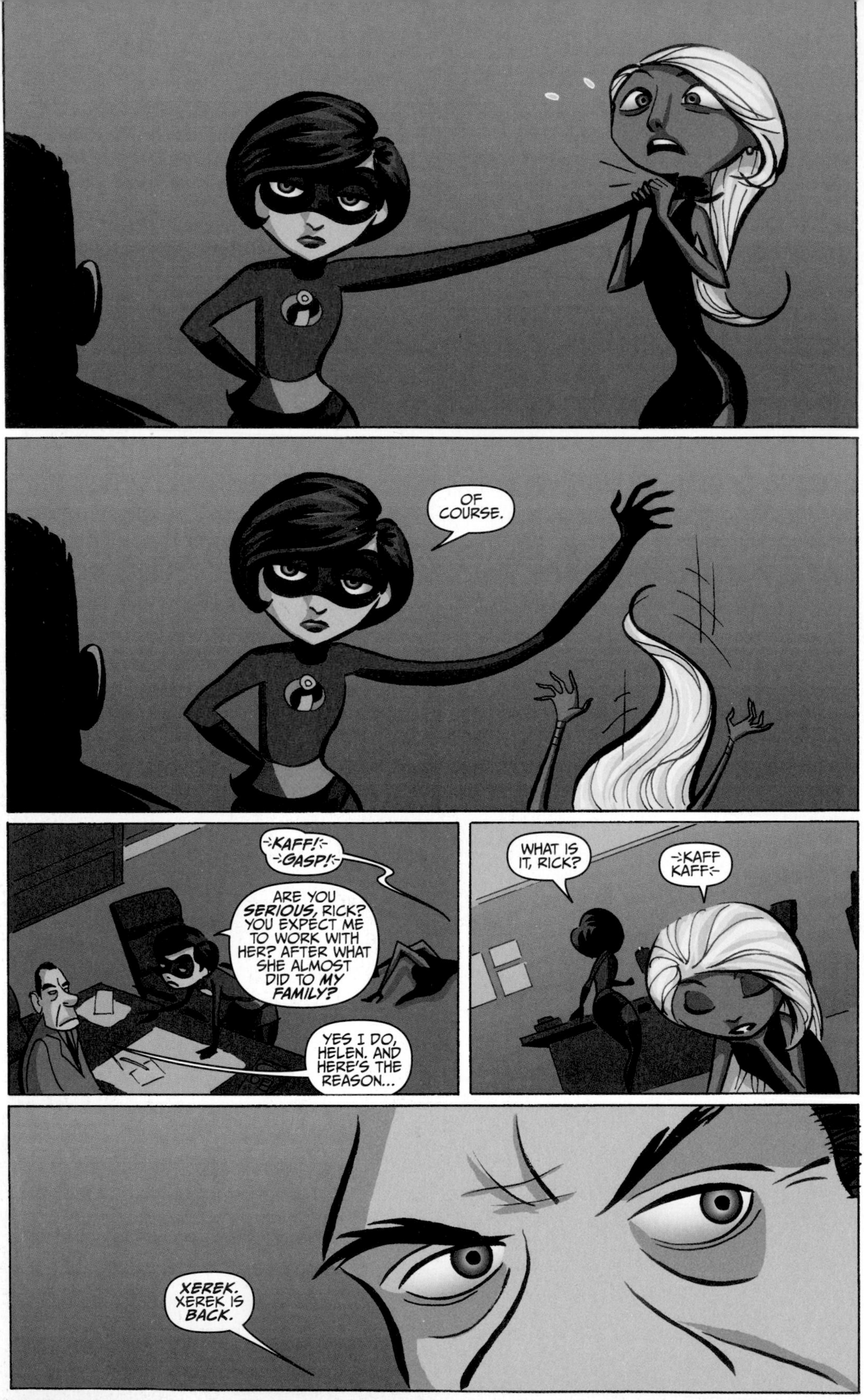
OF COURSE.
-KAFF!- -GASP!-
ARE YOU SERIOUS, RICK? YOU EXPECT ME TO WORK WITH HER? AFTER WHAT SHE ALMOST DID TO MY FAMILY?
YES I DO, HELEN. AND HERE'S THE REASON...
WHAT IS IT, RICK?
-KAFF KAFF-
XEREK. XEREK IS BACK.

THE GRAND TOURNAMENT

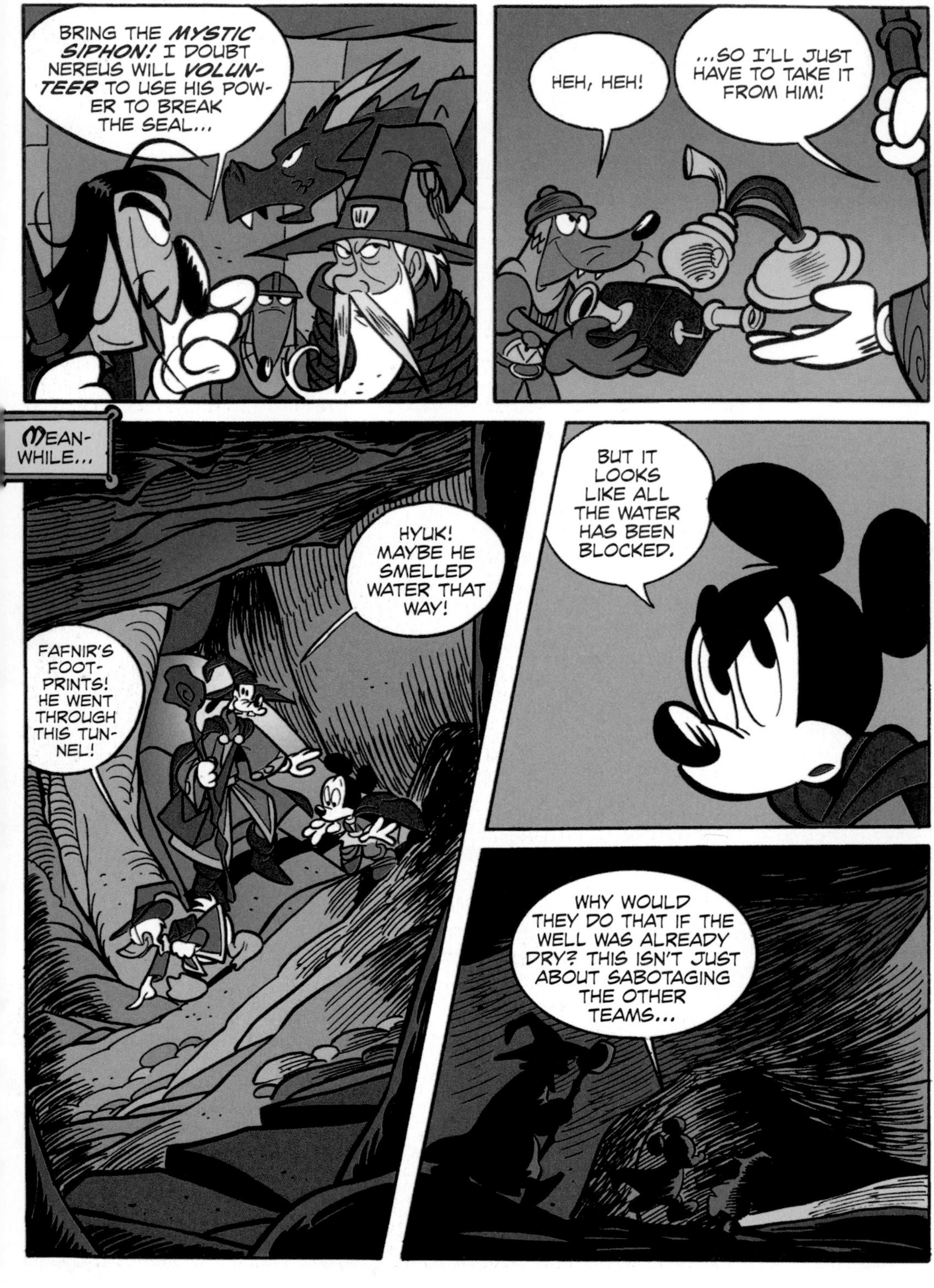
BRING THE MYSTIC SIPHON! I DOUBT NEREUS WILL VOLUNTEER TO USE HIS POWER TO BREAK THE SEAL...
HEH, HEH!
...SO I'LL JUST HAVE TO TAKE IT FROM HIM!
MEANWHILE...
FAFNIR'S FOOTPRINTS! HE WENT THROUGH THIS TUNNEL!
HYUK! MAYBE HE SMELLED WATER THAT WAY!
BUT IT LOOKS LIKE ALL THE WATER HAS BEEN BLOCKED.
WHY WOULD THEY DO THAT IF THE WELL WAS ALREADY DRY? THIS ISN'T JUST ABOUT SABOTAGING THE OTHER TEAMS...

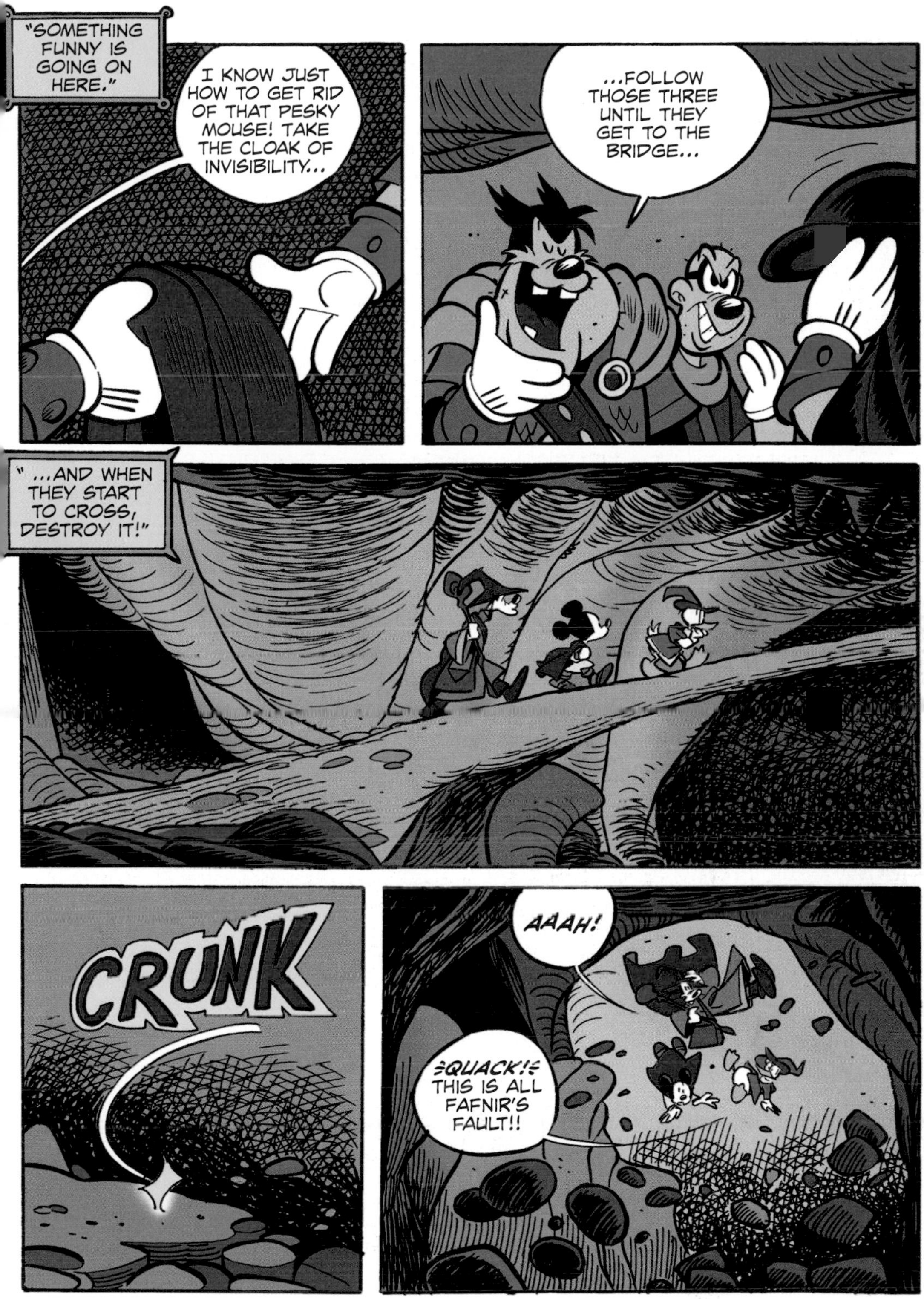
"SOMETHING FUNNY IS GOING ON HERE."
I KNOW JUST HOW TO GET RID OF THAT PESKY MOUSE! TAKE THE CLOAK OF INVISIBILITY...
...FOLLOW THOSE THREE UNTIL THEY GET TO THE BRIDGE...
"...AND WHEN THEY START TO CROSS, DESTROY IT!"
CRUNK
AAAH!
QUACK!
THIS IS ALL FAFNIR'S FAULT!!

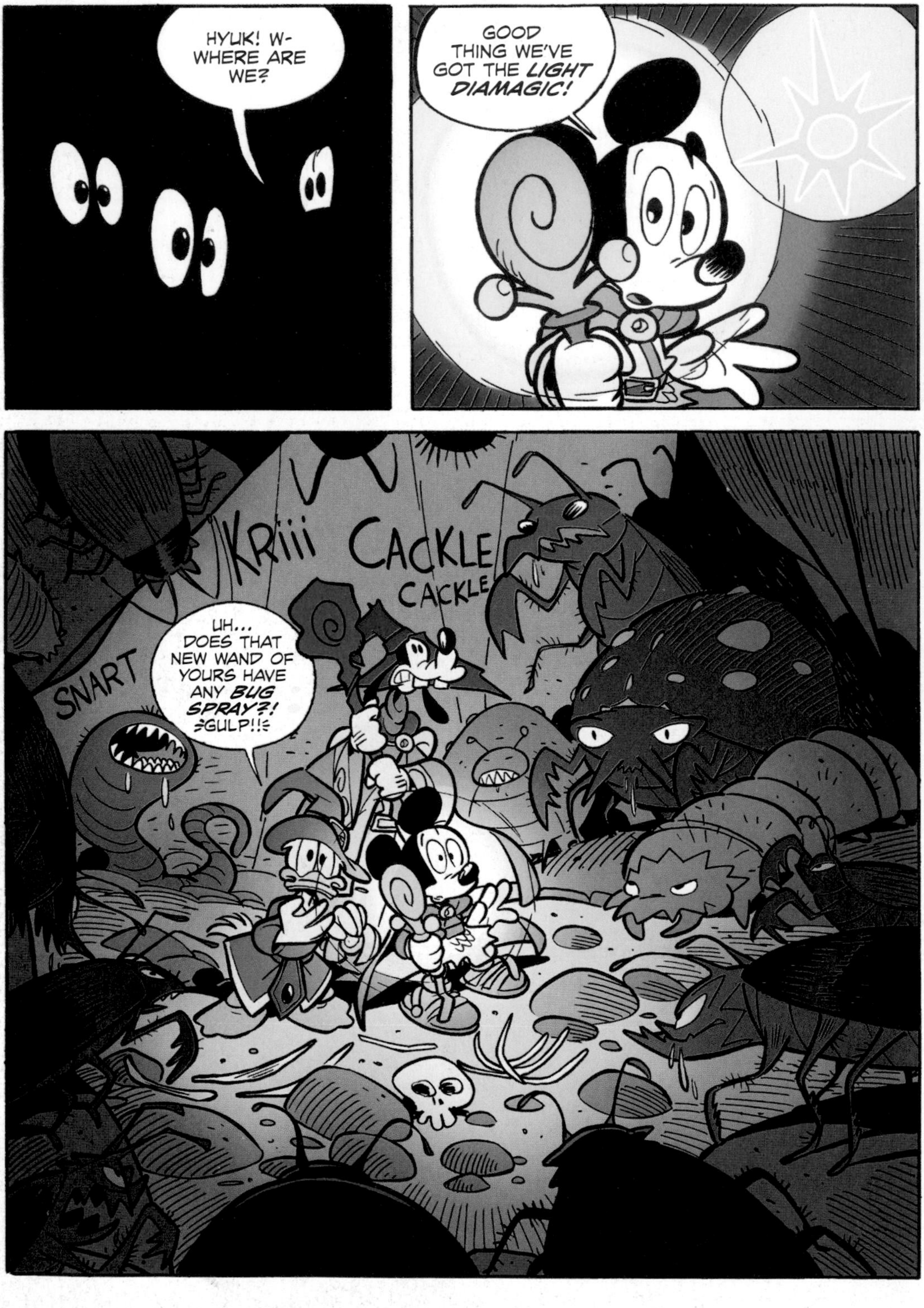
HYUK! W-WHERE ARE WE?
GOOD THING WE'VE GOT THE LIGHT DIAMAGIC!
KRiii
CACKLE CACKLE
SNART
UH... DOES THAT NEW WAND OF YOURS HAVE ANY BUG SPRAY?! GULP!!

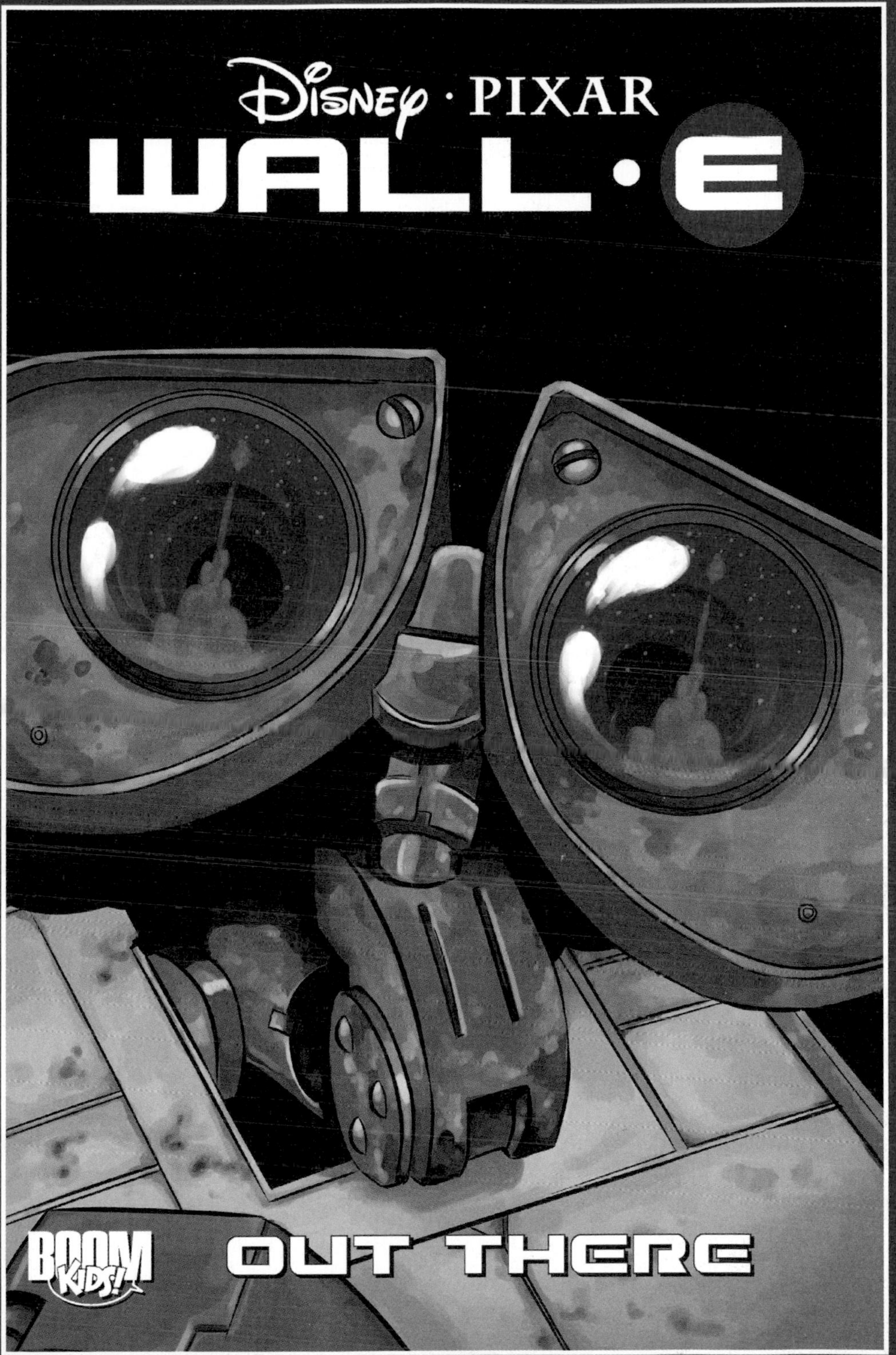
DISNEY · PIXAR
WALL·E
BOOM KIDS!
OUT THERE

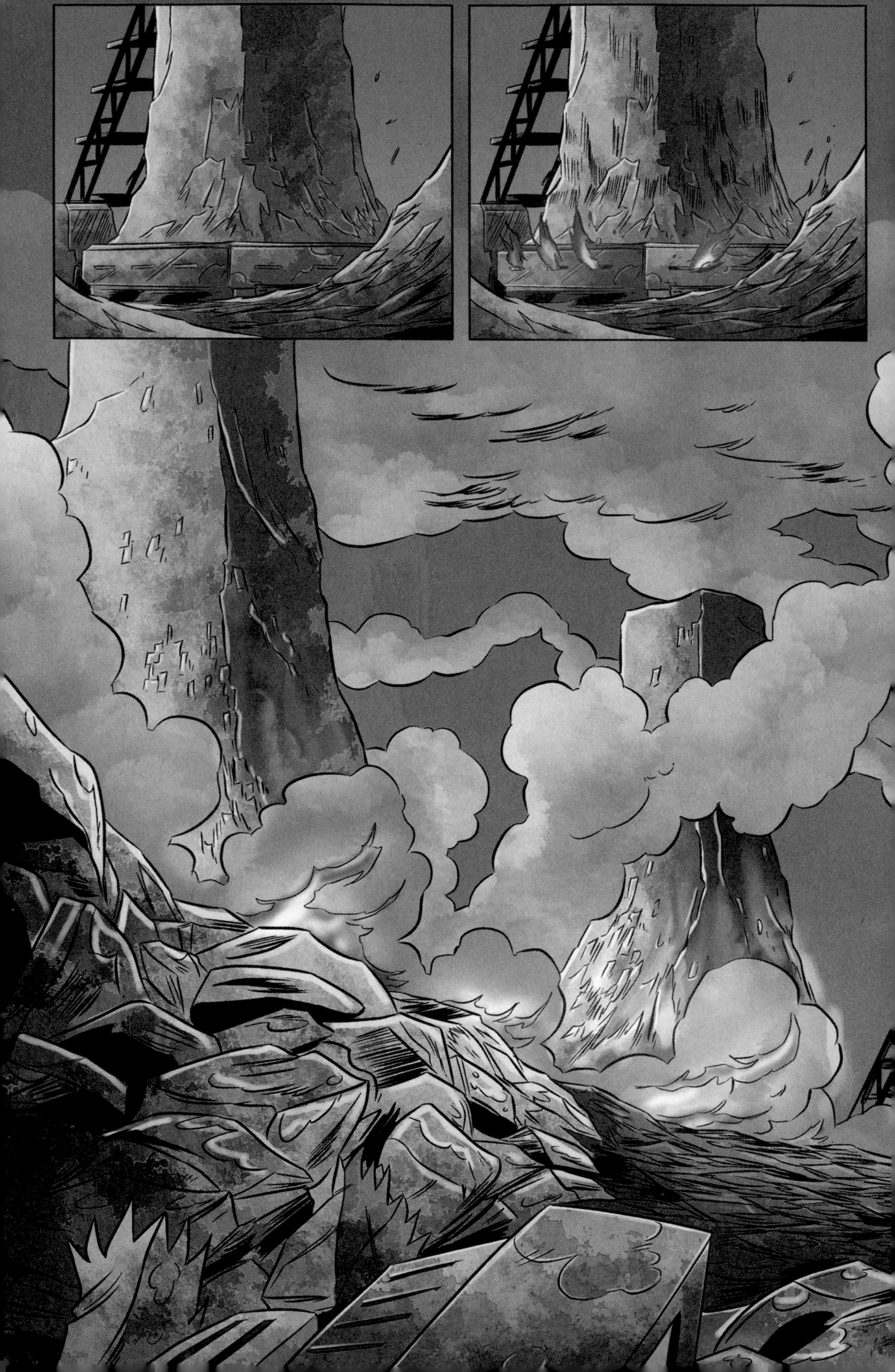

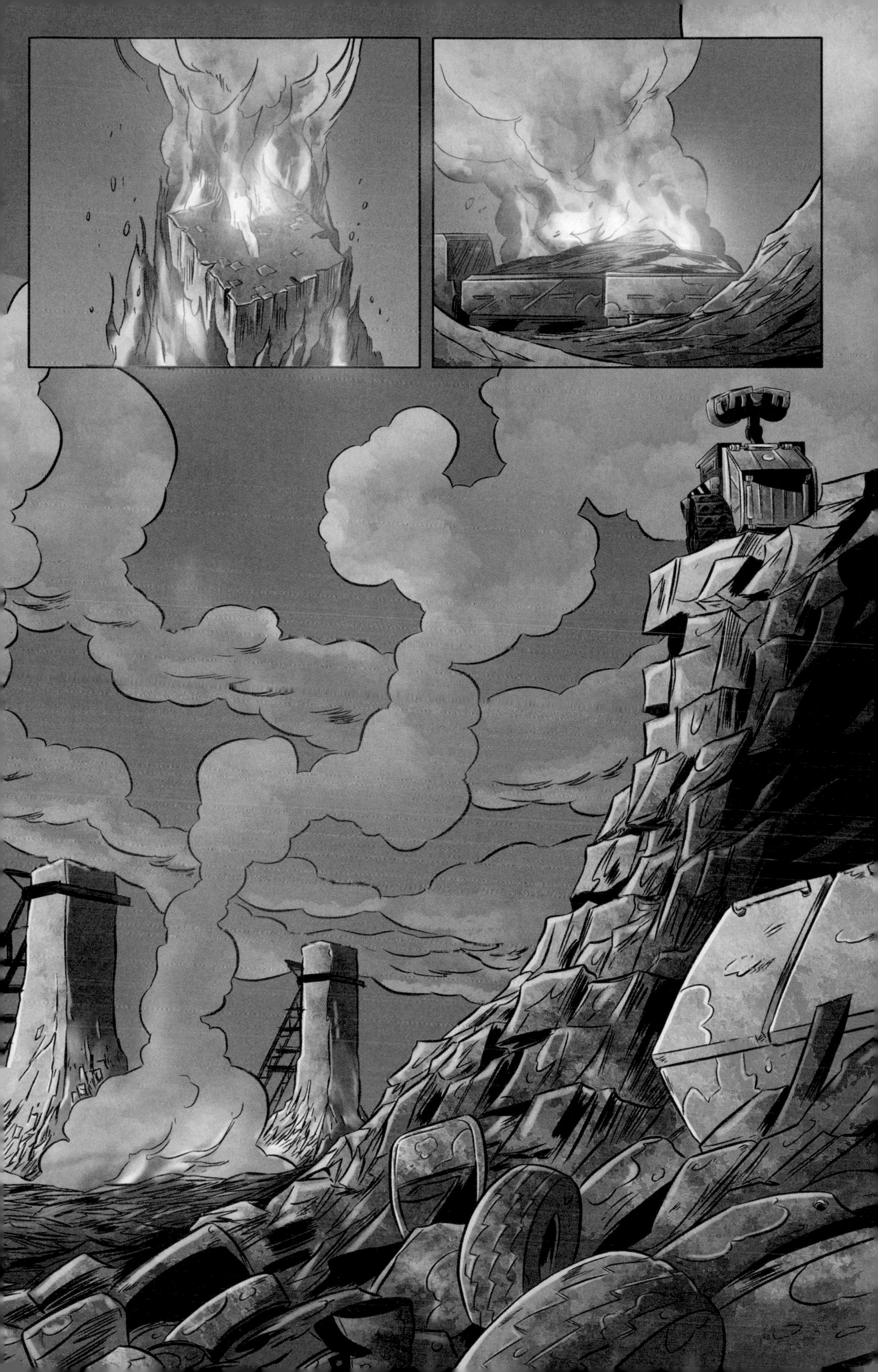

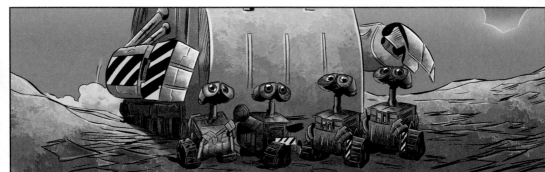

KLIK

BWOOOMM

KLIK

BWOOOMM

KLIK

BWOOOMM

HMMM?

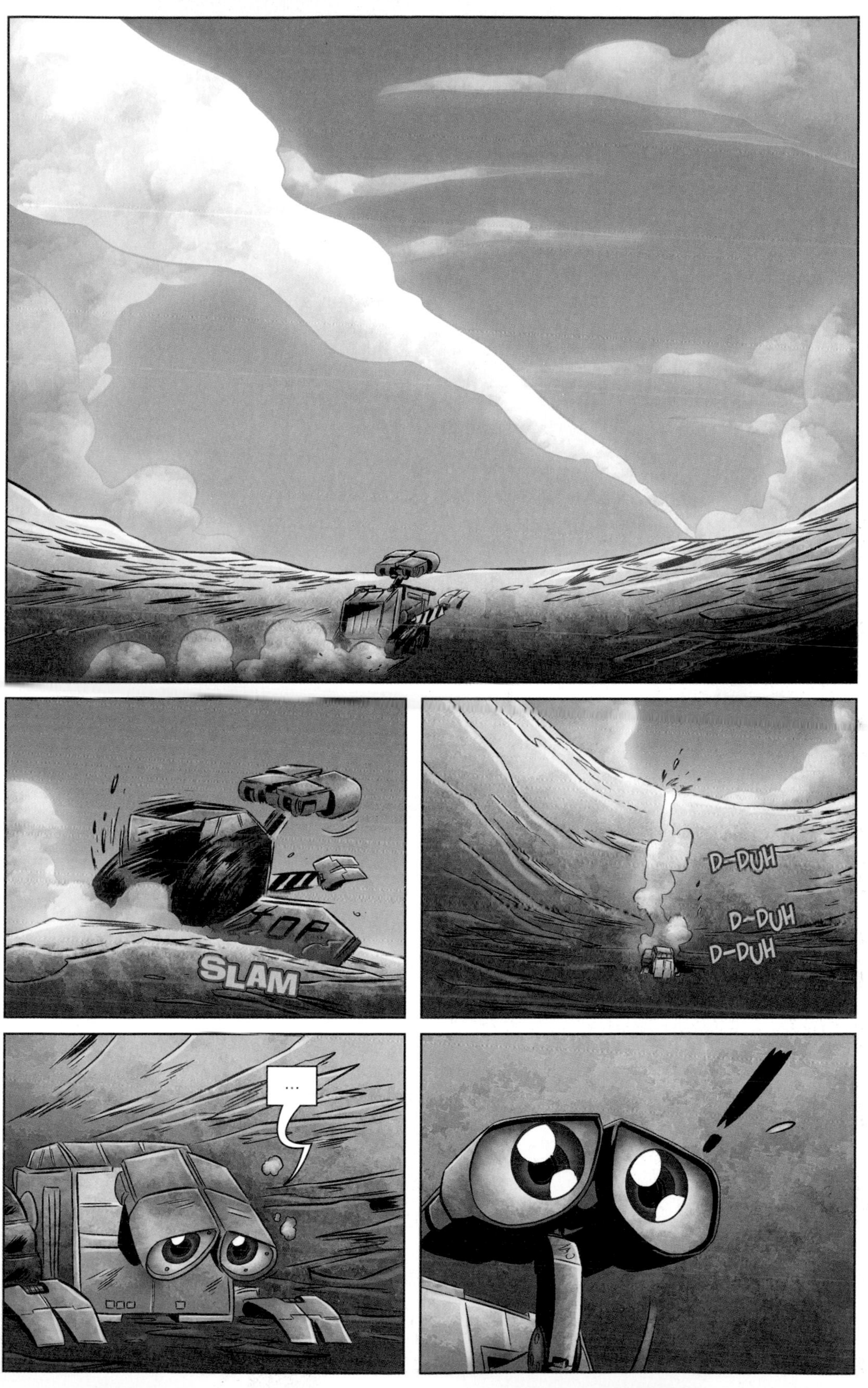
SLAM
D-DUH
D-DUH
D-DUH
...
!

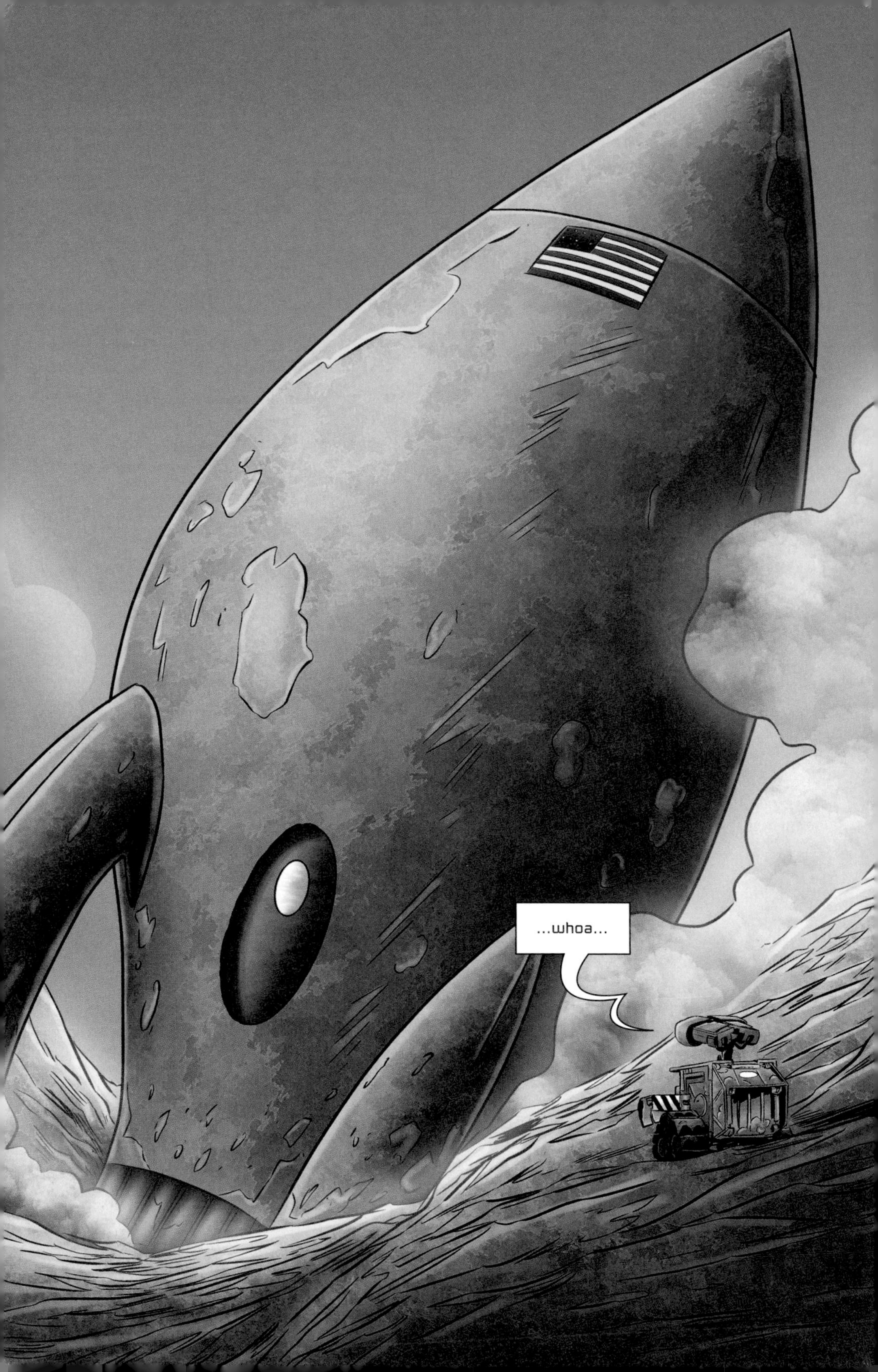
...whoa...

GRAPHIC NOVELS AVAILABLE NOW!

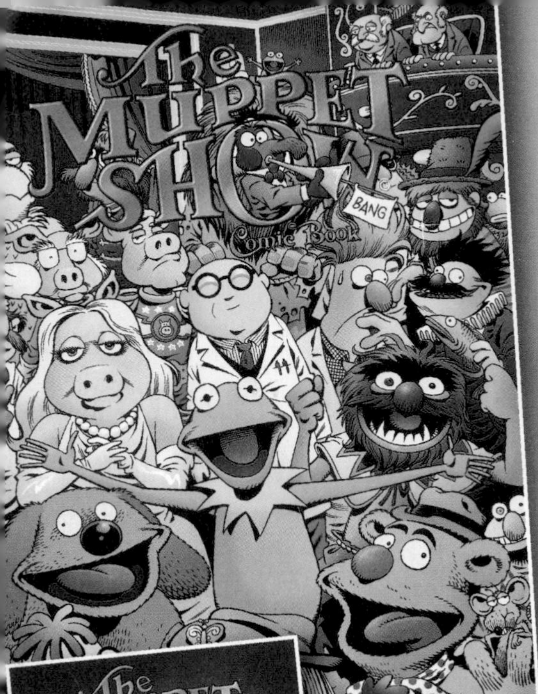
The Muppet Show
Comic Book
BANG

THE MUPPET SHOW COMIC BOOK: MEET THE MUPPETS

Collecting the first four issues of the Eisner Award-nominated THE MUPPET SHOW COMIC BOOK, written and drawn by the incomparable Roger Langridge! Packed full of madcap skits and gags, this trade is certain to please old and new fans alike!

SC $9.99 ISBN 9781934506851
HC $24.99 ISBN 9781608865277

THE MUPPET SHOW COMIC BOOK: THE TREASURE OF PEG-LEG WILSON

Scooter discovers old documents which reveal that a cache of treasure is hidden somewhere within the Muppet Theater...and when Rizzo the Rat overhears this, the news spreads like wildfire! Can Kermit keep everyone from tearing the theater apart?

SC $9.99 ISBN 9781608865048
HC $24.99 ISBN 9781608865307

THE MUPPET SHOW COMIC BOOK: ON THE ROAD

With the Muppet Theater destroyed, the Muppets take their act on the road...but with two very familiar hecklers in every town, will the show be a hit, or will our Muppet minstrels be run out of town in tar and feathers? Also: PIGS IN SPACE!

SC $9.99 ISBN 9781608865161

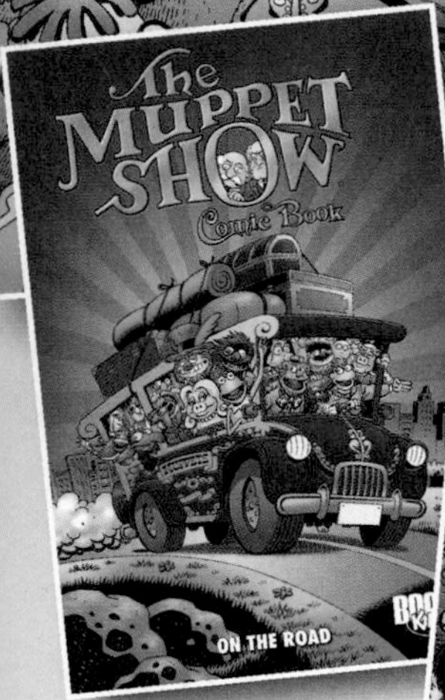
The Muppet Show
Comic Book
ON THE ROAD

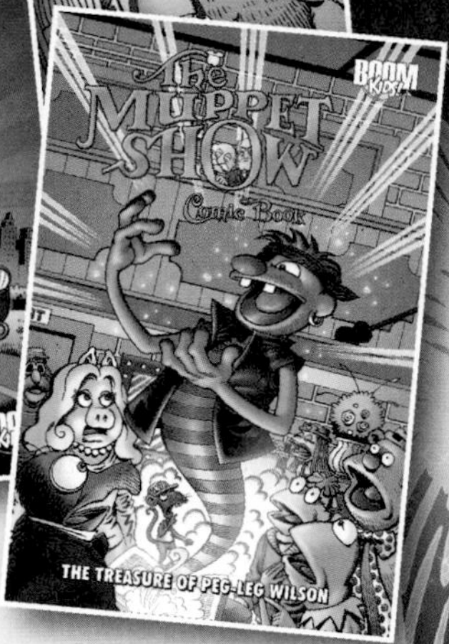
The Muppet Show
Comic Book
BOOM Kids!
THE TREASURE OF PEG-LEG WILSON

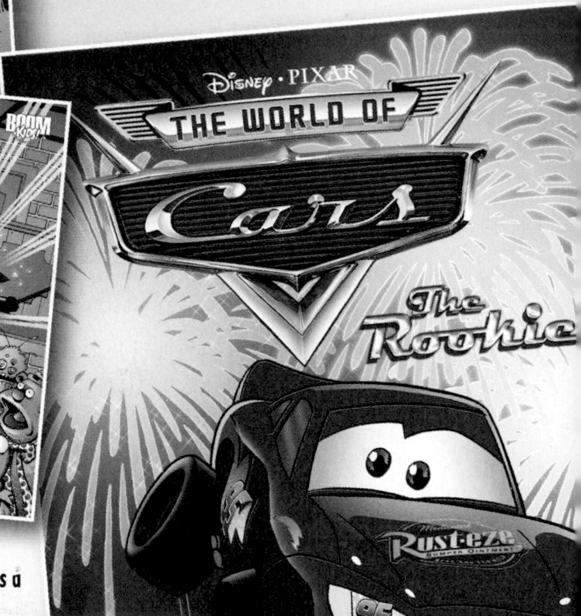
Disney • PIXAR
THE WORLD OF
Cars
The Rookie
Rust-eze
95

CARS: THE ROOKIE

See how Lightning McQueen became a Piston Cup sensation! CARS: THE ROOKIE reveals Lightning McQueen's scrappy origins as a local short track racer who dreams of the big time... and recklessly plows his way through the competition to get there!

SC $9.99 ISBN 9781934506844
HC $24.99 ISBN 9781608865222

CARS: RADIATOR SPRINGS

Lightning McQueen is hanging out with his friends at Flo's V8 Café when he realizes that everyone knows his story...but he doesn't know anyone else's! Lightning wants to know how his friends ended up in Radiator Springs...and more importantly, why they decided to stay!

SC $9.99 ISBN 9781608865024
HC $24.99 ISBN 9781608865284

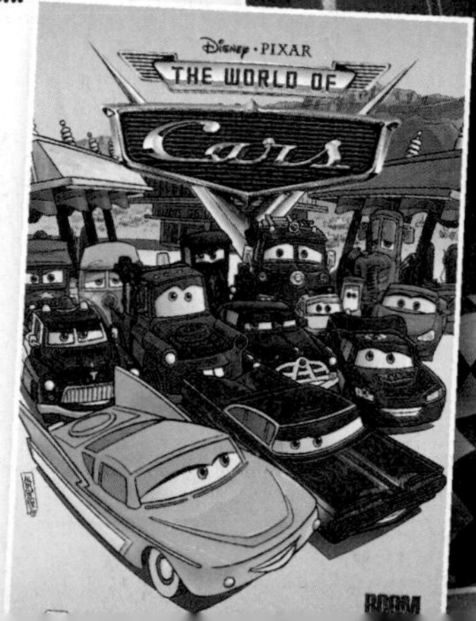
Disney • PIXAR
THE WORLD OF
Cars

WALL•E: RECHARGE

Before WALL•E becomes the hardworking robot we know and love, he lets the few remaining robots take care of the trash compacting while he collects interesting junk. But when these robots start breaking down, WALL•E must adjust his priorities...or else Earth is doomed!

SC $9.99 ISBN 9781608865123
HC $24.99 ISBN 9781608865543

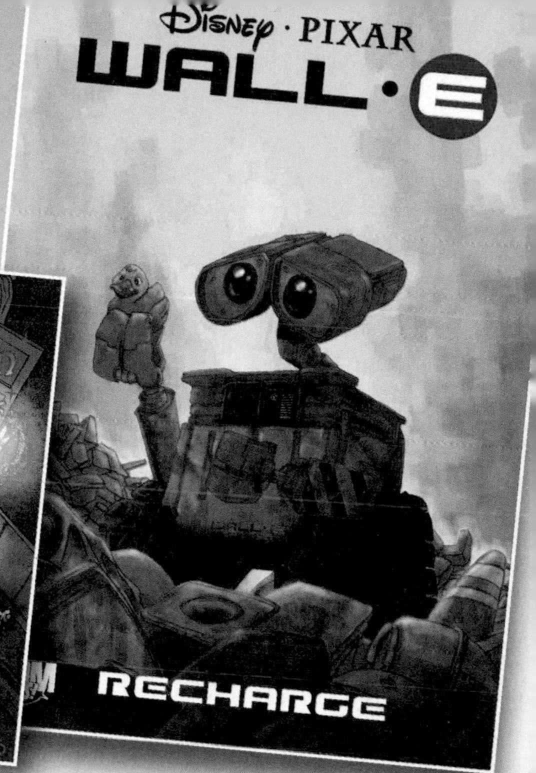

Disney · PIXAR
WALL·E
RECHARGE

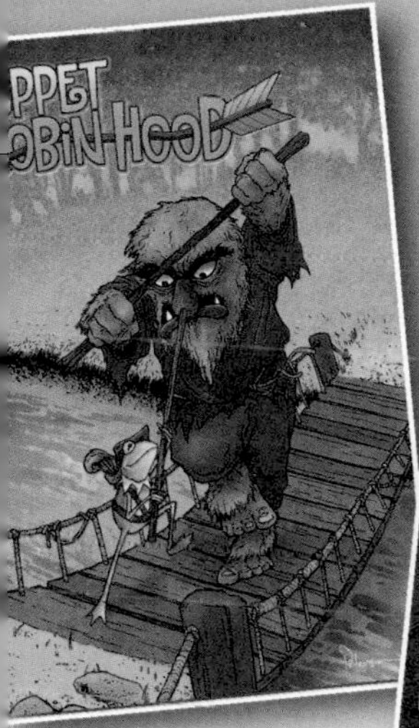

PPET
OBIN HOOD

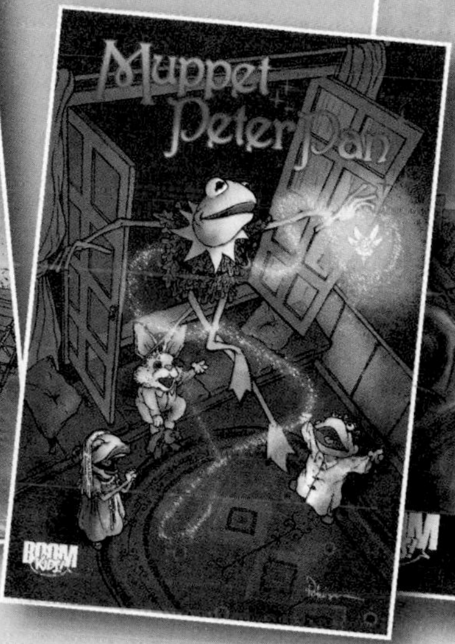

Muppet Peter Pan

MUPPET ROBIN HOOD

The Muppets tell the Robin Hood legend for laughs, and it's the reader who will be merry! Robin Hood (Kermit the Frog) joins with the Merry Men, Sherwood Forest's infamous gang of misfit outlaws, to take on the Sheriff of Nottingham (Sam the Eagle)!

SC $9.99 ISBN 9781934506790
HC $24.99 ISBN 9781608865260

MUPPET PETER PAN

When Peter Pan (Kermit) whisks Wendy (Janice) and her brothers to Neverswamp, the adventure begins! With Captain Hook (Gonzo) out for revenge for the loss of his hand, can even the magic of Piggytink (Miss Piggy) save Wendy and her brothers?

SC $9.99 ISBN 9781608865079
HC $24.99 ISBN 9781608865314

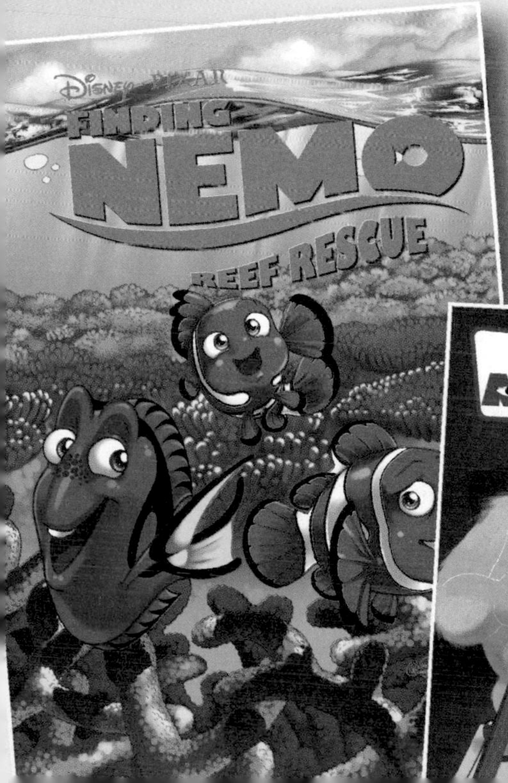

FINDING
NEMO
REEF RESCUE

FINDING NEMO: REEF RESCUE

Nemo, Dory and Marlin have become local heroes, and are recruited to embark on an all-new adventure in this exciting collection! The reef is mysteriously dying and no one knows why. So Nemo and his friends must travel the great blue sea to save their home!

SC $9.99 ISBN 9781934506882
HC $24.99 ISBN 9781608865246

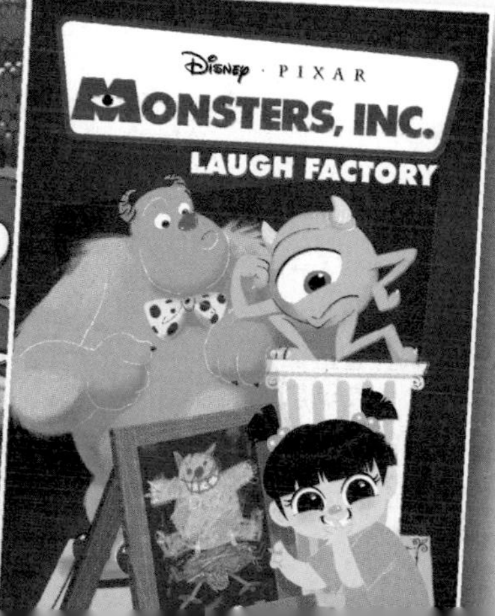

Disney · PIXAR
MONSTERS, INC.
LAUGH FACTORY

MONSTERS, INC.: LAUGH FACTORY

Someone is stealing comedy props from the other employees, making it difficult for them to harvest the laughter they need to power Monstropolis...and all evidence points to Sulley's best friend Mike Wazowski!

SC $9.99 ISBN 9781608865086
HC $24.99 ISBN 9781608865338

DISNEY'S HERO SQUAD: ULTRAHEROES VOL. 1: SAVE THE WORLD

It's an all-star cast of your favorite Disney characters, as you have never seen them before. Join Donald Duck, Goofy, Daisy, and even Mickey himself as they defend the fate of the planet as the one and only Ultraheroes!

SC $9.99 ISBN 9781608865437
HC $24.99 ISBN 9781608865529

UNCLE SCROOGE: THE HUNT FOR THE OLD NUMBER ONE

Join Donald Duck's favorite penny-pinching Uncle Scrooge as he, Donald himself and Huey, Dewey, and Louie embark on a globe-spanning trek to recover treasure and save Scrooge's "number one dime" from the treacherous Magica De Spell.

SC $9.99 ISBN 9781608865475
HC $24.99 ISBN 9781608865536

WIZARDS OF MICKEY VOL. 1: MOUSE MAGIC

Your favorite Disney characters star in this magical fantasy epic! Student of the great wizard Nereus, Mickey allies himself with Donald and teammate Goofy, in a quest to find a magical crown that will give him mastery over all spells!

SC $9.99 ISBN 9781608865413
HC $24.99 ISBN 9781608865505

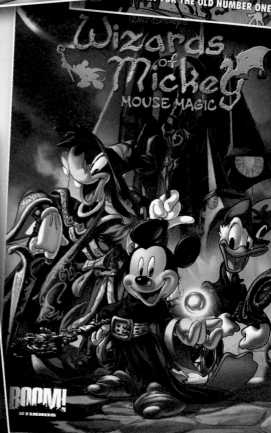

DONALD DUCK AND FRIENDS: DOUBLE DUCK VOL. 1

Donald Duck as a secret agent? Villainous fiends beware as the world of super sleuthing and espionage will never be the same! This is Donald Duck like you've never seen him!

SC $9.99 ISBN 9781608865451
HC $24.99 ISBN 9781608865512